ROYAL
AIRS

Ace Books by Sharon Shinn

THE SHAPE OF DESIRE
STILL LIFE WITH SHAPE-SHIFTER

TROUBLED WATERS
ROYAL AIRS

MYSTIC AND RIDER
THE THIRTEENTH HOUSE
DARK MOON DEFENDER
READER AND RAELYNX
FORTUNE AND FATE

ARCHANGEL
JOVAH'S ANGEL
THE ALLELUIA FILES
ANGELICA
ANGEL-SEEKER

WRAPT IN CRYSTAL
THE SHAPE-CHANGER'S WIFE
HEART OF GOLD
SUMMERS AT CASTLE AUBURN
JENNA STARBORN
QUATRAIN

Viking / Firebird Books by Sharon Shinn

THE SAFE-KEEPER'S SECRET
THE TRUTH-TELLER'S TALE
THE DREAM-MAKER'S MAGIC
GENERAL WINSTON'S DAUGHTER
GATEWAY

ROYAL
AIRS

Sharon Shinn

ACE BOOKS, NEW YORK

THE BERKLEY PUBLISHING GROUP
Published by the Penguin Group
Penguin Group (USA) LLC
375 Hudson Street, New York, New York 10014

USA • Canada • UK • Ireland • Australia • New Zealand • India • South Africa • China

penguin.com

A Penguin Random House Company

This book is an original publication of The Berkley Publishing Group.

Ace Books are published by The Berkley Publishing Group.
ACE and the "A" design are trademarks of Penguin Group (USA) LLC.

Library of Congress Cataloging-in-Publication Data

Shinn, Sharon.
Royal airs : an Elemental Blessings novel / Sharon Shinn.
pages cm. — (An Elemental Blessings novel)
ISBN 978-0-425-26171-2 (hardback)
1. Magic—Fiction. 2. Fantasy fiction. I. Title.
PS3569.H499R69 2013
813'.54—dc23
2013027604

FIRST EDITION: November 2013

PRINTED IN THE UNITED STATES OF AMERICA

10 9 8 7 6 5 4 3 2 1

Cover illustration © Jonathan Barkat.
Cover photos: sunset and clouds © Pavel Vakhrushev/Shutterstock;
stormy clouds © Shebeko/Shutterstock.
Cover design by Judith Lagerman.
Interior text design by Tiffany Estreicher.

To Margaux, who never has time to read,
and Denise, who sometimes does.
You have both been blessings in my life.

Who's Who in Welce

THE PRINCESSES

JOSETTA, daughter of Queen Seterre and Navarr Ardelay
CORENE, daughter of Queen Alys and Darien Serlast
NATALIE, daughter of Queen Romelle and an unknown lover
ODELIA, daughter of Queen Romelle and King Vernon
MALLY, the decoy princess for Odelia

THE PRIMES

ZOE LALINDAR, *coru*. Daughter of Navarr Ardelay, wife of
　　Darien Serlast, mother of Celia
NELSON ARDELAY, *sweela*. Father of Kurtis and Rhan, brother to
　　Navarr, uncle to Josetta and Zoe
MIRTI SERLAST, *hunti*. Aunt of Darien
TARO FROTHEN, *torz*. Distant relation of Romelle
KAYLE DOCHENZA, *elay*

THE POLITICIANS

DARIEN SERLAST, regent of Welce
QUEEN ELIDON, King Vernon's first wife
GHYANETH, prince of Berringey
FILOMARA, empress of Malinqua

Random Blessings

ELAY (AIR/SOUL)	HUNTI (WOOD/BONE)	SWEELA (FIRE/MIND)
joy	courage	innovation
hope	strength	love
kindness	steadfastness	imagination
beauty	loyalty	clarity
vision	certainty	intelligence
grace	resolve	charm
honor	determination	talent
spirituality	power	creativity

CORU (WATER/BLOOD)	TORZ (EARTH/FLESH)	EXTRAORDINARY BLESSINGS
change	serenity	synthesis
travel	honesty	triumph
flexibility	health	time
swiftness	fertility	
resilience	contentment	
luck	patience	
persistence	endurance	
surprise	wealth	

Quintiles & Changedays

The calendar of Welce is divided into five quintiles. A quintile consists of eight "weeks," each nine days long. Most shops and other businesses are closed on the firstday of each nineday.

The first quintile of the year, Quinnelay, stretches from early to deep winter. It is followed by Quinncoru, which encompasses late winter to mid spring; Quinnahunti, late spring to mid summer; Quinnatorz, late summer to fall; and Quinnasweela, fall to early winter.

The quintiles are separated by changedays, generally celebrated as holidays. Quinnelay changeday is the first day of every new year. Since there are five changedays, and five seventy-two-day quintiles, the Welce year is 365 days long.

Money

5 quint-coppers make one copper (5 cents → 25 cents)
8 coppers make one quint-silver ($2)

5 quint-silvers make one silver ($10)
8 silvers make one quint-gold ($80)

5 quint-golds make one gold ($400)

ONE

Rafe shuffled the deck for the third time and handed it to the woman on his right so she could cut the cards. It was clear the other three players distrusted him, and even the card cutting didn't reassure them he wasn't cheating. But they were too convinced that the *next* hand would be the winning one to call him out or stop the play. They merely watched him with a narrowed suspicion and nodded to indicate they were still in the game.

Rafe dealt the cards slowly, deliberately, making sure all his movements were visible. As it happened, he knew how to slip a trump from the bottom of the deck, how to hide a wildcard up his sleeve, but he didn't bother. Not with this particular group—two elay men barely in their twenties and a wild-haired sweela woman who was probably his stepfather's age. None of them could play half as well as they thought they could, but all were too caught up in the gambling fever to admit it. Rafe shrugged to himself. That was an elay man for you—a dreamer, a misty-eyed romantic with no practical sense. And all the sweela souls he'd ever encountered were so impetuous that they ignored their impulses to cold reason whenever the stakes were high. Of course Rafe was winning handily; it would be *more* astonishing if he were losing.

Once the cards were dealt, everyone gathered them up and sorted them into suits. Rafe kept his expression amiable but impassive as he looked over his hand. Two wildcards; that was a stroke of luck. Only two trumps; a potential disaster. Ah, but he had six cards in the suit of skulls. He could probably turn that to his advantage.

As his opponents frowned over their own cards, each trying to formulate a strategy, Rafe glanced casually around the bar. The clientele tended to turn over pretty quickly as the night progressed; he liked to keep track of who had walked in while his attention was elsewhere. He liked to guess who might be interested in playing a round of penta with him, who might be desperate, and who might be trouble.

Trouble came with some regularity to this little bar, which was situated solidly inside the crowded, noisome slum district of the city of Chialto. But it was actually one of the more respectable establishments, given its location just south of the Cinque, the five-sided boulevard that made an inner loop around the city. Traders' sons and merchants' wives felt safe enough to come here for a night of excitement that might include high-stakes gambling, high-proof liquor, illegal drugs, and companionship that could be purchased. As long as they stayed within hearing range of traffic on the Cinque, they didn't need to worry overmuch. But farther south, a little closer to the canal, and the illicit thrill could turn into a grim struggle for survival. No one walked *those* streets just for fun.

Tonight, at least so far, the bar was relatively quiet. The public space consisted of one big room, crowded with tables and a half dozen booths against the far wall. It was windowless here on the street level, so no matter what the time of day, the smoky oil-lamp illumination made patrons fail to notice how long they'd been sitting there, drinking or playing. The clientele was largely male, though a few women were always part of the mix. Some, like the one at his own table, were leathery old crones with a lifetime of hard experience chiseled into their faces. More were younger, prettier, plumper, not yet ruined by a brutal life, though clearly in peril of encountering a disastrous end.

Well, who isn't? Rafe thought, turning his attention back to his tablemates. "Everyone ready to bid?" he asked.

One of the elay men nodded vigorously. He was a slim, pasty-faced blond with full, sensuous lips; Rafe had mentally dubbed him the Loser, since his reckless style of play was all but guaranteed to leave him bankrupt before the night was over. "*More* than ready," the Loser exclaimed. He seemed almost feverish with excitement. Rafe assumed he had drawn the majority of the trump cards, and wasn't hiding that fact very well.

"I suppose so," said the other elay man, whom Rafe was calling Sad Boy because of his morose expression. Sad Boy had actually won a few hands by retaining trumps when Rafe had not expected him to, which argued a certain unexpected skill at the game, but his betting had been so erratic that he hadn't profited much by his victories.

Sweela Woman merely nodded, so they all called out their bids and laid down the proper cards. Rafe had the low cards in flutes, roses, and horseshoes, which made the others smile; on the face of it, he had the weakest hand. Sad Boy had the low skull and Sweela Woman the low fish. No wonder the Loser was grinning like a fool, and pushing a stack of quint-silvers to the middle of the table. He probably had high cards *and* trumps.

It would be a pleasure taking his money.

Sad Boy and Sweela Woman made more conservative bets. Rafe offered a slight shrug, which he hoped they would interpret as disappointment over a bad hand, and pushed a silver toward the pile of coins. "Looks like it's your play," he said to the Loser, and the game was on.

It unfolded almost exactly as Rafe had anticipated, with the Loser scooping up the first four rounds with ill-disguised triumph, and recklessly expending his trumps without any regard for which cards it would be prudent to hold in reserve. The Loser was clearly astonished when Sad Boy won a play and wrested control of the game for the next two discards, and even more astonished when his next trump was overmatched by Rafe, who had been keeping track. No trumps, no wildcards left.

"Skulls," Rafe said, and laid down the eight. Sad Boy and Sweela Woman tossed in skulls, and the Loser pouted and flung down the three of roses. Rafe spread the rest of his cards on the table. "I think the remaining rounds are mine," he said in a pleasant voice.

Sweela Woman groaned and Sad Boy actually laughed. "I wondered where all the skulls were!" he exclaimed. "All I had were flutes and roses, and they didn't do me a damn bit of good."

Sweela Woman was watching Rafe appraisingly. "Even if you've been cheating all night, you weren't cheating on that hand," she said. "You're brilliant at this game. I suppose you know that."

He smiled at her. He'd always rather liked the sweela folks he'd encountered. They tended to be self-absorbed and overbearing, but embued with a certain irresistible charm. As if it never occurred to them that, despite their loud voices and arrogant attitudes, people might not like them.

"Since much of my income depends on being brilliant at penta, I am aware that I play it well," he replied.

"Hell of a way to earn a living," she said.

Rafe shrugged and gathered the cards, straightening them into a neat pile. "Every job has its downside," he said. "The ills of gambling are no worse than those of working in a factory ten hours a day, building smoker cars for rich people."

Sweela Woman laughed at that, and even Sad Boy looked amused. The Loser frowned, leading Rafe to guess he was one of the rich folks who owned an *elaymotive*. In the past five years, the gas-powered vehicles had gone from being gape-worthy curiosities to commonplace carriages, though horse-drawn conveyances still accounted for three-quarters of the traffic along the Cinque.

"Never did want to spend much time working myself to the bone just so a rich man got richer," Sweela Woman agreed. "But I still don't think a gambler's life is the one for me."

Rafe shuffled the cards, loving the quick, ruffled sound they made as they interwove. "You might like it better than you think," he said. "Gambling favors the folk of mind and fire."

"Gambling favors the cheaters," the Loser muttered.

In response, Rafe offered him the deck. "You deal," he invited. "Count them first, make sure they're all there. What can I do to convince you I play a fair game?"

The elay man hesitated, as if thinking up tests. His friend said in a tone of great irritation, "Either trust the man and play, Edwin, or don't trust him and walk away. Frankly, I think he's honest."

"But he keeps *winning*," Edwin complained.

"I think it's more that we keep losing."

Rafe left the cards on the table and leaned back in his chair, crossing his arms on his chest. Let them see him relaxed and sure of himself; let them believe he didn't care whether or not they played one more hand. In truth, he'd prefer to win another few silvers, even a quint-gold or two. He rented a small apartment on the third story above the bar, paying by the nineday, and the money was due tomorrow morning. He had enough to cover it, but he might go hungry a day or two until he had another run of good luck.

The elay men were now arguing in earnest, keeping their voices low enough that Rafe could pretend he wasn't listening. Since there was a break in the action, Sweela Woman opened her handbag and pulled out a small, delicately carved box. Rafe wasn't surprised when the lid opened to reveal a couple of small, gilded bags and a ceramic cup no bigger than a thimble. She carefully opened each bag, shook out fine white powder from one and coarsely ground green leaves from the other, and combined them inside the cup. As soon as the ingredients began to curl with smoke, she dumped the mixture into her wine and began to slowly sip it down.

Once *that* particular drug took hold, Rafe thought, she'd have the energy and focus to play for another five hours.

The men were still arguing, so Rafe glanced around the bar again, noting that it had thinned out a little. He guessed it was two or three hours past midnight, and most of the casual visitors had already called it a night. The ones left were the professionals and the diehards, too drunk or too stupid to go home. Or unlucky enough to have no home to go to.

Movement caught at the edge of his vision and he shifted to get a better look. A young woman was coming in through the front door— *slinking* in would be a better way to put it, opening the door just wide enough to admit her small frame and then skulking along the wall until she came to an unoccupied booth. She dropped onto one of the benches and shoved herself back until her hunched shoulder hit the wall. Then she seemed to draw herself together in a tight ball and ducked her head down, trying—or so it seemed—to make herself invisible. She even leaned down to blow out the guttering candle on her table, to put herself in shadow as much as possible.

Rafe continued to watch her from the corner of his eye, not wanting to draw attention to her by staring outright. Though she would be something to stare at. Her trousers and tunic were lacy, delicate, and highly expensive items, though they were ripped and muddy, as if she'd fallen down during a mad run for freedom. Her bare arms bore fresh cuts and scratches; her thick red hair was a wild mess. She wasn't wearing any visible jewelry, but Rafe fancied he could spot a little lumpiness on the undercurve of her bosom, which should have been lusciously smooth. His bet was that she had stuffed a necklace down the front, and maybe a bracelet or two, when she realized she was making a detour through rough territory.

He could only guess what disaster had sent her off into the night, but that she was in dire distress was clear enough. She looked like she couldn't be more than fifteen, was rich as a queen, and was pretty close to terrified. Surely she knew she was in absolutely the wrong part of town for her age, sex, and social standing. Surely she knew that any of a dozen hazards could sweep her into calamity before the night was even an hour older. This place could not have been her intended goal, and Rafe thought she must not have the faintest idea what to do next.

But she didn't look entirely defeated. He watched as she examined the welter of plates and silverware left at her booth by the last patron. He thought at first she was trying to gain the nerve to eat some of the less-poisonous-looking scraps, so he almost laughed when the first thing she picked up was a dinner knife, sharp enough to cut fried meat. Actually, she found *two* knives among the dinner dishes and briskly pocketed both. Rafe silently applauded.

Next she sorted through the soiled napkins, grimacing a little at the unidentifiable stains. Rafe watched as she turned herself sideways in the booth so she could draw up her left leg, bringing that foot close to her body. She rolled back the silken edges of her fancy leggings and used the napkins to bind her ankle, biting her lip as she did so.

Ah. So her dash from danger had resulted in a twisted or sprained ankle. Rafe guessed that adrenaline had kept her going when there was no choice but to run, but if she'd sustained a real injury, the pain was going to become excruciating pretty quickly. That would make it difficult for her to flee again if fresh trouble presented itself here in the little tavern.

As it most probably would.

Not until she had armed herself and taken care of her ankle did the runaway survey the table again to consider her food choices. She was so obviously a well-bred girl—maybe even from one of the Five Families—that Rafe would have expected her to prefer starvation to eating off of strangers' plates, but she surprised him again. She picked through the scraps, ate a few roasted vegetables and a strip of discarded meat, and drank without hesitation from a glass half full of water. His opinion of her went up several notches. Whoever she was, this girl was a fighter.

A slight clatter across the bar caught her attention—and Rafe's. They both glanced over to see one of the serving boys gathering plates from some of the other unoccupied tables. That would be a complication for her. As soon as she was discovered, the owner would expect her to pay for something or leave. Rafe thought she had come to the same conclusion. He saw her delicate face pull into a frown as she drew herself farther back into the shadows to try and figure out what to do next.

"Well, all right, then, another hand, but if he wins that one, too, I'm gone," Edwin said suddenly in a defiant voice. He had spoken loud enough to make sure they all heard; clearly the private colloquy was over.

Feeling great reluctance—but not showing it—Rafe withdrew his attention from the runaway and presented a genial countenance to the table. "I can't promise to lose just to continue the game, but I'm happy to play another round," he said.

"*And* I'm dealing," Edwin added, still in that belligerent tone.

Rafe pushed his sleeves back and placed his hands palm-up on the table, so everyone could see he wasn't hiding any cards. "Happy to have you do it," he said. "Let's play."

As it happened, he *did* lose the next round, and only partly because he thought it would appease the whining elay boy. Partly it was because half of his attention was on the redheaded girl who huddled in the booth trying to elude discovery. He couldn't help it; his attention was caught. He wanted to see what happened to her.

And he wanted to make sure it wasn't anything too terrible. His chivalric impulses were rare but powerful. All he had to do was imagine his younger brother stumbling through the slums and he couldn't turn away from whatever lost soul he'd encountered. He'd handed out money more often than he could afford, intervened in a handful of fights, even offered the occasional stern lecture. He'd stopped mocking himself for these grand and probably wasted gestures. They were the price he exacted of himself for living the life he'd chosen.

So if anyone threatened the little runaway, he'd have to intervene.

He was so distracted by his thoughts that he misplayed a trump and heard Edwin the Loser crow in satisfaction. "My hand, I believe," the elay man said grandly as he raked in the pile of coins. "Anyone care for another one?"

"I'll play as long as you want!" exclaimed Sweela Woman. The drugs had brightened her eyes and brushed more color into her cheeks; she was grinning maniacally. Rafe figured she'd feel like strung-out death in the morning, but that wasn't his concern.

Sad Boy nodded without much enthusiasm. "Why not?"

Rafe nodded at Sad Boy. "Your deal, I think."

He had even worse cards this round, but it hardly mattered; the game couldn't keep his attention. In the past few minutes, the redhead had had a low-voiced argument with the serving boy, which she appeared to have won, because the boy tramped off to the kitchen and returned moments later with a steaming mug. The girl must have had enough coins to pay for that much, earning herself the right to stay at the table another hour or so. But her luck was no better than Rafe's. A thin, weasally man from another table had spotted her during the transaction. As soon as she was alone again, he slithered over to her booth and dropped down next to her on the bench, effectively pinning her in place.

Rafe, playing his hand almost at random, watched as he made her some kind of offer and she vehemently refused. The man pressed for a different answer, and she dumped the contents of the mug into his lap. Even from across the bar, Rafe could hear the man's howl of pain.

"You don't crack a smile all night, but you lose a wildcard to a high trump and you're grinning like a fool?" Sweela Woman demanded.

He turned his smile on her. "There's no other way to respond when you become the plaything of fate," he said. "You laugh, or you die."

Edwin grunted. "That kind of attitude, I'd have expected you to be dead a long time ago."

"Not at all," Rafe said, shaking his head. "I've thrived."

The random motion or the long night had caused a lock of hair to come loose from the ponytail he habitually wore, and he absently pushed it back behind his right ear. Sweela Woman's overbright eyes sharpened as she stared at the sight suddenly exposed to view. He smiled faintly and fingered the triangular points sliced into the outer curve of his ear. There were five, and each one had been set with a small gold hoop.

The serrated edges he'd had since he was a baby. The hoops he'd added himself, an act of defiance against the world. *If I'm forced to be different, then I'll celebrate my differences.* It was a credo he wholly believed in—though he generally preferred to keep his ear covered just to avoid conversation about it.

"I bet there's a rare story there," Sweela Woman observed.

"Rare and rarely told," he replied, still smiling at her. The others hadn't even noticed his ear, and he casually brushed his hair back in place to cover it up. "As I'm sure some of *your* more interesting tales are."

With a sweela mind's quick understanding, she realized he wanted to change the subject, so she cheerfully did. "I bet I can guess your blessings," she said. "Luck, am I right? You look to be mostly coru. Luck and resilience and charm." She grinned at him. "A little sweela fire thrown in."

In this situation, he routinely lied, sometimes claiming one set of blessings, sometimes another, depending on his audience and his mood. "Close enough," he answered. "Luck and resilience and honor."

Sad Boy didn't look convinced. "Any man can claim a blessing. That doesn't mean it was actually bestowed on him, or that he lives up to it if it was."

That made Rafe laugh out loud. "True enough," he said, tossing the three of skulls onto a pile of flutes. He might go the whole hand without taking a trick; this night had taken a decided turn for the worse. "Do you live up to yours?"

Now the sweela crone was swaying in her seat, either moved by some internal music or too dizzy to sit upright. "I do," she cackled, tossing out a high flute and taking the hand. "Grace and contentment and courage."

He couldn't tell if she was joking, picking the three blessings that probably described her least, or exposing her own personal irony for all of them to enjoy. It didn't matter. It didn't matter that she then led with a trump, which would take his own final trump and ensure he didn't win *any* points for this hand. It didn't matter that Sad Boy groaned and Edwin said angrily, "Is *everyone* at the table cheating?" Rafe was watching the redheaded runaway, and her life had suddenly gotten very perilous.

Two men had joined her this time, one sitting beside her, one across from her. A third had sidled up to loiter at the head of the table, opening his coat and setting his arms on his hips to prevent other patrons from watching the action inside the booth. Which was clearly some kind of forceful persuasion—maybe a knife to the jugular, a concoction down the throat, or a pair of hands around the neck, tight enough to render her unconscious without killing her outright.

"Excuse me for a moment," Rafe said politely, throwing down his cards and shoving away from the table. In a matter of seconds he was at the other booth, elbowing the lookout aside and slamming his hands down on the table loud enough to make the dishes rattle.

Everyone stared at him in astonishment—the girl, the men, the people sitting nearby. In this instance, the more attention the better, so he raised his voice to make sure anyone who was interested could hear.

"What's going on here?" he asked. "You boys find yourself a little unwilling sport tonight? You planning on dragging her out of here to do—what? Rape her? Kill her? Hold her for ransom?"

A few of the patrons behind him started muttering. They were all career drunks and reprobates but not wholly bankrupt, ethically speaking. They didn't mind a little free-for-all over marked cards or a flirtatious woman, but they didn't approve of unprovoked brutality or crimes that reeked of true evil. Not this crowd. Not this close to the Cinque.

The one sitting across from the girl bared his teeth in a snarl. He was the biggest one of this band of ruffians, the ugliest and meanest. "What's it to you?" he growled. "Take care of your own business, and I'll take care of mine."

Rafe shook his head, smiling slightly. Straightening up, he held his hands just so, fingers spread, barely touching the tops of his thighs. It would be clear to all of them that he was preparing to draw a weapon. Fighting had never been Rafe's style; he was more likely to rely on quick wits and cold nerve. But anyone who lived in the slums knew how to protect himself, and Rafe could handle a knife well enough. Three to one—horrible odds, but it was late enough in the evening that Rafe figured *someone* else would join in a rumble just for the fun of it.

"Tonight my business is spoiling your game," he said. "Leave the girl alone."

The thug who had been guarding the table came at him suddenly from the right, aiming a blow at the side of Rafe's face. Rafe punched back, hard, following up with a kick to the groin, and pulling his knife free for good measure. Someone behind him laughed. The brute staggered to an unoccupied table and leaned against it, coughing and wheezing.

"Leave the girl alone," Rafe repeated.

A shape bulked up behind him, and he turned his head just enough to see Samson, the bar owner and Rafe's landlord, standing at his back. Samson wasn't too sentimental. He might not have put a stop to an abduction if it had been conducted quietly enough, but he couldn't abide much ruckus; it drove away business.

"Leave her alone," Samson repeated. He was a big man, black-haired and burly. All muscle and all hunti. It was pointless to offer him physical opposition. "Go on home for the night, Becko. You know I don't like trouble."

For a moment, Becko's snarl intensified, but it was all bravado. He jerked his head toward the door and motioned for Rafe and Samson to step back. Then he and his partner pushed themselves out of the booth, collected their friend, and stomped out the front door, slamming it as they went.

Samson didn't even watch them go. He was eyeing Rafe, though his gaze flicked twice to the girl huddled in the booth. "What about her?" he asked.

"I'll take care of her," Rafe said.

"I don't like trouble," Samson repeated.

"There won't be any."

Samson watched him a moment longer, nodded sharply, and stalked back to the kitchen. Rafe slipped onto the bench where Becko had perched just a minute ago and gave the girl one comprehensive glance. "Looks like you're having an interesting evening," he said.

Staring back with a mix of defiance and uncertainty, she lifted her hand to show him one of the dinner knives clutched in her fist. He admired the fact that she didn't indicate she had a second weapon stashed away somewhere. Fierce enough to fight, smart enough to keep something in reserve. Even without the red hair, she would have been easy to pick out as sweela. "Who are you and what do you want from me?" she demanded.

"My name's Rafe Adova. I rent a room here, and I play cards for money. I saw you come in and I thought it looked like you were having a bad night."

She lowered her hand to the table, but kept her grip on the knife. "That's one way to put it," she said bitterly.

"You don't have any reason to trust me, but I'd like to help you."

"Why?" she asked suspiciously.

"To annoy Becko," was his prompt reply.

That made her laugh, but quickly enough she frowned again. "Why really?"

He shrugged and, unexpectedly, gave her the truth. "Because it's easy enough to do. Because once in a while when I needed help, a stranger gave it to me. And other times when I needed help, no one stepped forward. And I remember what all of those times were like—the times I got help and the times I didn't."

She was listening closely, as if he was speaking in riddles and her only chance of survival was to solve them. "How would you help?" she asked.

"If nothing else, I can find someone to carry a message for you," he said. "If you want, you can go up to my room—"

"I hardly think so," she interrupted.

He shrugged. "Or I can wait with you here so no one else bothers you. The place never closes. We'd just sit here till someone shows up to get you."

"I was trying to find my sister," she said abruptly. "But I got lost."

"If you crossed the Cinque to end up here, you got *really* lost."

"I meant to cross the Cinque," she said impatiently. "This is where she lives." She looked around expressively. "Somewhere in the slums."

Even his professional impassivity cracked at that. This gently bred rich girl had a sister who lived by the southern canals? Was the sister a prostitute? A dealer in drugs and illegal substances? It was almost impossible to credit.

"Excuse me for saying so," he observed, "but if she lives here, she might not be the best one to seek shelter with."

The redhead surprised him with a grin. "She's not that kind of person," she said. "But that's funny."

"So," he said. "What do you want to do next? Are you willing to trust me?"

She studied him for a long moment. Her brown eyes were large and expressive, and her face showed every nuance of her warring doubt, hope, and fatalism. She would make a terrible card player. "I don't see that I have any choice except to trust you, so I will. Can we send a messenger to J— To my sister?"

Interesting that she didn't want to offer a name; that meant she thought he might recognize it, which meant she would lie about her own name as well. "I'll grab one of the serving boys," he said.

But before he'd even stood up, his way was blocked by Edwin the Loser, who'd stalked over to glare at him. "Are you going to finish the game or not?" he demanded.

"I'll be there in a minute," Rafe said, unfolding himself from the bench. He was at least four inches taller than the elay man, and much less ethereal; Edwin backed off fast. Rafe took a moment to rifle in his pockets and tossed a few quint-silvers on the table. "I'm going to send a kitchen boy over. Tell him your message and give him two coins. Use the rest to buy yourself something to eat."

"I have money," she said instantly.

"No, you don't."

She stared at him mutinously for a moment, then dropped her gaze. "I'll pay you back."

"You certainly will." He started to move away, then stepped back. "I'll be right over there if you need me. As soon as I've finished the game, I'll come and sit with you until your sister—or whoever—shows up. Everything will be all right."

"I hope so," she said in a low voice. He nodded and turned away again, but her voice drew him back. "Rafe!"

He was surprised she remembered his name. But then, she was full of surprises. "Yes?"

"Thank you."

"I haven't done very much."

"Yes, you have." She hesitated a moment, then said, "I'm Cora."

Sure you are, he thought. "It's been interesting to meet you, Cora."

Her expressive face showed a faint hint of laughter. "It's going to get more interesting, I'm afraid."

He lifted his eyebrows. Now that was an intriguing thing to say. "I can't wait."

TWO

Rafe had resigned himself to the notion that Cora's dramatic introduction into his life would ruin his concentration enough to make him lose the next three hands, but, in fact, luck ran fairly evenly among the four players. By the time they were all ready to quit, even the jacked-up sweela woman admitting to exhaustion, Rafe was neither as far ahead as he'd have liked or as far behind as he'd feared. Could have been worse ways to end this night.

"A pleasure playing with you," Rafe told the others as he pocketed his cards and his coins. "I'm here most nights if you ever want to try your luck again."

Sad Boy shrugged and the Loser looked disdainful, but Sweela Woman said, "I just might be back later this nineday."

"Be glad to see you," he answered.

He was even gladder to see them all gone, ducking out through the door into the gray light of very early morning. He left a few coppers on the table for the serving boys, stood up and stretched, and shook his head to clear it. Normally this was the time he'd head upstairs for a few hours of sleep. But today, of course, he had a runaway with an assumed name to look after until help arrived. He grinned, shook his head again, and made his way through the mostly empty bar to the booth where Cora waited.

She was sitting sideways on the bench, her head against the wall, her legs stretched out before her, and she was fast asleep. From the plates arrayed before her, he could see she'd made short work of a hearty meal. He also guessed she'd secured another knife for herself, because he didn't see one on the table. He grinned. Heiress of the Five Families or not, this one had no doubt been a holy terror from the day she came squalling into the world. This might not have been the first time she'd run away. Probably wouldn't be the last.

He caught the attention of a passing servant who was taking advantage of the thin crowd to wipe down tables and sweep up debris. "Could you bring me one of those meat pies and a glass of beer?" he asked. "Thanks. And bring it to me quietly."

That last admonition had been in vain because as soon as he slid into the booth, Cora woke up. It only took her a moment to blink her eyes and remember where she was, and then she sat upright and dropped her feet to the floor. He saw her wince with pain when she jarred her ankle.

"Unless your sister brings a conveyance of some sort with her, you won't be leaving this bar today," Rafe commented. "Can't imagine you could walk more than five feet on that sprain."

Her lips tightened. "I've been thinking the same thing."

He shrugged. "My offer is still open. You can have my room." When she instantly looked suspicious, he added, "I'm not going to ravish you. I've never been interested in the very young and very unwilling."

"Glad to hear it," she said tartly. "You'd be surprised at the number of men who are."

"Not surprised," he said. "I'm just not one of them."

"I think I'd rather sit here," she said. "At least until J— At least until my sister comes."

On the words, his food arrived, smelling delicious. Samson had a questionable moral code, but he was an excellent cook. "Still hungry?" Rafe asked the girl. "Want anything else to drink?"

"Just water, if I could. Thank you."

Silence fell between them while Rafe dug into the meat pie. He was hungrier than he'd thought. Or it had been a longer night than he'd anticipated. Or both.

Cora was the one to speak first. "So I've been wondering what kind of man you are," she said idly. "Coru? Maybe sweela. Definitely not hunti."

"Somebody else recognized me as coru tonight," he said.

"So what are your blessings?"

He was too tired to lie, so he gave her the truth. "I don't have any."

"What? Why not? *Everybody* has blessings."

"I don't."

She narrowed her eyes and thought that over. "Well, even if your parents didn't pick blessings for you like they *should* have, nothing's stopping you from pulling your own blessings now," she said. "How old are you?"

He laughed. "Twenty-seven. How old are *you*?"

"Seventeen," she said impatiently. Older than he'd thought, but still ungodly young. She didn't waste time getting to her main point. "This would be an excellent year for you to pull your blessings. Twenty-seven is a *very* propitious number, because it's nine threes! It might have been better when you were sixteen or twenty-four, because eights are even better than threes. Maybe you could wait till you're thirty-two."

Rafe had grown up in the country, where people had a healthy respect for all the superstitions of Welchin life—the elemental affiliations, the random blessings, the powerful numbers of three and five and eight. But they weren't as *fanatical* about the traditions as the people in Chialto were. They did believe that newborns should receive their own random blessings within five hours of birth, but out on the farms it was sometimes hard to find the three requisite strangers and a nearby temple. They often made do with friends and whatever collection of coins they could scrape up amongst themselves.

He found it amusing that—with all the other topics that should be weighing on her mind—Cora was worried about Rafe and his lack of blessings. So he was laughing at her when he replied, "Maybe I'll do that."

"Of course, you shouldn't pull them yourself," she said. "Ask strangers. Or ask *me*. I'd go with you right now, if there was a temple nearby. And if I could walk."

He toyed with his empty glass of beer, feeling strangely sober all of a sudden. "I did that, actually. A couple of times. Can't remember how old I was, so maybe it wasn't one of the *propitious* years, but I went to a temple and had strangers pull coins for me."

"See? You do have blessings. What were they?"

He lifted his eyes to meet her interested gaze. "Ghost coins. All of them."

She sank back against the bench, surveying him with narrowed eyes. "That almost seems impossible," she said.

"Seems like a stupid thing to lie about."

"You said you did it a couple of times."

He nodded. "Same thing happened. Ghost coins. Every one."

There were dozens of temples all around Welce, some big, some small, some full of incense and rich woven rugs, others austere and chilly. What they had in common were five benches—one for each of the elemental traits—where visitors could sit to meditate themselves back into balance; a tithe box where they could drop donations to pay for the privilege of entering; and a big barrel of metal coins, each stamped with one of the blessing glyphs. There were forty-three specific blessings, so all the barrels held multiples of each, and they were constantly being replenished as visitors kept the coins they were particularly happy to receive.

But some of those disks stayed in the barrels for years, for decades, picked up and dropped back in again, worn smooth by many hands and constant churning. You couldn't tell what blessing they were supposed to confer, unless it was the questionable one of mystery. It was supposed to be bad luck to draw one for a newborn. Bad luck, maybe, to draw one for anybody.

"Well, that *is* a little strange," Cora allowed. "But I bet I'd pull something different for you. I bet my sister would."

He was amused again. "Somehow, I don't think we'll be making a trip to a temple together anytime soon." She looked like she was going to say something else, so he jumped in with a question of his own. "What are *your* blessings?"

She held out her right hand and spread her fingers to show off three rings, one in copper, one in silver, one in gold. Instead of being stamped with glyphs, each ring had the blessings carved out of them, to reveal the smooth skin beneath. "Imagination, courage, and intelligence," she said.

He wasn't qualified to judge on the first attribute, but he'd bet she had the other two in abundance. "Sweela and hunti," he said. "I would have said you were all sweela."

She grinned. "My mother's sweela and my father is hunti, so it's not really surprising that I have both kinds of blessings." She twisted the gold ring on her finger and added, "Although my sister has three elay traits, and she is *completely* elay in personality, but her mother is hunti and her father was sweela. So you never know."

The sister was sounding more and more like a madwoman. The elay folks were all odd, in Rafe's experience—melodramatically soulful or weirdly empathetic or giggly and ridiculous. He couldn't remember meeting a single one that he'd actually liked. And this one, who lived in the southern slums and was very likely a harlot, would probably prove to be the craziest one yet.

Then he registered what Cora had just said. "Wait a minute. If your mother is sweela and your father is hunti—and it's reversed for your sister—you aren't really related."

For a moment, she looked alarmed, as if afraid she'd betrayed something, then she relaxed again. "We're stepsisters."

"Is your mother married to her father, or is it the other way around?"

Now she was laughing. "It's actually more complicated than that."

"So you don't really have a sister at all."

"Oh, I have plenty of sisters. I'm just not related to most of them by blood."

He settled back more comfortably against the booth and gave her a crooked smile. "You know, I don't care who you are, why you're here, or what you're lying about. But, damn. You've got me pretty curious about how exactly your family is connected."

"I'm sure your family is just as interesting."

"Hardly. My mother's dead, my stepfather and I aren't close, and I only see my brother a couple of times a quintile. I don't really *have* much of a family."

Cora rested her chin in her hand. "Sometimes I think that would be easier. There are days I'd like to see all of them swept away in the Marisi River."

"Is that why you ran away? Family problems?"

Her delicate face, which had grown animated and open, now closed into a scowl again. "In a way. But it's complicated."

You keep saying that, he started to reply, but he never got a chance to say the words. The door opened, and spring stepped inside.

Of course, that wasn't what really happened. A fair woman in a plain white tunic came through the door and stood there a moment, looking around. Unlike Cora, who had entered as unobtrusively as possible, this newcomer didn't seem to notice that she drew all eyes her way, didn't seem to care. It was hard to say what exactly made her so hard to look away from, though maybe it was simply the light. She hadn't closed the door behind her, so the early morning sunshine had followed her inside and pooled around her white clothes, her ashy-blond hair. Maybe it was the swirl of fresh wind that danced in behind her, chasing out the stale odors of smoke and fried meat. Maybe it was the sheer incongruity of her presence, because Rafe had never seen anyone who looked *less* like she belonged in a southside tavern after a very long night.

If he'd had a roll of gold coins, he'd have laid them on the table at this moment and gambled them all. "I'm betting that's your sister," he said.

Cora turned in her seat and started waving wildly. "Jo—Josie! Here I am! Here I am!"

Josie—or whatever her name really was—instantly crossed the room, her eyes focused on her sister. Rafe found himself impelled to come to his feet in some wasted gesture of civility, but the blond woman had eyes only for Cora.

"What happened? Are you all right? I came as quickly as I could," she said, sliding onto the bench next to Cora and giving her a brief hug. But she pulled back almost at once and began to give the other girl a critical inspection. "You look like you've been in a brawl. Are you all right? What *happened*?" She glanced briefly in Rafe's direction. "Did he sell you any red gemstones?"

The complete non sequitur made Rafe frown and Cora grin, though it seemed to take her some effort. "No," she said. "Nothing like that."

Maybe it was a code phrase; he admired them for putting one in place. He said, "Let me excuse myself while you two talk."

Josie settled her gaze on him to appraise him more fully. Her face wasn't quite as delicate as Cora's, or her expression as lively; she looked grave and thoughtful and just a little sad. No, this wasn't the prostitute or the drug dealer Rafe had been envisioning. But she was certainly all elay. No doubt about that.

"Who exactly are you?" she asked in a courteous voice.

"He's the man who helped me," Cora interjected. "When this—this—*criminal* came over and tried to frighten me."

Josie was still watching Rafe. "Yes, that happens sometimes in the slums," she said. "That's why you shouldn't be here. What's your name?"

"Rafe Adova. I play cards."

"And you rescued my sister."

"Hardly that dramatic," he said.

"Oh, it probably was," she said, showing the faintest hint of a smile. "Things tend to get—exciting—when Corene is present."

"Josie," hissed Cora. *Corene.* Now that *was* a name he ought to recognize. Damn his slow thought processes after such a long night.

"It's the sweela gift," he said.

"At any rate, you know half the story, so you may as well know the rest of it. So what happened?"

Rafe slowly dropped to his bench again. Corene licked her lips and thought a moment, clearly editing out details. "There was a party at Rhan's last night. At the last minute, my mother decided not to go, so *he* and I were alone in the elaymotive together. There wasn't even a driver."

Josie nodded. Clearly she knew who *he* was.

"At first I wasn't paying much attention, but then I realized we'd been on the Cinque too long, we were way past Rhan's house," Cora went on. "When I demanded to know where we were going, *he* said there was a different party, he thought I'd like it, we were almost there. But I just thought—he seemed so odd—I decided I should get out of the car if I got a chance."

"A moving elaymotive?" Josie said faintly.

"Well, we'd come to a stop in bad traffic," Cora explained. "So I jumped out and ran as fast as I could. I *thought* I was going toward the river," she added. "Because I figured, if I could get to the Marisi, Zoe would be able to find me. But it was dark, and I got lost, and then somehow I ended up here on the southside. So then I figured I'd go looking for you instead. But I fell down, and I twisted my ankle, and I just came inside the first place I could find that looked halfway respectable."

Josie glanced around the bar again, showing no distaste for the sordid surroundings. "You made a good choice," she said. "There aren't a lot of places in this part of town where you would have been half so safe."

Corene looked over at Rafe. "Well, this one wasn't safe the whole time. These men came over and acted like they wanted to kidnap me or something, but that's when Rafe told them to get out."

Josie transferred her attention to him as well. "You did my sister a great kindness."

He shrugged. "It was easy enough to do."

"Since then, we've just been sitting here waiting for you," Corene finished up. "And now—now I just want to go home."

"Foley's already on his way to your father," Josie said. "He came here with me, but I sent him on with a message. Foley is my personal guard," she explained to Rafe.

"If you live southside and you only have one guard, I'm surprised you've survived longer than a nineday," he said.

That faint smile was back. "I don't live here all the time. And Foley is fairly formidable."

"But Zoe and my father aren't in the Chialto house right now," Corene objected. "They're staying with—someone else—on the other side of the canal."

"I know," Josie said. "It will take him at least a day to make it back. And if you sprained your ankle— Can you walk?"

"I don't think so. Not very far."

"Not sure you want to sit here in the bar for a whole day," Rafe said. "I offered your sister the use of my room upstairs. She seemed to suspect my motives at the time, but it was an entirely honest offer and it's still open."

"Thank you. This time we'll accept," Josie said. "We'll pay you, of course."

He smiled at her. He was tempted, so tempted, to say, *Play you for the privilege.* Whoever won five hands at penta would determine the cost of the accommodations for the night. But an elay opponent was always tricky, and this one would be harder to read than most. He could lose everything to her on a single turn of the cards.

"Of course," he answered. "Let me show you upstairs."

He paused to order bread and cheese from a serving boy, since Josie hadn't eaten and there was no food in his room, and then he shepherded the two women up the dark and narrow staircase. Corene refused to let him carry her, which would have speeded up the process enormously, and the server arrived with a tray of goods just as they made it to Rafe's door.

Five minutes later the three of them were more or less comfortably situated around a small table set right before the fire, which Rafe had built up hastily after they stepped into the room. He'd also given the women the only two chairs, while he perched on a battered trunk that held most of his possessions. He was relieved to see that the room was in relatively good order, but then, he was a fairly fastidious man. Even the bed was neatly made, though he couldn't remember exactly when he had last washed the linens.

"If you're tired, as I imagine you are, you can sleep while you wait," he said through a mouthful of cheese. "There's a room down the hall for washing up."

"I'm so tired," Corene said, yawning to prove it. "And my foot hurts."

"I'm fine," Josie said. "But you must be tired, too, if you've been up all night earning a living."

She didn't even say it sarcastically. "I might throw a blanket on the floor and nap for a few hours," he answered. "I usually don't have trouble falling asleep no matter where I am."

"We're still imposing on you most dreadfully. You've been so kind to my sister. I think you must be a very good man."

Something about that phrase must have triggered a memory in Corene's mind, because she looked up from her plate. "He doesn't have any blessings," she said. "Have you ever heard of such a thing?"

Now Josie's expression was speculative again. "Yes, of course. A lot of people here in the slums don't have any," she said. "Sometimes they let me pull coins for them. Those are always interesting experiences."

Ah—so that was it. This Josie was some kind of reformer, one of those maniacs and zealots who ministered to the poor. That explained her air of saintliness, though it didn't explain how she'd managed to stay alive for whatever period of time she'd been carrying out her mission. Even do-gooders tended to fare badly in this part of town. Only the tough survived, only the people who were both smart and ruthless. Right now he wasn't sure she could claim to have any of those traits.

"Can you take him to a temple?" Corene asked, yawning again.

"I think we have more pressing concerns at the moment," Josie replied.

"But I want to *see*. He says he's been to a temple, but he only pulls ghost coins."

That caught Josie's attention; she gave Rafe a quick, sharp inspection. But all she said was, "I suppose that means there's something mysterious about him."

He opened his eyes wide. "*Me?* I'm not concealing anything. Whereas your sister has been hiding a secret all night, beginning with her name, which clearly isn't *Cora*."

Josie looked amused again. "I'm surprised to learn she has such discretion."

So she wasn't disposed to share secrets, either. The less they wanted to tell him, the more he wanted to know. "I think I'll piece the clues together eventually."

"No doubt you will."

"But his blessings," Corene interjected, her voice stubborn. He thought she must be so tired and so overwhelmed that she had picked this one idea to anchor her thoughts to the present. "Can you take him to a temple later? Maybe while I'm sleeping? You pull the best blessings."

Josie sighed silently, as if capitulating, and then asked Rafe, "Do you have a sheet of paper? And something to write with?"

"Um—sure. Let me poke around a little."

He finally unearthed paper and ink, and cleared a space on the table for Josie to go to work. He wasn't surprised to see that she approached this odd, unimportant task with great precision, first marking off twenty-four squares on two separate pieces of paper, and then sketching a blessing sigil in each one.

"Do you know them all by heart?" Corene asked, watching in fascination.

"Of course. Don't you?"

Corene didn't bother to answer. "But why do you need forty-eight?"

"Forty elemental blessings. Three extraordinary blessings. Three ghost blessings. And two left over in case I make a mistake."

She didn't, of course, as Rafe could have predicted. When she was done, he had to hunt for a pair of scissors so she could cut the squares apart, and then look for a container to hold them. The sisters were busy folding the scraps into smaller shapes while he searched for a bowl or basket. The best he could come up with was a mug that had held ale at a not too distant date, but any leftover liquid had dried into a stain at the bottom of the cup.

He was heading back to the table when a knock on the door sent him that way. "Rafe," called one of the serving boys through the wood. "Samson sent up a loaf of bread if you want it."

Whenever Samson had leftover food, he offered it to his boarders at a huge discount, an arrangement Rafe appreciated. "Sounds good," he called back. Opening the door, he handed over a few quint-coppers in exchange for a slightly lumpy loaf. "Anybody want something else to eat?" he inquired as he turned back to his visitors, shutting the door quickly so the warmth from the fire couldn't escape.

But the sweep of the door sent an errant draft curling through the room, brushing most of the blessing squares off the table. More than half blew straight into the fire.

"Oh no!" Corene exclaimed, dropping to the floor and trying to rescue the ones that hadn't swirled into the flames.

Josie was laughing. "Maybe we're not meant to choose blessings for Rafe Adova after all."

Rafe set the bread on the table, along with the mug that was no longer needed. "There's still a few left," he pointed out, because three folded squares remained on the table. "Maybe those are mine."

"Maybe they are," Josie agreed. "And they've been chosen for you by the element of air."

"Maybe he's elay," Corene said, returning to her chair and reaching for one of the scraps of paper. She unfolded it eagerly, then stared at it wide-eyed. "Ghost," she said, showing them the empty square.

Despite himself, Rafe felt a prickle of superstition spiderwalk down his spine. Josie opened the second square. Not a mark upon it. Silently, she handed the third one to Rafe, and he smoothed it open.

Another ghost. If the element of air had chosen his blessings, it had gifted him with absolutely nothing.

THREE

Corene protested for about five minutes, but Rafe wasn't surprised that Josie convinced her to lie on the bed, where she almost instantly fell asleep. Rafe should have been just as tired, since he'd been awake since noon of the day before, but he found himself oddly energized. As if he'd just had the first glass from an excellent bottle of wine, and it was glittering through his veins. He was pretty sure the intoxicant in this case was the young woman sitting so primly at his table, looking utterly incongruous yet perfectly at ease.

He had been gone for a few minutes, cleaning himself up in the room down the hall, and now he dropped into the other chair across the table from her. He noticed that the fire was burning merrily; she must have added more fuel while he was out of the room. For someone who looked as dainty as an heiress, she possessed an impressive streak of practicality and a hard core of strength. Or so it seemed.

"Anything else I can do to make you more comfortable?" he asked.

"No, actually, I've been trying to think what *we* can do to make up for intruding on you. I'm sure you're exhausted, too, and would like to sleep in your own bed."

"I'm good for another few hours," he said. "But I suppose we're all trapped here until her father arrives."

"I know. I apologize again for the disruption to your life."

Out of habit, he pulled the ever-present deck of cards from a hip pocket and began shuffling them. "I find I'm not minding it much," he said. "It's made for a more than ordinarily exciting evening."

"You've been very kind."

He risked the question. "Even though I didn't sell your sister any red gemstones?"

She laughed. "So you caught that, did you? Some friends of ours taught us that phrase years ago. They were itinerant traders and sometimes dealt with unsavory characters. It's a way of asking if your friend or partner is in danger without letting anyone else understand the question."

He nodded. "I guessed." In the small silence that followed, the ruffling of the cards sounded very loud. "So how would you like to pass the time while we wait?" Rafe finally asked. "Do you play penta?"

She looked intrigued. "I never have. My mother always thought card games were vulgar."

He laughed softly. "Well, they're often played by vulgar people." Just to occupy his hands, he started laying the cards out in suits, face up on the table. Josie watched with seeming fascination.

"The artwork is very intricate," she said. "Do all decks look like this?"

"Some are more ornate than others. I tend to buy the beautiful, expensive ones." He shrugged. "I spend so much time handling them, I figure I might as well enjoy looking at them."

"So are there—five different kinds? No. Six. Seven?"

He neatened the piles and turned them to face her. "Five suits. One to match each elemental trait. Fish for coru, skulls for hunti, roses for torz. Horseshoes for sweela, though that's always seemed the weakest connection to me. I suppose because horseshoes are shaped in the fire." With a little flourish, he pushed the last pile closer to her hand. "And for your own element, flutes."

"What about all those other cards?"

"Three wildcards. Think of them as random blessings. Depending on the game, they can be more or less valuable to hold in your hand."

"And those?"

"Trumps. Nine of them. I don't know how they relate to the general blessings, but three times three is a lucky number."

"And you can play more than one kind of game with these same cards?"

"Dozens. Hundreds."

"Teach me one," she said. "Something simple."

He laughed. It was so unexpected that he should have expected it. This girl might be all elay, but she had a little of the coru element of surprise running through her veins. "All right. This is a game that even children can play. Trumps become their own suit, and the nine of trumps becomes the fourth wildcard. So all you have to do is match six of a kind . . ."

She was a quick study, mastering two easy games so rapidly that he taught her penta, since it had a subtlety that made it enjoyable whether the player was a novice or a professional. She even agreed to play for money—"as long as we keep it to quint-coppers and you don't cheat"—and laughed in delight the first time she won a hand. By that time, of course, she'd already lost a whole pile of quint-coppers, though he doubted they amounted to much more than a quint-silver. Hardly enough to cover the price of the extra loaf of bread Samson had sent to his room.

"I see how this could become addictive," she observed. "I keep thinking if I play just one more hand, I'll finally get the right cards."

"And that kind of attitude is exactly what keeps me employed," he answered.

She folded her hands and studied him. "So how does one become a professional card player?" she asked. "What road do you start down that winds up here?"

She didn't say it as if she pitied him or wanted to convince him of the error of his ways. Merely, she sounded curious. Elay women were creatures not only of air, but also of spirit. He had the sense she was trying to fix in her mind the precise pattern of his soul.

He gathered up the cards, since his hands felt empty without them, and began to idly shuffle and cut them, shuffle and cut. "My mother met an attractive man and found herself with a baby on her hands," he said.

"A common enough occurrence," Josie observed.

He nodded. "I get the feeling life wasn't very easy for her until she met my stepfather when I was a few years old. He'd come to Chialto for the work, but he was a country man at heart. All torz. He missed the land. When his sister asked him back to help run the family farm, he was glad to go, and my mother was glad to go with him. A couple years later they had a son, my brother, Steff. A couple years after that, my mother died."

He shrugged, a silent way of conveying what a time of pain and confusion that had been. All these years later, and he felt like he could still remember every day of that first awful year after his mother's death. "I hadn't liked farm life much to begin with, and pretty soon I couldn't wait to get away," he went on. "I wanted to get someplace where there was *life* and *chaos* and *music*. I wanted to go to the city. I left the first chance I could."

"How old were you?"

"Seventeen. Came to Chialto, drifted around, took odd jobs. Headed down to the harbor to work on the docks. Didn't like that, either. Came back to the city. Started playing cards to pass the time and ended up playing for money, when it turned out I was good at it. And here I am."

"Do you ever go back to see your family?"

"Sure. Steff's a good kid and I visit when I can. I think he's pretty lonely. The farm life doesn't suit him."

"I take it he's not torz."

"No, he seems to be coru, though as far as I can tell, no one in his father's family *ever* came from blood and water. So I guess it's no wonder that he doesn't fit in."

"To some extent, it doesn't matter who we are or where we came from—what kind of family brought us into this world," Josie said softly. "We become who we were meant to be, and all those other influences fall away."

He gave her a speculative look. "I suppose you're talking from experience?"

"Certainly I have turned out to be a much different kind of person than I was raised to be."

"I take it you spend time here in the slums doing some kind of reform work."

"Something like that," she said a little dryly. "A couple years ago, I bought an abandoned building and refurbished it. Turned it into a shelter with an infirmary, a kitchen, and a whole lot of beds. I provide a safe place for people to sleep if they're desperate and have nowhere else to go."

"Well, unless you have beds for a thousand people, I can't imagine you can take care of every desperate soul who ends up southside on an average night."

"Ah. Well. Some of the people *I* might consider desperate are perfectly happy with their lives. The ones who come to me are the ones who truly have no other options."

He gestured to indicate her plain, inexpensive tunic. "You're not dressed like it at the moment, but you look to me like someone who comes from money. I'm wondering how your family feels about this little project."

She smiled. "My mother is horrified. My brother-in-law brings fairly constant pressure on me to give up the work. My sister—she's proud of me, actually. She comes sometimes to help out."

He glanced toward the sleeping Corene. "A different sister, I take it."

"I have quite a few."

"That's what Corene said. She also said that the two of you aren't actually related by blood."

"We were raised as sisters until five years ago. The man we thought was our father turned out not to be. It's complicated."

"That's also what Corene said." He waited a beat, then added, "That's what *you* called her. *She* told me her name was Cora."

Now she was laughing openly. "She's being very mysterious. The sweela folk love excitement and intrigue."

"And I suppose your name isn't really Josie."

"Close enough. Josetta."

That's when it clicked in his head. *Corene. Zoe. Josetta.* "Slap me stupid," he breathed. "You're the princesses. The ones that weren't really the king's daughters."

"That's us," she said cheerfully.

He had been watching her covertly ever since she arrived, but now he stared outright. Oh, it had been such a scandal, though overshadowed by a *surfeit* of scandals that had all piled up at once four or five years ago. First the people of Welce learned that King Vernon was dying. Then they learned that he had been impotent all these years, and his three daughters—by three different wives—had been fathered by loyal courtiers doing their part to give the king his heirs. Then they learned that Vernon's fourth and youngest wife was carrying her second child and that *that* baby, miraculously, had been sired by the king.

A couple of quintiles later, the king had passed away, living barely long enough to hold his infant daughter in his arms. The five primes—the heads of the Five Families—had appointed a regent and an interim governing body that would rule Welce until the girl inherited her crown at the favorable age of twenty-four.

And while all of Welce waited for that child to grow up, what happened to the girls who had once been princesses? It had never occurred to Rafe to wonder before. He was at an uncharacteristic loss for words.

"I didn't think you'd be so shocked," Josetta said at last. "You don't seem like the type to fawn over royalty."

He pulled himself together. "I wouldn't know. I've never had the chance to converse before with someone in line for the throne."

"Anyway, I'm not really royalty. Surely you know the story? The bloodlines?"

He nodded. "But aren't you—I don't pay that much attention, but—aren't you and Corene both still part of the succession?"

"We are, but we're so much more removed from the crown now that Odelia's been named the heir."

"I wouldn't think you're so removed," Rafe observed. "Babies die all the time. People get trampled by horses—run over by elaymotives. They drown. Now I'm even more shocked that anyone is letting you roam around the slums unprotected. I'd think they'd have you locked behind the palace doors with guards standing over you day and night."

"I do have a guard with me day and night."

Rafe looked ostentatiously around the room. "Not that I can see."

She was trying to repress a smile. "He *was* with me. I sent him to fetch Corene's father. And I assure you, he was reluctant to go. He takes his duties to me very seriously."

"But one guard—in a place like this—it makes my blood run cold to think of what could happen to you."

"Now you sound like Darien."

"Darien," he repeated. "Darien Serlast? The regent?"

Josetta nodded. "Corene's father. My brother-in-law. And regent of the realm. He hates it that I spend so much time southside."

"I would think he would do more than just hate it. I'd think he would *make* you stay someplace safe."

"He doesn't have the power to make me do anything."

Rafe leaned back in his chair and surveyed her again. "Well, from what I hear, he does," he said softly. "He's a hunti man, right? He was practically running the whole kingdom in the days before anyone knew that Vernon was sick. He sounds to me like the kind of man who pretty much always gets what he wants."

"Let me put it differently," Josetta said. "For the first fifteen years of my life, I was afraid. I knew all eyes were watching me all the time. I knew I was expected to behave a certain way. I knew there were people who were eager to see me fail. I knew there were people who wanted me dead— people who tried to kill me, in fact, if you remember a certain regatta five years ago. My life was not my own and my life was not secure.

"Then Odelia was born, and the attention shifted. I decided I would no longer live to please other people. I would live up to my blessings. I would honor my elay heritage. And while this decision has not found favor with everyone, I have not changed my mind. It is very difficult to make an elay woman conform once she has decided she wants to be free."

"I can certainly see that," Rafe said, outwardly laughing, but inwardly feeling a touch of admiration. "I can almost pity poor hunti Darien, trying to contain a woman of air and spirit."

Josetta's smile was back. "Pity him even more for Corene, who is incorrigible, and for Zoe—his wife—who is the coru prime. *Nobody* controls Zoe. He is surrounded by women who won't do his bidding."

"He seems to have been a remarkably effective regent, even so. I suspect he is more powerful than you would like to admit."

"Powerful," she agreed, "and absolutely committed to the well-being of the realm. I like Darien very much. I just don't always do what he says."

The answer he was going to give was interrupted by a huge yawn. "Sorry," he apologized. "A rude way to treat royalty."

"I'm feeling exhausted myself," she said. "I think I'm going to curl up alongside Corene and see if I can sleep for a few hours. If you can make yourself comfortable, you might try to do the same."

A few minutes later, Rafe found himself in the distinctly odd position of trying to sleep in a room full of slumbering princesses. It was so unlikely as to be downright bizarre; he might wake up to find he had dreamed the entire evening. At least the room was set up to give the women a modicum of privacy, since the narrow bed sat in a curtained alcove and he had pulled the drapes shut once Josetta lay down. As for himself, he was making do with a blanket and a pillow on the floor in front of the fireplace. If he had been any less tired, he would have lain awake for hours, reviewing the events of the night, but as it was, he fell almost instantly asleep.

I t was probably three hours later when Rafe woke up, stiff and uncomfortable. A wooden floor made for a hard mattress, no matter how weary you were. He stretched, stifled a groan, and forced himself to his feet. He'd slept long enough to clear his head, but not long enough to erase his sense of wonder at the fact that royalty was sleeping in his bed.

He cleaned himself up in the chamber down the hall, changing clothes and shaving while he was at it. When he went back to his room to drop off his soiled garments, he hesitated a moment, then crept up to the drawn curtains and cocked his head to listen. Yes, he could catch the faint sounds of two people breathing in slightly mismatched rhythms. He was tempted to peek inside, and he might have, if they'd just been two ordinary girls who had, in some extraordinary fashion, become entangled in his life. But princesses. It seemed wrong to spy on them. Offensive. Treasonous, even. He turned away.

A glance out his window showed him a cloudy mid-afternoon sky; not too early to go downstairs and start earning the day's income. Josetta, he was certain, would instantly figure out where he had gone. She wasn't the type to worry if she woke up to an empty apartment. He would bet that very little rocked that girl off-balance.

It would be interesting to get to know her better. Or it would have been, if she hadn't been a princess. Which she was.

He gave his head a small shake and exited as quietly as he could. Downstairs, he found the place already starting to fill up with the afternoon regulars and the first vanguard of the evening crowd, the rich boys and the bored old men who thought an evening southside would get their blood racing or reverse their failing fortunes.

Rafe touched the deck of cards in his hip pocket, smiled impartially at the room, and made his way to his favorite corner table. Time to focus. Time to make new friends for the day.

The first set of players to join him consisted of a father and two sons—all of them torz, up from the country for the nineday, and still marveling at the sights the city had to offer. They were so wide-eyed and trusting that Rafe could have cheated them blind, but they were such a likable lot that he didn't have the heart. He won, of course, but he didn't beggar them in the process, unless they couldn't afford to lose three quint-golds.

"You'll find it's difficult to win a game against a professional gambler," he felt impelled to say as the youngest boy looked disheartened at losing the last hand. "It's not my place to offer advice, but you might try other districts of Chialto for better entertainment. Have you been to the Plaza of Men? You'll find some sport there. I'd get out of this part of town, if I were you."

The father gave him a keen look and heaved himself to his feet. "We were planning to make that our next stop. I just thought the boys would enjoy a chance to see the wilder part of town." He chuckled. "Things are very dull down where we live."

"Sometimes dull is preferable to dissolute," Rafe said. "There isn't much romance to debauchery."

"There isn't much romance to farming, either," said the youngest son.

"Probably pays better than gambling," Rafe said.

"On good days," the father agreed. "Well! Are we done here? Thank you for an instructive afternoon, young man."

They'd been gone about fifteen minutes when two sweela men and a coru girl came his way. The men appeared to be drunk already, though it wasn't even dinnertime; the woman was giggling so much that Rafe couldn't tell if she'd been drinking, too, or if she was just overdoing an assumed personality of foolish irresponsibility. She took the chair directly across from his and whined that she didn't have any money, so one of the sweela men dribbled a pile of coins in front of her, and she squealed with delight. Rafe kept his usual courteous mask on his face, but he conceived an instant and deep dislike of her. He always played to win, because his livelihood depended on it, but sometimes victory tasted even sweeter than other times. It would be delicious if he bested this woman.

Over the next half hour, the coru woman won three pots and Rafe collected only one, but his was by far the richest. It made her angry, and she flicked him a look of cold malice when she realized how masterfully she'd been outplayed. He pretended that he didn't notice. He couldn't afford to get into a private competition with her; he had to play the entire game against all opponents, or he would lose the whole thing.

They were halfway through the fifth hand—small pot, mediocre cards, a round that Rafe was willing to lose—when Samson approached their table. "Someone here who wants to talk to you," he said to Rafe in a low voice.

Rafe raised his brows, but Samson merely shrugged. Not someone the bar owner recognized, then, and not someone who seemed so dangerous that Rafe should slip quietly out the back door. "Then, friends, let me excuse myself. I'll be back as quickly as I can."

"Hey—what about the game?" one of the men demanded.

Rafe came to his feet and tossed his cards face up on the table. "I concede the hand. You can play it out, or split the pot among you."

Samson pointed to a booth along the side wall, and Rafe approached slowly, assessing the occupant as well as he could while he narrowed the distance. Male, probably in his mid-thirties, with dark hair and dark clothing. He sat very still, his hands folded before him, as if prepared to wait with unvarying patience until the world itself stuttered to a stop. But he wasn't torz, Rafe was pretty sure of that. This man looked to be all hunti, all stubborn unyielding determination. Rafe's least favorite type of gambler, because the hunti rarely gambled at all.

He slipped quietly into the opposite seat and leaned against the back, showing himself to be wholly at ease. In fact, he was tense all over, coiled as if to fight or run. Close up, the hunti man exuded a sort of implacable power, a certainty that whatever he wanted he would, without question, get.

Or maybe that was just the anger that he was clearly trying very hard, and without complete success, to hold in check.

Rafe figured there was only one man this could possibly be. And already Rafe didn't like him.

"I'm Rafe Adova. You wanted to speak to me?" he said in a neutral voice.

The hunti man stared at him with narrowed gray eyes. "I believe you have something of mine. And I want it back."

Rafe pretended ignorance. "Something you lost to me in a hand of cards? I normally sell all the jewelry I win, but if it's only been a day or two—although I can't say I remember you—"

"Don't play the fool with me," the hunti man interrupted. "You have my daughter. She came to this place last night, apparently in dire distress, and I understand *you* are the one who—took charge of her. Where is she?"

"Ah," Rafe said, resettling himself more comfortably. "She's safe. She's sleeping. I imagine it might be a couple of hours before she wakes up, so you could—"

"You will take me to her right now," the man said sharply.

Now Rafe leaned forward. He felt his own eyes narrow, his own voice roughen. "When she came here last night, she was obviously running from something—from *someone*," he said. "She didn't name him, so maybe that someone was *you*. I don't think I'm going to turn her over unless I'm sure you're not the one who tried to harm her—and unless I'm sure you can take care of her in the future. Because you're either one or the other. The man who tried to ravish her, or the man who didn't keep her safe."

For an instant, the other man blazed with such rage that he might have been the sweela prime, able to call fire at will. But oh no, he was pure hunti, strong enough to contain any rampaging emotion. His face tightened, smoothed out, gave nothing else away.

"Do you know who I am?" he asked in a soft voice.

"I'm guessing you're Darien Serlast."

"Then you know I only have to speak a word to have this building torn from its foundations." Probably right this very moment, too— Rafe guessed there was a contingent of palace guards outside, keeping the place secure while Darien Serlast did his business inside. He figured that Josetta's personal guard was among the soldiers who waited outside, because he didn't spot any newcomers inside the bar looking like they were ready to spring into action.

He kept his voice indifferent. "Go ahead. It's not my building."

"What do you want, Rafe Adova? Money? Name your price. I just want my daughter returned to me safely."

"What I want is to be sure *she* wants to be returned to *you*."

Something rippled across that cool face—surprise, maybe, perhaps even a hint of admiration. *A principled man here in the ghettos.* Darien Serlast seemed to grow even more still, more focused, as he studied Rafe for a long moment, not even pretending to be subtle about it. The gray eyes took in Rafe's clothing, his well-kept hands, even flicked to the right side of his face where Rafe would have sworn that unconventional ear was covered by a convenient swatch of hair. As a rule, Rafe was an excellent judge of character and mood, but he didn't have a clue what Darien Serlast was thinking.

Finally, the regent spoke, his voice still soft but utterly unyielding. "I believe if you ask her," he said, "you will find that she trusts me without reservation."

"I *would* go ask her," Rafe said, "but I'm afraid you'd follow me. So we're still at an impasse."

"Certainly there must be a way through it."

"Well—"

Before Rafe could complete his thought, he heard a woman's voice raised in relief. "Darien! You got here so fast!"

Again, spring swirled through Samson's tavern as Josetta moved into view. She practically flung herself across the room and into Darien Serlast's arms as he hastily stood up to embrace her. More slowly, Rafe came to his feet and observed them.

"Is she here? Is she all right?" the hunti man asked urgently.

"Yes, she's fine, she's sleeping. She had a scary misadventure. That awful man—"

Serlast released Josetta and sent an appraising look in Rafe's direction. "Not this one, I presume?"

"No, it was Dominic. They were alone in an elaymotive and he said something to frighten her, so she decided it would be a good idea to jump out at the first chance." Josetta's face revealed just how crazy she thought that was. "So she did, but she got lost and ended up southside, which is when she decided it would be a good idea to come find *me*. She was lucky she ended up someplace relatively benign."

Darien Serlast seemed more preoccupied with the first part of Josetta's speech than the last. "What did Dominic say to her?"

"She wasn't specific," Josetta said, sounding worried. "But I got the impression she's more afraid of him than she'd like to admit. Darien, you need to get her out of that house."

and hobbled away. Rafe involuntarily put his hand to his cheek and watched her go—watched all of them. Josetta met his eyes for a long, cool moment, then turned to follow the others out the door. Darien Serlast never bothered to look back.

Rafe figured it wasn't entirely his fault if he was a little unstable on his feet as he lurched back to his table of squabbling opponents. "Are you *finally* ready to play a few hands without jumping up every five minutes?" one of the sweela men demanded.

"Yes—absolutely—at your service," Rafe answered, willing his brain to clear and his nerves to steady. "No more distractions, I promise. Whose turn is it to deal?"

They played another two hours, fortunes changing hands a few times before Rafe finally swept up the final pot, glittering with silvers and quint-golds. The coru woman gave him an ugly look from under her heavy eyelashes; she had been so sure she would win the final hand that she had bet every last coin she'd won over the course of the night. That was what he'd been counting on, her confidence and her bravado. He took more satisfaction out of beating her than he did out of scooping up the money.

"Well, that's it for me," said one of the men, tossing his cards to the table in a show of bad temper. "Come on! It's late enough. Let's get out of here."

The three of them surged to their feet and instantly started bickering. Rafe paid no attention, simply pocketing the coins to count later. A yawn cracked his face open before he could look around and assess if any other likely opponents had strolled in while he was waiting.

He was so tired. It was hardly past dinnertime, but he could feel the weariness in his bones, in his brain. He'd almost lost that final hand with one careless discard. He'd better go to his room and sleep for a few hours, or he'd lose everything he'd won so far tonight.

Besides. There was some kind of reward waiting for him upstairs. He'd tried to pretend he wasn't curious about how much money Darien Serlast considered sufficient to pay for the rescue and safe-keeping of his daughter. But in truth, he was burning to know. He gulped the last of his beer, finished off a crust of bread, then pushed away from the table and headed upstairs.

His room had been tidied and his bed had been made—Josetta's thoughtfulness, he would guess, since Corene didn't seem like the neat-and-organized type. On the table by the fireplace someone had left a black velvet bag next to the stacked dishes and the three scraps of blank paper. Rafe hefted it, impressed by its weight. If it was filled with quint-golds, this was quite a haul. Two or three ninedays' worth of winnings.

He opened the drawstring and poured the bounty on the table in a clattering, glittering stream, then stood there staring. Not quint-golds, oh no—*whole* gold coins, each one enough to cover his expenses for a couple of quintiles. He could change his life with this kind of money. Put a downpayment on a building in a decent part of town. Invest in his own business. Buy shares in a merchant ship plying the waters to Cozique or Berringey. It wasn't enough to make him rich, but it was enough to put him on the path to making his own fortune.

Rafe had been casually kind a number of times in his life, but it had never paid off so handsomely. It was enough to make a man believe in the goodness of his fellow man. Enough to turn him elay.

Elay. Like the quirky blond princess. Whom he would never see again.

He shook his head and dropped the coins back in the pouch, one by one, listening with a sense of astonishment to each individual *clink*. It wouldn't be wise to leave the money in this room; it wouldn't be wise to carry it around with him. He had a small account with a banker situated up by the Plaza of Men. He would have to make a trip there tomorrow morning and deposit this incredible windfall while he pondered the best way to use it.

Not until he gave up the notion of staying awake any longer and headed toward bed did he remember that Corene had promised him her own gift of thanks. Bemused, rocking slightly with exhaustion, Rafe stood for five minutes, staring down at his pillow. Corene had left him her three rings of copper, silver, and gold, carved with the glyphs of imagination, courage, and intelligence.

Rafe could no longer say he didn't have any blessings of his own.

FOUR

Josetta had known that Corene's escapade would have serious consequences, she just hadn't expected that they would fall on her as well. Of course, that was often the way with Corene's adventures. Their effects rippled and swelled until they engulfed everyone in the vicinity.

"I don't want you going back there," Darien told Josetta the morning after he had swooped down to the southside bar to rescue Corene. The two of them were having breakfast alone in the pretty sun-filled dining room of Darien's house on the north edge of Chialto. Corene was never an early riser, and Zoe was sleeping late because she had been awake half the night with the baby. Josetta usually found it a rare treat to be alone with Darien, but she had forgotten how peremptory he could be. He was used to running the world, or at least Welce. It made him think he should run everybody else's life, too.

She stirred some crushed fruit into her water and asked mildly, "Don't want me going back where?"

"The slums. They're too dangerous."

"I've been working there for more than a year now, and I've never had any trouble."

"Yes, you have," he instantly disagreed. "The place has been robbed four times. You were assaulted on the streets just a nineday ago—"

"I wasn't assaulted. A beggar grabbed for my purse. Foley was right there to keep him away from me. I gave him a silver coin anyway," she added. "He was obviously starving."

Darien shook his head at such stupidity. "It is a mystery to me that you haven't been murdered twenty times over."

Josetta sipped from her glass and watched him over the rim, not allowing herself to show irritation. From the time she had been very young, she had known how to keep her temper. Navigating the shifting currents of palace intrigue had required a clear head and absolute concentration, and she had always been afraid of putting a foot wrong. "I think I was in far more danger when I lived at court and people were trying to kill me," she said softly.

He didn't take the bait. "Yes, and any princess might be the target of an assassination attempt at any time, but this is a different kind of danger," he said. "It's random and violent and comes from every direction. You've been lucky, but luck has a way of abruptly running out. You're not going back."

She smiled at him. "Darien. I appreciate your concern. But it's not your place to tell me what to do. As long as my mother isn't worried about me—"

"Your mother doesn't display enough good judgment on her own behalf to make her qualified to care for anyone else."

She went on as if he hadn't spoken. "And Zoe isn't worried about me—"

"Zoe," Darien interrupted, "has no sense of propriety whatsoever. Keeping *her* in check is more exhausting than watching over *you*."

Which was so true that Josetta couldn't help laughing. Although Zoe was the product of two of the Five Families of Welce—the Ardelays and the Lalindars—she didn't care a thing for societal rules. Maybe because she had been raised in obscurity while her father endured a long exile. Maybe because she was coru prime, and a woman of blood and water was contrary and difficult to contain. Maybe because she was Zoe.

"My point is that my blood relatives don't mind that I spend part of my time in the slums," Josetta said. "So I don't think it should be any of your concern."

He was silent for a moment, watching her out of those narrowed gray eyes. He wouldn't curse or shout; Darien, too, knew how to rein in his temper. That was one of the reasons she'd been so surprised, back there in the bar, to see the fury on his face when he was talking to Rafe Adova. She still wondered what the gambler had said to him.

"I would hate to think," he said, "that your little shelter would be closed or torn down for some kind of legal infraction."

She rested her elbows on the table and leaned forward, meeting his hard expression with a determined one of her own. Her mother was hunti; Josetta knew how to be as unmovable as stone. "Darien. If you shut down my shelter, I'll just go back to the slums and minister on the street corners. That's what I did before. I'll bring food, I'll hand out coins and clothing—I'll go with anyone who asks me to visit a sick girl or a hurt man. Do you think that's safer?"

His mouth tightened and he leaned back in his chair, still regarding her with a speculative expression. "I don't think you realize," he said, "how very valuable you are. Neither you nor Corene should be roaming around dangerous districts just waiting to be abducted."

"Foley is always with me."

"One man isn't enough. If you had three soldiers with you every time you stepped off the Cinque—" He paused and considered for a while, frowning.

It was difficult enough always including Foley in her calculations; operating with three guards would be cumbersome in the extreme. But she said in a conciliating voice, "Maybe we could talk about this some other time."

He nodded. "Very well. But I have a favor to ask you."

"Of course. What is it?"

"Stay here a few days instead of going to your mother's. Make sure Corene doesn't suffer any ill effects from this dreadful incident. She's more likely to talk to you than she is to either of us."

"Although I'm sure she doesn't tell me everything. But if you think it will do any good, I'll be happy to stay for a while." She loved her room in this house: It was a place filled with wind chimes and painted birds and soft white-and-yellow patterns. A peaceful elay room, crafted by a turbulent coru prime. Sometimes she felt guilty for liking this house so much more than her mother's.

Darien was still talking. "There will be more excitement in the next quintile or two. You might know that I have been negotiating treaties with various foreign nations, and I expect the prince of Berringey and the empress of Malinqua to each come visiting over the summer. Your presence will be essential while they're here. But even sooner than that—within the next nineday or two—Romelle is bringing Odelia to court. Naturally, I want you and Corene to attend all the dinners and receptions."

She was less thrilled with this part of his request, but, of course, she replied in the affirmative. Despite boasting to Rafe Adova that she ran her life to suit herself these days, she still couldn't imagine shirking her responsibilities as princess.

"Is Romelle really bringing Odelia this time, or will it be Mally?"

Darien smiled a bit sardonically. "Isn't that the point? That we don't know?"

"I thought *you* would know. If it's the real princess instead of the decoy, won't you want to marshal more guards?"

His smile grew wider. "But if I only bring out the palace guards when the real princess is present, doesn't that defeat the purpose of having a substitute in the first place?"

She laughed. "Of course! Then I'll expect to see the castle *overrun* with soldiers all looking very grim and attentive."

"I think they plan a stay of only three or four days. Mirti and the other primes have all agreed to attend—even Kayle is coming up from the coast, under heavy protest, I might add. So it will be quite the gala."

She couldn't help a small groan. "I hate these sorts of things."

"So does Zoe. So does everyone." He smiled. "But consider it an excuse to buy new clothes. Take Corene and go shopping."

She favored him with a mock scowl. "Are you trying to bribe me?"

"Whatever works to get what I want."

Corene was much happier than Josetta was at the prospect of shopping for new clothes—and attending events where she could show them off. So, shortly after she was up and dressed, the two princesses headed off toward the Plaza of Women. They would buy their formal tunics at one of the upscale emporiums in the shop district, but it was always fun to dig through the merchandise at the big open-air booths in the Plaza, looking for exotic accessories at bargain prices.

Foley accompanied them, of course; Foley always accompanied Josetta. A strongly muscled and mostly taciturn torz man somewhere in his mid-twenties, he had become her principal bodyguard when she was thirteen, and he had seen her through some of her most difficult years. She was used to him hovering behind her like a somewhat willful shadow, always keeping pace with her, always keeping her safe. He worked next to her in the southside shelter, traveled beside her in carriages and elaymotives; he never refused any commission she gave him. And yet there were days he was more a mystery to her than a hooded stranger she might pass on the street.

"Did Darien give you money? Because I have about three silvers left in my pockets, and *that* won't buy much," Corene said as they set out. They were riding in the smallest of Darien's many elaymotives, and the driver was carefully negotiating the heavy traffic of the Cinque. Foley sat up front with the driver, and two additional guards clung to perilous perches on the back.

"Yes, a couple of quint-golds for each of us," Josetta said. "Are you looking for anything in particular?"

They talked fashion for the rest of the short ride. Although she had tightly wrapped her ankle and rather ostentatiously brandished a cane one of the servants had found for her, Corene didn't seem to be suffering too many ill effects from her disastrous outing, Josetta thought. Still, with Corene, it was always hard to tell. Like her mother, Corene had delicate features and porcelain skin; her compact body looked both graceful and frail. But Alys was as tough as cured leather, and Corene was indomitable, or at least she pretended to be. Josetta had seen her cry when she thought no one was looking. And then grow furious if someone tried to offer her comfort.

Once they arrived at the Plaza of Women, they alighted and strolled around slowly enough to accommodate Corene's ankle. It was a big open space—or would have been, if it hadn't been densely packed with covered booths, unshaded tables, carts and stands and noisy peddlers, all hawking a sumptuous variety of merchandise. It was a perfect day in late Quinncoru, sunny, warm, and somehow playful. Everyone—the merchants, the shoppers, the children darting through the crowds and chased by exasperated mothers—seemed to be in a cheerful mood.

"It'll be Quinnahunti soon. We should buy jewelry for changeday," said Corene, glancing up at Josetta. Corene had always been the small, pretty one, Josetta the tall, ungainly one. Though Josetta had come to like her height and the impression of strength it gave her. "Did you see what Keeli wore last year on changeday? A necklace hung with tiny little skulls and bones! It was creepy but—I kind of liked it."

"Over there," Josetta said. "Someone selling jewelry."

They tossed through piles of cheap rings and bracelets, then moved on to a booth where a vendor fresh from the western provinces was selling polished wooden boxes with hidden compartments. "A nice gift for a hunti man," Josetta observed, though neither of them made a purchase. But at a neighboring stall she was won over by a coin-sized metal disk stamped with the image of a towering, flowering tree. Another hunti symbol. She bought it for her mother to add to Seterre's collection of charms.

Corene wandered away while Josetta was paying the vendor, but when Josetta caught up to her, she wasn't picking through scarves or fabrics at another booth. She was standing quite still, staring thoughtfully at the large raised dais where the blind sisters sat, listening to secrets.

Josetta glanced between Corene and the seers, three large, soft women who operated here in the Plaza every day, trading in knowledge. They knew everything about everybody; you could buy information with a coin or with information of your own, depending on which was more valuable.

Josetta had never had occasion to visit them herself, though she knew Zoe had. And probably half the residents of Chialto. If you wanted to find out if a man was honest, if you wanted to find out if a lover was faithful, you came to the blind sisters. If you wanted to spread the word that a merchant had cheated you or a banker had lied to you or your long-lost son had been recovered—

"Corene?" Josetta said uncertainly.

Corene was wearing a small smile of satisfaction. "I think I'm going to make a visit to the blind sisters," she said. "Would you like to come hear what I tell them?"

"Did you tell Darien you were going to do this?"

"It just now occurred to me."

"Maybe you should wait. Maybe you should see if he would prefer to handle this matter another way."

Corene's smile had grown to a wicked dazzle. "I don't feel like waiting," she said, limping straight toward the raised platform that held the sisters, her cane making a staccato sound against the hard ground. Josetta trailed helplessly behind.

It was less than five minutes before one of the blind women was free, and Corene climbed carefully up the stairs, then plopped herself down in front of the seer. Josetta followed more slowly and knelt behind Corene, a little to one side. Corene and the blind sister both sat cross-legged on the warm wood of the planking, Corene staring fiercely at the sister and the large woman staring sightlessly back.

"I have a story to tell you," Corene said. "Do I just say it while you listen?"

"What do you want to buy with your story?" the woman answered in a deep, peaceful voice. "Is there something you want to know in return?"

"I don't think so," Corene said. "I just want you to spread this story to anyone who asks."

"I'm listening."

"There's a man named Dominic Wollimer," Corene said, her voice confident and precise. "He's married to a woman named Alys, and I used to live with them. Whenever he caught me alone in the house, he would back me into a wall and put his hands all over me. Twice he came into my room at night and climbed into bed with me, but he was so drunk that I could run out of the door before he came after me. After that I had one of the maids sleep in my room. A few days ago he tried to kidnap me. I don't know what he would have done with me then. He's bad. Everyone should know just *how* bad."

Josetta was staring at her, dumb with horror, but the blind sister just nodded, her face still serene. Josetta imagined the old woman had heard worse atrocities over the decades. In fact, Josetta had, too, during the quintiles that she had worked in the slums, but she hadn't heard anything so bad that had happened to *Corene*. Well, since that time five years ago when Vernon had tried to marry her off to the corrupt old viceroy of Soeche-Tas . . .

"As it happens, I have a story it might interest you to hear," said the old woman. "I think the price of the two pieces of information is relatively equal, so no money needs to change hands."

"All right."

"This Dominic Wollimer. He has just purchased a very large share in a factory down by the southern port."

"A factory that supplies elaymotive parts?" Corene asked. Most of the manufacturing down at the docks was centered around the smoker cars; anyone who hadn't already bought into the transportation business was desperately trying to rectify the omission now.

"No. A textile plant that processes cotton. His partner didn't think Dominic's credit was good enough, so he had to put down cash. All in gold pieces."

"Darien will want to know that," Josetta whispered, and Corene nodded. Social ruin, financial ruin—any way they could harm Dominic sounded appealing.

"Thank you," Corene said, using her cane to push herself to her feet. Josetta rose more nimbly. "Don't forget to tell everyone what I told you."

The two princesses had turned toward the stairs when the sister said, "One more thing."

They both looked back at her. "Yes?" Corene asked.

"His wife. Alys. She's expecting a child."

For a moment, Josetta thought Corene had turned to ice, she stood so still and turned so cold. When she spoke, her voice was as chilly as the Marisi in winter. "Really? When is the baby due?"

"At the end of Quinnasweela or the beginning of Quinnelay."

"Oh, I'm sure she'll do everything in her power to make sure the baby is born in Quinnasweela," Corene said. "She wouldn't want anything but a child of fire."

"Sometimes the baby has something to say about that," the sister replied.

"You don't know Alys," Corene said. "Thank you. Do I owe you anything for that piece of knowledge?"

The blind woman waved a hand. "Soon enough everyone will know. It is information with very little value."

Corene fumbled in her pocket anyway, and leaned over to press one of her silver coins in the old woman's hand. "Value enough for me," she said. "Thank you again."

Josetta thought Corene looked a little unsteady as they climbed down the stairs, back into the color and gaiety of the Plaza. She wanted to hover close, take Corene's hand, suggest they sit down a moment, perhaps find a refreshment stand. But Corene's pale skin had flushed; the ice had melted in a fiery surge of temper, and Josetta figured she wasn't safe to touch.

Probably not safe to speak to, either, not if she didn't want to cause a scene right there in the middle of the Plaza. Alys pregnant! It seemed like such a stupid, careless thing for the queen to do, because a baby complicated everything. It tied her inextricably to Dominic, so she would not be able to cast him off if news of his sins spread far enough to turn him into a liability. It limited her freedom, during the duration of her pregnancy, at least, and Alys *hated* to be left out of any plan. It diminished her political power, because there were always people who considered a pregnant woman or a new mother to be vulnerable and soft. Those people didn't know Alys, of course, but they could be excused for discounting her during her maternity.

But Alys was never stupid or careless. Alys never did anything by accident. Could it be that she *wanted* this baby, that she loved Dominic Wollimer and was choosing this way to show it? And did that mean she would love the baby, too, smother it with delighted kisses, shower it with unfettered affection? As she had never smothered or showered Corene?

Josetta took another look at that set, sad, angry face, and decided she wouldn't say a word.

In silence, they examined the goods at a few more stalls, moving more slowly as Corene began favoring her wounded leg more obviously. Finally, after Corene paused to rest against a merchant's broad table, Josetta said, "I'm getting tired. Are you ready to go back?"

Corene nodded, then said, "Could we stop at a temple first?"

"You want to pull some blessings?"

Corene gave her a swift, unhappy smile. "It seems like the sort of day when I should, don't you think?"

"I think any day is a good one to seek out blessings."

"I don't know how to find the nearest temple."

Josetta grinned and put a hand to her heart. "Elay, remember? I know where every temple in the city is."

They took the elaymotive as far as they could through narrow, tangled streets until it became easier to get out and walk the last few blocks. The brief rest in the car seemed to have given Corene renewed strength, and she barely limped as they made it to the temple.

It was a small, pretty one made of veined gray stone and covered with vines. In the front played a dainty fountain decorated with butterflies; a smoky oil lamp hung just outside the door. All five elements subtly laid out to greet visitors before they'd even stepped across the threshold.

Darien's guards stayed outside, but Foley followed them in, ducking his head at the low lintel. There were only three other people inside, all of them congregated on the torz bench, which wasn't uncommon. People frequently paused at a temple to meditate themselves into a state of balance, which theoretically meant they would spend equal time contemplating each of the five elements. But there was something comforting about the element of flesh and earth, something that made you feel whole and alive and connected to everyone else in the room, in the city. People tended to strike up spontaneous friendships with other visitors; there were dozens of stories about romances blossoming at the torz station in some temple or another. Almost no one lingered on the sweela bench, but the torz section always collected a crowd.

Corene dropped the last of her coins in the tithing box and headed straight for the barrel in the middle of the room. Then stood a moment, staring down at the tumble of blessings. She lifted her hand as if to plunge it in, then let it settle back down at her side, empty.

"You pick for me," she said to Josetta in a low voice. No one liked it if anyone spoke above a whisper in the temple.

But Josetta was staring at Corene's hand, bare of all jewelry for the first time Josetta could remember. "Corene—where are your rings? Your blessings?"

Corene gave her a saucy smile, the first sign of spirit she'd shown since they'd left the seers. "I gave them to Rafe Adova."

"You gave them—"

"Because he didn't have any of his own."

Josetta stared at her, too stunned to reply.

Corene tossed her head. "Maybe he can sell them. Or maybe he can keep them. It was just—I mean, who doesn't have blessings? It was too sad."

"But Vernon had those made for you. When you were a girl."

Corene's face hardened. "My *mother* had them made for me. Anyway, they were getting too small for my fingers. I've had them enlarged three times already. It's time for new ones."

"New *blessings*?" Josetta had never heard of anyone denying their original random blessings and acquiring a whole new set. Of course, people liked to draw daily blessings as often as they could, hoping for a little insight into whatever vexing problem faced them at the moment, but that was different. That wasn't an attempt at a wholesale makeover; that was just a wish for guidance. A little worried, she glanced around the temple. "If that's really what you want, maybe we should find three strangers. Or maybe we should wait till a propitious day—Quinnahunti changeday, for instance—"

"No. Now. You." Corene smiled at her again, though Josetta read strain in her face. "Elay, remember? You always draw the right ones."

Josetta nodded, hiding her sudden surge of anxiety, and slowly dipped her hand into the pile of metal disks. Each one was a blessing, after all; no matter what she chose, Corene would have something uplifting or encouraging to cling to. Unless she pulled a ghost coin. Unless she came away with only a mystery in her hand.

She closed her eyes and concentrated, feeling the coins slide through her fingers, slippery as koi, cool as winter. Most people, she knew, just dug casually through the barrel, snatching up any old blessing, but she had always found the process to be a more mystical one. Her hand would encounter dozens of coins, all of them friendly and eager, like curious puppies, but her fingers wouldn't close around any of them. And then suddenly a metal edge would brush against her palm, so hot she would almost gasp. *That* was the blessing, she knew, the right one for this person at this time.

Her hand had pushed its way almost to the bottom of the container when she felt the first molten disk burn against her skin. She grabbed it and quickly pulled it out, but Corene shook her head when it was offered to her.

"I want to see all three at once," she said.

So Josetta pocketed the first one and laid her hand gently on the top of the mound of coins. A second blessing instantly smoldered against her skin, and she hurriedly dropped it in her pocket with the first one.

It took a little longer to uncover the third blessing, stubbornly tucked against the side of the barrel, but blazing with a defiant, unmistakable energy of its own.

Josetta collected all three—inexplicably cool now, or maybe they had only seemed warm—and held them out to her sister. "*You* read them," Corene said.

"Clarity," Josetta said, examining the first one.

Corene made a face. "That would be nice."

"It's a sweela trait, though. The blessings still recognize your fiery soul." She held up the second one. "Change."

Corene nodded decisively. "Good. I'm ready for something new to happen."

"A coru trait. Not something I ever associate with you."

Corene laughed. "That's why it's called change."

The third coin held a much more familiar sigil. "Courage," Josetta said with a smile.

Corene's expression relaxed into a mix of relief and delight. "My favorite of all my old blessings," she said. "I'm glad I got to keep one of them."

"Corene—"

"Don't," Corene said fiercely. "I *wanted* new ones. I'm *happy* with new ones. Let's stop somewhere so I can buy charms. This time I'll wear my blessings on a necklace, like you do."

"All right," Josetta said helplessly.

Corene turned to Foley, who had waited patiently this whole time. "What about you, Foley?" she asked. "Would you like a new blessing?"

"I'm always happy to receive a daily blessing from a princess's hand."

"Then we'll each draw one for you," Corene said.

Josetta dipped her hand in the barrel and almost instantly found a single metal disk, warm and insistent against her skin. She knew before she pulled it to the surface what the glyph would show.

"Loyalty," she told him with a smile. Every time she pulled a blessing for him, this was the coin that came into her hand. If she pulled three, sometimes one of them would bear the symbol for honesty or steadfastness, but those were rare. "Keep it or toss it back?"

He grinned in return. "Toss it back. I have plenty of those."

Corene was already digging through the barrel, and she laughed when she looked at the coin she'd pulled out for Foley. "It's a coru kind of day," she said, showing them the symbol. "Travel."

He nodded at Josetta. "Maybe you're about to embark on a journey."

"Back to the shelter. That's the only trip I plan to take."

"Now you," Corene said to Josetta. "Do you want us to pick, or do you want to choose your own?"

"I'll draw one, but each of you should, too. I like it when my blessings are influenced by the people around me."

Corene wasted no time plunging her hand in the barrel and bringing out a coin. "Strength," she said. "If it means strength of will instead of physical strength, I'd say that's pretty accurate."

Josetta nodded at Foley and, as seriously as he did everything else, he bent to the barrel and sorted through its contents until he found a coin that felt right to his hand. "Surprise," he said.

Which, in and of itself, was surprising. Josetta didn't remember ever receiving that blessing before, although it fell on Zoe practically every time she visited a temple. "It *is* a coru kind of day," she said. "Though I suppose everyone's life holds a surprise now and then."

"Now you pick one," Corene said.

Josetta slid her hand back into the delicious coolness of the stamped disks, feeling them frisk across her wristbone and along the delicate skin of her forearm. Without warning, one of the coins came to life against her palm, hot as a brand; when she pulled her hand out, she wasn't surprised to see her skin slightly reddened from the contact. Well, she supposed it made sense that a sweela blessing would burn any hand it came to.

"Love," she said, showing it to her companions.

"A very good blessing! One we should all receive from time to time," Corene pronounced.

Josetta nodded and prepared to throw the coin back. But she could still feel a fugitive heat under the stamped surface of the metal, like a lump of coal still glowing with the promise of fire. Hoping neither Corene nor Foley noticed, she slipped the disk into her pocket.

"Time to go home, I think," she said.

"Oh, yes," Corene agreed. "We got everything we came for."

FIVE

The small elaymotive was even more crowded for the return trip to Darien's, since they were sharing it with all their new purchases. Josetta directed the driver to take them to the servants' door at the back of the house, where they handed their bundles over to Calvin. He was one of the two attendants who had come with Zoe upon her marriage, though he and his wife were clearly more Zoe's friends than servants. A thin, white-haired, irrepressible old man, Calvin still looked like a vagabond despite nearly five years of living in the regent's well-appointed mansion.

He was invariably cheerful and full of gossip. "Corene's mother is expected to arrive in about five minutes, and Darien's waiting in the *kierten*," he told them as he took charge of their packages. "I think everyone in the whole house plans to hide in the hallway or on the stairs so they can hear the fight."

Josetta glanced at Corene, not sure how she'd take this news after the revelations of the day, but the other girl was smiling. "Well, I want to hear it, too," she said.

"Wouldn't miss it," Josetta said.

Foley stayed behind, but Calvin led them through the narrow service hallways to a small waiting room just off the *kierten* itself. Corene had relinquished her cane, but now and then she leaned a hand against the wall to improve her balance as they walked.

Zoe was in the waiting room already, and she grinned widely when they stepped inside. "I was afraid you wouldn't make it back in time," she whispered. "Come stand over here—you should be able to see everything."

Holding back giggles, Josetta and Corene joined her at the door and peered out into the *kierten*. Every house had one, of course—an empty area just beyond the entrance, a place to greet visitors or display subtle reminders of wealth—but Josetta particularly loved the one in Darien's house. It was an open well of space, as high as the three-storied building, topped by a cupola of leaded glass. Today sunlight poured through the glass in blinding columns of light; on stormy days, the rain rattled against the panes like gravel kicked up by a wagon's passing. On nights when the moon was full, if you timed it just right, you could see the heavy globe make an arc over the apex of the glass and then majestically sail out of sight.

The rest of the *kierten* was outfitted with small graceful touches—a miniature fountain, a red rug, a flowering plant with long, trailing leaves—but no one ever noticed those. The glass, the light, the very design of the space was what caught and held everyone's attention. It was a *kierten* made for an elay soul, and Josetta still believed Darien had bought the house to please her.

A smoker car growled up the road and the three of them tensed, but it passed without pausing. Zoe smothered a laugh and turned to face Corene and Josetta.

"Darien told me I could confront Alys if I wanted to, but I figured I was safer if I was out of sight," she said.

"Maybe *Alys* will be safer," Josetta retorted.

"Right. That's what I meant," Zoe said with an unrepentant grin. It was hard to imagine anyone who looked *less* like a woman of power and influence. She was tall and lanky, with straight dark hair and no sense of fashion, and the only jewelry she usually bothered to wear was the bracelet holding her three blessing charms. She liked servants better than most of their masters, abhorred any kind of grand social gathering, and could hardly bring herself to spend a quint-gold, remembering the long poverty-stricken days in exile. But she was coru prime; she could call water to a dry well, bid waves to dance on the ocean. She could flood the Marisi or prison it in its own banks, refusing to let it pour through its accustomed channel. She had done both of those things, in fact—once to save Corene, and once to save Josetta.

She had a robust and outspoken dislike for a hefty percentage of Chialto's finer families, but she absolutely despised Alys.

"Shhh," Corene breathed, waving them to silence. "I heard an elay-motive."

They strained again to decipher noises coming from the front of the house, and were rewarded by the sound of a brisk knock. Even before anyone could reasonably have answered, the knock came a second time, quick and impatient.

They all held their breath as they peered through the crack to watch Darien cross the *kierten* with an unhurried stride. He opened the front door and a small redheaded woman swept in.

Even at this afternoon hour, she was exquisitely dressed, in a sleeveless beaded tunic over diaphanous trousers so sheer they were merely wisps of fabric. She wore a flimsy printed scarf across her shoulders and no overtunic, leaving her more bare than Josetta had ever seen anyone in public. Anyone who wasn't as delicate and well-formed as Alys would have a hard time carrying off such a revealing style.

Normally she sashayed into a room with a swaying, seductive step, well aware that her very presence would draw all eyes, but she never bothered trying to charm Darien anymore. So today she just strode in and stood there, her arms crossed and her face showing exasperation.

"*Now* what is it?" she demanded.

Darien offered her the formal bow that anyone, even the regent, must give to a queen. Josetta studied his face as he straightened and looked down at Alys. He was wholly in control of his emotions; he wore a hunti man's mask of stone. "I just wanted you to know," he said in a perfectly calm voice, "that Corene won't be returning to your house. Please have her belongings sent here."

Alys dropped her arms and stared up at him in disbelief. "That's ridiculous. Why would you say that?"

"Dominic Wollimer tried to assault her a couple of days ago when they were alone in a car. Therefore, I am removing her from his presence. Send her clothes and other things here."

Now Alys's face flushed with heat. "How dare you accuse Dominic of misbehavior? He's my *husband*!"

"And as such, I hope he makes many trips to your bedroom and satisfies all your carnal desires, which heretofore have been insatiable." Darien spoke the insult in an absolutely uninflected voice. "But I won't have Corene exposed to him again. She's never returning to your house."

Another moment, Alys stared at him, and then she loosed an angry bark of laughter. "Because he—what? Tried to kiss her in the car? I'm sure he was just trying to show her affection. Maybe he was clumsy about it."

"She was afraid of him, and with good reason," Darien said. Josetta wondered if he suspected some of the things Corene had shared with the blind seer. Certainly she wouldn't put it past Darien to have spies in the Plaza, carrying information to him the moment the sisters acquired it.

Alys tossed her hands in the air. "'Afraid'! The minute a woman knows a man wants her is the minute he's utterly in her power. She should have been *glad* he took an interest in her. She could have gotten him to do anything she wanted."

Beside her, Josetta felt Corene grow stiff and brittle, heard Zoe stifle a gasp of indignation. Darien's face still kept its impassive expression, but his eyes showed a murderous rage.

"She's seventeen years old. He's forty—and your husband. Surely you would not condone any physical contact between them?"

Unexpectedly, Alys laughed. She came a step closer and laid her palm against his cheek. "Oh, Darien. Such a prude. Or is it that you're such a romantic? What do you think is so magical about the act of sex? It's bodies doing what they're meant to do. A woman who understands how to use her body has far more power and far more potential than a woman who doesn't. Corene shouldn't be afraid to experiment with hers."

Darien calmly wrapped his hand around Alys's wrist and pulled her fingers from his face. "If you want to speak with Corene, you come to my house and speak to her under my supervision," he said, each word so cold it was practically coated in frost. "If you attempt to talk to her at any public function, I will have you removed from the event. If Dominic Wollimer tries to speak to her in public *or* in private, I will have him arrested. If he touches her, I'll have him killed."

Alys blazed up in fury, wrenching her hand from his hold. "I hate you!" she cried. "How can you threaten me like that? Even you—even *you*, Darien, prancing around as regent and playing at politics and thinking you can force everyone to do your bidding—even *you* can't go around killing people just because you want to!"

"I think you'll find that I can," was his cool response.

She hit him, a quick strike on the shoulder with her balled-up fist. He didn't move to avoid it, didn't react when the blow fell. "Someday," she panted. "Someday, Darien, it won't be *you* pulling all the strings. My time will come."

"That may be," he said. "But it's not your time now. Are we clear?"

"I hate you," she said again.

"I don't think you could possibly hate me as much as I hate you," he replied. "Are we clear? Do you understand me?"

"Oh, I understand you. I've always understood you," Alys said grimly. She stalked toward the door, flung it open, and paused for a single parting shot. "Your mistake is that you've never understood me." With a final flick of red hair, she was gone.

Josetta pulled back from her crouch at the doorway, feeling sick to her stomach. Zoe pushed the door closed with a faint *click*, then leaned against the wall.

"That wasn't as entertaining as I thought it would be," Zoe said.

Corene shook her head. Her expression was tight, her whole body coiled with tension. "Dealing with my mother usually isn't," she said.

Zoe reached for her, and Corene flinched away. Zoe pushed herself from the wall and put her hands more insistently on Corene's shoulders. This time Corene held fast, but her eyes were focused on the floor.

"You have to listen to me," Zoe said in a quiet, intense voice. "She's your mother, and if you want to love her, you can go ahead and try. But she's not a good person. She doesn't have your best interests at heart. She's selfish. She's ambitious. She's ruthless. And I think she will use you— use anybody—to get what she wants."

Corene's voice was muffled. "I know all that."

"Just because she would throw you away doesn't mean you're worthless," Zoe added. The word made Josetta wince, made Corene jerk her head up. Oh, but Zoe was right, Josetta could see it in Corene's eyes. *Worthless* was exactly how she was feeling.

"I am," Corene whispered. "I'm not a princess anymore. I'm not the heir. My mother doesn't want me. I don't know what I'm supposed to be."

Josetta came up behind her, wrapped her arms around Corene's waist, laid her head on those fiery curls. "*I* want you," she said fiercely.

Zoe lifted one hand to brush it across Corene's cheek. "Oh, and *I* want you," she said in a soft voice. "You're my daughter's sister, my husband's child. The blood that runs through their veins is the same that runs through yours—I can feel it when I put my hand on your skin. You're a Serlast, one of the proudest families of the realm. And you are—magnificent. Beautiful. Clever. Brave. My daughter is going to want to be just like you, I know it already."

"Although maybe not quite as dramatic," Josetta said against Corene's hair.

She felt Corene shake with a tentative laugh. "I can't help the dramatic part," she said. "It seems to just happen around me."

Zoe leaned forward to kiss Corene's cheek, then for good measure she threw her arms around Josetta and Corene and gave them both one good squeeze. Corene squealed in protest as she was crushed between their bodies, and they were all holding back smiles and tears as they broke apart.

"So my prediction is that she won't send *any* of your clothes and things over here, what do you think?" Zoe asked.

"She'll do it," Josetta said. "She won't want to give Darien an excuse to come to her house and start rifling through it."

Corene shook her hair back and pasted a defiant smile on her face. "I say, who wants those old tunics and trousers?" she said. "Time to buy a whole new wardrobe."

Josetta stayed at Darien's house through the end of the nineday, but only because she was still worried about Corene. Otherwise, she'd have been gone shortly after Alys made her memorable appearance. Her life had grown so unadorned in the past quintile or two that she was no longer comfortable with opulence. She couldn't help thinking about how many people down at the shelter could have dined on the leftovers from each of their meals. She couldn't stop imagining the wide hallways and gracious drawing rooms organized into makeshift beds and infirmary rooms.

Zoe was the only one who really shared her interest in working with the poor, because Zoe had been homeless herself, though never entirely without resources. During the rest of that nineday, they spent many hours playing with the baby and talking over plans for expanding the shelter. Buying a new facility to hold more beds, perhaps. Maybe even setting up banking facilities for a few of the more ambitious souls who wanted to start small ventures that might help them buy their way out of poverty.

"But it all takes time, and I keep running out of it," Josetta said with a sigh. "And then Romelle will be coming to town, and I promised Darien I'd attend all the events. I think he's just trying to find ways to keep me away from the shelter, even though I told him he'd never be able to do that."

Zoe laughed. "Oh no, you don't understand. If Darien can't get you to do what he wants, he'll do something *else* to achieve his desired end. He'll work around you, but he'll still get his way."

"Then I can't wait to see what he has in mind."

She found out on firstday when she and Foley gathered up their things, slipped out of the house before anyone else was awake, and caught an elaymotive omnibus to take them down to the southern edge of the Cinque. Of course, there was no public transportation through southside itself, but there wasn't much danger at this hour of the morning. They walked briskly through the nearly deserted streets, stepping around mounds of trash, mosaics of broken glass, and the occasional snoring drunk lying in the middle of the road. Now and then they passed a tumbledown building where the doors or windows were open, or a tired woman was sweeping debris off the stairs. But otherwise, this part of the city could have been uninhabited.

The shelter was one of the few buildings that showed tentative signs of life, with moving shadows visible through the windows and the faint scent of baking bread escaping from the kitchen in back.

It was a long, narrow, two-story structure that at one point had housed six small and horribly rundown apartments. Josetta had plowed more money than Darien thought was reasonable into buying it, rebuilding it, and adding amenities. Now, on the ground floor, there was a sizable main room laid out with five long tables where meals were served. Shelves against the walls were stocked with food and clothing and medicines that anyone could have simply for the asking. There was a large kitchen, a small office, and an infirmary with six private cubicles, each with its own narrow bed. On one end of the building was a public bath; on the other end, a small temple. On the second story were two dormitories, one for men and one for women. They had to be accessed by separate outside entrances to reduce the possibility of commingling. The upstairs level also held four small bedrooms for Josetta and the rest of the staff; these were served by a private interior stairwell of their own.

Since the place had opened, Josetta had never had fewer than ten people staying overnight. She generally dished out between twenty and fifty meals a day. She'd lost count of the number of people she'd treated for broken bones, knife wounds, and lung diseases, and she'd never paid attention to how many tramped through the baths.

It had been Zoe who suggested the baths, as well as an exterior spigot where people could fill water containers. The canal and a complex aqueduct system carried water to most parts of the city, but many of the underground pipes that served the slums had broken long ago, never to be repaired. Of course, lack of water was never a problem when Zoe was around. She had located, or created, an aquifer below the cracked streets, and drew its contents upward to a private well. Josetta sometimes thought that the easy availability of water was the single most important gift she had been able to offer the community she served.

"Looks like the place has stayed intact while we've been gone," Josetta observed to Foley as she stepped up to the heavy front door.

"You have good people working for you," he said.

More people working for her than she realized, it turned out. The minute they were inside, she was greeted by Callie, the thickset, no-nonsense, middle-aged woman who functioned as housekeeper and chief cook and nurse and tireless assistant. She and her two children had been the first people Josetta had ever housed at the shelter, one cold Quinnelay night when the youngest boy had a fever and the older one was half dead from exposure. The oldest boy had signed on to a merchant ship a quintile ago, but Callie and her other son, Bo, were two of Josetta's most reliable workers.

"Who are these men? How long are they going to be here?" Callie greeted her as Josetta stepped into the main room. Callie had just carried a large platter of eggs and meat out from the kitchen and set it on a sideboard buffet. There were five or six patrons sitting or standing by the long tables, waiting to serve themselves, and they shuffled toward the food as Callie strode over to Josetta.

"What men?" Josetta asked, eyeing the people in the food line. Two were male, but they looked like the shelter's typical visitor, a little stringy, a lot ragged, not entirely clean.

Callie jerked her thumb toward the far end of the building. "Cleaning sinks and showers. I told them if they were going to hang around here, they'd have to work, or I wasn't feeding them. Or letting them spend the night, either."

"I don't know what you're talking about," Josetta said.

"They told me they were here for you. I thought you'd know."

Josetta glanced over her shoulder to exchange a look with Foley. "Let's find out who they are," she said, and he followed her down the cramped hallway that led to the bath area. It was a large, utilitarian room of inexpensive stone floors and head-high stone dividers, offering up to a dozen people privacy at any one time. The best part about the room was its steamy warmth, a temperature it maintained even on the coldest day. Because Zoe had managed to tap a *hot* underground spring when she had gone rummaging around looking for water.

Despite the fog, it was easy to spot the two newcomers who were wrestling a hose in place so they could, yes, scrub down some of the stone stalls. They were both barefoot and stripped of everything except their dark trousers, but those trousers looked to be fine and well-made. Josetta was even more baffled as she approached them.

"Excuse me," she called over the sound of the jetting water. One of them reached over to turn off the spray, and they both turned in her direction, bowing their heads in respect. "Who are you? Why are you here? I mean, I'm happy to have you volunteer, but—"

Behind her, Foley spoke in a low voice. "They're Darien Serlast's men. I recognize them."

"Darien—"

"That's right," one of them piped up. "The regent sent us here."

"Why? For how long?"

The men exchanged glances. "It's our permanent assignment now," one of them said helpfully. He looked to be about Foley's age, in his early twenties, still young and enthusiastic about the notion of defending the crown. "You know how some guards serve at the palace, and some serve at the regent's house, and some patrol the Cinque at night? We're here."

"Half a quintile at least, because that's how long an assignment lasts," the other one explained. "After that, we might be moved somewhere else and two new guards put in our place."

"Or we might stay," said the first one. "If you like an assignment, you can ask to stay on. I like it," he added.

The other one waggled his head. "I don't know. I didn't think we'd have to be mucking around in the showers. Or doing laundry. But she said that was part of the job."

"She" must be Callie, who was obviously going to get full value out of any able-bodied man who showed up on her doorstep like a gift. "I didn't ask the regent to send me guards," Josetta said. "It was thoughtful of him, I suppose, but—I'm going to send you back."

"You can't," said the young one cheerfully. "We only take orders from the regent. And Captain, of course."

"We were assigned to this place," said the older guard, and Josetta heard hunti finality in his voice. "And we'll stay till we're assigned someplace else."

She stood there a moment, feeling helpless and more than a little indignant, before she spread her hands in resignation. "Callie can generally speak for me," she said at last. "If she asks you to do something, please do it. As long as it doesn't interfere with your *assignment*, of course. And I'll take the matter up with Darien the next time I see him."

She turned to go, surprised to see a grin on Foley's face. "I would have thought you'd be as annoyed as I am," she said once they were in the hallway, out of earshot of the guards. "Or *insulted*. Darien clearly thinks you're not skilled enough to keep me safe."

"The regent's right. One man is never enough to keep anyone safe."

"Oh, so you think it's a good idea for him to set up an *armed outpost* here?"

"I wish he'd done it a year ago."

Josetta shook her head in exasperation, and then laughed. "I bet they didn't count on the manual labor, though. Callie will have them scrubbing floors and changing linens, just like all of us do."

"Won't hurt them," Foley said. "And it will make for lighter work for the rest of us."

Indeed, over the next three days, Darien's guards proved to be welcome additions to the small staff at the shelter, though Josetta did her best to resist liking them. They spent most of their time patrolling the neighborhood, but when they were actually at the building, they willingly pitched in. The younger one, Caze, was handy with carpentry tools; he rehung a sagging door and made repairs to the stairwell to the women's wing. The older one, Sorbin, proved to be a competent cook who could take over the whole kitchen if need be. Both of the guards used their free time to show self-defense skills to Bo and the other two workers—rather fierce young women with painful personal histories. And even Josetta had to admit it was handy to have them around when a brawl broke out during dinner one night. Foley and Bo probably could have subdued the two men who suddenly started going at it over an insult no one else heard, but Caze and Sorbin broke up the fight and ejected the combatants with a professional ease that prevented the event from escalating into a frightening scenario.

Josetta didn't *need* the extra guards. But it turned out she didn't mind having them.

Caze and Sorbin quickly fell into the habit of making their last patrol of the day somewhere around midnight. Josetta generally spent those final hours working in her tiny office, answering correspondence, checking inventory, and balancing accounts. Foley usually prowled around the main room, folding blankets, straightening chairs, and otherwise putting things to rights. When Josetta was finished for the night, they would lock most of the interior and exterior doors before going upstairs.

The big door that led from the street to the central room was always left open so that the shelter could serve as a haven to anyone who was desperate enough to need one in the middle of the night. More than once Josetta or Callie had gone downstairs in the morning to find someone sleeping under a dining table, a half-eaten loaf of bread in his hand. Josetta had warned Caze and Sorbin that they needed to return by midnight or be stuck sleeping on the main room floor with any other lost souls who wandered in.

She left the temple unlocked, too. But then, she didn't think there was a temple in the city that ever barred its doors.

Josetta was just tallying her last accounts when she heard men's voices raised in the main room, accompanied by clattering sounds as if someone had stumbled into a piece of furniture. She grabbed her lamp and headed into the main hall.

Caze and Sorbin were back from their rounds, but with an interesting addition: Sorbin carried the limp form of an unconscious man over his shoulder, and he was bracing himself against the weight as Foley hurriedly unlocked the door to the infirmary. Caze strode over to Josetta.

"We heard the sounds of a fight, and we investigated," he said. "Three men attacking this one fellow, so we chased them off. Can't tell how bad he is—he's unconscious, and he's bleeding pretty hard on one side. He's still alive, though."

"Don't think he would be if we hadn't shown up," Sorbin added. "They looked serious enough to be planning murder."

"Go wake up Callie," Josetta told Foley, and he disappeared. She followed Sorbin and Caze into the infirmary and waved a hand at one of the empty alcoves. "Put him here. Can you fetch hot water? Thank you."

They nodded and marched down the hall, but Josetta was already focused on the injured man. She didn't bother glancing at his face, because her more immediate concern was the blood welling up from his left side. She lifted his shirt to reveal a long gash that ran across his rib cage and plunged deeper just above his hip. The attacker had probably aimed at his heart, but the man had managed to deflect the blade or turn out of its direct path. The wound was still bad enough—and still bleeding.

She grabbed a clean rag from a pile of folded scraps and held it over the wound, bearing down with steady pressure. She could feel his chest rhythmically rise and fall with his breathing; she thought he was in pain, but not enough to indicate an injury to a lung. While she kept her hands in place, she made a quick visual survey of the rest of his body. His trousers were torn and muddy, as if he'd been knocked to the ground and kicked hard, and his right arm, which was missing a sleeve, was bruised and scratched. But there were no other major wounds immediately visible. He might have a concussion, but there wasn't much she could do about it at the moment.

Now she glanced at his face, but it was hard to make out his features because the skin was so reddened and bruised and because his head was turned to one side. Oh, but that angle showed her something very interesting indeed—his exposed right ear, half cut or torn from his head, and circled with a dried rivulet of blood. She was so surprised that for a moment she slackened her pressure on his ribs. That ear was curiously deformed or decorated—the outer ridge had a serrated edge, as if someone had cut tiny triangles out of the cartilage, and each of the five remaining points had been pierced with a delicate hoop earring that looked like real gold. Josetta couldn't remember ever seeing such an affectation before, and it looked like his attackers hadn't, either. Judging by the blood left behind, one of them had tried to hack off his ear as a souvenir.

There were voices in the main room and then Callie burst in, wearing a tattered robe over a cotton nightdress. "So how is he?" Callie demanded, winding her gray-black hair up into a bun. "Bad?"

"The chest wound seems to be the worst of it," Josetta said. "But I think he's unconscious, so he's probably had a blow to the head, too."

Callie nodded and began gathering up cloths and medicines. Caze brought in a couple of buckets of steaming water but instantly left again, because the small space was just too crowded. Josetta stepped away from the narrow bed to let Callie work, and spent the next thirty minutes as the other woman's assistant, washing, holding, handing instruments over, while Callie cleaned and bound the injury.

"Well, I don't think he'll die," was her assessment at the end. "But I don't like that he hasn't woken up. And what's this? His ear?"

"It's strange, isn't it?"

"Guess someone thought it was pretty enough to cut off and take home. Give me some of that ointment and a couple of long strips of cloth, and I'll bind it back up. I think we can save it, if it doesn't get infected."

Josetta moved behind the man to tie back his dark shoulder-length hair, then supported his head while Callie wrapped it with gauze.

Finally the older woman said, "Not much else we can do for him tonight. His heartbeat is strong, that's good, and his breathing. I guess we'll see. Here, let's get this bloody shirt off of him."

The shirt was ruined anyway, so it was easier to cut it off than help him out of it. His bare chest showed more contusions and a dozen shallow scrapes through a thin covering of dark hair.

"More jewelry," Callie commented, flicking her finger at a fine silver chain hung with several charms. "Maybe the thieves were after this as well. You can't wear real gold in the slums."

Josetta was staring at the necklace and its three pendants—actually, three rings—one copper, one silver, one gold. She knew those rings and the glyphs carved out of them. These were blessings. Corene's blessings.

She bent down to peer into the man's battered face, recognizing it now even through the puffiness and bruising. Rafe Adova, her sister's rescuer. Someone wanted him dead.

SIX

I'm still alive was Rafe's first thought when he fought to open his eyes. It was a moment before he could recall all the details of the last few hours, but he distinctly remembered the flood of adrenaline as he suddenly realized he was under attack and sorely outnumbered. His mind played back disjointed images, shadowy strikes, an arm lifted, a face snarling, everything backlit by the insufficient light of a chilly half moon.

His second thought was that he hurt so much, he'd almost rather be dead. His head was throbbing and his left side felt as if it had been set on fire and splashed with vinegar. Assorted aches in every other part of his body set up their own whimpers of distress, but it was his head and his rib cage that really made him long for oblivion.

He concentrated on taking a few shallow breaths to accustom himself to the patterns of pain, and then he tried shifting position to see if he could do it. It was like being flayed with white-hot knives. Panting, he lay still a moment and considered.

Where *was* he? He would have sworn his attackers—whoever they were—were trying to kill him, though he had no idea why. Had they left him for dead? Had some kind soul found him, battered but still breathing, and brought him to a place of safety? He could hardly believe such a haven existed anywhere in the southside, but he could feel the bandages wrapped around his head and torso. He could smell the sharp odors of medicinal scents. He could only see out of one eye—he *hoped* it was because the other one was bandaged—but he could make out a small, sunny room stocked with baskets of medical supplies. He was clearly in an infirmary of some kind and he assumed it was the morning after his beating.

Oh, if his gambler's luck had held true, he was at the shelter that Princess Josetta ran down by the canal. He had certainly been in its vicinity the night before. He had made it his business to locate the place the very day after the royals had vanished from his life. Not that he was spying on the princess. Not that he intended to walk through that heavy door one day and greet her, ask if Corene had recovered from her adventure, invite Josetta to play another hand of penta. He was curious, that was all. He just wanted to see the sort of place a dispossessed princess might design once she hatched some crazy scheme about caring for the poor.

In the past nineday, he'd strolled by it a couple of times—well, maybe four or five times. He hadn't caught a glimpse of Josetta during any of those casual viewings, but recently he'd seen a man he took to be her guard, so he knew they were back on the premises even though they'd been gone for a few days. He'd been only a block or two away last night when the three men jumped out of the shadows and proceeded to pummel him senseless.

What *had* they wanted?

Rafe struggled again to shift positions and accidentally kicked over a metal bowl that sat on a table nearby. It hit the floor with a metallic clamor. Well, *that* would fetch someone to check on him, no doubt. Grimacing against the pain, he pushed against the bed again and finally managed to sit upright.

He was still trying to use his one good eye to get his bearings when someone swept back the rough curtain that seemed to serve as a door. Disappointment stabbed through him when he didn't recognize the woman who stepped in.

"So you're awake," she said briskly, coming close enough to put a hand against his cheek. Her skin was a lot cooler than his, so he probably had a fever. "I'm Callie. How do you feel?"

"Miserable," he said. "Where am I? What happened to me?"

She peeled back an edge of the bandage over his face so she could examine both of his eyes. He immediately felt more alert when he had all of his sight back. "Some men attacked you in a back alley, but a couple of the folks who work here chased them off," she said. "You're in a shelter that takes care of the hurt and sick and poor. How's your head? Where's the pain? Do you feel like you're going to throw up?"

"My *ear* hurts," he said. "And the back of my skull. But, no, I'm not going to throw up. I'm not dizzy. I don't think I have a brain injury. How bad is the wound on my side?"

"Bad enough," she said. "You won't be walking too far for the next few days. But the fact that you're moving and talking now makes me think you'll be all right."

"Well, that's good news," he said. "Thank you for your care."

"Are you hungry?"

"Starving."

"I'll be back in a minute." She turned to go and briefly turned back. "In the corner—a chamber pot if you need it. If you can't stand on your own, I can help you. And there on the table is a pitcher of water if you want to wash up."

"If I can't stand up on my own, I'd rather be dead," he responded in a polite voice. Callie looked faintly amused as she ducked out through the curtain.

It was an ordeal to climb off the bed, try to catch his balance, then take a few unsteady steps through the small space to conduct his sketchy ablutions. But his head felt distinctly clearer when he dropped back onto the mattress, stretched out his legs before him, and supported his back against the wall. He could piss without help and he could damn well feed himself. And before a day was out, he was going to walk out of this place under his own power.

The curtain swished open again, and Princess Josetta walked in, bearing a tray of food. Rafe instantly changed his mind about wanting to leave the shelter in the near future.

"Majesty," he said. "I hadn't expected to see you again so soon. Or quite like this."

She laid the tray carefully across his lap. "Wait just a moment," she said, disappearing briefly and returning with a somewhat battered wooden chair, which she pulled up next to the bed. "What happened to *you?*" she demanded.

He shook his head and spoke around a mouthful of bread. It was at least as good as what Samson provided; someone at the shelter was an excellent cook. "I don't know. I was going home last night and three men jumped me. I thought they were going to kill me, to tell you the truth."

"That's what Sorbin said."

"Who?"

"One of the two men who apparently saved your life."

"I need to thank them profusely. Maybe give them a reward."

"Not necessary. They're men Darien Serlast has sent to watch over me."

He finished another big bite of food and grinned at her. "The regent has put you under guard? You don't sound too happy about it."

"Happier now that they've proved their worth by saving your life. Do you have any idea why those men would have come after you?"

"None."

"They weren't people you'd played cards with—people who didn't like losing, maybe?"

"I didn't get a really close look at them, but no, I didn't recognize them. And I didn't recognize their language."

She tilted her head to one side. "Language?"

It was the first time this morning his memory had supplied that detail. He concentrated, trying to reconstruct the unintelligible shouts. "They weren't speaking Welchin," he said. "So maybe they were telling me why they wanted to kill me, but I couldn't understand them."

"And they weren't speaking Coziquela, either?"

He shook his head. In the past ten years, as trade with other nations had become a bigger part of the Welchin economy, there had been a huge push to ensure that most schoolchildren studied the language of Cozique, the country that dominated international commerce. Rafe hadn't learned it when he was growing up in the country, but in the years since he'd lived in the polyglot slums, he'd become fairly fluent.

"So you have no idea what your attackers wanted?"

He shook his head again. "I didn't even win much at cards last night, so they wouldn't have any reason to kill me just for the money I had on me."

"Would they have had any reason to cut off your ear?"

Automatically, his hand went to his right ear—or, rather to the bandage around it. "Is that what happened? Someone tried to chop it off? No wonder it hurts."

"That's what it looks like." She waited a moment, and when he didn't speculate, she said, "It would certainly make an unusual trophy. If someone liked to carve people up for that reason."

Now he couldn't help laughing. "It certainly would."

She tilted her head again and waited. He thought he could outlast her, could match her gravity with calm silence of his own, but it turned out he couldn't. He chuckled and shook his head.

"My ear's been like that since I was still a baby," he said. "My mother said she came home one day and found that my father had taken me to some crazy woman who would—would brand your baby in some fashion so that you would never get him mixed up with somebody else's kid. She said it was one of the reasons she left him."

"It seems like this single reason would be sufficient," Josetta murmured. "That's barbaric."

"Yeah. I've gotten tired of the comments and the funny looks, so mostly I wear my hair long to cover it, but sometimes I'm careless." He shrugged. "So somebody may have seen it and decided to keep it for his own. Though that's a pretty thin excuse for murder."

"So is every other excuse for murder," she said. "Maybe they just wanted the jewelry. I noticed that you were wearing quite a few earrings, and all of them gold. Not exactly the best way to escape attention."

He grinned again. "Well, I figured if I was going to be an oddity, I'd be an oddity with pride," he said.

Unexpectedly, that made her smile. "Embrace the differences that make you unique," she said. "Yes. We all need to do that, but sometimes it's difficult."

He glanced around the small room, but he was imagining the entire building. A princess running a salvation project in the slums. He'd call that unique. "You've seemed to manage it on rather a grand scale."

"Maybe. But it hasn't been easy."

Before he could answer, the curtain twitched back, and a young man stepped through. He was maybe fifteen or so, big-boned and wide-faced. He looked enough like Callie that Rafe figured him to be her son, and his first words confirmed that.

"My mother says I should take the patient to the baths so he can wash off the blood," he said. "And then she'll come back and check his wounds and bandage him up again."

Josetta nodded and stood up, though Rafe wanted to protest the very notion of her leaving. "Thanks, Bo. I've got work to do myself." She glanced back at Rafe. "If you can walk under your own power, you can help yourself to anything that you need on the shelves in the main room. If you can't, just call out and someone will come find you. I'll check on you later." And with a brisk nod, she was gone.

Rafe was left with the much less interesting Bo. "Bath? That sounds good," he said. "I don't know how far I can walk, though."

Bo nodded. "Lean on me."

Cleaned up, dressed in ill-fitting clothes of Bo's providing, and back in his infirmary room, Rafe found himself feeling both better and worse. He hadn't been able to wash up as thoroughly as he would have liked, since he wasn't allowed to take off the two biggest bandages without Callie's supervision, but soaping up in the wonderfully steamy baths was an almost divine experience. Rafe didn't have any inhibitions about public nudity, so it didn't bother him that there were about ten other people, men and women, using the facility at the same time. He was comforted by the thought that none of them looked much better than he did, though their assailants appeared to have been poverty and bad luck rather than would-be murderers. He would probably recover sooner.

The cleansing had improved his mood, but the expedition had drained his energy and reawakened the pain in every bruise and gash. He lay back on his narrow bed practically panting with discomfort. Callie reappeared a few minutes later, checked his many hurts, and pronounced herself pleased with his improvement.

"I think you'll feel better tomorrow," she said. "Why don't you sleep for a few hours? Someone will call you for dinner."

He hadn't planned to obey her directive, but the need to heal was the most powerful soporific ever invented; he was asleep within ten minutes. He didn't wake again until early evening, or so he judged it to be by the quality of light peeking in through the window and the scent of cooking drifting down the hall. His assorted injuries still ached enough to make him curse as he pushed himself upright, but his mind seemed clearer and he felt steadier on his feet. Progress. Always a good sign.

It was easy to find the main room, somewhat romantically lit with a mix of candles and lamps and the fading daylight. Gaslight was all the rage in the wealthier parts of Chialto, but such innovations were rare in the slums. Rafe braced himself against the beams of the doorway and looked around. There were about fifteen people clustered around the five tables. He recognized some from the baths, but some appeared to have wandered in just for the meal. Bo and Callie were setting up platters on a sideboard, helped by two young women who looked like they also might be permanent staff. He didn't spot anyone who looked like he might be a royal guard; maybe his rescuers were off saving other unfortunate fools from death and dismemberment. Neither did he spot anyone who looked like Josetta. His interest in the meal dropped considerably.

There appeared to be no organizing protocol, so he served himself at the buffet, chose a seat at random, and nodded politely at the five people sharing his table. Two men, two women, one child; only the boy and one of the women looked connected to each other. None of them talked much, and Rafe followed their example. It wasn't the worst or most uncomfortable dinner he'd ever had, but it was hardly the most enjoyable, either.

Things improved once the meal was over, though. Most people cleared out as soon as they were done eating, but a few still lingered at the tables. Two were men about Rafe's age, one was a stringy older fellow who appeared to be on borrowed time, and one was a woman who might be forty and only recently weaned from some kind of drug addiction.

Rafe reached into the pocket of his borrowed trousers for the deck of cards that he had transferred from his own ripped and bloodied clothing. "Anyone interested in a game of penta?" he asked.

All of them, it turned out, were.

No one in this group had any extra money, not even a quint-copper; so, instead of coins, they used dried beans the stringy old man borrowed from the kitchen. It took the pressure off the need to win, so Rafe played carelessly, betting big when he didn't have the cards for it and laughing when he lost. The woman was unexpectedly good at the game, raking in pot after pot. Rafe was watching her pretty closely and he was fairly certain she wasn't cheating.

"You could make yourself a whole kettle of soup with your winnings," the old man observed when she won the last hand. "Next time we should bet with carrots and turnips. You can make a whole *meal*."

"Used to play a little professionally," she said. "Before—" She shrugged and didn't finish, but all of them could fill in that blank for themselves.

One of the younger men stretched his arms over his head and yawned hugely. "Bedtime for me," he said, and the others murmured their agreement. Even Rafe, who had spent half the day sleeping, admitted he was tired again already.

The others headed outside to the stairways that, he had been told, led to upstairs dorms. Rafe turned toward the infirmary until the sound of voices at the main door shifted his attention that way. He pivoted to see who might be walking in at this late hour.

It was the princess and three guardsmen, and as much as he hated the idea of Josetta wandering around the slums at night, he had to admit that these three looked capable of defending her against all comers. None of them wore royal livery, but two of them were formally dressed in close-fitting jackets and trousers that would keep out of their way if they had to fight. Clearly, those were the regent's men. The third—the big, silent fellow Rafe had already identified as Josetta's personal guard—wore a looser tunic and a generally more casual air. But he looked like he'd be a handy man to have around during a brawl.

"You're still awake," Josetta said, coming his way. "How are you feeling?"

"Beat up but better than this morning," he said. He nodded at the guards, who were all eyeing him with varying degrees of interest. "Are these the men who saved my life?"

"Caze and Sorbin are. Foley wasn't with them, but he would have jumped right in if he had been."

"I don't think I can even express how grateful I am to both of you."

"Part of the job," Sorbin said.

"Glad we were there," Caze added.

They exchanged a few more words before the three men headed toward the interior stairwell and Rafe turned back toward the infirmary. Josetta surprised him by following him to his room.

"How are you really?" she asked. "I notice you're moving very carefully."

He was too tired to stand, so he sank to the narrow bed and nodded. "My ribs hurt, my head hurts, and I'm so mad to be weak and helpless that I want to punch somebody. Except I'm too weak to punch anybody," he added. "But I'm trying to be thankful I'm alive."

She smiled. "Better in the morning, I'm sure."

"You'll have to tell me what I owe you for the food and the care."

She opened her hands in a gesture of benevolence. "Nothing. Caring for people in need is what this shelter does."

"Well, you're spending plenty of money on food and medicines, and you have to be getting it somewhere," he said.

"We have donors who believe in our cause. And, of course, I have money of my own."

"Maybe I'd like to be a donor. I recently came into a little cash."

She smiled again and leaned against the doorframe. She looked almost as tired as he felt. He wondered what she'd been doing all day. "I think you must have much better uses for your windfall. Maybe you should invest it in something."

"Maybe I should," he agreed. "I've been trying to think what."

"Something that appeals to you," she suggested. "If you like gold, for instance, buy a share in a mine. If you like spices and rare foods, find a ship's captain who sails to Cozique. And I know a couple of independent traders who buy and sell goods all over Welce. They're very astute—I promise you'd get a return on your money if you invested with them."

She had mentioned those traders on the very first night they met. He wondered how a princess came to be friends with people in that social class, but he decided not to ask. "You know what fascinates me?" he said. "Those smoker cars. I'd bet you any sum of money that transportation is the field where people are going to get rich in the next ten to twenty years."

"So buy a share in an elaymotive factory," she said.

He laughed. "Is it as easy as that? Just walk in the door and start throwing coins around?"

"I can introduce you to Kayle Dochenza, if you like. He's the one who invented smoker cars," she explained. "He'd be happy to take your money."

He just looked at her for a moment. This time he couldn't stop himself. "So. You're a princess. But you live in the slums. And you're friends with a couple of small-time traders. And you know factory owners and mad inventors. You're full of endless surprises."

Her face was alight with laughter. "Well, it's not surprising that I know Kayle Dochenza. He's the elay prime, and I've been around him since I was born."

That made more sense. "I suppose you know all the primes. I hadn't thought about that before. I suppose this Kayle Dochenza likes you because you're elay, too."

Looking thoughtful, she resettled her spine against the door. "Actually, it's interesting. He's an odd man—really odd. I wouldn't say I ever really *registered* in his mind until the past couple of years. I think most people don't make an impression on him until they do something drastic. But when I opened the shelter, that caught his attention. The elay traits are air and *spirit*, and the shelter appealed to his spiritual side. He's been one of my staunchest supporters." She grinned. "So he likes me *now*."

"Well, now you make me want to meet him, even if I don't give him money," Rafe said. "I've encountered my share of odd people. I'd like to see what makes him so strange."

She was laughing again. "Good! When you're well enough, we'll drive down to the port. That's where all the factories are."

He raised his eyebrows. "Do you have an elaymotive? Can you actually drive it?"

"I don't own one, no, but we could hire one. Or borrow one of Darien's. And I *have* driven one, but not lately. Foley can drive, though."

He lifted his hands in submission. "I have to ask. *When* did you learn to drive a smoker car?"

She tried to keep her face prim, but the smile kept breaking through. "When I spent a winter with the independent traders, of course. Corene and I both did. It was back when everything was happening at once—

the king was dying, the city had flooded, Corene was in danger—and Zoe decided it was best to get us out of Chialto. So she sent us off with Jaker and Barlow, and we spent half a quintile driving around the countryside. We both loved it. Corene and I had never been very close until that Quinnelay, but after that, everything changed."

"You know, just from the bits and pieces you've let fall, I think you must have led the strangest life."

"Sometimes I think so, too," she agreed. "And that's why I've ended up here."

He shook his head. "That doesn't follow."

She pushed herself away from the wall, clearly planning to depart. "I didn't have much say in all the things that happened to me before. Once I decided I wasn't going to let anyone else control my life, I had to decide what I thought would make my life valuable. And that's why I started the shelter. So, while my life still might be peculiar, it's peculiar in ways that *I* have chosen. I assure you, it makes all the difference."

"Makes sense," he said. He was trying to decide what might make his own life valuable. Offhand, he couldn't think of anything.

"Good night, Rafe. I'll see you in the morning."

"Good night, Princess Josetta."

It was actually closer to mid-afternoon before he encountered Josetta again, since some other priority kept her away from the shelter for the early part of the day. So Rafe submitted to more ministrations from Callie, shared a couple of meals with an assortment of down-on-their-luck companions, and played a few of hands of penta just to pass the time. The pain was almost as bad as it had been the day before, but his strength was returning. If someone would help him back to Samson's, he thought, he'd be able to take care of himself within a day or two. Though the stairs would be an ugly bitch.

And he didn't really want to leave the shelter.

Though that wasn't a thought he wanted to examine too closely.

He was sitting in the main room, shuffling his cards and practicing illegal dealing moves, when Josetta and Foley stepped in from outside. Sunshine trailed in behind her, or maybe it was just that she always seemed wrapped in fresh air and light colors. Foley headed straight to the kitchen, but Josetta paused to talk to him.

"Poor Rafe! Couldn't find anyone willing to lose his fortune to you?"

He grinned up at her, his hands still ruffling the deck. "A fortune of two quint-silvers, maybe. Hardly worth the effort. A few of us played for beans and nuts earlier, and we might get up a game tonight if you want to join us."

"Maybe I will," she said. "Those are my kind of stakes. How are you feeling?"

"Better than I did, worse than I'd like."

She nodded. "It would probably do you some good to get up and move around. Can you walk more than ten feet?"

For an answer, he pushed his chair back and stood up, more or less solidly. "You want to go strolling through the neighborhood? You might need someone else to be your bodyguard."

She gestured toward a part of the complex he hadn't visited yet. "Not far. Just to the east edge of the building. There's a temple there. I thought I could try to pull blessings for you."

That made him lift his brows. "There's an idea. Though if ghost coins come up again—"

"I don't think we *have* any of those in our temple. So it should be interesting to see what we get."

"Then let's go."

They moved at his maddeningly slow pace out the front door and away from the corner of the building that housed the baths. Rafe hobbled along carefully, the fingertips of his left hand trailing along the pitted stone of the building to help him keep his balance. A narrow strip of gravel separated the building from the street, but in many places, the layer of rock was so thin he was practically walking on dirt. Rafe was pleased to see a few hardy weeds poking their heads up from the packed earth, unfurling their leaves, offering the occasional garish red blossom. Even here, in the most unlovely part of the city, defiant stray scraps of beauty flashed their irrepressible colors. It almost made him feel hopeful.

"In here," Josetta said, directing him to an unpainted wooden door so low that he had to duck to enter. The space inside was maybe eight feet square and serenely austere. There were two small windows admitting a minimum of light, a well-scrubbed stone floor, and unadorned walls of the same gray stone. Instead of the traditional five benches, this temple sported just one, a continuous circular shape broken only by the door through which they entered. Sections of it had been painted in the prescribed colors—black, blue, green, white, and red—for visitors who wanted to move from element to element and meditate themselves into tranquility.

In the middle of the stone floor was a squat barrel that might once have been a wine casket, and it was filled almost to the top with battered coins.

The brief excursion had tired him, so Rafe sank to the white part of the circular bench. The elay section. "Cozy," he offered, looking around.

"Small," she amended. "But it serves its purpose." She considered him a moment. "Are you willing to have me draw all three coins? We could bring in Callie or Foley or one of the girls, if you would like to proceed in the usual fashion."

"Oh, no. I like the idea of receiving all my blessings from the hand of a princess."

She smiled and stepped closer to the keg, stirring the coins with her right hand. "I think I'm very good at it," she said. "Because I'm elay, not because I'm a princess! I feel as if the proper coins make themselves known to me. I don't know how it works for anyone else, but I feel a certain warmth in the ones I'm meant to draw—"

Her voice trailed off and she concentrated, mixing the coins with more determination. Rafe wondered what would happen if none of the blessings declared themselves to her. Would she admit defeat? Concede that his was a soul so lost not even the elements would claim it? Or would she just close her hand over a random disk and force an imperfect blessing on him?

"There," she said suddenly. "And—another one. And this one is almost hot to the touch! So that's three."

She pulled her arm from the barrel, her fingers closed tightly over her selections, then came to sit next to him. A floral scent drifted through the small temple, then was gone.

"Open your hand," she directed, and laid the first coin in his palm. It felt cool against his skin. "Huh. That's interesting," she said.

He examined the forceful, jagged symbol stamped into the metal. "What is it?"

"Synthesis. One of the extraordinary blessings."

"So it's not affiliated with any of the elemental traits?" he asked. When she shook her head, he added, "What does it mean?"

"It's a blessing people sometimes receive when they're overseeing a huge project, something where they have to draw a lot of different components together. One of my mother's friends—a theater director—said he pulls synthesis when he's putting together a big production. But it can have a broader meaning than that. It might signify that you spend your whole life balancing different forces and making them work together as a whole."

He glanced from the coin to her face and back to his hand. "Right. I don't think that's it. In this case."

She laid the second coin in his hand. "Another extraordinary blessing. Time."

"Oh, that's a good one, right? It means I'll have a lot of time—a long life."

"It can mean that," she acknowledged. "Or it can indicate that a certain time has come. That now is the moment for something to begin."

"Synthesis," he said with a grin. "Now's the time to put those pieces together."

She held up the last blessing and studied it for a moment. Rafe thought she looked a little nonplussed, so he said, "What is it?"

"The third extraordinary blessing," she said. "You have no elemental affiliations at all."

He was damned if he could remember what the third extraordinary blessing actually was, even when she handed it to him and he studied the glyph. The highly stylized image might have been a clenched fist or just a series of slashing lines. "What does it mean?"

"Triumph."

He raised his eyes to her face again. "That seems highly unlikely."

"I've never seen that happen before," she said. "I've seen men reach into the basket a dozen times and pull out the same coin every time. I've known women who never drew any blessing but torz for their entire lives, whether they were picking coins for themselves or someone else. But I've never seen anybody draw only extraordinary blessings."

"Let me try," he said. "Throw them back in and let's see what *I* pull out."

"All right," she said.

"Although I don't think any of them will feel hot to my fingers," he added.

"Let's see."

He came to his feet and managed the few steps to the barrel, where he rested against the rim as he gave the whole pile a good mixing. Then, not stopping to think much about it, he pulled out three blessings, one right after the other. Limping back to sit beside Josetta, he handed her the three disks. She studied them only briefly before she burst out laughing.

"What?" he demanded. "Did I really get three extraordinary blessings again?"

She shook her head. "Not at all," she said. "You pulled beauty, grace, and joy."

"So why is that funny? Because I don't seem to embody any of those things?"

"Because they're all elay blessings. Because they're all mine."

SEVEN

Josetta was right. Kayle Dochenza was the strangest man Rafe had
ever encountered.

They met up with the elay prime after a pleasant drive along
the well-maintained road that followed the Marisi River south from
Chialto all the way to the sea. The land was low and gentle, covered with
hardy, uninspiring vegetation that was the only thing that would properly grow in the sandy soil, or so Josetta informed him. Now and then,
on the two-hour excursion, they passed clumps of civilization that had
grown up around small businesses designed to service the heavy-duty
wagons and elaymotives that hauled equipment up and down this road.

"This used to be the most desolate stretch of land," Josetta said.
"But ever since Kayle built his factories down at the port, it's been
building up. Every time I come this way, I see something new."

The rest of their conversation was similarly impersonal, because
they had an audience for the whole drive. Not only Foley, who seemed
perfectly at ease driving the smoker car, but also Caze; Sorbin had
stayed behind to watch over the shelter.

What it meant to Rafe was that, although he got to spend time with
Josetta, it was wholly chaperoned.

The port itself was a revelation. Rafe had been there before, but not for at least five years, and he couldn't believe how it had grown. Tall-masted ships still dominated the landscape, crowded up against the wharf at the very southern edge of land, with the limitless blue miles of ocean stretching out behind them. But everywhere he looked, there were big, hulking structures that clearly were factories, dozens of smaller buildings that might be homes or offices, and half-built constructions that could be anything. The wide streets were clogged with carts, elay-motives, and pedestrians, every block worse than the Cinque on a parade day. The place was louder than the Cinque, too, with people shouting, workmen clanging, and ferocious grinding noises bellowing forth at rhythmic intervals from some of the factories.

"It's a little overwhelming," Rafe said.

Josetta nodded. "This is the first time I've come here without Darien or Kayle. I *think* I can find my way."

"What's that smell?"

"Kayle says it's heated metal combined with the compressed gas they use to power the cars. And a little dead fish odor thrown in. It's awful, isn't it? But you get used to it after a while." She leaned forward to give directions to Foley. "Turn here. And then—see that big building with the yellow roof? That's where we're going."

Rafe would have enjoyed a chance to explore the factory itself, but they were met at the door by an efficient servant who took one look at Josetta and said, "Please come with me, majesty." Caze and Foley had stayed behind with the car, and the servant's expression said he wished Rafe had done the same, but no one barred his entry. He followed the other two down a narrow hallway and up a twisted stairwell to a small, hot, cluttered office whose windows overlooked the sea.

Every surface in the room was covered with papers and small-scale reproductions of elaymotives in various stages of completion. Some of them were models Rafe had seen driving the streets of Chialto. Some were completely unfamiliar—and some were surely impossible, sleek tubular bodies adorned with feathery metallic wings. Rafe couldn't resist picking up one of those fantastical specimens and manipulating the wings, which moved with a surprising smoothness. Was Kayle Dochenza truly trying to design an elaymotive that would fly? Now *that* Rafe would like to see.

A bustle in the hallway made him hurriedly put down the model and spin to face the door just as a man walked in. The newcomer was tall and absurdly thin, not like a starving beggar but like someone who often forgot to eat. His clothes were finely made but poorly cared for, stained in spots and unraveling in others. He had a shock of white-blond hair, also unkempt, and there were fingerprint smudges on the lenses of his glasses. If he'd been standing on a street corner in Chialto, Rafe would have thought he was a madman.

The elay prime didn't seem to realize there were two people in the room. At any rate, he didn't even glance at Rafe as he greeted the princess. "Josetta. Was I expecting you?"

She kissed him on the cheek. "No, I'm a surprise! I hope you don't mind."

"Many things are surprises to me," Kayle said. "I only mind the bad ones."

"I hope you've been well," she said. "I haven't seen you in a quintile, I think."

"Oh, well, what's a quintile?" Kayle responded. "Sometimes I feel like I am holding something in my hand, just glancing at it for a moment, and then I look up and a nineday has passed." He brushed a hand through the unruly hair. "I don't sleep sometimes, for all the thinking," he said earnestly. "Do you think other people have silence in their heads?"

Yes, Rafe certainly would consider him a madman.

"I think sweela folks are always arguing with themselves, if there's nobody else around to argue with, so *they* hear a lot of voices," Josetta replied serenely. "But I think they like it."

A smile lit Kayle Dochenza's face, rendering him a little less bizarre. "I always forget you had a sweela father," he said. "You are so unlike Navarr Ardelay. Well, of course, I didn't like him, so I don't think of him at all if I can help it."

Josetta seemed amused rather than offended by that remark. "Kayle, I want you to meet someone. He recently came into some money and thought he might invest in one of your factories."

Kayle nodded. "Good, good, I'm always happy to have more money. Bring him by sometime."

Rafe couldn't help it; he glanced over both shoulders as if to verify to himself that he was actually in the room. What—this crazy old man wasn't just ignoring him, he actually couldn't *see* Rafe?

Josetta's voice was gentle as she gestured in Rafe's direction. "I *did* bring him, Kayle. He's right over here."

Kayle's dreamy expression vanished; he stared at Rafe with blue eyes that abruptly turned knife keen. Rafe had the uncomfortable sensation that those eyes were boring straight into his soul. How would his spirit be weighed by the elay prime? Right now it felt heavy and miserable in his chest. His breath came slowly, in deep, difficult pants. He wanted to look away from Kayle Dochenza but he couldn't.

"You're a stranger here," the prime said at last, still staring.

Rafe could barely get enough air to speak. "I haven't been to the port in years. I live in Chialto."

Kayle made an impatient, jerky motion with his left hand. "No. To Welce. That's why I didn't realize you were here."

Rafe was wholly confused. "A stranger to Welce? No, I was born here."

"Well, you weren't, and neither were your parents," Kayle answered.

Rafe cut his eyes over to Josetta, and she shook her head slightly. *Don't argue with him right now.* So he just said, "And that's why you didn't notice me? Because I'm not a native?"

Again, Kayle made a choppy gesture. It was clear he was often frustrated in his attempts to explain what very strange thoughts went through his head. "Breathing. I hear everyone's breathing—or I feel it—it is part of the very air around me. You could blindfold my eyes and set me in a room and I could tell you how many people were there just by the inhalations and exhalations."

Rafe glanced uneasily at Josetta. "It's true," she said.

"I can put my hand on a man's chest and stop his breath altogether," Kayle added, a little too proudly, Rafe thought. "Actually, I don't even have to touch him."

Maybe it was Rafe's imagination, but for a moment he would have sworn his lungs did seize up; he opened his mouth and no air would come in. Kayle regarded him fixedly for another five seconds, and then glanced away. Immediately Rafe felt the breath rush back into his body. He tried not to feel too relieved.

Kayle addressed Josetta. "I forget what we were talking about before."

"Rafe. He wants to invest in some of your inventions." She paused a moment, but didn't add the words Rafe was sure both of them were thinking: *Unless you don't want a foreigner's money.* Rafe swallowed another protest.

But Kayle was nodding. "Excellent! I have great plans! Bigger machines, smaller ones." His hands traced appropriately sized circles in the air. He was the most restless man Rafe had ever come across. It seemed possible he was never entirely still. "And faster ones! You'll be surprised at the velocity."

"I like the idea of speed," Rafe said.

Now Kayle shook his head and began picking his way through the cluttered office, touching one model, then another. "But that's not where the excitement is," he said. "Not on the ground." He lifted one of the sleek winged cars that had fascinated Rafe. "In the air. *Flying.* That's the future of transportation."

Rafe sucked in his breath. "Really? You can get something like that to fly? Oh, I'll give you every quint-copper I ever earned if I can ride in one of those things."

Kayle flicked him a glance of real amusement, then set the model down again. "Not that one. Too heavy and the wings—well, they aren't right. Too much flapping, not enough gliding. We're working on better designs."

"I'm in," Rafe said.

Josetta cast him a worried look. "It sounds like it might be years before you have a successful vehicle. That can fly."

"Oh, yes. Five at least. Maybe ten," Kayle said, nodding.

"Then I wonder, Rafe, since you don't have an excess of cash on hand—perhaps you would be wiser to put your money on something a little more certain?"

Kayle made a scoffing noise. "*Nothing* is certain. Fires could burn down every one of my factories tomorrow. I could be struck dead! Or I could go mad, which everyone has always said is very likely. He'd lose all his money then, too."

Josetta frowned at the prime. "You're not making a very good case for yourself."

Kayle flung his arms out. "You must invest out of *passion*! You must invest out of *desire*! The same way you invent. The same way you fall in love! If you are too careful, you end up with something timid and unimportant. Something you don't mind losing. And when was that ever something you wanted to fight for?"

"You're exhausting," Josetta told him.

Kayle opened his blue eyes very wide. "I'm merely telling you the truth."

"He's right. I have to love it. And I love the idea of flying," Rafe said. "How do we do this? When can I bring you my money?"

Kayle turned back to him, beaming. *He can see me now,* Rafe thought. "You can bring it anytime."

After all, they did get a tour of the factory—the one that built smoker cars, not the one that was building prototypes of flying vehicles, because that one apparently was some distance out in the countryside. Rafe lost track of all the hundreds of stages, thousands of parts, that were required to put together a single elaymotive. He and Josetta watched, fascinated, as workers forged metal, assembled gears, and outfitted wheels with spokes and rims. The noise was deafening and the scorched scents of metal and gas sent Josetta into a coughing fit. Still, Rafe was entranced. He could have stayed all day, watching the fantastic process of *something* being created out of nothing but will and imagination. Or he could have if his ribs and head hadn't started to throb with pain.

"You will come back to me when it is convenient," Kayle said to Rafe when he finally saw them to their smoker car. It was evident that Foley was relieved to see the princess, because he rushed to help her into the backseat, where she collapsed with another spasm of coughing.

"It might be a while," Rafe said. "I'm still recovering from injuries."

Kayle waved a hand. "There's time. Come when you can."

"I look forward to seeing you again," Rafe said, climbing in beside Josetta.

"That was interesting," she said, her voice practically a croak.

He pulled out a hip flask of water and handed it over. "Here— drink something," he said. "I think you'll feel better once we get away from the port."

No one talked much as Foley negotiated the crowded streets and Caze offered him advice like "Hey, did you see that fellow?" and "Too fast for this corner, too fast!" But ultimately they made it free of the city traffic and back to the much calmer, much emptier main road.

Josetta revived a little as their speed picked up and fresh air blew in, but Rafe saw Foley half turn a number of times to check on her. It irritated him; *Rafe* wanted to be the one to watch over the princess.

Caze slewed around in his seat. "What did you think of Kayle Dochenza? He's an odd one, isn't he? I've been up at the palace when he was one of the guests, and he was usually better than the paid entertainment."

Foley gave the soldier a quick, repressive glance. "He's the *prime*," he said sternly.

Caze shrugged as if to say, *And a prime can't be a crazy man?*

Rafe smothered a grin and said, "In my experience, anyone who's elay is *different* in some way you can't always put your finger on."

"Thank you," Josetta said sardonically.

"And the prime was as different as they get. But I liked him," he added.

He glanced at Josetta, who was watching him steadily. They were both thinking about Kayle's extraordinary observation, but it was clear neither of them planned to say anything in front of the others.

Caze shrugged, and resettled in his seat, facing forward again. "Well, give me a hunti man any day," he said. "That's why I'm happy to serve the regent. Give me torz, even give me sweela! But elay and coru—there's no understanding them."

Rafe smiled over at Josetta, who was smiling right back. "I don't know," he said in a soft, idle voice. "I think I'd like to try to figure some of them out."

It was nearly dark, and Rafe was nearly on fire with pain, when they made it back to the shelter. Though he hated the necessity, Rafe allowed Josetta to help him out of the elaymotive. She was still holding tightly to his arm as she leaned over to speak to Foley.

"You'll return the car to Darien tonight?"

He gazed up at her. "If you're not planning to leave the building again."

"I'll stay put. I promise."

"Then I'll be back in a couple of hours."

Trying not to lean on the princess too heavily, Rafe limped through the door into the main room, where Callie and Bo were cleaning up after the first round of diners and setting out food for the next wave.

"Pull up a chair if you're hungry," Callie called. "I'll bring meals out to you."

Caze bustled off to find Sorbin, but Rafe sank gratefully to the first chair he could find, which was at a table that was blessedly empty. Josetta dropped into a seat across from him. "It doesn't seem like it should be so tiring to just sit in a conveyance all day while someone else does the driving, but it *is*," she remarked. "And I'm not even recovering from mortal wounds!"

"I hate being so pathetic," Rafe said with a grimace. "I'd rather be dashing and manly."

Josetta was still laughing when Callie brought over a tray filled with plates and glasses. Plain food and tumblers of tepid water had never seemed so appetizing. "You were plenty dashing when you saved Corene, so you don't have to worry about that."

"You weren't even there when I confronted those ruffians," Rafe pointed out. "You didn't get to see me strut and threaten."

"Maybe you don't know this, but I'm not really impressed when people strut and threaten," Josetta answered. "I'm much more touched when someone is wounded and desperate."

He wolfed down the first bite of meat before answering. "Even to please you, I don't think I can promise to let myself get beaten up again," he said. "If that's what it takes to catch your attention, I'm not going to be able to do it."

She was eating more daintily than he was, but Rafe noticed that the food was disappearing pretty rapidly off her plate as well. "You've caught my attention in a number of ways," she said, her voice low enough that no one else could overhear. "I don't think I'll be forgetting you anytime soon."

Rafe swallowed another big mouthful. "So. What he said back there. About my parents. Do you think he was right?"

Without hesitation, she nodded. "The primes all have the power to read people, but in very different ways. My sister Zoe can touch a man and tell you who he's related to because she can analyze the blood in his veins. I don't know *how* Mirti and Nelson and Taro sort out who belongs to what family, but I'm certain they can do it." When he didn't answer, she studied him curiously. "Does it bother you? To know you don't belong here?"

He shrugged. "I've always been something of an outsider. I didn't fit in when I lived in the country. I live on the fringes here in the city. This news doesn't really change anything, but it makes me curious, I guess. I always thought my mother ran away from some farming homestead, maybe, came to the city to try to make her fortune, and ended up seduced and abandoned." He shrugged again. "Not a pretty story, but a common one. But if she came here from some other country—why'd she leave? Why'd she pick Welce?"

"And *where* did she come from?" Josetta asked. "Cozique? Malinqua? Both pretty long journeys for a woman with a baby."

"Soeche-Tas is just over the mountains," he suggested. "Maybe that's where she was from."

Josetta studied him a moment. "Maybe. But I've met my share of Soechins and you don't have their look."

"I suppose we'll never know."

"Could you ask your stepfather? Maybe your mother confided the truth to him."

"Could be. Though I think he would have told me the story by now if he knew it. He's a great believer in honesty no matter what the cost."

"That's right. You said he was torz. It's a typical failing."

"At any rate, at this point it doesn't matter much who she was. You said it yourself, the night we met. It doesn't matter what kind of family we're born into. What matters is what kind of people we become."

"I do believe that," she said, smiling now. "And trust me, I know how it feels to learn, very abruptly, that your parents aren't who you thought they were. But you're still who you made yourself into. Life just becomes a little more interesting, that's all."

"I think mine's been interesting enough lately, thank you very much."

She tilted her head to observe him. "Something tells me there are more unexpected developments to come. I hope they'll be fun to watch."

He observed her for a long moment before finally saying, "And I hope you're there to watch them."

EIGHT

The next morning, as she prepared to travel into the heart of Chialto, Josetta was surprised to learn that Caze and Sorbin didn't plan to follow her through the city like so many dogged shadows.

"We'll take you to the Cinque, just to see you safely out of the slums, but our orders are to guard the *shelter*," Caze informed her. "As long as Foley's with you, we're to stay here."

She could admire Darien's master hand at work; she could hardly object to the presence of his guards if they were standing watch over the thing she loved. Then again, maybe Caze and Sorbin just didn't want to accompany her because they knew where she was going.

To her mother's house.

Seterre had taken a place almost dead center in the city, a little south of the fashionable district where most of the well-connected families had their homes. The main advantage was that it was walking distance from the new Plaza of Arts that had sprung up in the past few years, largely because of Seterre's passionate support.

Of Vernon's four queens, Seterre had been the one who seemed most unsure of herself once the king died and all his secrets were revealed. Elidon, his first wife, had remained at the palace, serving as advisor to Darien and keeping herself deeply involved in Chialto politics. Romelle, the youngest queen, had retired to the country estate of the torz prime to raise her two daughters—and the decoy princess. Alys, of course, had continued to plot and stir up trouble. But Seterre had been at a loss.

Josetta couldn't remember how her mother had fixed on the idea of becoming a patroness of the arts. Maybe she'd gone to a theatrical production one night when she was bored; maybe a concertmaster had come to visit her one afternoon, begging for funds. At any rate, Seterre had become transformed. She had rented a quirky house with many rooms and levels, turning some into rehearsal studios, some into art galleries, some into music chambers. She had adopted a dramatic and colorful style of dress and added even more gestures and intonations to her animated manner of speaking. She was a little silly, Josetta thought, but she was happy, which made up for it. She had not been particularly happy at court.

"Darling!" Seterre greeted her when Josetta arrived for lunch the day after the expedition with Rafe. "You look so pale. Have you been working too hard? Come in and let me feed you something *sinfully* delicious."

"Wait—let me get a look at you," Josetta said, coming to an utter standstill in the middle of the *kierten*. Foley stood poised on the threshold itself, as if he was afraid to step inside. The big open space was unfurnished, as custom demanded, but it was hardly empty. A brightly colored mural—a street scene from the Chialto shop district—had been painted in one continuous picture along all four walls, incorporating the house's doors and windows into its whimsical design. Adding to the busy market feel were nine or ten lifesize figures made of cloth and wood, sumptuously dressed, arranged in conversational groupings or contemplative poses. One woman appeared to be starting toward the door, her arm lifted in an enthusiastic wave, her painted face breaking into a smile of delight. She was so lifelike, and she looked so much like Seterre, that for a moment Josetta had mistaken the doll for her mother.

But Seterre was even more gorgeously dressed. She spun around to show off the velvet folds of her turquoise tunic, heavily decorated with jewels and feathers. She had a matching clip in her thick blond hair. "Do you like it? I had it specially made."

"It's beautiful, but I'm afraid it's wasted on a lunch with me. Unless we're expecting company? In which case—" Josetta glanced down at her own tunic and trousers. She knew better than to show up at her mother's in the plain clothing she preferred at the shelter, so she was wearing fine silk and handmade shoes, but the pale pink was subdued and the embroidered accents were subtle.

"No, it's just the two of us, but I was hoping you would come with me tonight. There's a performance at a new little theater and I promised I'd attend. I could lend you something to wear," she added. "Just something with a little color."

Josetta thought about all the work awaiting her back at the shelter: the accounts to tally, the supplies to inventory, and the *very* interesting patient who had practically healed himself by willpower alone. She hesitated, gazing at her mother's hopeful face. "I'd love to come," she said.

"Excellent! Foley, you'll join us, I hope?"

"I'll certainly escort you there," he said in his courteous way. "But I'd rather wait outside to make sure there are no disturbances on the street."

"Excellent," Seterre said again. "But first—lunch!"

Foley bowed them out of the *kierten* and then disappeared—to the kitchen, Josetta supposed, or to the room that Seterre maintained here for his private use. It was off an odd little hallway that fell between the servants' quarters and the guest chambers, but a considerable distance from the rooms set aside for Seterre and Josetta. Like everyone else, Seterre wasn't exactly sure of Foley's place in her daughter's life.

Though that didn't keep her from trying to find out. In fact, he was her first topic of conversation once they were settled in a small, cheerful dining room that was relatively free of clutter. Food had been laid out and the servants had already withdrawn. Time for mother and daughter to share secrets.

"So?" Seterre inquired, arching her delicate brows over her blue eyes. "How's the situation between you and Foley these days?"

Josetta served herself a portion of some poultry dish covered in thick sauce. "Mother, you know you would be scandalized to hear I'd become involved with Foley."

Seterre made an equivocating motion with her head and spread her hands wide. She wore rings on every finger. "It might not be what I would want for you *permanently*, but if you took him for a lover one summer? Or even two? I don't see that it would do you any harm. Once you're married, you know, life can be very dull. You should take the chance to enjoy yourself while you're still unencumbered."

You took the chance to enjoy youself while you *were married,* Josetta was tempted to say, but she knew how her mother would respond to that. *I was fulfilling my duty to give the king an heir! I did not sleep with Navarr Ardelay merely for the pleasure of it!* Maybe it was even true. Though from everything Josetta knew about Navarr Ardelay, Seterre probably *had* enjoyed their nights together.

"No, nothing has changed between us," Josetta said, spooning some spiced berries onto her plate.

"It's strange. He's so devoted to you. And yet—" Seterre took a sip of fruited water. "Do you think he just prefers the company of men?"

"Maybe. Though he was with us when Corene and I were traveling with Jaker and Barlow, and *they're* a couple, and Foley didn't seem particularly interested in *them*."

"Maybe he's been damaged somehow. You know. So he can't quite function."

Josetta strangled a laugh. "Mother, I don't think this is an appropriate conversation."

"Maybe you just need to encourage him," Seterre said. "You're a princess. He's a guard. He doesn't have the nerve to speak his love."

Josetta toyed with her food. She had done just that two summers ago. Found a moment when she was alone with Foley and confronted him—practically offered herself to him, or so it had seemed at the time. *I'm not a princess anymore. I can choose who I want to be with. I trust you more than any man I know. If you want me, I will love you in return.* He had been almost appalled at the declaration—not, it seemed, by her boldness, but by the very notion that such a union could be possible. *I could not think of you in that way,* he had answered. *It would be like wanting a statue in the Plaza.*

Josetta had been depressed about it for a quintile. Like her mother, she had had trouble finding her way once Vernon was dead and everything was changed. She had been lonely, unsure of her place, wanting simply to make a choice, any choice, and move forward with her life.

She had thought that taking a husband and finding a house and producing babies would at least give her some direction.

Later, though, she was glad that Foley had turned her down, and surprised that there had been oddly little awkwardness between them because of it. Her life still might hold a husband and children someday—she hoped it did—but she had stumbled on a different kind of passion, and it was enough to sustain her for a good long while.

And she might meet more suitable men than Foley someday. Not, of course, that any of them had come her way in the past nineday or so . . .

"I don't plan to encourage him," she answered at last. "I don't think Foley is the right man for me."

"Well, don't let Darien Serlast marry you off to someone *he* thinks is right for you. You know he's a schemer. I worry about how much influence he has over you."

Josetta smiled. "I think he would *like* to have influence over me."

That made Seterre laugh. "Oh, good! Ignore him as much as possible! The man is entirely too arrogant."

"He had an argument with Alys the other day, did you hear?"

Seterre was delighted. "Yes! You know my cook is friends with Zoe's maid, and she must have *run* through the streets to bring the news. *Everybody* knows. But is it true she's pregnant?"

"That's what one of the blind sisters told Corene. How did *you* hear?"

Seterre looked mysterious. "I have my sources."

"Do you suppose it was a mistake?"

"Alys doesn't make mistakes."

"But why would she want another baby?"

"She thinks it will be an asset somehow. She can marry it off to some heir or heiress of the Five Families, I don't know. Use it as a pawn in some dark scheme."

"What a repellent woman she is."

"I know," Seterre said cordially. "Some days when I'm feeling a little tired or unhappy, I think, 'At least I'm not living at court anymore. At least I don't have to see Alys every day.' Cheers me right up. I don't mind not seeing Elidon every day, either," she added.

"I like Elidon," Josetta said. "Although she's very—" It was hard to find a single word that summed up the intelligent, strong-willed, and confident queen. "Sure of herself," she ended lamely.

"I know! Can you believe she's elay? You'd think she was all hunti, because she can be so *inflexible*."

Josetta grinned, but said, "I think what makes her elay is her sense of vision. Elidon sees things—the whole world, all at once—in ways most of the rest of us never manage. She's not as *flighty* as elay people can be, but she thinks on a different plane."

Seterre sniffed and said, "Well, I'm just as glad to be living in a place where Elidon's *vision* doesn't have any bearing on my daily life."

"You do seem happier these days," Josetta agreed. "You seem like you've found the right place for yourself. Something all of us need to do."

"I hope your place isn't that dreadful little shelter in the city."

"I think it is, though. That's where *I'm* happy."

"But, darling—you know I don't like to criticize—but you can't spend your whole life there. You have to be part of society some of the time."

"I already promised Darien I'd come to court when Romelle visits."

"Yes, but more than that. If you're not going to run off with Foley, then you need to be thinking about other men. Wealthy men. Men from the Five Families."

"I'm only twenty. I don't have to marry for years and years."

"You don't even *have* to marry! But you will certainly want—companionship—and you're not going to find it down in the slums."

Josetta couldn't help envisioning Rafe Adova's smiling, roguish face. The man with a light heart, a curious mind, and the most extraordinary blessings. "Who knows?" she said. "Maybe I will."

J osetta stayed for the play, which her mother loved but Josetta found incomprehensible, then spent the night because Seterre seemed so woebegone at the thought that she wouldn't. But in the morning she couldn't be persuaded to linger past breakfast.

"There's too much work to do back at the shelter," she said firmly. *And too many interesting people to see. Unless they've already moved on.*

Rafe Adova was still there when she returned, though she had been right to worry he might be gone. He had clearly grown well enough to be restless. Her day was so chaotic she didn't have a chance to speak to him until after dinnertime, when he announced he planned to return to his own apartment above the bar where they'd met.

"I can feed myself, bathe myself, and tend to my own dressings," he informed her. It was late in the evening and everyone else had gone upstairs except for Caze and Sorbin, who were making one last patrol around the block. "Callie's given me some salve to take with me. I don't need to be cared for anymore—I'm just taking up space. So I'm leaving in the morning."

"We have plenty of beds. There's only one other person in the infirmary—as you must know, since you heard him screaming when we tried to patch him up! You don't have to leave if you're feeling at all unsteady."

It seemed his hands could never be idle. He shuffled his deck three times, four times, before looking up at her with a half-smile. "I'm not sure it's the wounds making me feel unsteady," he said.

The words hung between them as they watched each other long enough for Josetta to experience a little dizziness of her own. Then he looked down at his hands again.

"I've been away from my familiar life too long. I've lost the usual rhythm of my days," he went on. "I need to settle back in. Think things through."

Josetta nodded, showing a face of calm. "Of course. But I hope you'll come see us from time to time. Just to visit. Or to pull another blessing."

He shuffled the cards again. "I'd be glad to. If it wouldn't be an imposition."

"You'd be welcome."

"I could do something to earn a meal or two," he suggested. "Cook or clean. I don't mind scrubbing the floors."

"There's always work to do here."

"And if Steff comes to the city, I might bring him by."

It took her a moment to remember who Steff was. The half brother with the hardworking torz father. "I'd be happy to meet him."

"And if you need me—I mean, I can't imagine you would, but—you know where I keep my quarters. You can always find me there."

It was worse than the conversation with Foley two years ago. Each of them was breathless and nervous; each of them was trying to say something without saying it. Or maybe that made it better. At least this time she wasn't the only one struggling to understand an emotion.

"Deal a card," she said suddenly. "One to me, one to you."

His hands stilled completely. "Why?"

She smiled. "Whoever gets the high card gets to ask the other one a favor."

His eyes narrowed, half in amusement, half in speculation. "What kind of favor?"

She kept her face prim. "I think we can both be trusted not to request anything too outrageous."

Now the amusement deepened. She thought he might want to say *I'm not sure I can.* But he merely flicked one card to each of them. "Do you know what favor you have in mind?" he asked.

"Yes. Do you?"

He didn't answer, merely turned his card faceup. Four of roses. Josetta displayed her own card and started laughing. Four of skulls.

"We seem to have the oddest luck with runes and portents," she said.

"Two cards this time. High card or trump takes the hand."

Rafe turned up the five of horseshoes and the five of fish, while Josetta held the same cards in roses and flutes. "You're doing this on purpose," she accused. "Just to extend the game."

"I'm not," he protested. He squared the deck and set it between them on the table. "Let's just keep drawing cards one at a time until someone wins."

She cut the deck first and reordered it. "Just to be sure," she said, and he laughed. The first thing she pulled from the stack was a wildcard. "Oh, I think I've got you!" she crowed—but he turned over a wildcard of his own.

"I *know* you did something to the deck," she said.

"I wish I knew how to arrange it *this* well," he answered. "I'd never lose another game."

They drew, and drew again, matched over and over until only about a third of the deck was left. They hadn't drawn a single trump. "This one will do it," Rafe said under his breath as Josetta reached out a hand.

She gave him an inquiring look. "How do you know? I've started to believe we'll be tied to the very end."

"All that's left are the single cards that don't have a pair because we've already drawn all the matches—the five of skulls, the two of roses and so on. And the trumps. And one wildcard."

"Really? You remember that?"

He shrugged. "I always remember every card that's played in any game. So pick yours."

She turned up the high trump. "Ha! I win!"

But he had the last remaining wildcard. "I match you."

Laughing, she folded her hands before her on the table. "Perhaps neither of us is supposed to win. Or we both are."

"What do you mean?"

"We each get to ask the other one a favor. Or perhaps it's not a favor, it's a gift."

He considered that. "I admit I'm curious what you have in mind."

"Then it's a deal?"

He nodded.

She tried to speak nonchalantly, though she felt she was being bold as a harlot. "Come back once every nineday. Have dinner with us. I'm afraid if you just say, 'Sure, I'll stop by sometime,' you really won't. But if you promise to eat with us every firstday, for instance, you'll feel more obligated."

His eyes narrowed; he watched her again with a look that was half speculation and half surprise. Trying to decide how much to read into her offer, no doubt. Then he smiled. "You're right. I probably would have convinced myself that you were only being polite when you told me to stay in touch."

"So you'll do it?"

"You'll get tired of me if I'm here that often," he said.

"Maybe," she said. "If I promise to *tell* you when I get tired of you, will you agree to a schedule?"

Now he laughed. "You're different from other girls," he said.

"I know."

"But I'd like to know that I'm going to see you again," he added. "Firstday it is."

Josetta tried not to show just how delighted she was by his response.

"Excellent! We always have our best meals on firstday—still nothing fancy, but Callie makes a special effort."

"I'm not coming for the food," Rafe said.

She smiled. "Of course not. For the companionship." He looked like he might add something, but when he didn't, she prompted, "And what was the favor you were going to ask me?"

Now his smile was a little wicked, a little rueful. "I have to think of a new one. The old one was predicated on the belief that I'd probably never see you again."

That pulled her eyebrows right up to her hairline. "*Really.* Well, now you have to tell me what it was, even if you ask for something else."

He seemed to think it over a moment, the smile lingering. Then he shrugged and stood up, motioning her to her feet. "Can't think of anything else I'd want," he said, and stepped forward and kissed her. His mouth was brief and gentle against hers. She felt his finger under her chin, tipping her face up, but other than that he didn't touch her.

When he stepped back, he was no longer smiling. "Still want me to drop by for dinner?" he asked in a husky voice.

For a minute, she was that most curious of creatures, an elay woman who couldn't draw breath. But she managed to get the words out anyway. "Even more."

That made him laugh again. He scooped up his cards, dropped them in a pocket, and shook his head. "Then I'll see you on firstday," he said. "Looking forward to the visit." And he sauntered back to the infirmary without a backward glance.

In the morning, Rafe Adova was gone.

NINE

Every time Josetta stepped inside the palace, she had a moment where she succumbed to black depression. Even in the huge, high-ceilinged *kierten* with its white-stone floors and its bubbling fountain, its gracious proportions and its echoing emptiness, she felt trapped. She felt desperate. She felt lonely and afraid.

Until her circumstances had changed, until she was no longer the eldest heir who *had* to live at the palace, Josetta hadn't realized that there were any other ways to feel.

These days she was still figuring out what she wanted her life to be, but she knew it would be better than it had been five years ago.

Now, at least, she only had to return to court life for special occasions, like today's events to celebrate Romelle's visit. Josetta had spent the night at her mother's, and they had hired a smoker car to carry them up the steep road to the palace. It was situated in a natural plateau halfway up the mountain that stood guard over Chialto, and it was visible from almost any vantage point in the city. It was sublimely picturesque, with the severe peaks behind it and the spectacular waterfall of the Marisi River beside it. Outside it was constructed of warm, golden stone and fluted turrets; inside it was neatly divided into public and private spaces, residential wings, kitchens, large ballrooms, small studies, and, of course, that magnificent *kierten*. It was a beautiful, welcoming place, stocked with every luxury, and Josetta hoped she never had to spend another night there in her life.

"Very nice," Seterre murmured as they strolled through the *kierten*, sampling the refreshments and assessing the decorations. "I might have brought in more of those small flowering trees—it *will* be Quinnahunti changeday, after all; you have to play up the symbolism. And the colors are a little restrained. Elidon never did have much sense of style. But still. Very nice. And the food is quite good."

There were probably three hundred other people milling around inside and another hundred outside in the courtyard, or strolling around the nearby lake that had been formed by the falling water. For once even Seterre's flamboyant costuming did not look out of place, Josetta thought. Every visitor wore clothing worthy of a coronation; the glitter of jewels could have illuminated an underground passage.

"How long do we have to stay?" Josetta asked.

"Well, since we're attending the dinner after all the public events this afternoon, I'd say quite a long time."

Josetta groaned.

She brightened up a few minutes later when Zoe picked through the crowd to greet them. "I hate these events," she announced, pushing her dark hair behind her ear. "I only came today because Taro Frothen accompanied Romelle, and Darien says if the torz prime can haul himself all the way in from the western provinces, the coru prime can drag herself two miles."

"Josetta has been complaining, too, but I rather like all the extravagance," Seterre said, waving her hands. "I don't miss living here, but I do miss the excitement sometimes. Have you seen Romelle?"

Zoe nodded. "Yes, Darien and I were up here last night for a much quieter dinner with Romelle and Taro and Elidon."

"Talking politics," Seterre said. She sounded a touch wistful.

"Well, *they* did. I was just bored."

"How is she?" Seterre asked. "I was always so fond of her, and I haven't seen her in a quintile, at least. She's the only one of the other wives I actually miss."

"I thought she seemed a little harried. Natalie doesn't travel well and Odelia was getting over some kind of stomach ailment, so I think the journey was taxing. And Romelle is not overfond of court life, either, so she wasn't entirely happy."

"So is it really Odelia?" Josetta asked. "Or Mally?"

"I don't know. Both girls were paraded through the dining room, but neither of them climbed into my lap, and if I can't touch them—" Zoe shrugged.

"Surely it's Odelia. She brought Mally last time," Josetta said. "The last two times."

"Well, it better be Odelia at least *some* of the time," Seterre said. "If that girl is going to be queen, she has to learn court rules and court etiquette. Romelle can't just keep her there on Taro's farm, learning about nothing but hay and corn."

Zoe was amused. "She's not even five yet. Plenty of time to learn."

Seterre looked a little superior. "A princess is never too young to start preparing herself for her responsibilities, and her mother should know that."

Zoe didn't reply; she never bothered to compete with Seterre, who still, after all this time, drew great satisfaction from knowing she had once been the wife of a king. Zoe was a prime, of course, and that was all very well, but Seterre made it clear it was much more impressive to be royalty.

Josetta always suspected it was only *her* existence that convinced Zoe to make any effort with Seterre at all. Zoe was always friendly enough to Seterrre, but Josetta didn't think her sister really liked her mother. She never asked.

The crowd shifted and parted, and a low murmur rippled from the front of the room to the back. Josetta stood on tiptoe to get a better look at the hallway that led to what used to be the king's quarters. It was now the wing of the palace where visitors stayed and Romelle took rooms whenever she was in town.

"There they are," Josetta said. She could just glimpse a knot of people emerging from the hallway and moving slowly through the mass of people. She could make out Elidon, Darien, Romelle, two nursemaids, two little girls, and a handful of guards holding the crowd in check. "It's going to take *forever* for them to make it around this whole room."

"Well, I'll have plenty of opportunities to gawk at the queen and her daughters," Zoe said. "I think I'll wait in the courtyard. There's going to be music. And entertainment, Darien said."

"Yes! A few of the actors I know are doing comedy sketches—just silly little scenes, you know, to keep people amused. When Darien asked if I was acquainted with anyone who might be suitable, I could hardly pick from all my friends!"

"What fun," Zoe said. Josetta was sure she was trying to hold back a laugh. "Let's go see them."

The weather was fine, the actors were entertaining, and there was more food outside, so Zoe and Josetta didn't go back into the palace for the next two hours. Seterre had elected to stay in the *kierten*, where there was a better chance that someone important might see her, but Corene joined them about twenty minutes after they'd stepped outside.

"I still don't like Natalie," she remarked. "She's just so irritating."

"I don't remember *you* being a very pleasant little girl," Josetta said without heat.

"I didn't *whine*."

"You were mean."

Corene rolled her eyes. "And you were always afraid of everybody."

"With pretty good reason, as it turned out," Zoe said.

"Do you like Odelia?" Josetta asked.

Corene wrinkled her nose. "I don't know. She's not as cute as Celia."

"Well, nobody's as cute as my darling little girl," Zoe said.

"I don't think Romelle likes her, either," Corene added.

"What a thing to say!" Josetta exclaimed. "Of course she likes her own *daughter*."

"Then why doesn't she ever hold her?" Corene demanded. "Did you ever notice that? It's always the nursemaid carrying Odelia everywhere. Never Romelle."

"She has to greet people and shake hands and all that," Josetta said. "Hard to do if she's holding a child. Or even just holding her hand."

"She did it with Natalie," Corene said positively. "She never put that girl down. Don't you remember?"

"Well, Natalie cried a lot," Josetta said. "Romelle was always picking her up to comfort her."

"I bet Odelia cries, too," Corene said. "But Romelle doesn't hold *her*."

Josetta glanced at Zoe, expecting her to say, *Don't be ridiculous.* Or *Things were different back then.* Or *Natalie was just a baby, and Odelia's four years old.* But Zoe was frowning. Zoe was thinking it over.

"Corene has a point," Zoe said slowly. "Last night at dinner, Odelia dumped a whole plate of food in her lap and started crying. Romelle didn't even look over. The nurse is the one who took care of her."

"Then it must be Mally," Josetta said.

"Even so," Corene said. "She should *pretend* to like her. I mean, isn't that the point? So that no one knows if it's the real heir or not?"

Zoe nodded. "I'll mention it to Darien and see what he thinks."

"Better be sure," Josetta suggested. "Try to find a chance to touch Mally—and make sure she *is* Mally."

Corene's voice was hard. "Right. Because who would ever believe a mother wouldn't like her own daughter?"

The long public day was followed by a long private reception—well, "private" in the sense that there were only about fifty people in the room and it was actually possible to find someone to talk to that you knew.

Although not necessarily someone that you liked. For more than a half hour, Josetta was trapped in the type of conversation she hated the most, with two young men from rich and prominent families. They spent the whole time vying with each other to see who could pay her the most extravagant compliment or impress her the most with his wealth and possessions.

"I told my father, 'I don't *need* my own elaymotive,' but I'm glad to have it, of course. He turned over a little property to me last year—it's small, hardly more than a hunting lodge, but now I can drive out there anytime I want," said the one she thought was remotely related to Kayle Dochenza.

"Oh, you've got a country house?" said the one who might be part Lalindar. "I've got a place in the city, not far from the Plaza. Well, you know, my father brought me into the firm last Quinnelay. It seemed the right time to set up my own household."

You're wasting your time, she wanted to tell them. *I don't care about your cars or your properties or your bags of gold. What have you done with your life? What are you going to do with it? That's all that matters.*

But she smiled politely and offered the appropriate responses and escaped the first chance she could. She spent a much happier half hour talking with the sweela prime, a big, bluff, outgoing man whose boundless energy seemed only slightly dampened by the fact that he was pushing seventy. Nelson Ardelay was her uncle and fond of her for his brother's sake. Though, really, Nelson had such a warm personality that he could manage to be fond of almost anybody, she thought.

Except, as it turned out, one of the king's former wives. "Ah, excuse me, my dear, I have to go perform an unpleasant chore," Nelson said regretfully. "I see Alys headed in Corene's direction, and I promised the regent I would help keep them apart."

Josetta quickly scanned the crowd; yes, there was Alys, angling through the throng to where Corene was laughing with Nelson's sons. Like Corene, like Nelson, they were red-haired, headstrong, and sweela. Ever since Zoe had brought the Ardelays back into favor five years ago, Kurtis and Rhan had been popular at court, and Corene in particular had an affinity for them, despite the fact that they were twice her age.

"Alys will be furious if you stop her from talking to Corene."

"Well, it doesn't bother me to make a scene in public," Nelson said cheerfully. "I think that's why Darien asked me to be watchdog. I would purely love to drag that woman out of the room, cursing and shrieking."

It didn't come to that, though there was certainly a stir when Nelson intercepted Alys and she realized why. Corene realized it, too, Josetta could tell. The girl stood silently with Kurtis and Rhan, observing the low-voiced argument that ended with Alys stalking from the room. Rhan excused himself and went after her; he had always been the Ardelay who had the easiest relationship with Alys. He was the youngest of the brothers, just over thirty, with a reckless charm that made him the perfect man to soothe the feelings of the enraged queen.

Corene watched both of them until they disappeared out the main door. Her face was so fierce Josetta was sure she was fighting back tears. She pushed her way politely through the crowd to Corene's side, arriving just as Zoe did. They knew better than to try to offer comfort or commiseration, and so did Kurtis. So instead they engaged in only slightly awkward banter until life came back into Corene's expression.

"I suppose you've heard the news," Kurtis said after a few minutes. "The crown prince of Berringey will be here sooner than anyone thought. Bringing, it seems, a sizable entourage."

"How soon?" Zoe asked. "I was hoping to go up to my grandmother's house after changeday."

"Well, since I think he's arriving for changeday, you'd better not."

Zoe groaned and Kurtis laughed. "Taro was pleased. He hates to travel into Chialto, and he wasn't looking forward to doing it twice in a short stretch of time. Now he says he'll stay long enough to greet the man, and then go back to his farms for the next quintile."

"Why can Taro get away with that sort of behavior and I can't?" Zoe demanded.

Kurtis tapped his chin. "Why would that be, I wonder? Because—I don't know—you're married to the regent? And you have to *pretend* you know how to behave in society, even if you don't?"

"I think it sounds like fun," Corene finally spoke up. "A prince! I'm so tired of princesses. Is he young and handsome?"

Kurtis looked amused. "He might be. I know he's unmarried."

"Then I agree with Corene," Josetta said. "It does sound like fun."

The reception was followed by the real business of the evening, when the primes joined Elidon and Darien and Romelle for a conference in a private room of the royal wing. Everyone else mingled a while longer before setting off for home.

Before Zoe joined the others, she found a chance to speak to Josetta. "Stay until we're done. Tell your mother we'll bring you home."

"If you want," Josetta said, a question in her voice.

Zoe glanced at Corene. "Keep her company. Make sure she's all right. I think we'll be done in an hour. Or two."

"Did you get a chance to hold Odelia?" Josetta asked in a low voice.

"Not yet. Maybe tomorrow. Thank you," Zoe said, and hurried off.

Corene was sitting on an ornate, embroidered divan at the far end of the reception room, and Josetta dropped down beside her. The servants moved quietly around them, picking up plates and dropped silverware.

"I'm fine," Corene said in a distinct voice. "Don't be worried about me."

Corene had never been the type to respond well to sympathy. That wasn't how you let her know you cared about her. It had taken Josetta forever to figure that out. "I'm not," she said, lowering her voice conspiratorially. "I had an idea! Maybe we could see if Natalie and Odelia are still awake. They're our sisters, after all, so, of course, we'd want to visit them. And then we'd still be with them when Zoe's done and she can come find us, and *then*—"

Corene's eyes sparkled and she practically bounced to her feet. "Oh, yes, let's go!" she exclaimed.

The royal wing was vast and multistoried, so it took a little wandering through gorgeously appointed hallways to find the suite of rooms where Romelle and her daughters were staying. Two guards at the closed door advertised the presence of high-ranking visitors, and commotion within indicated that the children were still awake. Josetta could hear the sound of Odelia wailing and Natalie announcing, "I am the *princess* and I do *not* have to go to bed when you tell me."

Corene grinned at the soldiers. "Oh, good. We'll get a chance to see them before they fall asleep," she said, heading right in, Josetta at her heels. Neither guard moved to stop them.

They followed the sounds of distress through the *kierten* to the nursery. The two nursemaids on hand appeared young, overworked, and overmatched.

"Oh, aren't you having a time of it!" Josetta exclaimed. "I'm Josetta and that's Corene. We came to say hello to our sisters—you don't mind, do you? Maybe we can calm them down for you."

It was clear the maids would have liked to refuse, but they didn't have any clue how to gainsay royalty. Within a few minutes, Josetta and Corene had taken charge. Corene dropped to the floor, heedless of her beaded tunic, and put her face close to Natalie's ill-tempered one.

"Do you think that's how a *princess* behaves?" Corene demanded. "Let me tell you how you're supposed to act when you're in the palace."

Josetta had taken Odelia—or Mally—from the nursemaid's arms and settled the little girl on her hip. The sheer novelty of the experience caused the child to stop crying as she stared at Josetta out of huge, tear-filled brown eyes.

"I don't know you," the child said in an accusing voice.

"We're stepsisters," Josetta said.

"I don't know what that means."

"It means that we're not really related but we can pretend we are. We're in the same family. It means we have to stick together, especially here at the palace."

The little girl scowled. She had dark ringlets, just now damp with the exertion of screaming, and a child's flawless skin. "I don't like it here," she said.

Josetta started strolling around the room with her, swaying a little as she moved. "No? I lived here when I was your age, and I didn't like it, either! Too many people and too many rooms."

"And my stomach hurts," the little girl said ominously.

Josetta hastily looked around for some kind of receptacle. "Do you think you're going to throw up?"

"Maybe."

"Do you want me to set you down?"

"No. I like you."

Josetta kissed the top of her head. "And I like you."

"What's your name?"

"Josetta. What's your name?"

For a long time, the little girl just stared back at her out of those huge eyes.

"Do you know your name?" Josetta asked softly.

The little girl finally nodded. "I'm Odelia."

Josetta couldn't tell if it was true.

Their plan worked. Zoe found them in Romelle's rooms a little more than an hour later. "You *are* here!" she exclaimed. "I had to ask five people if they'd seen either of you. Of course, Foley was the one who actually knew where you'd gone."

By this time, Josetta was perched in a rocking chair; on her lap was the drowsy child, sucking a thumb and fighting off sleep. "People used to keep far closer track of us when we lived here," she observed.

Natalie and Corene were in another corner of the room, where they had been practicing correct manners for a princess—how to bow, how to offer a hand, how to communicate disdain with a single glance. No surprise that both Corene and Natalie had been especially enthusiastic about that last one, which was not an element of deportment Josetta had ever encountered before.

"Zoe's a prime," Corene whispered to Natalie. "Show me how you would greet *her*."

Natalie scrambled to her feet, still game despite the lateness of the hour. "She's not as important as a queen but still very important," she rattled off, offering an impressively deep bow. "So I must be very nice to her."

Zoe responded with an even lower bow, acknowledging a near heir to the throne. "I hope you are nice to everyone, princess," she said.

"I am nice to people if I *like* them," Natalie retorted. "And if they aren't always telling me what to do and what not to do."

"Sometimes if you *pretend* you like them, you can trick them into letting you do what you want," Corene informed her. "You like to pretend, don't you?"

Josetta and Zoe traded a look, half amused, half appalled. Josetta wondered what other kind of disastrous advice Corene had offered the young princess while she had been too busy to pay attention. "All done for the night?" Josetta asked Zoe. "The whole kingdom straightened out?"

Zoe sighed. "We have to come back tomorrow, though Kayle is even less happy about it than Taro."

Josetta pushed herself to her feet, a delicate maneuver with the child in her arms. "If you have to come back tomorrow, we should probably get going," she said, keeping her voice casual. "Would you like to say good night to the princess?"

Zoe came close enough to make another deep bow, then extended her hand. The girl watched her with some suspicion, keeping her thumb in her mouth, but offered her other hand to be kissed. "Sweet dreams, majesty," Zoe said.

There was a swirl at the door, then Romelle was inside. "Goodness, you're *all* here? I thought you'd left hours ago. Natalie, darling, why aren't you in bed? Odelia—get your fingers out of your mouth! How many times—where are the nursemaids? Lanni! Jilla! Come get these girls to bed!"

Five minutes of chaos later, the nursemaids had regained control of the nursery, while Romelle had ushered her visitors to a sitting room that opened off the little *kierten*.

"I don't mean to sound rude, but I have to send you all home. I'm so exhausted, and then there's *tomorrow* and the day *after*," Romelle said, sounding almost as petulant as her daughters.

"I know. We're all tired," Zoe said sympathetically. "But, Romelle. I need to ask you something. Is there any reason you brought Mally with you this time instead of Odelia?"

Josetta froze to the floor and saw Corene do the same. They both watched the queen intently. Fleeting emotions crossed Romelle's face—astonishment, then fear—then a sort of brazen defiance. She lifted her chin and said, "I don't know what you mean. That's Odelia."

"Don't lie to me," Zoe said quietly. "You know all I have to do is lay my hand on hers and I can tell she's not your daughter."

"I ought to know my own child! And that's Odelia!"

Zoe regarded her for a long, steady moment, but Romelle maintained the look of indignant certainty. Zoe shrugged. "All right. I'll see if Mirti or Nelson or Kayle can visit her tomorrow. Let's see what the other primes say."

Now fear showed again on Romelle's face, but she hid it quickly by putting her hands to her forehead. "This is a ridiculous conversation. Zoe, please just go away. I have such a headache, and everything you say makes it worse."

"I'll go," Zoe said, still in a gentle voice. "But the questions will only start again tomorrow."

Romelle didn't answer. The three of them stepped into the corridor, past the guards, down the hallways, and toward the main *kierten* of the palace.

"Zoe!" Corene hissed as soon as they were out of earshot of other servants, guests, or soldiers. "What did all that mean?"

Zoe shook her head. "I don't know, but we have to find Darien. And Taro. And any of the other primes who haven't left yet."

They were in luck, because they located Darien in the great entrance hall, talking with Nelson Ardelay and the hunti prime, Mirti Serlast. It was late enough that the gaslight had been turned low, and the immense space was filled with shadows and echoes. A few of those shadows were royal guards, keeping the midnight watch. One was Foley, standing near the main doors, waiting with his usual patience. Josetta flicked him a brief wave as she and her sisters hurried up to the others. She thought that, at this late hour, even their soft-soled shoes sounded loud on the marble floor.

"There you are," Darien said, greeting them with a smile. "I thought maybe you'd bribed one of the palace grooms to take you home."

"Darien, we need to talk," Zoe said without preamble. "Mirti—Nelson—you, too. Are either of the other primes still here?"

"Taro must be on the premises somewhere, since he's staying here," Mirti observed. She was a thin, stringy woman with gray hair and an obvious disdain for fashion. She was Darien's aunt and usually his staunchest supporter, but like anyone with hunti heritage, she could be unyielding. Once she made up her mind, it was like asking an oak to turn into a rosebush to get her to change it.

"What's wrong?" Darien asked. He glanced at Josetta and Corene. "And should we discuss it somewhere else?"

"We already know," Corene informed him with a smirk.

"Send someone to get Taro," Zoe said, "and let's find a private place to talk."

A few minutes later they were in one of the small meeting rooms that clustered along the first story of the palace. Zoe didn't bother sitting in one of the comfortable chairs or leaning against one of the scattered tables.

"We were just upstairs saying good night to Romelle and her daughters," she began. "I had an opportunity to hold the youngest princess—long enough to realize it's Mally who's come here this time, not Odelia."

"Mally frequently substitutes for Odelia," Mirti said. "That is the point of having a false heir on hand."

Zoe nodded. "When I asked her why she had brought Mally instead, Romelle became very affronted and told me it *wasn't* Mally."

Mirti frowned. "That makes no sense. She must realize you would *know*." Her gesture included Nelson. "Any of us would know."

"Exactly," Zoe said. "So why bother to lie? Why pretend the impostor is the genuine child?"

"I assume you asked her that," Darien said.

"Of course. And she told me to leave because she had a headache."

Although Josetta generally kept silent when she was privileged to overhear serious conversations among the primes, Corene piped up at this point. "I don't think she's brought Odelia here for at least a year," she said.

That got everyone's attention. "Why do you think that?" Darien demanded.

"Because of the way she acts with Mally. Like she's mad at her all the time. That's how she's acted the last few times she came to court."

Nelson spoke up. "I know it was Mally the last time Romelle was here," he said, his voice slow, as if he was remembering. "Kurtis had brought his twins to court, and they wanted to meet the princess, so Romelle sent her to our table. I knew instantly that she was the decoy, but I didn't tell the twins that, of course."

"When was that? The beginning of Quinncoru?" Mirti asked. When they all murmured assent, she said, "And the time before that, she also brought Mally. I remember, because it was during the regatta, and we spent some long, dull hours in the pavilion waiting for the boats to cross the finish line. I helped Romelle feed the princess, and I could tell who she was."

"So when *did* we see Odelia last?" Darien demanded.

No one could answer for sure, and they all glanced from one to the other, their faces concerned. It was as Mirti had said. It didn't make sense.

There was a knock at the door and then Taro Frothen shouldered his way inside. He was a big man, brown all over, even less fashionable than Mirti, but full-bodied and comfortable and reassuringly serene. He was the one person Josetta knew whom no one despised. People might mock him, in a friendly way, for his rumpled clothing and slow manner of speech, but they couldn't help liking him anyway.

"You all look pretty earnest for such a late-night conversation," he observed in his rumbling voice. "One of the guards said you wanted to talk to me."

"Yes, you have to clear something up for us," Mirti said in her impatient way. "We all know that the little girl upstairs is Mally, not Odelia, but Romelle is claiming otherwise. Furthermore, between us we think we've figured out that Odelia hasn't been here for at least a few quintiles. And we'd like to know why—and why Romelle would lie about it."

"Ahhhh," Taro said, dropping his big body into one of the plush chairs that everyone else had ignored. "There's a tale."

"Then tell it, please," Darien said, taking the chair beside the torz prime. The others followed suit, though no one else relaxed into the furniture the way Taro did.

"Odelia was last here—let me think about it—in Quinncoru of last year," Taro said.

"Quinncoru! But that's *more* than a year ago!" Mirti exclaimed. "That's unacceptable! The heir to the throne *must* come to Chialto with some frequency! There is so much to learn—"

"She's still young," Taro interrupted gently. "Plenty of time."

"Yes, but Mirti's right," Darien said. "When Romelle announced she wanted to raise Odelia in the country, the primes and I agreed with great reluctance. It's essential that a child be familiar with court life from a very early age, because it is a complex society that is not easy for strangers to navigate."

Josetta shared a look with Corene. They'd been born at the palace and lived there every day until the shocking truth of their parentage was revealed. They'd learned how to navigate the treacherous currents of court life, all right, but the personal costs had been high. Josetta had always been envious of Odelia—and glad for her, too—because she got to spend the majority of her life somewhere less poisonous. Maybe that meant she'd grow up with a clean soul and a whole heart.

"So I assume something happened to make Romelle uneasy about bringing Odelia here," Mirti said. "What was it?"

"She was at a reception. One of the endless events that you insist on holding whenever she's in Chialto. And she was in conversation with some well-dressed woman whom she didn't recognize. And the woman smiled and said, 'Don't you ever worry about what might happen to your daughter if someone didn't want her to take the throne?' At first Romelle wasn't sure she'd heard correctly. She said, 'What do you mean?' And the woman said, 'If certain people set themselves against little Princess Odelia. If they wanted to get her out of the way.' And she handed Romelle a packet and walked off."

"That's ridiculous," Darien exploded. "If someone made a threat like that—she should have come for me immediately! She should have called for a guard! If we'd stopped that woman—"

"What was in the packet?" asked Nelson, who had been uncharacteristically silent up to this point.

"She didn't look right away," Taro said. "First she ran up to her rooms, terrified, but Odelia was sleeping in her bed and the maids said no one had come in. Nothing at all was amiss. Only then did she open the packet and find—a lock of hair."

"Odelia's?" Darien said sharply.

Taro nodded. "She wasn't sure, of course, until she came to find me. She handed me the packet and asked if I knew who the hair belonged to. When I answered, 'You've cut off one of Odelia's curls,' I thought she would faint from fright."

"Let me say it again," Darien said, even more grimly. "This news should have been brought to me instantly. I would have found the woman—or at the very least I would have doubled the number of guards at the palace—"

"I'm not sure any measures you could have taken would have been enough to reassure Romelle," Taro said. "But she feels safe when she is on my property. She knows that I could call a boulder to crush a man if I had any reason to do so—not that I ever have. She believes Odelia is safe there, and it will take a powerful inducement to convince her to put Odelia in danger. No matter how many guards you whistle up."

Mirti, who always saw through all the clamor and clutter straight to the heart of matters, summed it up. "Then we have two serious problems. One is that someone has made a threat against Odelia's life. And the other is that Odelia cannot—*cannot*, Taro, and you know it—live her whole life sequestered away from the palace and still be considered a candidate for the crown."

"In both cases, the answer is heightened security," Darien said. "And despite your ability to—to—kill men with random rocks, I hope you have fortified your property while Romelle lives with you."

"I have."

"And I will investigate this threat as thoroughly as I can, but—a trail that is more than a year old? It will not be easy to track."

"Look at it from the other direction," suggested Nelson. Naturally, it was a sweela man who approached the problem as an intellectual puzzle. "Who might want Odelia dead? Who might benefit?"

Darien spread his hands. "Anyone who sponsors a different candidate for the throne. Hardly a short list!"

"And yet, Odelia was essentially unharmed," Zoe observed in a considering voice. "If a mysterious woman cut Odelia's hair off, she could certainly have smothered the child in her crib." When everyone cried out at that, she added impatiently, "Well, she *could* have. But she didn't. She just wanted to frighten Romelle. Maybe she just wanted to keep her out of the city. Undermine her position with the primes and the regent and the governing council."

Now they were all staring fixedly at Zoe.

"Are you saying—" Mirti began, then stopped, appalled.

Zoe shrugged. "Who doesn't have nearly as much power now as she used to? Who is not only vengeful and ambitious, but has access to the private corridors of the palace? Who would do something like this?"

"My mother," Corene said.

Darien's hands were clenched. "I'll murder her."

"You don't have a shred of proof," Mirti said. "Just because you hate her doesn't mean she's guilty of every crime in the city."

Zoe opened her eyes wide. "There *wasn't* a crime. There's nothing to prosecute, because no harm was done. There was just intimidation and suggestion. Who's skilled with those particular weapons?"

This time nobody answered, but Josetta knew everyone was thinking the same thing.

"I'll look into it," Darien said. "I'll have another conversation with Alys and see where it leads. I wouldn't have thought any meeting could be worse than our last one, but I see I was wrong."

"What do we do in the meantime?" asked the always practical Mirti. "Allow Romelle to pretend that the false princess is the true one? Allow her to hide Odelia on some isolated farm away from all society and sophistication?"

"It's not as remote as you make it sound," Taro drawled. "We even have gaslight. And elaymotives."

Darien pressed a hand to his temple. *And I'm sure he thought his life would get easier once Vernon died,* Josetta thought, feeling a little sorry for him. Darien had kept all of the king's dreadful secrets and never let them break him, but she had to think even a hunti man would wear down after a while.

"I don't know what we do next," Darien admitted. "But I think first we need to let Romelle know that we're aware of the substitution. We understand why she thinks it's necessary, but we can't allow the situation to continue indefinitely. And we must assure her that we can keep the true princess safe."

Taro sighed heavily and hauled himself to his feet. The rest of them more slowly followed suit. "I'll go tell her," he said. "No doubt Zoe's visit has left her in a frenzy anyway."

As soon as he was out the door, Mirti wiped a hand across her face. "I'm so tired I could lie down here on the floor and fall straight to sleep," she said. She maintained quarters in the palace, so she didn't have far to go before she could seek her bed. "Go home, all of you! We'll talk more in the morning."

"Hold on a moment," Nelson said, catching at Darien's arm to keep him in place.

"What is it?"

Nelson waited until the sounds of Taro's footsteps had faded away. "People like to say the sweela primes can read minds, which we can't," he said. "But we can tell when people aren't speaking the truth."

Darien just stared at him mutely, waiting for the blow to fall.

"I don't know why, and I'm not sure about exactly what, but Taro was lying."

TEN

Rafe was a little surprised and a little relieved to learn that Samson hadn't given his room away while he'd been missing.

"Thought you'd be back," Samson greeted him when he showed up at the tavern six days after he'd been there last. He inspected Rafe's lingering cuts and bruises. Rafe had dispensed with the head bandage days ago, making sure his hair covered the half-healed ear, but his appearance was still a little rough. "Looks like you've been mixing it up with a few folks," Samson observed. "Becko and his ugly boys?"

Rafe shook his head. "Strangers, if you can believe it."

"Any of them look as bad as you do?"

Rafe laughed ruefully. "I don't think so."

"You're too soft," Samson said. "And you owe me a nineday's rent."

Rafe handed over the money, bought a loaf of bread and some fruit a day away from rotten, and headed up to his room, thinking over Samson's comments. He'd always considered himself as hard as he needed to be—a reasonably good fighter, a shrewd thinker, a man who could take care of himself. He'd always been good at sizing up opponents, whether on the street or across the card table, measuring his strengths against another man's weaknesses, and exploiting those weaknesses when he had to.

But he'd never been ruthless. He'd never been brutal. He'd seen those traits on display plenty of times in other men, and he'd deliberately turned away. Did that make him soft? Or did that make him a better man than the people he saw around him every day?

Did that make him a better man than his circumstances had led him to believe?

He let himself into his room and made one slow, thorough inspection. Yes, there were a few careless souvenirs of an imperfect search made by Samson or one of his lackeys; he wouldn't have expected any differently. Samson had to know what kind of valuables might be lying around upstairs, didn't he, in case the absent tenant never returned, in case city guards came calling with news of a crime? Only a few things were missing—some loose coins he kept in a bottom drawer, a woman's ring he'd won a few ninedays ago and never bothered to sell. Small items he'd never miss or at least not bother to argue over.

He sat at the small table by the unlit fire and made a brief, not particularly satisfying meal.

If he was too soft, how could he toughen up?

If he was too good for the life he was currently leading, how did he find his way into a better one?

How good would he have to be to return to Josetta on something closer to equal terms?

The last question made his lips twist in a wry smile. He might claw his way out of the slums through some combination of luck and hard work, but he would never be fit to approach a princess as an equal. Insanity to think so.

He finished his abbreviated meal and touched his pocket just to make sure his cards were there. But his fingers felt forgotten shapes through the thin fabric, and he pulled out the three coins he had drawn from the barrel in Josetta's temple.

Synthesis. Time. Triumph.

A man with those three blessings might do anything. If a blessing possessed any power, any magic at all.

Rafe slipped back into his ordinary life as if he had not been knocked completely askew by the events of the past nineday. He played cards most of the night, slept most of the day, won more than he lost, and spent every last quint-copper he brought home. He was restless, though, and that was new. He'd always been able to endure the dullest conversation, the slowest night, with natural equanimity. But now boredom was his constant companion, sitting beside him as he shuffled the deck, waiting for the next game to start, matching him stride for stride when he strolled down the streets. He was jumpy, he was impatient, and he only managed to hide his tension because he was very good at concealing his thoughts.

He knew, though, what was putting him on edge. It was the countdown of the days, one gone, then two, then suddenly seven. Two more and it would be firstday again, and he had promised to take dinner with Josetta at the shelter.

He was sure she remembered the invitation. He was sure she remembered the kiss. He was certain she expected him to show up anyway. He knew that only his own death would prevent him.

On the eighth day, he gambled hard and won big, a pile of silvers and quint-golds that any reasonable man would carry right over to a bank the following morning. But Rafe headed instead to the Plaza of Women with its endless booths and vendors. He couldn't return to Josetta empty-handed. But what kind of present did you buy for an elay woman? He wasn't used to shopping for *anyone*. He had no idea what kind of gift would be appropriate.

He wandered for at least an hour, bewildered by the unending variety of merchandise, from severely practical hand tools to purely ornamental glass figurines. He stood for a long time in front of a booth lined with small mesh cages, each filled with a live fluttering prism of butterflies in all colors and sizes. Butterflies were elay, weren't they? Would Josetta be delighted by their delicate, powdery wings and jewel-bright colors? Maybe—but she was just as likely to be horrified at their captivity and set them all free. Rafe moved on.

He tried for a while to find gifts that would match her own particular blessings—beauty, grace, and joy—but he couldn't think how to translate them into concrete objects. In the end, he selected items that were more about him than they were about her, but they had a sense of rightness to them.

In a musician's stall he found a tiny toy flute, the size of his little finger, made of chased silver and set with topaz stones. "It's not meant to be played, though it *will* produce a few notes," the vendor told him. "It's just supposed to be pretty."

"It is that," Rafe agreed, handing over his coins.

Fish were easy to come by—almost too easy—he didn't find one he actually liked until he spotted a jeweler who'd laid out rows of bracelets. One was hung with dozens of fish-shaped charms, some carved from onyx or carnelian, others cast from silver or gold. When he lifted the bracelet from its velvet cushion, the charms all chimed together with a happy sound.

"I want this one," he said.

He was taken by a wreath of red silk roses, small enough to set on a woman's head like a crown, and he couldn't resist a whimsical reproduction of the royal palace constructed from miniature horseshoes and leather cord. He'd doubted he would find a skull that was a suitable present for a gently bred young woman, but Quinnahunti changeday was just around the corner, and there were skeletons everywhere. The skull he finally selected had been carved from some gorgeously veined piece of hardwood and burnished to a high shine; its blank face somehow possessed an expression of contentment, as if it had looked on a lifetime of failures and successes and had finally won through to peace. Rafe held it in his hand a long time, just because he liked the feel of the wood, and he was smiling when he finally made his purchase.

Unusual courting gifts, maybe, but they suited him. He hoped they would suit Josetta as well.

There had to be thirty people crowded into the main room of the shelter on the evening of firstday, and more of them were arriving every minute. Rafe headed straight back to the kitchen and offered his services to Callie.

"I'd be grateful," she said. "Can you carry that pot in? Then come back for the bread."

When Josetta showed up a half hour later, Rafe was hustling between the kitchen and the dining tables, wearing one of Callie's aprons, and holding a pan full of dirty dishes. *There's a nice, romantic picture for you,* he thought ruefully, nodding at her across the tables. But she looked pleased, or so it seemed. Glad to see him working for the common cause.

Or maybe just glad to see him. Five minutes later she had joined Callie and the girls in the endless exchange of full and empty platters, clean and dirty plates. Bo stood at the sink washing dishes as fast as he could, while Foley tended items in the oven. Of Caze and Sorbin there was no sign.

"Is it always this crazy on firstday?" Rafe demanded when there was a brief lull.

"It's because changeday is almost here," Josetta explained. "More people come into the city for the holiday."

"And because it's warm weather," Callie put in. "More people living on the streets. In the cold weather, a lot of them find places to stay, even with relatives they hate. In the summer, they work up the courage to leave."

It was another hour before things really settled down—most of the tables empty, most of the food eaten. Josetta took off an apron she'd tied over her tunic and brushed a strand of hair from her eyes. "Hungry?" she asked Rafe.

"Starving, actually. If there's anything left to eat."

Callie pointed to a covered roasting pan sitting on the edge of the stove. "I always hold a little in reserve for us. We can't care for others if we don't take care of ourselves."

Josetta and Rafe filled their plates and carried them out to the dining area, choosing spots at a table where no one else was sitting. Under his arm Rafe carried a wrapped bundle full of Josetta's gifts, which he'd stored in the kitchen while they worked. Full dark had fallen by now, so the big room was lit with flickering candlelight that softened the hard edges of the utilitarian space and painted dancing shadows on Josetta's face.

She smiled and toasted him with her water glass. "I'm so glad to see you again," she said.

"You didn't think I'd come, did you?" he challenged. "Even after I promised."

She moved her head in an equivocal motion. "I thought you might show up at midnight and stay a half hour. I didn't expect you to roll up your sleeves and start working."

"Trying to impress you."

"Good job." She took a small bite before asking, "How have you been feeling? Are your wounds healing up all right?"

He moved his shoulders in an experimental shrug. "The one in my side still bothers me, especially if I get too tired. But it's not infected or anything. I think my ear's fine."

"Maybe Callie can take a look at them. Since you're here."

"Since I'm here," he echoed. "What about you? How's your nine-day been?"

She looked for a moment as if she were reviewing recent catastrophes. "Full of unexpected and not always pleasant events."

When she didn't elaborate, he said, "Princessy stuff, I guess."

"And sister stuff."

"Is everything better now?"

"Not really."

"Can I—I mean, it seems unlikely, but can I do anything to help?"

Her face softened into a smile. "If I think of anything, I'll keep the offer in mind."

"How's Corene?"

She looked worried again. "I'm not sure. Lately we've learned some things about her mother that have . . . well. She always knew Alys was selfish and manipulative, but she always thought Alys cared for *her*. Now she's not so sure. And I think it's really hurting her. Not that she'd ever say so."

He remembered the night Corene had slipped into Samson's bar, how she'd armed herself with a couple of table knives because she had no other weapons. "She strikes me as someone who always fights back," he said. "No matter what kind of blows she sustains."

Josetta nodded. "That's a pretty good description. Describes Alys, too. I think sometimes Corene wants to be like her mother, and sometimes she's afraid she is."

Rafe shrugged. "She'll have to sort that out. Like everyone else does."

She smiled again, a little sadly. "As you and I have said before."

Rafe picked up the bundle, essentially one long swatch of scrap fabric carefully wrapped over the assortment of gifts. "I brought you something," he said. "To thank you for taking care of me while I was here."

For a moment, she gazed down at the lumpy package. "I know I should tell you that you don't owe me anything, but I'm consumed with curiosity," she said at last. "What kind of gifts would Rafe Adova buy someone? I have to find out."

He grinned. "Anyway, it's rude to turn down a present."

"And I would never want to be rude," she said. She was already untying the knot that held the whole collection in place, and she unrolled the fabric slowly, exclaiming in a low voice as each separate item was revealed.

As soon as she uncovered the flute, the one at the very heart of the bundle, she started laughing. "A deck of cards! You brought me the five suits!" she exclaimed. "Oh, I loved all of them anyway, but that's so clever!"

"I know some of them are a little strange," he admitted. "I mean—a skull—"

"No, but it's so *beautiful*. And he looks so wise—it is a he, don't you think?—as if he has learned all the secrets of life. But then the roses. And the palace! And the bracelet is so charming. Zoe will want to steal it from me, because she thinks every coru item should belong to her. But I think this is my favorite of them all." She put the tiny flute to her lips and looked enchanted when she produced three sweet notes. "Oh, and it actually plays! I *love* this."

Her reaction pleased him to an absurd degree; he thought he might actually be beaming. "It was fun to shop for everything," he said. "Once I decided what I was looking for."

"It's funny," she said, "because I have something for you, too. Not a gift exactly. Well, sort of."

His curiosity burned even hotter than his delight at this announcement. "Now I know how you felt," he said. "I have to know. What does a princess consider a suitable gift for an aimless drifter?"

She pulled a slim leather coin purse from a pocket of her tunic and handed it over. "Something very elay, I'm afraid."

He opened the clasp and poured the contents into his palm. Three wide rings slid out, all of them too small to fit on his little finger. One was gold, one silver, one copper, and the outer circumference of each one was stamped with a different symbol. He rubbed his finger along the engraving on the gold. "Are these—they look so much like the pictures on the coins—"

She nodded. "Your blessings. Triumph and synthesis and time. I thought you could wear them on the same necklace where you've hung Corene's rings."

His hand went automatically to the silver chain around his throat and he pulled it free of his tunic. "Maybe I should give these back to her."

Josetta shook her head. "Oh, no. She was so pleased with herself that she thought to give them to you. Anyway, she's long since replaced them."

He was busy stringing the new rings onto the chain and refastening it around his neck. "Thank you," he said. "A couple of ninedays ago, I had no blessings, and now I have six."

"Maybe eventually you'll acquire the whole set."

"Maybe." He folded his hands before him on the table. "Thank you," he said again, more seriously. "It was a thoughtful gift. And I can't tell you how pleased I am to learn that I *was* in your thoughts this past nineday. I can't really guess why."

He hadn't phrased it as a question, but she answered readily enough. "Because you're interesting to me," she said. "And because you're different. You're not smooth and polished like the men I know at court— ambitious and political, always trying to impress me or obtain some advantage. You're not desolate or desperate, like so many of the men I see here. You're something else entirely. You don't really have a solid place in this world, but you seem comfortable wherever you are." A smile swept across her serious features, lighting the room more than candleflame. "And you have such extraordinary blessings! I think you're going to have an extraordinary life. It's just hard to guess how."

"It was pretty ordinary until I met you."

"Then maybe the blessing of time is about to come into play."

At that moment, the door pushed open, and Rafe was spooked enough by the conversation to swing around, staring, wondering if destiny was about to stride through. But it was only Caze and Sorbin, back for the night after a final patrol.

"Hey! Rafe! Good to see you!" Caze greeted him in his friendly way. "Stay long enough for us to eat, and then we can play a round of penta!"

So the guards joined them, and then Foley joined them, and then Callie and Bo joined them, and then all seven of them sat in on a game that lasted past midnight. Between the eating, the talking, the playing, and Callie's insistence on examining his injuries, which she pronounced satisfactory, Rafe didn't get another five minutes of solitude with Josetta. No chance for another exhilarating exchange of personal observations, no chance for another even more exhilarating kiss.

But it was all right, or almost. "You'll be back again next firstday?" she asked as they all clustered at the door to wave him off into the night.

"I will."

"We'll see you then."

It was strange, he thought, walking home, adroitly dodging the drunks and firmly refusing the prostitutes, strange to have something laid out in front of him that he looked forward to so much, that he desired so much, that he could actually feel its presence as a weight drawing him toward the future. He couldn't remember the last time anticipation had exerted such a powerful pull on him that it could reshape time, rendering some days negligible and others momentous. He couldn't remember the last time he had been so conscious of being alive. Of wanting something from his life.

Of wanting *something*.

So how did a nobody gambler turn himself into a man of substance? He amassed money and prestige, Rafe figured. On secondday, he withdrew most of his windfall cash and boarded one of the public elaymotives that traveled regularly between the Plaza of Men and the port. The vehicle wasn't nearly as comfortable as the one Josetta had provided for the previous trip; it was crowded and noisy and made frequent stops at little crossroads Rafe hadn't even noticed before. He tried not to look like a man carrying a fortune in gold in his shoulder bag, so he gazed out the window with an assumed expression of boredom and resisted the urge to constantly check that the clasp on his bag was shut. It was a relief to finally arrive at the harbor.

He had no trouble finding the hulking, stinking factory again, though it did occur to him to wonder if Kayle Dochenza was even on the premises—and if he would remember Rafe. "Tell him I accompanied Princess Josetta here a couple of ninedays ago," he told the skeptical servant who guarded the door. "Tell him we talked about an investment I might make."

Whether *Josetta* or *investment* was the magic word, it was only a few minutes before the man returned to say, "The prime will see you." Soon enough he was shown into the messy, overheated room with the magnificent view and the crazy occupant.

"Rafe Adova," Kayle Dochenza greeted him, bobbing his head in acknowledgment. His pale eyes blinked rapidly as he scanned Rafe from head to toe. "You said you'd be back, and here you are."

Rafe shook the bag over his shoulder. "I told you I had money to invest, and I brought it. I've never done this before. I don't know if we sign a contract or go to the Plaza of Men and swear an oath before witnesses at the booth of promises."

"Oaths are worthless," Kayle said, waving a bony hand. "If a man wishes to cheat you, he'll do it, no matter what vows he's taken."

It was a philosophy Rafe happened to agree with, but he asked the question anyway, wanting to hear how this odd man would reply. "Then how do you know who to trust?"

"I don't know how *other* people know," Kayle said. "But I can just tell. I am attuned to their essences." He tapped his own chest. "Man of air and spirit."

"You can tell, even with me?" Rafe said curiously. "Last time I was here, you didn't even know I existed."

"I perceive you now," Kayle said grandly. "And I can read you as well as I read any other man. I can see you don't always find it necessary to be honest, but you remain honorable. The two are often confused, but they're hardly the same thing."

Which Rafe thought was about as accurate an assessment as anyone had given him. "Well, I've already decided to trust *you*," he said. "So here's my money."

It actually took about a half hour to complete a formal transaction which—despite his posturing—Kayle did have witnessed by some kind of official-looking flunky who behaved with a cool efficiency that seemed foreign to Kayle.

"Would you like to see the machinery you're buying with your gold?" Kayle inquired once the banker type had left the office.

"Yes! Except—didn't you say the flying car was still ten years away from production?"

Kayle made one of his frequent gestures, as if trying to sweep up useful words that would help him explain complex concepts. "Of course I did, but there are prototypes. There are experimental vehicles. No failures, only designs that taught us something, whether or not they worked."

"Then let's go."

The experimental flying machines were housed in yet another factory, far enough from the bustling port that Kayle commandeered a small elaymotive and drove them there. He was a rapid and wholly terrifying chauffeur, apparently oblivious to the fact that there might be other vehicles—even people—on the road, but handling the car with such skill that he was able to steer past every potential calamity. Rafe was literally clutching the edges of his seat, hoping to hold fast in case they crashed or rolled; he hadn't felt this close to death since the night the strangers had jumped him.

Once they cleared the narrow, packed streets around the port, Kayle drove even faster. The roads were worse, but the hazards were fewer, so Rafe started to breathe more easily. But he was still hanging on in case they hit a bump and went flying.

They'd traveled maybe twenty miles from the harbor when a series of large, utilitarian buildings rose into view, practically the only things on the skyline for acres of flat, open countryside. The roads got better, not worse, on this final stretch, and Rafe was so surprised that he commented on it. Kayle nodded.

"Of course. There isn't much traffic out here, so we block the roads off when we need to and use them as running ramps."

"As what?"

Again, Kayle made that scooping motion, trying to snatch up the right words. "The flying machines. They need a long clear road to drive down at high speeds before takeoff."

"So you've done that much?" Rafe demanded. "You've put a prototype into the air?"

"For short periods of time," Kayle said. "We haven't figured out how to sustain flights for longer than thirty minutes."

"It's not going to take you ten years to figure it out," Rafe said.

Kayle gave him a quick sideways glance. He was smiling. "Maybe not."

It turned out there were three mammoth structures this far out from the port, sharing the road but widely separated from each other as if determined to keep their own secrets. "Nelson Ardelay and his boys own those two buildings," Kayle remarked as they drove by. "Actually, they own all the land out here outside of town. Brilliant investment, brilliant, and years before anyone else realized how valuable this land would be. All my property is in the port, so I have to rent space from them out here. Well, it's more complicated than that."

"No doubt," Rafe murmured.

"And this is my building," Kayle went on, driving up to the last, most isolated, and most unprepossessing edifice Rafe had seen here or in Chialto. It was huge, the size of four or five factories, made of what looked like lightweight metal soldered together in massive sheets. One whole wall appeared to be missing, though as they drew closer, Rafe realized that it was a wall that doubled as an entrance, and the gigantic doors had been rolled aside as if to allow some kind of monstrous creature to enter or exit.

Inside, he could glimpse three of those monsters, and he couldn't stop staring.

They didn't look all that different from the models he'd seen in Kayle's office, slim metal lozenges sprouting an assortment of wings held in place with various struts and cables. None of them were as chunky as the elaymotives; in fact, there was something about their smooth contours, especially from front to back, that made him think of sea creatures gliding effortlessly through the waters.

"And those things *fly*?" he breathed.

He could hear the amusement in Kayle's voice. "Not yet, but they will."

They spent the next two hours inspecting every inch of the three aeromotives, as Kayle was calling them, while Kayle and one of his mechanics answered all the questions Rafe could think of. He learned that the machines were crafted of a specialized new metal created to generate almost no friction even at high speeds and that the designer thought they'd solved the problems of liftoff but were now baffled by creating sufficient forward propulsion to keep the machines in the air.

"We know how to glide forever, at least in a favorable wind," said the designer, a pale-faced, dark-eyed woman with a fanatic's intensity. It was no great leap to guess she was wholly elay. "But height. Speed. That's what we can't get enough of."

They allowed Rafe to sit in the small, uncomfortable space built into each machine for the lucky—or insane—person who would handle the controls. This lever would tilt the plane from side to side, they told him; this one would bring the pointed nose up or down. This dial would add more fuel to the combustion chamber, and this gauge would show him how much fuel was left.

"What happens if you run out?" Rafe asked.

"You fall out of the sky," Kayle replied.

"Or glide," the elay woman amended. "If you're lucky."

Rafe glanced between them. "How many pilots have you lost?"

It was a moment before either answered. Maybe they were mentally adding up the number of crashes, the number of fatalities, the names of the fortunate few who had walked away. "Seven," Kayle said at last.

"We're hoping there will only be one more," the woman added.

Rafe couldn't help staring at her. "Why?"

"That would make eight. One of the propitious numbers."

"Maybe you won't stop till twenty-four," he said. "Also propitious."

Kayle nodded briskly. "Well, however many it takes."

"I hope you don't run out of pilots before you run out of aeromotives," Rafe said. "I imagine it's hard to find volunteers."

"We pay them," Kayle said, his eyes on Rafe. "Quite a bit of money."

Rafe stared back. He was still in the cramped, uncomfortable driver's box of the last machine, a long slim creature that glowed silver in the bright sunlight flooding in through the open door. It was smaller and seemed lighter than the other two; Rafe imagined it would be mercilessly bullied by a hostile wind, but easily carried by a friendly one. There was a long rip down the slanted wing on its right side, and a handful of Kayle's inventors were attempting to mend it with blowtorches and some kind of bitter-smelling chemical. The machine was utterly quiescent—Kayle hadn't even switched on its motor to let Rafe experience its rumble, as he had with the other two—and yet Rafe could feel its impatience coiled just under its prim metal skin. This was a creature that wanted to leap into the air and soar.

"It takes a certain type of person to pilot an aeromotive, of course," Kayle went on, as if Rafe had asked for a job description. "Someone reckless enough to take risks, but smart enough to avoid stupid ones. Someone who can think quickly in response to changing circumstances."

"Someone who's not afraid of heights," the woman put in.

"A gambler. Who's stood on a mountaintop," Rafe said.

"Yes," Kayle said. "Someone like that."

There was more to see in the factory—a whole room dedicated to parts fabrication and repair—but Rafe's mind kept drifting back to the implied job offer. What did Kayle Dochenza consider "quite a bit of money"? If seven men had died so far, how many had survived? What was the ratio, what were the odds? Rafe would like to impress Princess Josetta with his cool daring and his accumulated riches, but she wouldn't feel much admiration if he were dead.

His hand kept going to his pocket where he kept his favorite deck of cards. It was an old habit with him when he was restless, when he was itching to make a bet.

I'd do it if I thought I'd live through the experience, he realized. *Even if I'd never met Josetta. Just to see what it's like.*

He wasn't paying much attention when Kayle led him to an out-of-the-way corner in the fabrication room, and the designer laughed.

"This is your project, not mine," she said, leaving them without another word. Kayle didn't even glance after her.

"Another prototype," Kayle said, pointing to a contraption hanging from a row of hooks on the wall. It looked like nothing so much as a dog harness attached to the kind of yoke that horses would wear to pull a plow, except that a heavy cloth bag had been belted on top of the yoke. "Though this one would have no commercial application even if we could get it to work properly. And yet it haunts me."

Rafe reached out to brush a finger along the worked leather of the harness. "What is it?"

"A single-person short-distance propulsion device."

"You might have to speak more plainly."

Kayle enunciated with exaggerated precision, pointing to the various parts. "A man straps himself into this harness, holding the guidebar in front of him. Inside the combustion bladder are a number of chemicals, currently inert. When he introduces a final chemical, there's a powerful reaction. The bladder swells upward and the man is lifted high into the air. While the combustion continues, he has enough forward motion to travel a short distance, using the guidebar to control his direction."

Rafe fingered the leather with more reverence. "That would feel even more like flying than the aeromotive."

Kayle nodded. "Exactly what I thought."

"But it doesn't work?"

Kayle seemed to nod and shrug at the same time. "We've gotten a man off the ground a dozen times, but not as high as I expected. Twice he's achieved height, but no sustainability. It's pointless to introduce directionality if you don't have sustainability, but it's even more pointless to simply go up in the air if you can't send yourself somewhere else."

"How many people have died on *this* little contraption?" Rafe asked. "Because I don't see anything that would help you glide down, so impact has got to be a real problem."

Kayle nodded. "It would be, except the combustion slows at a perceptible rate. It doesn't just quit and send you plummeting to the ground. It *sets* you down. Though I admit a few of the landings have been rough. Some broken legs. But nothing fatal."

"So you have an easier time finding volunteers to test it out?"

Kayle shook his head. "Insofar as there is any prestige at all associated with carrying out experiments for a lunatic, most people prefer the glory that comes with the aeromotives. This—this little flying bag—is met with a certain amount of derision, even among my own inventors. But I am used to mockery. I never let it daunt me."

Rafe looked around the room, then through the connecting door at the three aeromotives, crouched in readiness before the wide entrance. "I don't think I'd bet against you," he said.

Kayle regarded him with those misty blue eyes. "No," he said. "But then, you do not seem like the type of man who has ever been afraid to gamble."

. . .

Rafe left without speaking the words that had risen to his lips a dozen times: *I'd like to pilot one of your aeromotives for you.* Kayle was right, he wasn't afraid to gamble, but he'd never been reckless about it. Or—that wasn't right. He'd been reckless plenty of times, but he'd never wagered more than he could afford to lose. Even the largest bet he'd ever made—the gold he'd invested in Kayle Dochenza's factory—wouldn't beggar him if he lost.

But betting his life? That wasn't something he'd contemplated before. There were probably safer ways of catching Josetta's attention.

Over the next two days, he turned the idea over and over in his mind, unable to decide whether or not to make the wager. He was grateful for the distraction when, late on that second day, he received a note from his brother. Like most of Steff's letters, it was brief and unhappy.

> *I hate it here. Nerri is having another baby. Are you ever going to visit again?*

"I'm going to be gone for a few days," Rafe told Samson the next morning. "Don't give my room away."

"How long is a 'few days'?" Samson wanted to know.

"I'll be back by firstday."

ELEVEN

Public transportation out to the western provinces had improved during the past five years, Rafe thought, but not by much. The big enclosed cabins pulled by elaymotives covered the distance more quickly than the old horse-drawn conveyances, but they were still at the mercy of bad roads and bad drivers and bad weather.

Fortunately, Steff's family didn't live at the extreme western edges of Welce, but owned property in the fertile midlands only two days outside of Chialto. Rafe hired a driver and a one-horse wagon to take him the final five miles of his journey, through endless fields of monotonous green. He made no attempt to identify the assortment of crops on lush display, though during the years he'd lived in this part of the country he'd done his share of plowing and harvesting. Hated every minute of it, too.

He did size up the sprawling farmhouse, which looked as if it had just gotten a fresh coat of paint and maybe a new chimney. Last time Rafe had been out here, his stepfather had proudly showed him the new wing built on in back, big enough to house any number of new babies and half the in-laws besides. He spotted a couple of other buildings that looked new—a toolshed, maybe, and a granary—though he had to confess they might have been on the property anytime these past three years. He didn't care enough for the place to pay attention.

It wasn't far from the dinner hour, still daylight at this time of year, by the time Rafe paid off the driver and strolled up to the front door. Most of the family members were probably still working in the fields, he realized, but his sharp knock on the open door elicited the sound of a woman's voice promising she'd be there momentarily. And before long Nerri appeared, looking flushed and frazzled and very pregnant.

She stared for only a second or two before she recognized him. "Rafe! I didn't know we were expecting you! Come on in."

He stepped into the *kierten*, a comfortably sized space made entirely of burnished wood planks—walls, ceiling, floor. He'd always felt like he was stepping inside a highly polished casket.

"You're looking well," he told her, and earned a grimace for that.

"I'm looking like a *cow*," she said. Her light brown hair was pulled back into a no-nonsense bun, and her swelling belly pushed against the loose fabric of her plain green top. She hadn't bothered with an overtunic and, indeed, looked like she was hot enough that she'd like to dispense with the clothes she *was* wearing. But she *did* look good—rosy, vibrant, full of life. "But it was nice of you to lie."

He grinned. "City manners," he said.

"Would you like something to eat or drink? How long are you staying?" she asked, leading the way into the kitchen. Rafe barely bothered glancing at the other rooms they passed, all of them familiar from his miserable years under this roof. Everywhere, the rich wood paneling was complemented by sturdy furniture and hand-sewn drapes over the wide windows. Intellectually, Rafe knew that it was a comfortable, well-maintained, even welcoming place, but he had so thoroughly hated living here that he still couldn't appreciate its unpretentious charms.

"Only a night or two. And I'm sorry to just show up like this. But I got a note from Steff and I realized how long it had been since I saw him—and I figured I could get here as quickly as a letter could."

The kitchen, like the rest of the house, was spacious and well maintained, floored with stone instead of wood, and redolent of baking meat. Nerri waved him to a long table where she prepared the food and fed the family.

"*I'm* hungry, of course—I'm always hungry—so I'm going to have a bowl of soup and some bread. Do you want some?"

"That would be great."

When they were seated across from each other at one end of the table, Nerri heaved a sigh. "Steff isn't happy here. No more than you were. Bors tells him he has to stay until he's eighteen, but I don't know that he will. Every morning I check his bed first to be sure he hasn't run off in the night."

"Where would he go?"

She gave him a quick, keen look. Her jewel-blue eyes were the only things about her that were actually beautiful. It was as if she'd hurried through the marketplace of physical attributes, resisting all the gorgeous hues and textures offered for hair and skin, but when some enterprising vendor offered her a choice of eye colors, she just couldn't help herself. "Well, my suspicion is that he would run to you. But my heart nearly stops when I think of a sixteen-year-old boy trying to make his way through that great city all by himself, looking for one man."

Rafe had to admit the prospect was chilling, though Chialto wasn't particularly dangerous if you stayed within the circle of the Cinque. "I'll talk to him."

Nerri leaned her elbows on the table. "Well, get him to think more than a few quintiles into the future, would you? He wants to leave the farm and make his own way, fine. But what does he want that way to look like? Does he want to sign up to be a soldier, take a job on a merchant ship, study a profession? We'll help him, but he needs a plan, or he'll just be adrift his whole life."

Rafe nodded. "As I know."

Her lovely eyes were on his face again. "I don't mean to be unkind, but you haven't made much of your life, Rafe."

"I know," he said again.

"If Steff *does* run away to you, I hope you have a place to offer him that's safe. That's secure. Where he might look for a decent job and make suitable friends."

She didn't end her speech on an interrogative note, but she didn't have to. She and Bors had visited him once in the city, and even Rafe had been embarrassed. They hadn't stayed, of course, not for longer than it took them to write out the address of a quiet hotel they'd found in the Plaza district. And Nerri was right. Steff couldn't stay with him, either. Rafe had never thought that far ahead, but he would never subject his younger brother to the rough education of the slums.

After a long silence, he answered, "I'll work on that."

"Good. Let me show you where you can sleep tonight. Steff will be so excited to see you."

In fact, the whole damn lot of them seemed pleased to have Rafe in their midst that night. Steff had greeted him with a wide grin but a punch on the arm instead of a hug. A gangly kid nearly Rafe's height, he was clearly conscious of trying to behave more like a man. The little ones—two boys and a girl ranging in age from eight to two—danced around him with truly exhausting energy, demanding that he look at this or answer that or show them another card trick *and* another one.

Even Bors had seemed glad enough to see him, clapping him on the back and managing a brief smile. Bors was big and brown and slow and certain, and the earth would have to cave in beneath his feet to get him to move from this place. He had no malice and no imagination, and to this day Rafe had no idea what Bors and his mother had ever seen in each other. His memories of her were few but vivid; she had been slim and sweet and brilliant and magical. What had drawn her to this severe and heavy man? Why had he wanted to hold on to her? Nerri was so obviously the woman he should have married in the first place.

"So what's going on in the wicked city?" Bors asked over dinner. It was the same question he asked every time Rafe saw him.

"The usual wickedness," Rafe replied with a smile. "Everyone is planning for the big changeday celebration. There's talk that the crown prince of Berringey is coming for a visit. There are more elaymotives on the street every day. Oh, and Kayle Dochenza—the man who invented smoker cars—he wants to invent cars that fly."

"I hope I live long enough to see that," Nerri commented, passing around a platter of meat. "I thought I'd be too terrified to ever ride in an elaymotive, but now I have, a dozen times, and I want one!" She gestured around the kitchen, where they were all crowded around the long table for the meal. "And did you notice? We have gaslight in the house now. Even gas for cooking on the stove! For the first nineday, all I could think about was how the whole place would catch on fire. But now I love it."

Conversation continued in this pleasant but impersonal way for the whole meal. Not until the dishes were cleared and Nerri was taking the younger ones off for their baths did Rafe get a chance to speak to Steff alone.

"Why don't you show Rafe the new grain thresher?" Bors said. Steff was dragging his brother out the back door toward one of the new outbuildings before Rafe even had a chance to respond with an insincere, "That sounds interesting."

"The new *grain thresher*," Steff burst out once they were out of earshot of the house. "The new *irrigation system.* My life is a nightmare. If people aren't talking machinery, they're talking weather. I honestly think I'll go insane if I'm here through one more harvest."

They circled around to the back of the new shed, where a padlocked door kept the equipment safe from thieves, but it was clear neither of them had any interest in going in. Rafe leaned his back against the sun-warmed wall and grinned sympathetically at his brother.

"I understand *exactly* what you're going through," he said. "But Nerri says your father wants you to stay another year or two."

"I don't think I can stand it! Rafe, you have no idea—"

"I do," Rafe interrupted. "The labor's hard, the conversation is dull, the kids are annoying, and you feel like you're the only living creature surrounded by people made of stone or clay. No one else is real. Or if they're real, they certainly don't understand you."

"Yes—right—exactly! I can't stay another year or two. I'm not sure I can stay another day."

"So you leave. What then? You come live with me in the slums? Learn how to win at cards, or maybe how to steal a man's wallet when he's not looking? Sell illegal medicines to rich folks from the city? Sell *yourself*? Plenty of people, men *and* women, would love to buy time with a good-looking kid like yourself."

Steff looked first irritated, then disgusted. They'd had variations of this conversation before, except never so explicit. "No—of course not— I could get a real job, couldn't I?"

"Sure, if you had any particular skills. Or any idea what kind of career might appeal to you and applied yourself to learning it."

"So then—you're saying—"

"I'm saying plan to stay here another year, but think about what you want to do next. Don't waste the time being mad and frustrated. And try not to drive Bors crazy while you're here."

Steff threw his hands in the air and slouched against the toolshed with a *thump*. "I didn't expect a lecture from *you*."

"That's the end of the lecture, such as it is. Tell me what else is going on with you."

Teenagers could always be counted on to talk about themselves, so Steff launched into a long and animated description of the indignities he'd suffered as an unpaid farm worker, as well as some of his more enjoyable activities with friends. Rafe listened, laughed, and commented appropriately, but the entire time half of his mind was running on another track.

How can I create a safe home for Steff in the city?

He had been on his own for so long it hadn't occurred to him that he might have to tailor his life to meet anybody else's needs or expectations. He'd had no incentive to better himself or his situation. Even now, he felt a tiny bit resentful at what he might have to sacrifice, what he might have to change wholesale. At the same time, he felt himself standing a little straighter, bracing his shoulders to accept a new weight.

He felt a touch of excitement as well. They were all part of a pattern, perhaps—Josetta, Kayle Dochenza, Steff. They were showing him the shapes and colors of a new life, if only he could figure out how to put the disparate puzzle pieces together. If only he could figure out exactly what he wanted and how to get it.

By the time Steff and Rafe made it back to the house, most everyone else had gone to their rooms. Rafe remembered that, too, from his years at the farm: Sunset meant bedtime, no matter how early it came; and dawn meant it was time to rise and get to work. He was certain it was largely a rebellion against this implacable diurnal clock that had turned him into a man who pursued most of his activities at night.

Bors was the only one still awake, and he was standing in the kitchen, yawning mightily. "Best get to bed, son. Early day tomorrow," he said to Steff and the boy stomped off, his expression mutinous but his mouth shut.

The minute he was out the door, Bors waved at the table where he'd set out some homemade wine and a couple of squat glass tumblers. It was clear he'd been waiting for Rafe to return; otherwise, he'd probably already be asleep. "Pretty good vintage from two years ago," he said. "Would you like to try a glass?"

"Be glad to," Rafe said, and they took their places across the table from each other. The wine was sweeter than Rafe liked, and full of sediment, but it was better than no wine at all, so he praised it highly and received a second glass for his pains. Bors, who rarely drank, took a second glass himself.

"Nerri says she talked to you," Bors said abruptly.

Rafe nodded. "That's right."

Bors shot him a heavy look from under those heavy brows and spoke in a heavy voice. "He doesn't want to stay. Don't want you to think we'd push him out, but I don't think we can hold him back."

"I never thought you would push him out." Rafe managed a grin. "You didn't push *me* out, though I have to think you were glad when I left. But I always knew you'd have let me stay as long as I wanted. As long as I did my share, of course."

Bors nodded. "There'd be a place for you here anytime you wanted—and work for you to do, too. But you weren't meant to be a farmer, and neither is Steff. I worry about him. He's not like me. He wants things I never wanted." He leveled a longer stare at Rafe. "Maybe you'll understand him better if he comes to you. But it's not so easy to try to raise a boy. You have to give him some direction or he'll end up—" Charitably, he didn't finish the sentence.

"Nerri said much the same thing. I'm taking it all to heart, I assure you. I know I'm not the best role model."

Bors took a sip of his wine and changed the subject. "So how are things with you? Still getting along all right?"

Rafe meant to say *Yes* and leave it at that. Bors always asked a variant of the same question and Rafe always replied with polite generalities; but tonight, unexpectedly, the truth crossed his lips. "Getting a little restless," he admitted. "Asking myself questions. Maybe I'm older than Steff, but I don't seem to have a much better sense of direction."

Bors's brown eyes were alight with comprehension. "Met a girl, I take it."

Rafe laughed. "Is that such an obvious corollary?"

Bors smiled slightly. "Women are about the only thing I ever knew could make a man stop and think, even if he wasn't keen on thinking before."

"Somehow I find it hard to picture you as young and rash and thoughtless," Rafe retorted.

Bors's smile widened. "I had my days."

"So were you in your wild phase when you met my mother?"

Bors thought that over, taking Rafe's question seriously. "Looking for reasons to settle down, I expect," he said at last. "I'd been living in the city because I thought every man should get some experiences his father had never had, and my father had never set foot in Chialto. But I missed the land more than I thought I would. I just hadn't been able to convince myself that it wasn't a defeat to go back home. Then I met your mother, and you. I never saw any two people who needed a home more than you did. So it all came together for me. Provide for her, provide for you, and get what I wanted for myself, even though I hadn't been able to put it into words."

And that, Rafe thought, neatly answered the question he'd had earlier in the evening. Of course that was how those two unlikely people had come together. They gave each other reasons to change; they gave each other the strength to continue. They each had what the other needed. "My memories of her aren't that clear," he admitted. "But I would have thought she was more of a city girl—that she wouldn't have loved the farm life any more than I did."

"Some truth to that," Bors said. "I think she missed almost everything about Chialto. The markets. The pretty things you could buy. The special foods you could eat. All the excitement—all the things *you* like about the city. But she felt safe on the farm, and that made it all worth it for her."

"Safe?" Rafe repeated. "What was she afraid of?"

Bors shrugged. "Just the general ills of the city, I think. She'd seen some violence in the streets. She knew a girl or two who had been attacked." He nodded across the table at Rafe. "Said she'd heard of children being snatched away from their mothers, sold as laborers or worse. She was always watching you, like she was terrified someone would steal you away. Once we moved to the farm, it was like she finally relaxed. She said no one would be able to find you out here."

More and more baffling. Unconsciously, Rafe put his hand up to smooth the edge of his serrated ear, run his finger around the mostly healed cut between the cartilage and his scalp. "Someone said something strange to me the other day," he replied slowly. "He said he didn't think either my mother *or* my father was from Welce. Do you know anything about that?"

Bors's forehead furrowed in concentration. "It might be true," he said. "She always believed your father was a foreigner, though she never supplied too many details. I had the sense he was a wealthy man, maybe a merchant from somewhere overseas, and she got caught up in some girlish notion of romance. Which didn't last too long after you were born." He jerked his chin in Rafe's direction. "After he cut up your ear that way and maybe did some other unsavory things."

"And then abandoned her."

Bors looked uncertain. "Or she left him. She had the strength of will to do it."

"So *he* came from somewhere else. What about her?"

"Well, there was always a bit of mystery about her. She had an accent when she spoke, you know, though she told me she had been raised by a maid who was from somewhere else—Malinqua, maybe, though I don't remember. She actually spoke Coziquela more fluently than Welchin. But I thought that must be the way rich families raised their children. It was always clear she came from money."

Rafe leaned his elbows on the table. "But you never met any of her family, did you? Never knew that much about her."

"I knew they disowned her when she turned up pregnant," Bors said bluntly. "I knew she never wanted anything to do with them again, after the way they'd treated her."

"Didn't you ever ask her for more details?"

Bors shrugged. "I didn't need to know them. I didn't care what her background was." He studied Rafe for a moment. "Why are you suddenly so interested?"

"I told you. Someone said he thought I was a stranger here."

Bors could hardly have appeared more skeptical. "And how would *he* know?"

Rafe laughed. "It was Kayle Dochenza. The elay prime. He says he can sense the essence of a man, and mine's foreign."

Bors was thunderstruck. "You've met a *prime*? How did you manage that?"

"That girl you were guessing about. She knows him. She introduced me."

"No wonder you want to impress her."

"Anyway, he seemed pretty certain. Though I have no idea if primes really have the ability to trace bloodlines and heritage, like this one claimed he could."

"What does it matter?" Bors asked. "Even if you knew you were from Soeche-Tas or Berringey, what would change? Unless you wanted to travel there and try to track down your father—but that would be an awfully cold trail by now."

"That it would," Rafe agreed. "I was just curious."

"Better to look forward to the future than back to the past," Bors told him. "That's what I always say."

Rafe nodded again, using a joke to cover his disappointment. "And as *I* always say, I think you're right."

Rafe stayed another full day to spend more time with Steff, then caught a public omnibus that would get him back to Chialto before sunset on ninthday. Of course, he'd forgotten that before another firstday rolled around, he would have to endure Quinnahunti changeday. Well, he hadn't *forgotten*, precisely, he just hadn't factored in how much it would disrupt his life. The omnibus was packed with boors and yokels headed to the city for the festivals; there was barely room to breathe, let alone space to sit. If Rafe hadn't been determined to make it back to Chialto in time for dinner with Josetta, he would have leapt from the vehicle and *walked* back to the city.

Things were no better, of course, once they crossed the canal into Chialto proper, because every street, every building, every scrap of green lawn was bursting with five times the usual number of people. Quinnahunti changeday was the year's most joyous celebration. Tomorrow the streets would be thronged with vendors, entertainers, and ordinary folks devouring whatever they had to offer. There were usually marvelous displays up at the palace—light shows visible from every corner of the city—and dozens of street fairs closer at hand. It was a prosperous day for pickpockets and prostitutes, who in their various ways preyed on the happy, drunken, or uninhibited souls roaming the streets looking for adventure. Generally speaking, it wasn't quite as busy an occasion for career gamblers, who found their usual targets distracted by other pursuits. There had been some changedays that Rafe hadn't even bothered to leave his room.

Once the public conveyance turned onto the Cinque, Rafe fought his way off and finished his journey on foot. He made it to Samson's place just as night was closing in, to find the tavern stuffed with loud and rowdy patrons. "Good thing you're back," Samson observed. "I was about to give your room away to a family in town for the big festival. Don't suppose you'd want to make yourself a couple of quint-golds by renting out your bed for a couple of nights."

"I'm not that hard up for cash," Rafe replied. "So, no."

Samson nodded. "Well, step carefully when you leave in the morning. There might be people bedded down in the hall."

Rafe couldn't tell if he should laugh or groan, so he just collected his dinner and carried it up to his room. Once he'd firmly locked the door behind him, he pulled back the curtains and stared through the gathering dark at what revelry he could see in the streets below. Mostly what worked its way up to him was noise, not light—the sounds of people laughing, shrieking, cursing, singing, breaking glass, breaking promises, breaking hearts. Probably breaking a few heads, too, he thought, and wondered how many of the hurt, sick, lost, and lonely would make their way to Josetta's shelter tonight. He wondered if she was there, just a few streets away, or up at the palace, where there were surely official celebrations she had been asked to attend. He wondered what she was viewing, what she was experiencing, if she was thinking about him the way he was thinking about her.

Probably not. He turned away from the window and settled in to his supper.

TWELVE

I t was almost impossible *not* to dislike the crown prince of Beringey.

Darien had insisted that a royal contingent be on hand to welcome the prince when he arrived at the palace courtyard two days before changeday, so there they all were—Josetta, Corene, Natalie, Mally, all four queens, all five primes, and assorted other members of Chialto's ruling families. Josetta had been informed that her job was to make sure Alys kept away from Corene, but it didn't prove too difficult. Alys was far more focused on the visitors than she was on her daughter, and she did her best to be at the forefront of the crowd when the prince and his escort arrived.

They made an impressive sight—four huge, highly decorated carriages pulled by matched teams of plumed white horses and accompanied by at least fifty soldiers in gold-and-white uniforms. By contrast, the Welchin guards looked a little drab in their dark livery lightened only by shoulder patches with the royal insignia, a small rosette featuring the five intertwined colors of the elemental affiliations.

"Has he come to start a war?" Zoe muttered to Josetta and Corene as they clustered at the very back of the crowd. "How many guards does one man *need*?"

"How do they keep white uniforms clean if they've been traveling?" Josetta wondered, which made the others giggle.

"I don't like him," Corene announced.

Zoe glanced at her. "You haven't even laid eyes on him yet."

"I can already tell that he's arrogant. He thinks he's important."

"I suppose a crown prince *is* important," Josetta acknowledged.

"There's a difference between *being* important and *acting* that way," Corene said.

Zoe was laughing. "I can almost hear Elidon teaching you that lesson."

"Well, I think she was right!"

The lead carriage was the largest and most heavily ornamented, so they assumed it was the one that held the prince, but the door to the second one opened first. Three servants bustled up to the main carriage; one positioned a footstool right under the door while another reverently pulled it open. It was another five minutes before the prince stepped out and, standing on the footstool, looked around.

He was sumptuously dressed in what looked like cloth of gold heavily decorated with jewels, lace, and intricate embroidery. The stiff metallic trousers were tucked into gleaming black boots buckled with gold; across the bright jacket lay a purple sash glittering with more gems. His head was wrapped in a cloth-of-gold turban set with an amethyst the size of an egg. Wisps of black hair escaped around the edges, somewhat softening the effect. By Welchin standards, he had an exotic look, with deep olive skin and huge dark eyes tilted slightly upward at the outer corners. A handsome man, or he would have been, if his expression hadn't hovered somewhere between haughty and discontented.

"Oh, tell me I wasn't right," Corene breathed.

Zoe, never impressed by excess, was trying to muffle a laugh. "He's almost a caricature of a prince, don't you think?"

"Except he seems to be taking himself very seriously," Josetta said.

"*How* long is he staying?" Corene demanded. "This might be the worst Quinnahunti ever."

The prince's first hour at the palace was spent meeting the Chialto elite. Darien had settled him in an ornate chair on a dais in the great hall; four of the prince's resplendent guards stood right behind him, and another six were stationed around the dais. Josetta didn't know if the prince wanted them there to protect him or merely to give him consequence.

The gathered Welchins queued up to present themselves, with members of the royal family in the lead. Darien performed the introductions.

"Josetta, this is Ghyaneth Werbane Kolavar, crown prince of Berringey," he said when she stepped up. She made her deepest bow, the one she would have offered to Vernon had he still been alive. "Prince, this is our eldest princess, one of those in line for the crown."

The prince held out his hand, gloved in purple leather, and she touched it briefly with her fingertips as she straightened from her bow. "It's a pleasure to meet you," she said in Coziquela. "I hope the travel has not been too tiring."

Up close his dark eyes were startlingly beautiful, a complex brown flecked with gold and sharp with intelligence. He stared at her with disconcerting intensity. "Travel is always tiring," he said in the same language, though his accent was much different. "I prefer to stay in Berringey."

Well, how did she answer that? *Why didn't you stay home, then?* "I hope the sights you see on your journey make the exertion worthwhile," was all she came up with.

"So far I have not been much impressed with Welce," he said. "It is a small country, is it not? The mountains are pretty, but the countryside is dull, and there is too much of it."

"We are mostly a farming nation, but we have turned our fertile land into a great resource," Josetta replied civilly enough, but inside she was starting to laugh. Oh, if Elidon could only hear her now, parroting back the history and commerce lessons she had despised so much! "We sell our grain and produce to many other countries, and even during droughts we have never had a serious famine. This prosperity has kept us peaceful through countless generations."

Prince Ghyaneth's sulky face looked even more dissatisfied. "Yes— you are right—a nation that cannot feed itself sometimes experiences great turbulence. And sometimes becomes dangerously dependent on its neighbors."

Again, she wasn't sure how to answer him. "So we take pride in our self-sufficiency," she said.

"It is good to be proud of something, I suppose. How old are you?" he demanded abruptly.

"Twenty. How old are *you*?"

He looked annoyed, as if she was rude to ask or stupid not to know already. "I am twenty-five. I have traveled to eighteen different countries and met the ruling families of each. How many countries have *you* been to?"

"None," she said, keeping the smile on her face with some difficulty, "but I have met the viceroy of Soeche-Tas and his entourage." *And I disliked them all, possibly even more than I dislike you.*

"A princess should not be so provincial," he said.

"A prince should not be so rude," she replied.

There was a moment's silence while he tried to assimilate the fact that he had been insulted, and in such a cordial voice. Then his handsome face gathered into a scowl and he sat up a little straighter in the ornate chair. "You should not say such things to me! I am a guest in your house!"

She wondered how much of their conversation anyone else could hear. Surely Darien must not be close enough to catch their words, or he would have stepped in by now. Corene would be crowing with delight if she had managed to hear even half of it.

"I am polite to anyone who is polite to me," she said. "But you haven't been."

"It is not rude to speak the truth," he said.

"Sometimes it is."

He sat back in his chair, curling his fingers around the carved armrests, and regarded her for a moment from those dark eyes. "I want you to sit beside me at the dinner," he said suddenly.

She felt her eyes widen in dismay. "What? Why? I believe all your dinner companions have already been decided."

"One of them can sit elsewhere. I want to talk to *you*," he said.

She knew without asking what Darien would say to that, so she summoned a courteous smile. "Then, majesty, I will be happy to provide conversation."

. . .

Of course, it was another hour before the meal was served, and the Welchins spent that time gathering in small groups and comparing their first impressions of the visiting prince. Josetta wasn't surprised to find that her mother had been won over by his regal bearing and air of entitlement.

"He's very handsome," Seterre observed. "And he holds himself like a king, did you notice? Vernon was always a bit too eager to have common men and women approve of him. I think this Ghyaneth will make a formidable ruler."

"Did you flirt with him?" Josetta teased.

Seterre laughed and fanned herself with her hand. "Of course I didn't! I might be his mother's age! But I did compliment his taste in clothing and said that I had always had great admiration for Berringey's culture, and he told me I was very kind."

Corene's assessment more closely tallied with Josetta's. "What a slit-shafter," she remarked.

The phrase was so vulgar that Josetta actually gasped. "*Where* did you learn such an ugly expression?" she demanded.

"Barlow said it that winter when we were traveling. He wouldn't tell me what it meant, though, so I had to ask Calvin. He tells you anything."

"If Darien hears you talking like that, he'll—I don't know what he'll do. Drown you in the Marisi."

"Like my father doesn't say such things when he thinks we can't hear him."

"A princess is different."

Someone came up behind them, resting one hand on Josetta's shoulder, the other on Corene's arm. "A princess is always different," said Alys. She leaned over to kiss Corene on the cheek. "Hello, darling. Did you enjoy meeting the very surly prince of Berringey?"

Not attempting to be subtle about it, Josetta pushed between Alys and Corene, shoving her sister behind her back. "You know Darien doesn't want you to talk to her," she said bluntly.

Alys laughed, but her lovely face was bright with anger. "And I know I don't require *Darien's* permission to speak to my own daughter whenever I want," she replied.

"Not here. Darien won't allow it."

Alys's mouth set and her green eyes narrowed, but she still managed to smile. She had always been the most poisonous when she was pretending to be sweet. "You won't get far in life, Josetta, if you allow other people to do your thinking for you," she said. "Everyone pretends Darien is so wise, but he has fumbled so often, made so many mistakes. Do you really want to tie your fortunes to his? Shouldn't you start thinking for yourself? I often wonder if you have more spirit than anyone realizes. But maybe you *are* just the scared little elay girl you always appeared to be."

Behind her, Corene lifted a small, cold hand and pressed it between Josetta's shoulder blades. It might have been Corene's way of offering Josetta her own strength, but Josetta didn't think so; it felt more like Corene begging her not to back down, not to give way.

"I would trust Darien's counsel over yours on any day in any quintile you could name," Josetta replied, not raising her voice in the slightest. "Why would I listen to you? You're selfish and you're cruel. If you want to talk to Corene, come by the house someday when Darien's there." She casually turned away, draping an arm over her sister's shoulders. "They're serving wine over by the fountain. Let's get some."

Alys grabbed Josetta's arm, jerking her back. Her beautiful face flamed with fury. "I want to talk to Corene *now*," Alys spat out in a low voice. "You're too shy and nervous to let me cause a scene—on the very night the prince of Berringey arrives—when all of Welce wants to glitter and shine for him!"

"Just let her say whatever it is she wants," Corene muttered.

Josetta still stood between the two of them, her body a bulwark for Corene, an obstacle for Alys. "See, that's where you're wrong," Josetta said quietly. "I don't care if you make a spectacle of yourself. I don't care if everyone in the whole room starts pointing and staring. Things like that don't bother me anymore. So throw a tantrum if you want. Corene and I are getting something to drink." She turned away again and practically dragged Corene across the floor.

Her shoulders were hunched against the possibility of onslaught—she really thought Alys might start hurling objects or shrieking invective—but the queen didn't try to stop them this time. Corene didn't say a word until they had paused by the great basin of the fountain, where servants were serving glasses of wine and small tidbits of food.

It was so unusual for Corene to remain silent that Josetta thought maybe she'd handled the whole thing wrong. "I'm sorry if you *wanted* to talk to her," she said finally, after sipping half of her glass.

Corene shook her head. Her eyes were cast downward, as if she was fascinated by the pale gold of the wine in her goblet. "I wonder what she wants, though."

"To make you feel bad, probably," Josetta said with some heat. "To embroil you in some scheme. To encourage you to flirt with some hideous old man because he's rich."

Corene smiled reluctantly. "She wasn't always like that."

Josetta took another sip and decided not to contradict that.

Corene sighed. "Or maybe she was. I always thought she was so beautiful. When she hugged me or told me she loved me, I thought I was beautiful, too."

"You are. Much more than she is."

"She used to tell me I would be queen. I mean, she must have started whispering it to me when I was in the cradle. I always believed it, *always*, even when I got old enough to realize that you were the oldest, *you* were the most likely heir. I even said that to her once, and she said, 'Josetta will never wear the crown. She doesn't have the heart for it.'"

"When did you start thinking she might be wrong?"

Corene laughed sharply. "When I was almost married off to the viceroy of Soeche-Tas. But my mother said it only proved she was right, since I *would* be ruling over a great nation, it just wouldn't be Welce."

Josetta studied her sister for a moment. Corene was deceptively delicate; behind the heart-shaped face, locked within that small frame, was a soul of unflinching fierceness. But Corene had been looking a lot less sturdy in the past few ninedays. "Do you still want to be queen? Of Welce? Of anywhere?"

"I want—" Corene hesitated a moment, and then plunged on. "I want to know where I'm supposed to belong. Odelia has replaced me and my mother doesn't want me—"

"Of course she does. It's just that—"

Corene went on, unheeding. "I'm not a prime, and I'm not an heiress from one of the Five Families, and I'm just not sure what I'm supposed to be *doing*. I feel like I'm—I feel like I'm flailing."

Josetta had to swallow a laugh, because *flailing* was melodramatic, even by Corene's standards. "You're seventeen," she said gently. "You have years to figure it out."

Corene finally looked up, her face a study in protest. "I want to know *now*," she said.

There was a shuffle and commotion up by the dais, and Darien spoke loudly enough for his voice to carry through the hall. "Dinner is being served," he announced. "Please, would you all follow Prince Ghyaneth and me into the dining room?"

"You can figure it out some other time," Josetta said. "What you need to do *now* is go eat dinner."

Honoring the prince's wishes, Darien seated Josetta on Ghyaneth's left at the circular table that sat on a raised platform in the middle of the dining hall. There were eight people at this table, of course, and eight at the five other tables arranged like spokes of a wheel around the central one. Josetta heard Darien explaining to Ghyaneth how the people of Welce arranged their lives by threes and fives and eights, a piece of information that seemed to strike a chord in him.

"In Berringey, the number twelve has mystical powers," he replied. "But we do our best not to invoke it except under extreme circumstances. It can be destructive if it is not controlled."

"Very interesting," Darien said. "In Welce, we find our lives out of balance when they are not ruled by our propitious numbers."

"Give me some examples," Ghyaneth demanded, and Darien obliged with a few of the histories Welchin children learned in school.

This won't be so bad if Darien does all the talking, Josetta thought, glancing around at the rest of her tablemates. Romelle sat across from the prince in the seat of highest honor, as proxy for the heir, who had been put to bed an hour ago. All the other queens had been relegated to one of the lesser tables, even Elidon. The rest of the places at Ghyaneth's table were taken up by Mirti Serlast, Kayle Dochenza, Taro Frothen, and Nelson Ardelay.

"Where's Zoe?" asked Mirti, who was seated to Josetta's left.

"Having a lovely time sitting next to Kurtis and his wife," Josetta answered, "where *I* should have been."

"That's what I meant," Mirti said impatiently. "Why are *you* here?"

"The prince requested my presence."

Mirti looked intrigued. "You managed to charm him even during that brief introduction? I wouldn't have thought it possible."

Josetta summoned a look of indignation. "I didn't realize you thought I was *that* boring."

Mirti grinned. "You're delightful, naturally. But I would have thought he was a man not easily won over."

They had to speak in low voices and in Welchin because, of course, the prince was sitting inches away. But he and Darien had moved on to another topic—agriculture, from what Josetta could overhear. She hoped she was not going to be asked to weigh in with observations about crops and livestock.

"No, I don't think he is," Josetta agreed. "He seemed to find me annoying more than appealing."

"Some men like a challenge," Mirti observed. "Like a bit of spice."

"That doesn't usually describe me."

"No, but you're a little wayward," Mirti said. "People think they know what to expect from you, and they're usually wrong."

"I suppose everyone can surprise you from time to time."

Mirti grinned again. "Not me. Hunti through and through. You always know what I'm thinking and what I'm going to do next, and I never suddenly turn into someone you don't recognize." She nodded in the direction of her nephew. "Darien's the same."

"I find it very comforting, sometimes, to have a few absolute certainties in my life," Josetta said.

"This young man seems to *think* his life is full of certainties," Mirti answered. "He seems very sure of himself."

"Maybe his life hasn't been as tumultuous as mine."

Their private discussion was broken up by footmen climbing to the platform and serving the main course. Conversation was sporadic and general for the next half hour, as everyone tried the food and proclaimed it excellent—even the prince, who was unfamiliar with some of the selections.

"I like this very much," he said after he'd sampled a sugared fruit compote. "What is it made of?"

Darien's attention had been claimed by Nelson, so Josetta answered. "A kind of berry that grows only in our northern provinces," she said. "It's too tart to eat unless it's prepared just right, but it's very popular."

"We have nothing like it in Berringey. Perhaps this is something we might trade for, your nation and mine."

"I'm sure the regent would be happy to provide *crates* of berries for you to take back with you. I believe my sister owns acres of land devoted to just this one crop."

"Your sister," Ghyaneth repeated. "Princess Corene?"

Josetta smiled. "She's one of my sisters, but I meant Zoe Lalindar. The coru prime, and the regent's wife. She's my sister, too."

Ghyaneth shook his head, and the amethyst in his turban winked in the gaslight. "I can't keep track of all your tangled bloodlines. There are too many sisters and half sisters and princesses and heirs. It's very complicated."

"It *is* complicated," Josetta agreed. "I suppose things are much simpler in Berringey?"

"Drastically so," Ghyaneth replied. "I have only one heir, my cousin Siacett. She is five years older than I am."

"Doesn't that make the people of Berringey a little nervous?" Josetta asked curiously. "In Welce, everyone worried when King Vernon only had one daughter, then only two. It's the reason he took so many wives—they wanted him to have five children, or eight. In case something happened to me or Corene."

Ghyaneth stared at her as if she were mad. "*More* heirs?" he demanded. "But didn't he think that was dangerous?"

"What? Dangerous? How?"

"Every additional heir is another potential threat to the throne," Ghyaneth said condescendingly, as if the fact were so obvious he couldn't believe he had to explain it. "Factions arise. Loyalties divide. The only way to keep the kingdom united is to concentrate everyone's attention on a single successor."

"Now, *that* seems dangerous to me," Josetta responded. "What if some fever swept through the palace, and you and your cousin both succumbed? Where would the kingdom be then?"

He shook his head. "Siacett is kept sequestered on an estate far from the royal city. We cannot be destroyed by the same catastrophe, whether it is illness or fire or some other hazard."

Sequestered didn't sound like very much fun, Josetta thought. "So you never get to see her?" she asked. "That's a little sad. Don't you miss her?"

He gave her a superior smile. "Hardly. She would do anything in her power to see me dead."

"*What?* Why?"

"Because she wants to be queen, of course," he said. "We are all bred to be very ambitious—it is what makes us so powerful and so dangerous. She has spies all over the kingdom. She undoubtedly knows that I am out of the country even now, and she is taking the chance to amass support. There are already those who would back her in a bid for the throne—her husband's family, mostly, and their allies."

"She is married, then?"

"Yes, and has three children."

"And that's how all of them live? On some isolated estate, under guard, because you're afraid she might try to overthrow you someday? That seems like a wretched life."

"Oh, once I marry and have children, she and her family will be put to death," he said.

Josetta could only stare at him in mute horror.

"I can see you find our customs shocking, but I assure you our system is very sensible," Ghyaneth went on. "Whoever is on the throne marries and produces several children. He usually has a living brother or sister, and that sibling also marries and produces children. As you say, a nation becomes uneasy when there is any doubt about the succession, and we want there to be plenty of heirs when they are young, because childhood is a chancy time."

"It seems like adulthood is a chancy time in Berringey as well," Josetta managed.

He permitted himself another of his superior smiles. "Once the children reach an age where they seem healthy, the king or queen picks the two likeliest, and the rest are put to death," Ghyaneth continued. "At this time, if there are any other living heirs—siblings or cousins—they are expected to take their own lives as a gesture of fealty to the crown."

Josetta was staring at him. "And they *do* this? Willingly?"

Ghyaneth seemed amazed by her stupefaction. "Of course they do. Their first loyalty is to the throne. They want to see Berringey strong, and it cannot be strong if there is constant war over who should rule the country."

"But then—you said—" Josetta rubbed her index finger across her forehead. It was too difficult to comprehend. "Your cousin is plotting against you. It doesn't sound like she is entirely committed to the idea of sacrificing herself."

Ghyaneth's face darkened. "No. She is greedy and ambitious, and she cares only for herself and her glory, not the good of Berringey."

"Maybe she just doesn't want to die," Josetta suggested. "Have you told her you'll let her live if she'll just emigrate to Malinqua or Soeche-Tas?"

"She couldn't be trusted," he replied. "She would agree to exile, and then continue plotting to raise armies against me. Siacett is the perfect illustration of why it is dangerous for any kingdom to produce too many heirs. She is willing to tear Berringey in two just to see herself on the throne."

Josetta took a deep breath. "Well. I have to admit my sympathies are with Siacett, just a little. But now *I'm* confused about *your* bloodlines. If everyone's killed off when they're just children, how can you have a cousin? Shouldn't the only other heir be your brother or sister? Shouldn't your aunt or uncle and all *their* children have been put to death once you and your siblings were born?"

"Yes, and they would have been, but my father was quite old before he sired me, and he never produced any other children," Ghyaneth said. "Years before I was born, my grandmother insisted that my aunt and uncle both marry and have children, to make sure of the succession."

"Aunt *and* uncle? There were three competing heirs? I'm shocked."

"My aunt and uncle were twins. My grandmother couldn't choose between them," Ghyaneth said, sneering at her weakness. "But all of them are dead now, except for Siacett and me. And her family, of course."

"I have to say, I'm a little surprised Siacett could find someone willing to marry her," Josetta observed. "If he thought he *and* his children would all die once you started producing heirs."

"He gambled that he might win it all instead of losing everything,"

Ghyaneth explained. "If I drown at sea or die in some accident—if I fail to produce children of my own—my cousin will take the throne and he will sit beside her. An ambitious man would be willing to take that risk."

"I'm not sure I would," Josetta said.

He looked surprised. "Really? I would. If Siacett had been the crown princess and her sister her heir, I would have been willing to marry her sister. Yes, and I would have gladly taken my own life if it turned out Siacett was fertile and able to bear the next generation of rulers."

"How unfortunate, then, that positions were not reversed," she murmured.

He looked at her suspiciously, thinking he had been insulted again, but not sure how. Josetta wasted a moment hoping Darien or even Mirti would lean in and engage the prince in conversation, but they both seemed pleased to allow her to manage the bulk of the entertaining, so she cast about for other topics.

"Let's talk about something else!" she said, trying for a light tone. "You mentioned that you had traveled to eighteen other countries. Tell me about them. Which ones did you like best and why?"

"I like Berringey best, of course."

"Of course you do," she replied, thinking: *You are the most tedious man!* "But certainly you must have found something to appreciate in the other places you visited. The food? The fashions? The landscape?"

"Cozique was quite striking, at least along the coastline," Ghyaneth answered, almost unwillingly. "But the food was terrible."

One of the first comments he had made to her when they met was that the countryside of Welce was dull; perhaps he was particularly sensitive to the beauty of his surroundings. "I've heard that Malinqua is a lovely place, especially in the spring."

His handsome face chilled with anger. "We do not visit Malinqua, or even speak of it," he said darkly.

Oh, she'd stumbled into that one! "I'm so sorry," she said quickly. "As I told you, I've done so little travel that I don't know what—"

"We *used* to trade with them," he burst out. "Until their ambassadors proved to be completely untrustworthy. Utterly without honor."

She was torn between the desire to change the subject and the hope of learning something useful. Darien had said he expected to entertain

Malinquese visitors within the quintile; it would be good to know exactly how their dishonor manifested itself. "I'm horrified," she exclaimed, hoping she didn't overdo it, though Ghyaneth seemed immune to melodrama. "What did they do?"

He folded his lips and shook his head. "My father wouldn't wish me to speak about it," he said at last.

Too bad. Josetta sipped from her glass of fruited water and tried a smile. "Then let's talk of more pleasant things," she said. "Tell me what you do to entertain yourself in Berringey."

The dinner finally ended, though there had been moments when Josetta had thought it might not. She escaped home with her mother to gossip for a couple of hours before going to bed. Unfortunately, there was a full slate of events lined up for the next day, but she thought it might not be so bad if she could manage to avoid any more one-on-one conversations with the sulky prince.

Ghyaneth had expressed a desire to tour Chialto, so Darien had arranged for a fleet of elaymotives to circle the Cinque and pause at some of the more interesting sights. Because they were to be in such public places, Ghyaneth insisted on being accompanied by twenty of his guards, so they formed quite a cavalcade as they made a slow circuit around the city. They also created a stir at the Plaza of Men when the prince decided to patronize a few of the booths, and his guards closed around him in a tight phalanx. Even so, he managed to visit some of the more famous attractions. He even wrote his name on a document at the booth of promises, though he refused to tell anyone what vow he had committed to paper. But he seemed pleased with himself when he emerged and climbed back into his *elaymotive*.

Josetta had managed to avoid being in the lead conveyance with Darien, Zoe, Ghyaneth and two of his advisors, which meant the trip was much less stressful than dinner had been, but also less interesting. She found herself staring out of the window a great deal and playing idly with the fish charms on the bracelet Rafe had given her. She probably should have been attempting conversation with Romelle, her carriage-mate, but the queen seemed just as happy to be left to her own thoughts.

A traffic snarl stopped them for nearly twenty minutes when they were traversing the southernmost leg of the Cinque, and Josetta amused herself by wondering how Darien was explaining away the ramshackle buildings and desolate alleys visible even this close to the road. Then she spent time wondering what Rafe Adova might be doing at this exact moment. Was he still sleeping at this early afternoon hour? Was he awake and carrying out the mundane tasks of ordinary life, mending clothes or laying in groceries? Or was he already sitting downstairs in Samson's tavern, shuffling his cards and waiting for the first customer to arrive? The bar wasn't that far away. She could slip from the carriage and walk there within fifteen minutes. It was possible no one would even notice she was gone.

Almost as soon as she had the thought, the smoker car jolted to life again and the caravan moved forward. Josetta sighed and leaned back against the cushions. It was starting to feel like a very long day.

Quinnahunti changeday was even longer, but at least it was more fun. The royal festivities were held at the palace, of course, where both the courtyard and the *kierten* had been transformed with banners, ribbons, flowers, colored lanterns, and other decorations. In fact, the courtyard seemed a miniature replica of the Plaza of Women because it had been filled overnight with dozens of merchant booths selling clothes and jewelry and other trinkets; dancers and jugglers moved through the crowd, offering entertainments. There was even a small stage that had been erected right beside the lake, and a dozen benches set up before it. Seterre told anyone who would listen that she had personally selected the actors who performed a series of short comedies to the delight of the crowd.

The nighttime light show was the best part of Quinnahunti changeday, though, and everyone happily gathered outside to watch the wild colors play over the sturdy canvas of the palace's pale stone walls. The light show had been a tradition for six or seven years now, ever since Kayle Dochenza had invented a way to mix pigments into some kind of gaseous medium. Josetta knew Kayle considered it the most minor of his inventions, but she had to admit that it might be her favorite. Bright colors wreaking glorious havoc against the dour night—naturally such a contrast would appeal to her elay soul.

"There's another dinner tomorrow," Darien reminded her once the display was over and they were all bundling themselves back into carriages or heading inside, if they happened to be staying at the palace overnight. "A smaller group this time—we won't even use the main dining hall. I'd like you to come a little early to talk to Ghyaneth."

She shook her head. "I can't. I have a commitment tomorrow night."

Darien looked at her as if she had just spoken in Soechin and he'd never learned a word of the language. "Then break it," he said. "It couldn't be more important than dinner with a visiting head of state."

She just laughed at him. "It is to me."

THIRTEEN

There had been any number of small crises at the shelter while Josetta had been trying to charm Ghyaneth Werbane Kolavar. Callie had handled most of them with her usual brisk efficiency, but there was a banking tangle that Josetta had to straighten out personally and a handful of thank-you notes she had to write to a few particularly generous donors. Then there were just the ordinary, everyday tasks that always piled up and never got done because there simply weren't enough hands. So Josetta spent several hours restocking shelves in the main room, changing sheets in the infirmary, putting away laundry that someone else had washed and folded, and working beside Callie in the kitchen to assemble a particularly fine dinner.

Because it was firstday. And dinner on firstday was special.

As he had last time, Rafe Adova showed up early and stayed late. He spent the first two hours meekly doing Callie's bidding, carrying pots and platters to and from the dining room, helping to serve the *masses* of people who must have come to the city for changeday and had not yet mustered the energy to head back to their homes. Rafe was more cheerful about the extra work than the rest of them, Josetta thought. She herself was tired and irritable, and the imperturbable Callie actually snapped at a little girl who asked for another piece of bread. But Rafe worked without pause and without complaint all through the long evening.

Eventually every person had been fed, every pan had been washed, and the workers could take the time to sit, relax, and devour their own meals. Josetta had to admire Rafe's casual canniness: He waited until the others had clustered together at one of the tables before carrying his own food to a different one. When Josetta joined him a moment later, they finally had an opportunity to be alone. Well, alone in a large room with a half dozen people near enough to eavesdrop, if they were so inclined. But it still felt like privacy.

"If you ever decide to give up gambling, you can come work for me here," Josetta told Rafe as they finished eating. "I don't pay a lot, but you could live in the dorm, too. Think of all the money you'd save on rent."

"I don't pay Samson that much, to tell you the truth," Rafe answered. "You'd need a better incentive than that."

She laughed. "Oh, *would* I? What kinds of inducements are you looking for?"

He laughed back. "Opportunities to meet all your rich and powerful friends, of course. I can't think of anything else that would draw me back here on a regular basis."

She felt a little breathless. She half wanted him to say *A chance to see you every day*, and half feared how she might feel if he spoke the syllables aloud. Even unsaid, the words glittered in the air between them. "Kayle told me that you came to see him."

"Did he? Should I be flattered that you and the elay prime were talking about me?"

"Well, we were at an *excrutiatingly* boring dinner when we were having the conversation, so we were desperate for any topic that would get us through another five minutes."

He grinned. "He took me out to his aeromotive factory. I can't tell if he's brilliant or absolutely insane."

"No, that's the problem with Kayle. With most of the Dochenzas, in fact. But I do like him. When I can understand what he's talking about."

Rafe leaned his elbows on the table and looked like he was debating whether or not to tell her something. "He didn't actually offer me a job," he said finally, "but I think he'd give me one if I wanted it."

Josetta felt her eyebrows lift. "Doing what?"

"Piloting his prototype aeromotives."

The breath went right out of her at that. "Piloting—flying them? Up in the air?" When he nodded, she said, "But isn't that dangerous? I mean, *really* dangerous?"

He nodded again. "They've lost seven fliers. One of his assistants thinks they'll stop at eight—because, you know, it's a *propitious* number."

She could hardly believe it. "Are you that much in love with danger?" she demanded. "I mean, the life you lead now isn't exactly safe and calm. People seem to want to beat you up on a regular basis. But it's like living inside a banker's vault compared to flying one of Kayle's experimental machines."

"No, in fact, I think I have a pretty healthy desire to live," he responded. "But I need to—I don't want to—" He paused a moment, seeming to think over what he wanted to say. "You see them all the time, southside. Old men, skinny as sticks, sitting in the darkest corner of some dark bar. Shuffling their cards. Waiting for the next stupid torz farmboy to come in and gamble away the profit on whatever crop he just sold at market. They look like ghosts. No, they look like those slimy little bugs you see if you turn over a rock in a garden. Small and squirmy and afraid of daylight."

Still leaning on his elbows, he lifted his gaze and trained it on her. "I don't want to be one of those men. But I only have two choices. Die in some bar brawl when someone accuses me of cheating—or find a way out. What other kind of work can I find? I'm not trained for anything. But I learn fast. I don't mind danger. And I *like* Kayle Dochenza's crazy machines. I keep thinking this might be just the kind of job I need to move me out of here."

Josetta held her breath through most of his speech, which was delivered in a quiet and sober voice. Not much posturing with Rafe Adova, not much ornamentation. Although she was petrified by the thought of Rafe risking his life in one of Kayle's experimental death-traps, she wholly understood now why he would want to do it. She also, for the first time, understood how Darien felt when *she* had taken up residence in the slums. Shocked and terrified and, maybe, a little proud.

She could hardly tell him not to do it. Not when she understood why he wanted to.

"I think it's a splendid idea," she said, "though I'm scared to death for you."

"Really?" He looked inordinately pleased. "I thought you might try to talk me out of it."

"Well, I won't agree to go flying *with* you, so don't even think about inviting me."

He laughed. "Only room for one person in the driver's box."

"When will you go flying for the first time?"

"I haven't even asked for the job yet! And I imagine I'd need some training. And that's assuming Kayle Dochenza is willing to hire me. Maybe I misread him. He's not an easy man to understand."

"No, I think he'd hire you tomorrow. He likes you."

Rafe looked pleased again. "I *am* moving up in the world," he said. "A prime likes me. And a princess likes me." He glanced at her. "I think."

She smiled back. "I think she does."

He leaned back in his chair, clasping his hands behind his head, an exaggerated pose of a man sure of himself and his place in the world. "So that's what *I've* been doing in the nineday since I saw you last," he said. "How have you been occupying yourself? How was your change-day? You said you were at a boring dinner."

So she told him about Ghyaneth's visit, and he told her about his trip to see Steff, and they talked a little more about Kayle and his flying machines and what it might be like to live in the port town.

"But even if you do it," she said in a warning voice. "Even if you take a job with Kayle and move down by the harbor. You have to come back here on firstday for dinner."

"I will," he said. "I promise."

All in all, it was a lovely interlude, made even lovelier when she finally walked Rafe to the door and he kissed her on the cheek before ducking out into the night. Josetta was smiling in a silly girlish way when she closed the door and turned back into the main room. In the shadows she could just make out Foley standing at the base of the stair-well, watching to be sure she made it safely to bed.

"Don't tell Zoe," she said.

"I won't," he said. He didn't sound shocked or amused or jealous or even worried. He merely waited until she'd blown out all the candles, then followed her up the stairs.

I t turned out Foley didn't have to tell Zoe about late-night flirtations with attractive vagabonds because Josetta accidentally told her sister herself. Even worse, Corene was in the room.

They were at Darien's for the afternoon, "resting up for the horrors to come tonight," as Zoe put it—another formal dinner, followed by a theatrical production Seterre had helped put together. It was supposed to feed the visiting prince the whole history of Welce in two dramatic and entertaining hours. As far as Josetta had been able to ascertain, only Seterre was looking forward to the performance.

The three of them were lounging in the room Darien had specially built for Zoe. It featured windows on three sides to let in oceans of sunlight, and it was decorated in the aqueous blues and greens that soothed the coru soul. But its primary attraction was the low circular fountain that ringed the room like a tame indoor river, gurgling over rocks and hissing through simulated rapids. On hot days, Zoe had been known to wade through the fountain or actually plop herself down on one of the larger boulders and get soaking wet. Corene and Josetta were more likely to dangle their feet in the water by sitting on the small metal bridge that connected the room to the rest of the house. They had become less excited about this activity once Zoe introduced fish into the river.

"I can't believe we have to endure another dinner," Corene com-plained. "Isn't the stupid prince leaving soon?"

"The day after tomorrow—but he's coming back," Zoe informed her. She glanced over at her baby, sleeping beside her on a sofa cushion, but making little mewing noises in her dreams. "Don't you wake up, Celia darling. Not yet."

"He's coming back? Why?"

"When he leaves, he's only going as far as Soeche-Tas. And when he returns, he plans to meet with Kayle and talk about some of his inventions. Elaymotives, mostly. Apparently he's asked Kayle to come visit him in Berringey, but Kayle refused outright. I think he's happy to export his ideas to other countries, but not if he has to cross the sea."

"I don't think Ghyaneth will enjoy visiting Kayle's factories," Josetta remarked. "They're hot and *loud* and full of these awful smells."

Corene, who had been lying on her back on a low divan, turned over and propped herself up on her elbows. "You went to visit Kayle's factory? *Why?* I can't imagine anything more dull."

Josetta didn't have a lie ready and she stumbled through her reply. "I was taking—someone I knew wanted to meet Kayle, so I said I'd introduce . . ." *Him.* "This person," she ended lamely.

Now Zoe rolled to a more upright position, clearly intrigued. "Some person you know? From the slums? Because I would think everyone else you've ever met in your life has been acquainted with Kayle as long as you have."

Corene's eyes grew wide with speculation. "Is she right? Truly? Someone you met down at the shelter? Tell us everything about him. It's a him, right? Who else would care about a stinky old factory?"

"There were plenty of women working there," Josetta said, hoping to turn the subject. The fish bracelet on her wrist had never seemed so heavy. She held her hands absolutely still so the charms didn't chime together and draw her sisters' attention, eliciting another spate of questions. "Not all of them were elay, either. I think there are plenty of sweela folks who are just as entranced as Kayle is with his elaymotives."

"We don't care about those people," Zoe said. "Who did you take to meet Kayle?"

Josetta glanced at Corene and gave up. She'd always been a hopeless liar. "Rafe Adova."

Zoe looked bewildered, but Corene bounced to a sitting position, positively delighted. "Rafe!" she crowed. "So you've seen him since that night?"

"What night? Who's Rafe?" Zoe demanded.

"The man who rescued me," Corene said. "He's *much* more handsome than the Berringey prince."

"The man who—the gambler? Who lives in a tavern? *That's* who you've been secretly meeting with?"

"I haven't been 'secretly meeting' with him," Josetta said, though the evolving friendship did have a clandestine feel. "He came to the shelter one night when he'd been in a fight and needed someone to patch him up." All right, that wasn't strictly the truth, but she plunged on. "And he mentioned that he was trying to decide how to invest the reward money Darien had left him. He's interested in the elaymotives, so I offered to introduce him to Kayle. That's all there is to it."

Corene and Zoe traded glances. "Is that all there is to it?" Zoe asked.

"No," Corene said positively. "She likes him. I can tell."

Josetta mustered indignation. "Corene!"

Zoe leaned back against her cushions, amused now, not nearly as alarmed as Darien or Seterre would have been. Well, Zoe had a healthy disregard for class distinctions and societal expectations. She'd spent years camped on the border of poverty, and she had her own criteria for judging a person's worth. "I always thought it would have been Foley that Josetta ran away with," she said. "To the outrage of her mother and all the Five Families."

Corene shook her head. "Foley's not in love with her. He never was."

"How would *you* know?" Josetta demanded.

"Well, we spent all that time together when we were traveling with Jaker and Barlow. I saw how Foley treated you."

"You were, what, twelve years old? You had no idea what might be going on."

"How did he treat her?" Zoe wanted to know.

Corene waved a hand. "Like a precious object. Like something he had to keep safe. Jaker said—"

"Jaker! You and Jaker talked about Foley and me?"

"Of course we did. Jaker said he acted around you the way Barlow acted around some expensive new cargo they'd just acquired that he wanted to get safely to its destination. So he watched over you and worried over you—but he didn't plan to keep you for himself."

Zoe nodded. "That makes sense. Jaker's always been so insightful."

Josetta was ruffled at the whole conversation, but she hardly knew which part to protest against. She settled on, "I don't think I like being gossiped about."

"So then tell us what we want to know," Zoe invited. Celia hiccupped in her sleep and Zoe patted her on the back. "Tell us more about Rafe Adova! Have you seen him since you took him to the factory?"

"He dropped by the shelter the other day," Josetta said unwillingly.

"And what did you talk about?"

"Just—whatever people usually talk about."

"What have you found out about his background? His people?"

"Well, he's not secretly connected to one of the Five Families, if that's what you're hoping."

Zoe spread her hands in a gesture of innocence. "I'm hoping he's *not*. Or he would be a lot less interesting."

Josetta shrugged. "His parents are dead. He has a stepfather and a half brother who live on a farm in the western provinces. He's been living on his own in the city since he was seventeen—and it's just now occurred to him that maybe he should come up with a plan for his life."

"So he's going to invest in smoker cars," Zoe said.

Josetta laughed. She couldn't prevent herself from adding, "And he's thinking about signing on to pilot some of Kayle's aeromotives."

That really got their attention. "He wants to fly?" Zoe demanded.

"Then he's as crazy as Kayle," Corene said.

"Is he elay?"

Now Josetta shared a look with Corene, who was smiling. "No. When we met him, he didn't have any blessings."

"He has mine now, though," Corene said with satisfaction.

"Right. But whenever he pulled his own blessings, they were always ghost coins."

Zoe looked fascinated. "How unusual. I wonder what that means? Maybe *you* should try picking blessings for him."

"I did. Time. Triumph. Synthesis."

For a moment, Zoe and Corene just stared at her, clearly trying to work out what such a set of blessings might mean. "An extraordinary young man, it would appear," Zoe said at last. "I believe I will have to meet him."

Josetta couldn't decide if that would make things better or worse. "Darien met him," she said with a faint smile. "He wasn't impressed."

Zoe's own smile was wide. "I'm much more subtle than Darien," she said.

"You're not subtle at all!" Josetta objected. "You flood whole *cities* just to make a point."

Now Zoe was laughing. "Well, then, I'm more open-minded."

"*That's* true," Corene said. "Anyway, I think you'll like him."

Josetta didn't have to respond to that because Calvin came to the door, making so much noise as he clattered over the bridge that he had to be doing it on purpose. He loved this room and all its amenities; he was, like Zoe, coru to the heart.

"There's a visitor," he said, "but you aren't going to want to see her."

Zoe sat up in alarm. "Who is it?"

"Queen Alys. She wants to talk to Corene."

Josetta and Zoe glanced over at Corene, whose face had instantly assumed a neutral mask. Zoe said slowly, "Darien's gone. And he doesn't want Alys to see Corene unless he's here."

"You're here," Corene said. "He'd probably think that was good enough."

Zoe debated. "Do you *want* to talk to her?"

Corene shrugged. "She says she has something to tell me. I should probably hear it sometime."

"Maybe she'll apologize," Josetta suggested.

Corene threw her a mocking look. "Maybe not."

"You can meet her in Darien's study," Zoe decided. "That's private enough for a real conversation—but Josetta and I can be just outside the door, listening, if you want our help."

"All right," Corene said. Josetta still couldn't read her emotions—resignation, indifference, hope, anger? Maybe all of those. Maybe more.

"Calvin, can you take Celia to Annova? Then show Alys into the study and tell her Corene will be along shortly."

It was a few minutes before everyone was in place and Corene was heading to Darien's study, Zoe and Josetta creeping along behind her. Corene's back was perfectly straight and she never once looked behind her, but Zoe and Josetta exchanged a few glances. What was the girl thinking?

Corene let herself into the study, carefully leaving the door open a few inches, and Josetta and Zoe settled on either side of the frame. The melodrama made Josetta want to laugh until she remembered who was on the other side of the door.

"Hello, Mama," Corene said. "You wanted to see me?"

There was a rustle of fabric and the sound of quiet footfalls; Josetta imagined Alys crossing the room to take Corene in an embrace. "Darling! It feels like a quintile since I've had a chance to talk to you! I will never forgive Darien. I will never understand this game he's playing."

Corene didn't answer, and after a moment, Alys said, "Here, let's sit down for a few moments. Are you enjoying Ghyaneth's visit?"

"Well, I'm enjoying all the dinners and the parties, but I don't like the prince," Corene said candidly.

"No, he's a rather hateful thing, and very self-important. Still, powerful men often have flaws, and women simply must learn to work around them."

"I don't see why," Corene said. "I think women should just do what they want and not care what men think or say."

Zoe grinned at Josetta across the width of the door. *So do I,* she mouthed.

"Sometimes it's not that easy," Alys murmured. "Sometimes the power you have access to is indirect. Then you're forced to be—let us say—clever in how you deploy it. You can't be obvious. You can't be stupid."

Again, Corene remained silent. Alys waited for a moment, then sighed.

"Darling, you know what I need to ask you."

"No, I don't."

"I want you to apologize to Dominic."

"Well, I'm not going to."

"My pet, he's a powerful man. He does business with most of the primes; he has connections to all of the important families in Chialto. He's rich. Men like that must be treated well, because if you manage to win their favor, life becomes very easy."

"My life's already pretty easy."

"Corene, you have to apologize to him. You accused him of assaulting you, and you made him very upset."

Corene's voice was limpid. "Did it make him upset when I told the blind sisters what he did?"

"When you—*what*?"

"I told one of the blind sisters. I told her everything he'd done to me."

Zoe's eyes were wide with shock. Apparently Corene hadn't bothered to mention this to anyone else in the household. Josetta nodded. "I was there," she breathed.

Alys sounded first stunned, then furious. "You told— I can't believe— That must be why Lilias Ardelay wouldn't let us— How could you *do* such a thing! Corene, you go back there today, right now! You tell them you were making up stories!"

"I only told her the truth."

"You could ruin him, do you understand? Lilias is such a prude— and Riana Dochenza! Even worse! If they back out of their business deals—Corene, you have to recant."

"Mama, he came to my room when I was sleeping! He climbed into bed with me, he put his hand over my mouth so I wouldn't scream!"

"Your maid was there," Alys said impatiently. "Nothing happened. She told me about it the next day."

Zoe and Josetta were exchanging looks of horror. Inside the room, invisible to them, Corene sounded like she was almost crying.

"Mama, how can you love somebody like that more than you love me?"

"Darling, of course I love you more! But I *need* Dominic, don't you understand? And so I *need* you to make this right. I need you to go to the blind sisters, to tell them that you fabricated the whole story, and then come with me to see Dominic—"

There was a rushing sound, as if Corene had jumped to her feet so fast she caused the draperies in the room to blow. "I won't. And if anyone asks me, I'll tell them what he did. And if he ever tries to talk to me, I'll spit on him."

"You—selfish—bitch," Alys hissed, and slapped her.

Zoe was through the door before Josetta had even registered the sound of the blow. By the time she scrambled into the room a scant second later, Zoe had already pushed her way between mother and daughter and had obviously shoved Alys so forcefully that she had fetched up hard against Darien's desk.

"Get out before I have you thrown out," Zoe said in a dark voice.

Alys pulled herself upright, rubbing her thigh where she would no doubt have a spectacular bruise, and divided a smouldering look between the two erstwhile eavesdroppers. "I might have known there was no such thing as a private conversation in this house," she said.

"If you ever touch her again, I will boil the blood in your veins," Zoe promised.

Alys laughed and tucked her red hair behind her ears. "Oh, you will? I think the last time you threatened me, Mirti Serlast practically broke the bones in your body."

"This time maybe she'll help me destroy you."

An ugly expression crossed Alys's beautiful face. "You're already bent on destroying me, but you won't. You can't. I know a fact that will change everything. And then we'll see who falls down in the wake of the grand destruction."

None of them had had time to summon the servants, but suddenly Calvin appeared in the doorway with three footmen at his back. Josetta supposed he had been spying on them while she and Zoe had been spying on Corene, and she was grateful.

"Majesty, we've come to see you to the door," Calvin said in his affable voice, though he was having trouble hiding his smirk. He seemed like the only one who was actually enjoying himself. But then, Calvin found the human pageant endlessly entertaining.

"Oh, no need to throw me out," Alys said, straightening her tunic and giving her hair a light pat. "I'm leaving." She gave Corene one long, sorrowful look. "You have no idea how much you've hurt me. You've cut me to the heart."

Josetta thought Zoe would lash out at Alys again, but instead she turned her back on the queen and drew Corene close to her, shielding the girl's eyes against her tunic, trying to cover Corene's ears with one bent arm. "Don't listen to her—never listen to her again," she whispered over that bowed head. "She cares about nothing but herself."

"Majesty," Calvin said again. And with a huff of irritation, Alys stalked from the study and slammed the door. Josetta didn't even watch her go. She hurried over to where Zoe and Corene were huddled, putting her arms around both of them, adding her murmured reassurances to Zoe's soft voice. But Corene didn't look up. Corene didn't speak. It was hard to tell if she was crying or merely standing there, hoping that if she stood entirely still the world wouldn't split apart and swallow her whole.

FOURTEEN

It turned out Kayle had been expecting Rafe to apply for a job.

"Yes, of course," he said before Rafe had gotten out the first few words explaining how he wanted to pilot one of those sleek, magical, perilous metal creatures. They were standing in Kayle's messy office, although the elay prime wasn't really *standing*—the man couldn't seem to stay in one spot for longer than thirty seconds. "How quickly can you join us? There's a test flight tomorrow and I'd like you to be there."

"I'd love to go," Rafe said. "I didn't bring a change of clothes, but I suppose they have shops here where I could buy things."

"No. They're all horrible. Tunics made out of *seaweed*, or so you'd think. Although probably no worse than what you've got on now."

Rafe grinned. "I'm not very picky."

"We issue uniforms to the mechanics. Surely something will fit you. Do you have a place to stay?"

Rafe shook his head. "I thought if you hired me, I might find lodgings here. I have a room back in Chialto, of course, but—"

"Oh, you'll need to stay here. I own a building near the wharf that I rent out to some of the workers. I think there are a couple of open units. My man Darby can get you settled in. Be back here at sunrise tomorrow, and we'll drive out to the hangar. The flight is planned for sometime before noon."

Rafe glanced out one of the magnificent windows, which showed blustery skies, a storm-tossed sea, and ships of every size rocking on the choppy water. "Doesn't look like the best weather for flying. What if it doesn't clear up by tomorrow?"

For a moment, Kayle stood absolutely still and trained those wide blue eyes on him. "I believe I can be counted on to ensure calm weather for at least the duration of the flight," he said at last.

"Oh—you can—really? The primes can control the weather?" Rafe stammered.

Kayle looked faintly annoyed. "Everyone talks of *Zoe's* prowess, but really, every prime has some skill with his or her element," he said. "I could call up a *storm* if I wanted to, but I am much better served by still air and blue skies."

"Of course," Rafe said.

Kayle turned away from him, nervously tapping his desk, shuffling through papers. "Now, you may as well read the reports we have so far—it will start your training in a way—but where did I—ah." He located a thick file, bulging with loose papers and what looked like sketches and mathematical calculations. "This is more or less a history of our successes and failures so far. This will give you an idea of what to expect tomorrow."

"I can't wait to read it."

Darby was a thin, tight-lipped man of indeterminate age and nervous energy who accepted without comment his assignment to settle Rafe into one of the rental units. He consulted a ledger, retrieved a key from a safe, and escorted Rafe out of the office and into the crowded, noisy streets.

"Is it far?" Rafe asked him, lifting his voice to be heard.

Darby shook his head. "Down this street and one street over. You won't get lost."

Walking through the port town was a whole different experience from driving through in an elaymotive. The streets were uneven and oddly patchy—a few blocks constructed of cobblestone, half a block of brick, one long stretch in some kind of hardy amalgam—as if the city had built itself out from the sea in visible increments every time it needed to expand. The buildings themselves were similarly idiosyncratic, one-story wooden shacks side-by-side with tall stone structures designed for both strength and beauty. Nowhere did Rafe see a patch of grass or a cultivated acre of land. The few green things he spotted were defiant weeds and small, pale, twisted bushes that had improbably sprouted between gaps in mortar and blocks of stone. He wondered what the people in the port found to eat. Maybe they lived on fish and salt water. Maybe they subsisted on dreams.

Kayle's rental property was one of the newer and more attractive buildings, five stories tall and solidly constructed of honey-blond stone. Darby and Rafe followed a central stairwell to the third floor, which featured one long hallway with doors opening off either side. The door Darby unlocked led to a surprisingly airy space with enormous windows and a spare selection of graceful furniture. Right across the threshold, the *kierten* was delineated by a plush blue rug the size of a couple of grave plots; everywhere else, the flooring was a burnished hardwood.

"I assume you wanted a furnished place," Darby said. "There are empty rooms if you'd prefer."

"No, this is fine," Rafe answered. "I mean—I suppose I can afford it."

"Rent is taken out of your wages," Darby told him.

"Then this is perfect."

Morning arrived far more quickly than Rafe could believe. He was up and dressed and back at the factory just as sunrise was painting the eastern sky a vibrant pink. Ignoring Kayle's fashion critique, he'd spent part of the evening shopping for necessities, so he was wearing fresh if utilitarian clothing, and he'd made a hearty meal before leaving his room. He couldn't shake the notion that Kayle never bothered with food, and he figured he might need to fortify himself for the day ahead.

As before, the elay prime took the wheel and careened through the city streets, though there were fewer potential collisions at this early hour. "Did you read the reports I gave you?" Kayle demanded.

"Most of them."

"Tell me what you learned."

"You mean what *you've* learned?" Rafe said with a grin. "You've got to make the aeromotives lighter and get them to go faster if you want to travel any distance. So you're trying to find thinner, smoother material that's still strong enough to hold together under stress, and you want a more powerful fuel than the compressed gas you're currently using. You've figured out how to steer—mostly—but the aeromotives aren't nearly as maneuverable as the smoker cars."

"We need to gain more height *and* deliver more fuel without adding more weight," Kayle said. He glanced over at Rafe. "You're a slim man. That's good. One of our pilots was too big. Weighed well over two hundred pounds."

"What happened to him?"

"Crashed," Kayle said. "Died."

Rafe looked at his stomach. "I'm beginning to regret breakfast."

Kayle let loose a crack of laughter. "You won't be the one in the aeromotive today. But when you are—something to think about."

They arrived at the factory to find close to fifty people milling around in the open space before the movable door. Rafe thought that maybe half of them were engaged in essential tasks such as carrying fuel canisters and assorted cables; the others were there, brimming with excitement and curiosity, merely to watch. A whole team was vigorously sweeping debris from the roadway where the machine would gather speed before lifting into the sky. Kayle actually wrenched the elaymotive off the road and drove across the rocky ground for the final half mile, presumably so his wheels didn't introduce any foreign matter to the smooth surface. He was an even worse driver on the open ground.

Kayle had barely halted the elaymotive before he jumped out and began issuing commands. Rafe climbed out more slowly, then just stood there and watched the activity. The morning sun, still well below its zenith, shone eerily bright through an utterly cloudless sky; there wasn't a hint of wind. A surreal, suspended stillness hung over the scene, as if—despite the purposeful commotion—the whole world was holding its breath, waiting for something glorious or catastrophic to unfold under that intense sun.

It was another hour before anything interesting happened, and Rafe had settled himself on the ground to wait, leaning his back against one of the big spoked wheels of the elaymotive. But he scrambled to his feet when the great mobile doors were shoved open even wider and metallic glints in the interior darkness hinted that something very large was on the move. At first it seemed like nothing more than lights flickering across a shadowy liquid surface, and then the shadows took shape—a lean, cylindrical body with impossibly long, outstretched arms—before giving way to solid silver.

The aeromotive had been guided out of its housing.

It was being moved into place by a dozen workers, some tugging on cables attached to its wings and struts, others pushing it from behind. Rafe supposed Kayle didn't want to waste an ounce of fuel merely positioning it for takeoff. Its forward progress was uneven and accompanied by much shouting, which grew even more feverish when the aeromotive began wobbling toward the border of the roadway. Rafe imagined it wasn't easy to haul that creature back to the level surface once its wheels had dropped into soft soil. But a few more shouts, a lot more curses, and it was back on course, slowly rolling forward until it was a good thirty yards away from the building.

Rafe's attention was drawn to a man who strolled alongside the craft, his arm lifted just enough so his fingers could brush the sleek exterior skin. He wasn't helping with the manual labor, oh no. He was laying claim to the aeromotive with all a lover's possessiveness. He was overdressed for the intensifying heat of the day, in close-fitting heavyweight trousers and overtunic, sturdy boots and gloves; he had wound a long strip of light-colored fabric around his head and face, so that only his eyes and mouth were visible.

This was the pilot, Rafe had to believe, the man who would climb into that tiny driver's box and feel the great beast roar to life under his hands. He was dressed to protect himself against the wind of rapid passage and maybe against the hard burn of a disastrous landing, but he didn't look particularly worried. It was impossible to see his expression, of course, but there was something jaunty, almost arrogant, about the set of his shoulders, the lift of his head. Someone said something to him and he laughed. From the swaddling of silk, his eyes peered eagerly around, noting the angle of the sun, gauging the size of the crowd gathered to see him off. Something about his self-confidence, his swagger, made Rafe doubt he was elay, as you might expect an aeromotive pilot to be. No, this was a sweela man, Rafe would bet his life on it, a soul of reckless brilliance and limitless imagination. He believed he could fly, and so he very probably would.

Rafe had never in his life been so jealous of another man.

Someone called another order, and everyone stopped at once. The aeromotive shuddered to a halt, perfectly positioned in the center of the roadway, facing straight south, toward the sea. There was another flurry of motion as workers finalized some last-minute preparation, and then a man's voice sang out, "All clear! Ready to board!"

The pilot took a step away from the machine and raised both arms in the air, and the whole crowd cheered. Kayle broke free from a knot of his employees to offer the pilot a handshake and perhaps some final advice, and again the pilot laughed. One of the workers hurried over to cup his hands and boost the pilot into the driver's box. Only moments after he had settled in place, Rafe heard a low rumble, much louder than that of an elaymotive, and saw the aircraft begin to tremble all over. It was almost as if the inert metal construct had suddenly come to life.

All the bystanders scattered, falling back toward the building or to either side of the roadway, to give the aeromotive plenty of room. The rumbling grew to a roar, and suddenly the machine leapt forward, gaining speed at an astonishing rate. Faster, *faster*, and then abruptly it was airborne, a few feet off the ground and edging higher, its slim nose gradually lifting toward the sun.

Rafe felt a shout of triumph tear from his throat, but it was lost in the general cheering. Maybe thirty people raced after the aircraft, as if they could catch up with it, waving and calling after the pilot to speed him on his way. Everyone was staring after the diminishing silver shape; a few had their arms stretched out before them, strung with tension, as if they were helping to hold the machine in the air.

Keeping his eyes on that bright spot overhead, Rafe backed his way into the crowd, feeling the need to share the jubilation. The woman he found next to him had a severe fanatic's face. He thought she might be one of Kayle's elay inventors, certainly someone with more knowledge than he had.

"How long will it stay aloft?" he asked her. "How far will it go?"

Not looking at him, she shook her head. "We never know. Some craft never get off the ground. One flew halfway to Chialto and could have gone farther if it had had more fuel. One—we never found it. We don't know where it went down."

Rafe had read about that in Kayle's reports. Everyone seemed to think the pilot had plummeted to the sea, though the wreckage had never washed ashore. "If he returns safely, how soon can the machine be ready to fly again?"

She gave him one quick, appraising sideways glance. "Why—oh. You're Kayle's new recruit, aren't you?"

He couldn't help grinning. "How did you know?"

"You have the look of a man who would like to fly."

He wasn't sure exactly what that might mean, and he didn't want to ask, so they stood together in somewhat strained silence for the next twenty minutes, listening for sounds of the aeromotive returning. Someone else had sharper ears than Rafe did, though, because suddenly a man behind him shouted, "I can hear him! He's coming back!"

As one, the crowd moved off the roadway again, even farther back, hurrying to the dubious shelter of the factory wall. Rafe imagined that if the pilot lost control as he touched down, the aeromotive could plow right through the walls of the building and turn the whole thing to a twisted smoky mess.

"How easy is it to stop one of those things?" he asked his new friend.

She pointed. "He'll try to set down some distance away. Landing is almost as dangerous as takeoff—he doesn't want to be anywhere near the building."

Indeed, it soon became clear that that wasn't going to be an issue. While the machine was still at least a mile away, it started dropping rapidly, wobbling from side to side as if the pilot was fighting desperately to keep the wings level. Even from this distance, Rafe could hear the motor cutting in and out in an erratic fashion, as if it stalled, restarted, and stalled every few seconds. Around him, he could hear the sounds of people whispering, weeping, praying. His own lips were moving in soundless encouragement. *Come on come on come on.* His whole body was tight with cramps, as if simply by willing it, he could keep the craft aloft.

Then three things happened at once: The flying machine lost fifty yards in one sickening drop, the crowd moaned its fear in a single wordless gasp, and a wind rushed eastward across the open land and caught the craft in its chaotic swirl. The crowd gasped again, this time in hope, because the tumultuous pillow of air somewhat eased the machine's descent. The aeromotive made a half-spin in one direction, tipped its left wing dangerously close to the ground, righted at the last minute, and then fell to the earth. Its wild skidding motion flung it across the paved roadway, where it plunged into the rocky soil. The sound of screeching metal and collapsing struts carried with perfect clarity through the gusty air.

Even before the machine came to complete halt, everyone from the factory was racing forward, calling out questions, instructions, oaths, and prayers. Rafe ran with the others. At least a dozen of them, he noticed, were awkwardly burdened with buckets of water, the contents sloshing on their trousers as they ran. There was some possibility of fire, then, perhaps of a truly spectacular explosion. Rafe didn't suppose a few ounces of water would be enough to contain a real conflagration.

They all kept their attention on the wreckage as they charged across the open fields, but none of them saw what they were looking for: the pilot unstrapping himself from the driver's box and waving to reassure them that he had survived. Despite Kayle's best efforts—for surely it had been the elay prime who whipped up that helpful blast of wind— the machine had come down hard enough to jar a man's head almost off his spine. Or slam it into the metal edge of the box. Or leave him alive, but snap his back or break his neck. Every possibility worse than the last.

The first to reach the aeromotive was a girl who looked barely older than Steff. "He's alive!" she shouted to the onrushing crowd. The noisy cheer almost drowned out her next words: "But he's badly injured!"

Rafe pulled up and let the rest of the workers rush past him. He wasn't much of a hand in a sickroom, and surely someone on Kayle's staff was a medic. But a badly injured man couldn't walk on his own, so maybe somebody should fetch transport. He jogged back to where Kayle had left the elaymotive on the side of the road.

He'd driven a smoker car a few times—just because the technology fascinated him, just to say he'd done it—but he was hardly adept at the job, and Kayle's vehicle was fancier than the ones he'd rented. So it took him a couple of tries to turn the damn thing on, and he was clumsy enough at the controls that it went lurching across the countryside in an ungainly fashion. But he managed to avoid hitting anyone as he guided the elaymotive to the crash site and stood on the brakes to make it stop.

Around him, he heard a few approving murmurs: *Excellent idea. Quick thinking! Yes, put Arven in the smoker car and take him back to the hangar.* Rafe hopped out and said to anyone paying attention, "Someone else better drive it back, though, or he'll get bounced right out. How is he?"

Arven was pretty beat-up, it seemed—two broken legs, a broken collarbone, and a head wound that left him woozy—but whole enough to declare with conviction that the outing had been a success. Everyone else seemed to agree.

"He may have gone ten miles!" Rafe overhead one of the designers say. "*And* made it back!"

"Distance, direction, maneuverability, target goal achieved," someone else counted off. "Incredible."

"Will you be able to salvage the aeromotive?" Rafe asked. Because now that he got a good look at it, he found it even more amazing that Arven had survived. One of the wings had snapped in half and now bent forlornly to the ground; the struts supporting all the wheels had given way, so the belly of the machine lay flat on the ground. And there was a gash across the nose of the craft, a long rip right through the metal skin. To his untrained eyes, the thing looked irreparable.

But those who had overheard him were nodding. "Oh, yes. Anything that can be manufactured can be *re*manufactured. We can make it skyworthy again in a few ninedays."

"Arven won't be ready to fly again for longer than that," someone else objected. "So no need to rush."

A third person joined the conversation. "But the LNR is scheduled to take off next, isn't it?"

"That's right, the LNR."

"Oh, *that's* the one I want to see fly," the first man said in a reverent voice. "How long do we have to wait for Arven?"

"We need another pilot."

"We need a dozen other pilots."

"I'm almost ready to sign up myself just to see it in its natural element."

Don't bother, Rafe thought. He didn't know what an LNR was, but he knew absolutely that he wanted to be the one to send it slicing through the air. *I'm the new pilot. I'll fly anything in your whole damned factory.*

Today's exhibition, ending with an injured pilot and a twisted carcass of metal, hadn't done anything to change his mind. If anything, he was more excited than ever, impatient and eager to climb in the driver's box. He had found his passion. He wanted to fly.

Becoming an aeromotive pilot involved far more than buying fancy leather flying gear and developing an egotistical attitude. It involved a certain amount of tedious physical preparation, because it required serious strength to haul on the wheels and levers that controlled the craft. "You look like you've got the muscle mass of some of my designers, which is to say, none at all," Kayle informed him when Rafe questioned the necessity of the training exercises. "I admire your quick mind, but you need physical strength as well."

It involved even more tedious study of the specifics of every craft currently sitting in the big hangar. Kayle felt his pilots should have a thorough knowledge of how each machine was constructed, what the weak points might be, so they would better understand what could go wrong when they were high in the air and had to make rapid life-and-death decisions.

The most interesting part of the prep work involved practicing how to operate an aeromotive. Kayle—who seemed to possess half the property in the port city—owned yet another large building on the northern edge of town, this one a training facility. Complex ropes and pulleys hung from the ceiling and stretched from the walls, holding a replica driver's box twenty feet above the floor. A pilot-in-training would climb into the suspended capsule and engage the gears and levers, and the box would respond, turning right, dipping lower, trembling with simulated speed. It was as close to flying as not flying could be, and the experience left Rafe even more eager to take a machine for a trial run.

"So when will you fly your first aeromotive?" Josetta asked him over dinner on firstday.

He had by this time been training for six days, and he was sore all over. His arms and abdomen hurt from the physical workouts; after dozens of hours in the replica box, hauling on stiff levers, his hands were rough with blisters slowly turning into calluses. Even his brain hurt from trying to absorb the mathematical calculations of speed, fuel, and stress. Kayle had seemed shocked that Rafe planned to take a couple days off to recuperate.

And return to Chialto to have dinner with the princess, of course.

"I'm not sure," he replied. "Kayle thinks I need to build more strength in my hands and shoulders. *I* think I need to practice what it feels like to lose power all of a sudden and see if there's any way to bring the aircraft into more of a controlled crash. So the engineers at the training facility are devising ways to duplicate that sort of situation."

Josetta looked like she was trying hard not to appear frightened. He was pleased that she made the effort—and pleased to think she was worried about his safety. "If you let me know when it's going to be, I'll come out and watch," she told him.

It was hard to tell which outweighed the other, his surprise or his delight. "You would? That would be— I'd love that."

She gave him a half-smile. "Otherwise I don't suppose anyone would think to tell me if you'd been horribly injured in a crash, and I'd just be left to wonder what happened to you when you stopped showing up on firstdays."

He laughed, but she had a point. "I'll leave a note with Darby, telling him who to notify if something goes wrong."

"Who's—oh, Kayle's assistant. Right. Because I assume your brother would want to know, too."

He smiled at her. "But nothing will happen. So Darby won't be notifying anyone of anything."

Josetta toyed with the remnants of food on her plate. "So have you given up the gambling life altogether?"

He laughed. "Oh, I'd say flying an aeromotive is the biggest gamble of all."

She smiled reluctantly. "I mean, have you stopped playing cards as a way to support yourself?"

He leaned his elbows on the table. "For the moment. I've taken an apartment down at the port, though so far I've kept the one at Samson's just so I have a place to stay when I'm in the city."

"You could stay here," she suggested. "There's usually an empty bunk in the dorm."

His face showed his distaste. "Once you've lived on your own—even in a dump like Samson's—it's hard to go back to communal living, even for a night."

"I understand that," she agreed. "But it gets cumbersome to split your possessions over a couple of different households. I have one room at Darien's, one at my mother's, a suite at Zoe's house up on the river, and my bedroom here. If I wanted to, I could keep a room at the palace, too, but I try *never* to spend the night there."

"Why not?"

"I hate it there," she said softly. "I was so miserable when I lived at court. Every time I step back inside I just feel all the weight of those wretched days bearing down on me again."

"You're still an heir," he pointed out. "There's still the possibility you'd end up being named queen, and you'd have to live there again."

"Oh, surely not," she said. "There's Odelia—and Natalie—" Her voice trailed off and she looked, for a moment, decidedly uneasy.

"What's wrong?" he asked.

"Oh, just—remembering that Odelia was sick last time Romelle was in Chialto," Josetta said, so offhandedly that Rafe was sure she was lying. He didn't know why she'd bothered; he had no idea how to piece together the significance of anything that happened at court. "So I suppose you're right. Once you're in line for the throne, you're never really out of the shadow of the palace."

"But nothing will happen to Odelia," he said in a reassuring voice. "Just like nothing will happen to my aeromotive."

She smiled again. "That's right. Nothing to worry about at all."

FIFTEEN

Of course there was plenty to worry about, and Josetta couldn't imagine how Darien kept track of it all. The obnoxious prince of Berringey had finally departed with his many guards and attendants, though he still threatened to return. Even worse, Darien reminded everyone that the empress of Malinqua would be paying a visit sometime before Quinnatorz, so there would be at least as much pomp and celebration to welcome her.

And orchestrating the visits of foreign dignitaries was only one of the time-consuming tasks that had fallen to Darien recently; another was trying to keep a rein on Alys. Zoe and Corene were gone, but Josetta was in the house, when Darien summoned Alys and her husband for a confrontation.

"What are you going to say to her?" Josetta wanted to know. "Can I listen in?"

She'd expected him to say no, but his eyes narrowed as he considered it. "It might be useful to have a witness, even one clearly biased in my favor," he decided. "Even Alys is less likely to tell lies about me later if you're in the room."

"I won't say a word," she promised.

He gave a grim laugh. "You won't have a chance to. We'll be yelling at each other too loudly."

But Darien, at least, kept his cool during the tense, angry interview. Of course he did; Darien never lost control. It was Alys and Dominic who did all the shouting.

They gathered in Darien's study, where Alys and Corene had had their last disastrous conversation. Josetta sat at a small table by the window, laying out a solitary card game that Rafe had taught her, using a deck he had lent her when she admired its pictures. She stood up long enough to bow at Alys when the queen entered, and to favor Dominic with a nod. He was a beefy man with a ruddy complexion and dark hair; Corene had said once that he always looked greedy, no matter what the discussion. Josetta thought he looked smart but calculating. He smiled at her, which was more than Alys did, but she didn't smile back as she dropped back into her seat and resumed her game.

"Delighted, as always, to see you again, Darien," Alys said in her silky tones. She and Dominic took chairs across from Darien, who had seated himself behind a massive, scrupulously tidy desk.

"I feel certain your delight will quickly fade," he replied.

"Well now, well now," Dominic said in a placating voice. "We're all reasonable people here. There's no need to be arguing over—what *are* we arguing over?"

"We're not arguing," Darien said. "I have a question to ask and some information to share. That's all."

"A question?" Alys asked in a marveling, mocking voice. "But I thought the regent had spies everywhere and knew everything!"

"I would like to think so," he said. "But now and then I learn of events that happened without my observation. For instance, I wanted to ask you, Alys, if you ever thought it might be amusing to send one of *your* spies to the bedroom of Princess Odelia and—just for fun—cut off a lock of the girl's hair."

The silence went on for so long that Josetta looked up from her card game to see what expression Alys was wearing. The queen looked neither guilty nor panicked; her eyes were narrowed and she was watching Darien closely.

"Why, no," she said. "But I take it someone did? How very alarming that must have been for Romelle."

"As you say," Darien replied.

"I assume the princess wasn't actually harmed?"

"No. Which leads me to believe the visitor was merely intent on mischief. Which is why," he added, "I instantly thought of you."

"Oh, Darien," Alys said. "To think you still hold me in such high regard."

"So much so that any harm that comes to Odelia will instantly lead me to consider you the likeliest culprit."

Alys actually laughed. "I have no wish to harm the princess. Absolutely none. So if that's what this little meeting is about—"

"I only wanted to let you know I am paying attention," Darien said. "That's not the point of our conference at all." He tossed an envelope across the desk at Dominic. "Here's the real business at hand. I've purchased the mortgage on the house you're buying in Chialto. It now belongs to me."

Dominic first appeared wholly taken by surprise, and then furious. "You can't do that! I have a contract—I'll own it in five years!"

"The contract has been rewritten. I'm now your lender, and anytime I decide to foreclose, I can."

"So you'd turn us out in the streets?" Dominic blustered. "You would be willing to see the *queen* homeless?"

"Alys owns a small property in the middle provinces," Darien said coolly. "It belonged to her family before she married Vernon, and was bequeathed to her by the throne when Vernon died. She will never be homeless."

"If you think I will ever live anywhere but Chialto, you are entirely mistaken," Alys told him.

Darien shrugged and slid a somewhat bulkier package across the desk. "I've bought a controlling share in the cotton processing factory you've invested in. If I ever decide the business isn't functioning satisfactorily, I'll shut it down."

"Shut it down—but you could bankrupt me! I put more than half my assets in that business!"

"Where are you getting all this money you're flinging about?" Alys demanded. "Or were you stealing from Vernon all those years?"

"I borrowed cash from my wife, who is a very wealthy woman," Darien said. "The hunti prime insisted on contributing funds as well."

Dominic was getting angrier and angrier; Josetta had the sense that he could literally explode with rage. "So you *are* trying to destroy me!" he snarled. "Alys said—but I didn't believe her—and all of this over lies some little girl started spouting about me."

Darien passed him a tightly rolled scroll sealed with a wax wafer. "Here's a copy of the letter I've sent to the other four primes. I've also provided copies to Romelle and Elidon and Seterre, as well as members of the council. They've all been told the notes should remain unread until Zoe or I tell them the contents should be made public, but—" He shrugged. "People get curious."

Dominic looked fearful. "What does it say?"

"It details Corene's accusations against you, sworn before witnesses at the booth of promises."

Now Dominic appeared so stunned he was almost incapable of speech. "If you—but you—this letter—"

Darien enumerated on his fingertips. "If you ever—in public where I can see you or in private when I learn about it—approach my daughter again. If you ever speak of her to anyone else, and word makes its way back to me. If you ever lay a hand on another young girl, whether a maid in your household or a daughter of the Five Families, and I learn of the infraction. If any of these things *ever* happens, from now until I am dead, I will destroy you. That's all. That's what I wanted to tell you. Goodbye."

Now Dominic burst into fury, lunging to his feet and shouting in Darien's face, banging his fist on the table and screaming that he wouldn't stand for this abuse, he would call in his friends, he would start a campaign of retribution against the regent that would rock the whole city. *You have no idea how powerful I am, Darien Serlast!* Alys, too, was on her feet, but her words were low and bitter, almost indistinguishable beneath Dominic's rant. Josetta only caught a phrase or two, something like *I have outwitted you before, Darien. You mustn't think I've forgotten all your weaknesses.* Darien barely reacted; he didn't even stand. He just sat there gazing up at them, his hands folded before him on the desk, allowing them to shout themselves hoarse.

It was only a minute before four burly footmen entered the room and stood suggestively by the door, at which point Darien came to his feet.

"I think we all understand each other," he said pleasantly. "The servants will see you out." And he bowed to both of them and then simply stood there waiting until they finally snatched up their things and stalked for the door.

Where Alys turned for a final parting shot. "You're not as clever as you think you are, Darien," she said. "You make mistakes all the time."

"I do," he said. "And then I fix them, which is more than I can say for you."

She actually laughed. "Oh, no," she said. "This time I'm not committing any errors at all." And with that cryptic remark, she swept through the door, close on her husband's heels. Darien followed, probably to make sure they actually left the house.

For her part, Josetta couldn't speak, couldn't stand, couldn't move. She had always hated confrontation, always felt sick to her stomach when she'd been caught in the poisonous plotting carried out at the palace. For some reason, the casual brutality in the southside slums didn't affect her the same way, maybe because it was so direct and obvious. She couldn't tolerate these court games, couldn't scheme and counterscheme without check and without mercy. She sat at the little desk, staring down at the patterns of roses and flutes, and waited until she stopped trembling.

The other problem Darien was supposed to be solving was Odelia. As soon as Prince Ghyaneth headed over the mountains to Soeche-Tas, Romelle and her entire entourage decamped.

"We'd never see them in Chialto again if Romelle had her way," Zoe observed over a casual dinner one night. Well, it wasn't entirely casual, since Mirti and Elidon had been invited. Anytime there were two primes, two princesses, one queen, and the regent at a table, talk was bound to be political.

"Well, she *will* return when state affairs demand her presence," Darien said in his peremptory way. "And I've made it very clear Odelia must be in her train. We need to see the actual heir."

"I made the same point to her," Mirti said.

"And I," Elidon added. The eldest queen was a full-figured and forceful woman of great intelligence, patience, and subtlety. Aside from

Darien, she had always been the person Josetta was least inclined to cross. She was elay, but it hardly showed. "In fact, I made the point with so much emphasis that I believe she will comply with our wishes."

Mirti grinned over at her. The two women had always been allies, and since Elidon had been widowed, there had been much speculation that they were lovers as well. Josetta had even heard a few snickers about *this* being the true reason Elidon had never borne Vernon any heirs.

"Did you make Romelle cry?" inquired the hunti prime. "I thought you had vowed to stop doing that."

"Nonsense. I never promised any such thing."

"Well, I don't particularly need her weeping, I just want her to bring Odelia to court," Darien said. "I have developed a strong urge to verify with my own eyes that the heir to the throne is, in fact, healthy and strong."

"And if she brings Mally instead?" Zoe asked. Everyone looked at her, most of them frowning. Zoe went on, "If she truly believes Odelia is in danger, she'll leave the girl behind. That's what I'd do if I was worried about my daughter's safety. I wouldn't care what any of you said."

"So how do we counter that?" Darien said. "I can promise to put every resource at her disposal. I can send her a hundred guards. Odelia need never be more than six inches from a soldier."

"Maybe we're going about this the wrong way," Elidon said. "If Romelle believes someone threatened Odelia—and if, as seems highly likely, that someone was Alys—maybe we simply remove the threat. Banish Alys from the city."

There was a short silence as they all considered that. "It appeals to me, simply because I like the idea of Chialto without Alys," Mirti said. "But unless we have proof of her malice, I don't think we *can* banish her. She still has allies here. And we can hardly present ourselves as an impartial ruling body if we start getting rid of people just because we don't like them."

Now Josetta was watching Corene, whose gaze had dropped to her plate. Zoe watched her, too, but neither of them said anything.

"The fact is, even if she was living in the western provinces, Alys could hire someone to harm Odelia," Darien said. "Even if we bundled her off to Berringey, she could still be plotting."

"I suppose that's why the people in Berringey kill off all their heirs," Josetta said. "To stop just this kind of scheming."

"That's exactly why," Darien agreed. "It's effective, of course, but barbaric. I can't imagine that even Romelle would look with favor on such a policy."

"Well, I for one think Romelle is being unreasonable," Mirti said roundly. "Here are the facts. We have the power and the resources to protect Odelia as well as any child can ever be protected. And even so, no one is ever completely safe. People fall sick, they drown, they are run over by elaymotives, they are betrayed by their closest confidantes. You must accept these facts and move forward with your life."

"I agree," Darien said. "Now we must convince Romelle."

Josetta was heartily tired of all of them—Romelle, Odelia, Alys, Ghyaneth, every political topic endlessly rehashed at the dinner table—by the time she returned to the shelter a couple of days later. Unless she was suddenly summoned to the palace for some urgent reason, she thought she might stay southside until the empress of Malinqua arrived. It sounded deliciously relaxing to be free of the brangling and speculating for so long.

Of course, the shelter came with its own problems, and Josetta had neglected it so much lately that many had become critical. First among them was the fact that they were simply running out of room.

"I thought it was just the usual spillover from Quinnahunti, but we've been full every night since changeday, and more people are coming all the time," Callie told her. "I can *feed* them all, but I don't know where to put them at night. I've let some of them sleep on the floor in the dining room. When the infirmary's free, some of them sleep there. Last night, I think three men bedded down in the baths, and a woman and her baby slept in the temple. But it won't do."

"We need another dorm—a separate place," Josetta said. "We've talked about it before."

"You could buy one, *if* you had the money, but who'd fix it up? Because every single building in southside is falling down. Except this one."

"I hired workmen to renovate this place, and I can hire some again," Josetta said. "But it was so much work!"

"Make it a smaller place," Callie suggested. "Just rooms. Everyone can still come here for the meals."

"That makes sense," Josetta said. "So let's start looking for a place nearby."

"You still have to find the money," Callie objected.

Josetta thought of the mortgages and financial documents Darien had flung across his desk to Dominic. *My wife is a very wealthy woman.* "I think I'll find some backers," she said. "Let's look for the real estate first."

R afe Adova thought it was a fine idea for Josetta to buy more prop-erty in the slums, when she told him about her plans. "Well, let me rephrase," he said over dinner on firstday. "I think it's a terrible *mon-etary* investment, and I've started to pay attention to finances these days! But it's a wonderful thing for you to do. You want me to look at property with you?"

"If you don't need to hurry back to the port tomorrow to keep training."

He grinned. "I need the break. My arms are so sore I can hardly lift my fork."

They made quite the procession the next morning—Josetta, Callie, Rafe, Foley, and Sorbin—prowling the nearby streets and examining the empty buildings with an eye to remodeling them. Most were too small for their purposes; the bigger ones were generally in such bad shape it seemed safer to tear them down and start over. There was one building that they all liked—a three-story property with a stone foun-dation and solid wood upper levels—but it was occupied by a tailor and his sons.

"Think of that," Callie marveled as they stood outside and peeked through the grimy windows. "Those fine clothes that women buy in the Plaza for a few quint-golds. They're made here by an old man and a couple of boys. I'm surprised the girls of the First Family can't smell the stench of the slums on their pretty shawls."

Rafe had backed up into the crumbled street to stare up at the top two floors. "Do you suppose they use the whole building or just the bottom story? Maybe they'd rent out the rest of the place."

"We could certainly ask," Josetta said and opened the door.

At first, the tailor was not inclined to talk business. He was suspicious of strangers, particularly those who offered easy money, and he was clearly too busy to waste his time with charlatans. But once he realized that Josetta ran the nearby shelter, he begrudgingly invited her inside to talk.

"Wait—*all* of you are coming in? Oh, very well. But there's no place to sit."

Indeed, they all clustered by the door for their brief conference, though Josetta couldn't keep her eyes from straying to the cluttered but carefully laid out workroom. There seemed to be different stations for weaving, for dyeing, and for other more mysterious functions; their conversation was accompanied by the constant rhythmic clatter of a wooden loom.

It turned out that the tailor used part of the second floor as storage, but the whole top story was uninhabited. "I might be interested in renting that out to you," he said cautiously. "Maybe even part of the second story. But you'd have to build a separate entrance. I don't want any of your vagrants in here stealing my goods."

"We could do that," Josetta said. "May we tour the upper levels and see what condition they're in?"

"*All* of you?" the tailor asked again, but Josetta insisted, and the whole group climbed up to the second floor. It was conveniently divided into six smaller rooms, and only two of them were filled with giant spools of thread and dozens of bottles of dye. The other four were empty, except for dust and spiders and mounds of debris.

"Could fit three bunks in each room—tight quarters, but better than the streets," Callie said.

The third floor was a big open space, though not a very comfortable one. The ceiling was low, the windows were small, and here in early summer, it was already hot and close. Josetta imagined it was smothering during the warmest quintiles and frigid in the cold ones. Still. As Callie said, better than the streets.

"We could divide it in two," Josetta said. "Men on one side, women on the other."

"Is that safe for the women?" Rafe asked. "A man might be grateful for this kind of haven and still not be wholly trustworthy."

"We have dorm rooms just like this at the shelter," Josetta said.

"Sure. But Callie and Bo sleep there every night. If no one's here to enforce order—" He shrugged.

"Split them up," suggested Foley. He spoke up so rarely that Josetta always listened to him seriously. "Put all the men here, all the women and families back at the shelter."

"I like that," Callie said.

The tailor was frowning. "I haven't said I'll rent you the place yet."

"No, you haven't," Josetta said. "Let's talk specifics."

It was clear he'd done some calculations while they considered options, because he promptly named a rental fee per quintile. It was high, and Josetta counteroffered. "We'd be investing in structural improvements that would make it more attractive if you ever sold it, so we should figure that into our price," she said.

He snorted. "Who'd buy anything here in the slums?"

"*I* would," she said. "So you should give me favorable rental terms."

He laughed at that; she had the feeling he enjoyed a negotiation. "But you'll have laborers tramping in and out, disrupting my work and costing me money," he answered with zest. "So I should charge you *more*."

They continued to debate it as they headed downstairs, where Josetta was practically run over by one of the tailor's sons. The young man was hauling two buckets of water and cursing under his breath.

"What's wrong?" Josetta asked.

The tailor waved over at the biggest loom, now standing idle. "We bought that piece a year ago—steam-powered, faster than three men. We thought it would save us hours' worth of work a day. But to make steam, you need water, and it's almost as much trouble to fetch the water as it is to do the weaving by hand."

Josetta couldn't contain her smile. This was the wildcard, this was the high trump. "If I could guarantee you water," she said softly, "how would you renegotiate our terms?"

The tailor stared at her. "Guarantee me water? Southside, so far from the river or the canal? You can't."

"I can."

"I'd cut your rent by half."

"Then we have a deal."

. . .

During the short walk home, during which they all buzzed with satisfaction, Josetta found Rafe beside her.

"You can guarantee him water?" he asked without preamble. "How?"

"How do you think I got water at the shelter?"

He shook his head. "You paid someone to install the pipes for you?"

"My sister Zoe. The coru prime. She can draw water to her from anywhere in Welce."

"That's remarkable." He seemed to think something over. "And all the primes have that kind of magic? Because I swear I've seen Kayle Dochenza control the wind."

Josetta nodded. "And Taro Frothen could cause the earth to shake and the mountains to tumble down if he wanted to. I've never seen Nelson or Mirti play any tricks with fire or wood, but I'm sure they can."

"Will Zoe mind that you're trading on her power just to get a better rental rate?"

Josetta laughed. "She'll be delighted. I can hardly wait to tell her."

In fact, she didn't have to wait. Because Zoe—and Corene—were at the shelter when they arrived.

SIXTEEN

Josetta felt a confused swirl of uncharitable emotions—surprise, embarrassment, irritation, and a desire to hide. It was obvious Corene and Zoe had showed up hoping to find her entertaining Rafe Adova, and it was only sheer coincidence that he happened to be present this day. The one clear thought in her head was *I'm not ready for this*. But ready or not, here she was, trying to preserve her tranquility as her two separate worlds intersected.

Callie, Sorbin, and Foley disappeared the instant they recognized the exalted visitors, which left the four of them to stare at each other. Josetta felt compelled to speak first.

"Well! Look who's here!" she said, hoping her voice sounded friendly with just a note of inquiry. "Did Darien send you to check up on me?"

Zoe was trying to repress a grin, but Corene wasn't even making that effort. "We came to see if Rafe was here and he *is*!" she said in delight. "Hello, Rafe, do you remember me?"

He seemed wholly amused and utterly relaxed. Clearly *he* didn't mind that her sisters had come to call. "Of course I remember you, Princess Corene," he said. "I hope you haven't had any adventures lately."

"Well, I wouldn't mind a *good* adventure," she said. "But, no, life has been very dull. Even dinners with the prince, which you'd think would be more fun."

Josetta made introductions. "Zoe, this is Rafe Adova. The man who rescued Corene and is now planning to fly Kayle's aeromotives. Rafe, my sister Zoe Lalindar, the coru prime."

Rafe made a deep bow, as gracefully as he did everything else, and Zoe nodded back as befit her station. Royals and high-ranking members of the Five Families never indulged in casual contact with strangers, so no one extended a hand, but Josetta had to guess Zoe was dying for a chance to touch Rafe on the arm or shoulder.

"I've heard so much about you from Corene," Zoe said in her usual friendly way. "Josetta has been more reserved in her stories, but that just made me more curious."

Rafe slanted a quick look at Josetta. "I'm gratified to learn that the princess has spoken of me at all."

"She *didn't*," Corene jumped in. "We had to keep asking her questions!"

"I hope I sounded more interesting than the prince."

"A man with a kind heart, a gambler's nerve, and three extraordinary blessings," Zoe said. "Hard not to sound interesting."

Josetta turned toward Rafe. "She *seems* relaxed and amiable, but she can be intimidating. Actually, a little frightening. When she wants to be."

He looked even more amused, because anyone less frightening than Zoe at this moment would be hard to find. She was wearing her oldest and most unfashionable tunic, and she had barely bothered to style her dark hair. She looked like someone who might have sought help at the shelter a couple of years ago and returned now to show how she'd managed to pull herself out of poverty with some respectable job in the shop district.

"I'll be on my guard," he promised.

"We should sit down and talk—get to know each other a little," Zoe said genially. "Should we go inside?"

"Maybe we can get something to eat," Josetta said. "I'm hungry after all the walking around."

Rafe held the door open and the three women stepped inside, where it wasn't much cooler and certainly no more private. But clearly privacy was going to be in short supply in Josetta's future. Well, of course, it always had been. But she had thought, here in this part of town, she might be able to lead her life without constant observation . . .

"Walking around doing what?" Zoe asked.

"Looking at real estate," Rafe replied.

Josetta left the three of them to find a table and ducked into the kitchen to see if she could put together any kind of meal. She found Callie way ahead of her, cutting bread and arranging fruit on a tray.

"I don't have anything here fit to serve a prime!" Callie exclaimed in a low voice. "And a *princess*! Not even crushed fruit to stir into the water!"

"*I'm* a princess, and you feed me every day," Josetta countered. "Trust me, Zoe's not very picky. And Corene is adaptable."

Callie tried to shoo her back out into the main room, but Josetta needed a few minutes to regain her composure, and she had no fear that the others would have trouble making conversation. Not those three. Corene, who always spoke her mind. Zoe, who only respected boundaries when they didn't get in her way. And Rafe, who was at ease with anyone who crossed his path. *She* was the most awkward and unsure of the lot.

When she finally did carry a tray from the kitchen to the main hall, she found the others playing a card game. Of course. She began distributing plates and glasses while Rafe explained the opening moves to penta.

"Wait, start over so Josetta can learn, too," Corene said.

Rafe gave her a quick, smiling glance. "She already knows how to play."

Zoe gathered up her cards. "I'm sure she does," she said affably. "Josetta's always been a quick study."

"I'm just as smart as Josetta is," Corene said, her voice a little sulky.

Josetta seated herself next to Corene and picked up her own cards, sorting them into suits. "Yes, but you're more annoying," she answered, and Corene laughed.

The card game, she decided later, had been a masterstroke. It provided them with an activity to pursue as they got acquainted, which prevented the conversation from becoming strained or stilted. And it showed Rafe to his best advantage: He was not only knowledgeable about the game, he was also personable and entertaining as he told anecdotes about past opponents. He didn't attempt to present his life as other than it had been—sizing up strangers and winning their money—but he still came across as amusing, insightful, and intelligent.

"That was fun," Zoe said when Corene won the game on the last turn of the cards, though Josetta strongly suspected Rafe had been cheating on Corene's behalf. "I think that's how I'll make my living if I'm ever exiled again. Of course, I'll have to get better at it."

"You could hold tournaments down on the river flats," Josetta suggested.

Rafe had collected all the cards and he was now idly shuffling them, cutting them together, and shuffling again. "'Exiled'?" he repeated. "'Again'?"

Zoe nodded. "My father was expelled from court when I was a little girl and I went with him. When I came back to Chialto, I lived on the river flats for a while. I still miss the vagabond existence sometimes."

"Like, whenever princes from Berringey are visiting," Corene interpolated. "Maybe if he had left off his everlasting turbans for *just one day* I would have liked him better."

Rafe grinned at her, but addressed his next question to Zoe. "When did you become coru prime?"

"I don't know exactly when it happened, but I knew it *had* when I discovered I had the power to control the Marisi. To control all water, actually, but it was most spectacular when it was the river."

Rafe nodded over at Josetta. "Your sister promised a southside landlord that you'd bring water to his property. Can you really do that?"

Zoe nodded but looked at Josetta. "Why did you tell him that?"

"I want to rent it from him. We need to expand the number of beds we can offer. He was very excited at the idea."

"Take me over there. I'll do it today."

Josetta laughed. "It might be a few ninedays before we're ready for you."

"If you can bring water to the slums so easily, why haven't you done it before?" Rafe wanted to know.

"I have—more than once," Zoe said regretfully. "I've picked good spots and drawn up water for public wells. But in this part of town, unless someone is constantly watching over them, they tend to be vandalized. Refuse gets thrown down them—dead animals are tossed in. I haven't figured out how to keep them operating unless they're someplace like this."

"Well, I think our new landlord will be very protective of his water source," Josetta said.

Rafe still seemed intrigued by the notion of someone having so much influence over water. "So are all your blessings coru?" he asked.

"None of them," Zoe said, extending her hand so he could see the three charms hanging off her bracelet. "Beauty, love, and power were drawn for me when I was born. But virtually every time I pick a coin from a barrel, it's a coru one. Change, usually. Though my life has been very stable for the past few years!"

"When's the last time you pulled a blessing?" Josetta asked.

Zoe considered. "A while. Maybe not since Celia was born."

Corene had already jumped up. "Then let's go get blessings!" She gave Rafe an impudent glance. "I want to see if he's a ghost again or if he's still extraordinary."

Four people made for a tight fit in the small temple. It seemed less crowded when they all took seats on the circular bench, but then their knees practically touched the wine barrel in the center of the room.

"Who first?" Josetta asked.

"Oh, it has to be Rafe," Zoe said. "His blessings will be the most interesting."

"I think we should each draw one for him," Corene said.

Zoe nodded and said, "I'll start." She plunged an arm elbow-deep in the small keg and gave the coins one vigorous stir before pulling out a coin and handing it to Rafe.

He studied it for a moment before showing it to Josetta. "I think it's synthesis."

"You're getting better at recognizing them," she said.

"I've memorized the shapes of my own," he answered, touching his chest where his six blessing rings made a slight lump under his shirt.

"My turn," Corene said, leaning over the barrel. She withdrew one coin, tossed it back without looking at it, drew out another and threw it away.

"Corene," Zoe admonished.

"I'm just trying to see how powerful the extraordinary blessings are," she explained. "If one really wants to come to me no matter what I do." She picked a blessing with each hand, seemed to weigh them, then let the one in her left hand drop with a musical *clink*. She handed the remaining coin to Rafe.

Who laughed out loud. "Time," he said.

"This is remarkable," Zoe said. "I've never seen anything like this."

Rafe nodded at Josetta. "Now you."

As she always did, she dug her hand through the cool pile of metal and waited until she felt heat along her fingers. Almost immediately one of the coins scalded against her skin, so she quickly dug it out and handed it over to Rafe.

He showed it around the circle. "Triumph."

"So those are the only blessings anyone has ever drawn for you?" Zoe demanded. "Ghost coins or extraordinary blessings?"

"So far. I suppose someday things could change again."

"What happens when *you* pull coins out of the barrel?" she asked.

Rafe exchanged a smile with Josetta. "I've only done it once. It was interesting."

"How so?"

"I was sitting here," Josetta said, "and what he pulled were all of *my* blessings."

Zoe raised her eyebrows. "See what happens now when you draw one for each of us."

"Nobody look until we all have one," Corene ordered.

"I won't look, either," Rafe said, and ostentatiously covered his eyes with his left hand while his right hand sorted through the barrel. Once he'd distributed a coin to each of them, he waved his hands like a conjurer at a Quinnahunti fair.

"Reveal your blessings!" he commanded.

"Courage," Corene said. "My favorite."

"Power," Zoe said.

Josetta turned hers so everyone could see the glyph. "Joy."

Zoe leaned back on the bench so her spine rested on the wall, and regarded Rafe with narrowed attention. "This is very odd," she said, her voice unwontedly serious. "It's as if you don't exist in the common dimensions of Welce. It's as if you're—you're—a mimic or an echo. Something reflected or something seen through a curtain. Duplicating our motions and our mannerisms but not truly understanding why."

Corene frowned. "That's mean."

Zoe shook her head. "I don't intend it that way. I find that I like Rafe Adova. I just don't understand precisely how he fits in."

Josetta was silent, watching Rafe as he assimilated Zoe's words. Let him decide how much of his background to tell her; she hadn't gone into much detail when Zoe had questioned her the other day. He was quiet a moment, thinking it over, and then he nodded.

"I think I *am* something of a cipher," he said at last. "My mother never told me much about her own family, and she died before I knew I should be curious. All I knew about my father was that he left her when I was a baby—or she left him—after he did this to me," he added, sweeping back his hair to expose his right ear.

Corene and Zoe leaned forward to examine the precisely cut triangular pattern, defiantly decorated with the five gold earrings. "It's weird but I sort of like it," Corene said. "Does it hurt?"

He smiled at her. "Not now. I imagine I screamed my head off when it was done to me."

"Did she say *why* your father did that?" Zoe asked.

"So she'd never get me mixed up with anybody else's children. Also, I guess, so no one could steal me and then try to prove I wasn't her son."

Zoe was frowning. "So, really, you have no idea who your people are, your mother's or your father's."

"I asked my stepfather about it the other day, and he admitted he'd never asked my mother many questions. He seemed to think it was likely that my father was foreign—and *possible* that my mother was." He shrugged. "But Kayle seemed convinced they both were."

"Really? You were discussing your bloodlines with Kayle Dochenza?"

Rafe grinned faintly. "He said he couldn't hear me breathing."

"Ah." Zoe nodded; it seemed to make perfect sense to her. She scooted a little closer to Rafe on the curved bench. "If you like—if you're willing—I'd try to decode your blood for you," she offered.

Rafe drew back infinitesimally. "You'd—how would you do that?"

"Oh, don't be a baby," Corene said. "She won't hurt you."

"No, but, I mean—does she need me to bleed into something?"

Zoe was grinning. "No, no, I only have to touch you. Josetta may have mentioned that I can generally tell how people are related—well, it's hard to explain. I'm the coru prime. A woman of water *and* blood."

"So you just want to take my hand?"

"If you wouldn't mind."

He glanced at Josetta. "Only if you want," she said softly. "But that's how she learned she and I had the same father. That's how she learned Corene is Darien's daughter. By touching us. If I were you, I'd want to know. I'm glad *I* found out."

He nodded, took a deep breath, and placed his hand in Zoe's outstretched one. Josetta watched as Zoe closed her fingers over Rafe's and concentrated. She had seen Zoe do this a dozen times and had always been amazed at how quickly Zoe could find the genetic match in the blood.

If Zoe knew the person's family, of course. If Rafe's mother was a runaway from some provincial Welchin family, the chances were slim that Zoe had encountered any of her relatives. And if she had actually emigrated here from another country, well, Zoe would be able to tell him nothing.

But the look on Zoe's face was one of recognition—followed quickly by a puzzled frown. "How very strange," she said softly, dropping Rafe's hand.

Now they were all staring at her. "Well?" Josetta said impatiently. "Did you learn anything?"

But Zoe's full attention was on Rafe. "I met one of your family members just the other day," she said, her voice strained. "Not a brother, I think—a cousin, perhaps."

Rafe's face lit up with curiosity and excitement. "Really? You could tell that? Who is it? Can I meet him?"

"I don't think you want to meet him," Zoe said. "He was the crown prince Ghyaneth of Berringey."

For a moment there was utter silence in the little temple. "The crown *prince*," Rafe repeated. "Of Berringey. Are you sure?"

Zoe nodded. "Completely. I shook hands with enough of the Berringese contingent to be able to tell that no one else in the prince's train was related to him. There's a definite signature in the blood, and you've got it."

"But that's—I can't take that in," Rafe said. "I'm related to a *prince?*"

"You don't want to be related to this one," Zoe said.

Rafe looked at Josetta in a mute appeal for enlightenment. She said slowly, "Ghyaneth told me that in Berringey, once the crown prince or princess has survived to adulthood, it's customary for all the other heirs to kill themselves. Or, if they're not so cooperative, for someone else to kill them. So there are no rivals for the throne."

Now Rafe's eyes widened. "Wait. So. I'm related to this prince, but if he knew I was alive, he'd want me dead?"

"Exactly," Zoe said. "In fact, I'd guess that's why your mother ran away. Once she realized her son was due for murder in about twenty years, she took off with you in her arms."

"That probably explains the cuts on your ear, too," Josetta added.

Rafe lifted a hand to finger the edges, and Zoe nodded. "Right. Probably all the direct heirs are marked in such a fashion. So, even if they try to disappear, someone will recognize them, and do the crown a favor by killing them."

Josetta was frowning. "But was Ghyaneth's ear cut the same way? I think I would have noticed if it was."

Zoe shook her head. "You couldn't see his ears. He was always wearing one of those turbans, remember?"

"One of those *stupid* turbans," Corene corrected.

"But I'd guess his ear *has* been sliced in the same way," Zoe added. "All the Berringese heirs no doubt have similar markings."

Rafe shook his head as if to clear it. "I can't really absorb this," he admitted. "All this time—I mean, I'm nothing, I'm nobody, I'm a bastard who's taken up a career as a gambler—but I'm the heir to a *throne?* It's like one of those stories you tell yourself when you're a kid and you're thinking about running away from home because nobody appreciates you. I'm having trouble believing it's real."

"Well, I doubt you're a bastard," Zoe said. "I suppose the kings of Berringey take lovers now and then, but I bet they're *awfully* certain not to sire any troublesome children outside the marriage bed."

Josetta was frowning. "I'm trying to remember what Ghyaneth told me. His father was childless until very late in life, so his grandmother didn't murder her other two children as soon as she might have otherwise. So there was Ghyaneth's father and his younger siblings—a man and a woman. One of them had Ghyaneth's cousin, and one of them had you."

"I'm guessing it was the woman who was your mother," Zoe said softly. "As soon as they decorated your ear, she realized you'd been marked for death, just like she had. The minute she had a chance, she fled."

"I don't think so," Josetta answered. "Ghyaneth talked about his cousin—how ambitious she is, how she's constantly scheming to destroy him so she can be queen instead. She married a man who's equally ambitious and they have children together—and they did this knowing that all of them will die once Ghyaneth ascends the throne and produces heirs. Anyone who was bred in that atmosphere wouldn't run away. Or if she did, she'd run someplace where she could gather resources in her own bid for the throne. But this girl just ran."

"That makes sense," Zoe agreed. "So your father was the younger prince, and your mother was some nice aristocratic girl who was married off by a ruthless lord who gambled that a child of his line might one day wear the crown."

Josetta smiled at Rafe, who was still looking dazed. "So you see? Gambling is in your blood."

"Somehow, I don't think I've ever played for stakes so high."

Corene, who had been largely silent, suddenly demanded, "But do they know Rafe is alive? Are they looking for him?"

The other three exchanged startled glances. "They must know—they must be looking," Zoe said. "Unless she found a way to fake their deaths—which maybe she did—"

"They'll never stop searching," Josetta said grimly.

"But they don't know he's here in Welce," Corene said.

Rafe touched his ear again. "They do now," he answered. "Those men who jumped me in the alley—they saw the markings. They knew who I was."

"And they have undoubtedly sent word to Berringey by this time," Zoe said.

Josetta frowned. "I don't think Ghyaneth knew yet, though," she said. "He didn't act like he knew, and he's the sort of man who would be very righteous and angry. You know, 'You depraved peasants of Welce have shielded a pretender to my throne, and I'll have everyone in the whole country hanged.' But he didn't say anything like that."

"Then maybe Rafe got lucky," Zoe said. "Maybe these weren't royal spies combing the foreign shores for missing heirs. Maybe they were just Berringese mercenaries who happened to come across Rafe in a bar—and they knew how much his dead body would be worth."

"So either they'll try again to kill him—or they'll take whatever reward is offered for information about where he might be living now," Josetta said. "But why didn't they tell Ghyaneth while he was in Chialto?"

Zoe shrugged. "Didn't know he was coming? Sailed for Berringey instead?"

Josetta nodded. "At any rate, we have to assume that Ghyaneth will discover the truth sooner or later." She looked at Rafe. "And come looking for you."

He took a deep breath. He wasn't even trying to appear nonchalant, though Josetta did think he was making an effort to seem calm. "And here I thought I was risking my life by flying aeromotives," he joked.

"Probably a more enjoyable way to die," Zoe said.

Josetta appealed to Zoe. "So what do we do? How do we keep him safe?"

"We can't just let him be murdered," Corene added. "I mean—he's essentially a prince of a foreign nation!"

"Well, we wouldn't want him to be murdered even if he was just a nobody from the streets," Zoe said. She was smiling. This sort of chaos appealed to her coru soul. "But, of course, in the eyes of the world, he's suddenly a much more valuable man."

"He needs a lot of guards," Corene said. "Or maybe he should live at the palace! He'd be safe there."

"Sure, right, and then my cousin Ghyaneth would never figure out who I was," Rafe said scornfully. Then he came to a full stop. "My *cousin* Ghyaneth . . . I still can't believe it."

"Believe me, I understand what you're going through," Zoe said. "For years, my father and I lived in a tiny house on the edge of nowhere.

I knew that my family had been wealthy before my father was banished—but I didn't know I was the coru prime. I didn't know I'd be expected to come to Chialto and take my place at court. And once I did, there were a lot of days I just wanted to run back to the village." She laughed. "There are still days like that, actually. But the world shifts, when you suddenly realize you have power. Your responsibilities shift. You might not like it, but you have to assess your life with a wholly different set of measurements."

He shook his head. "I don't know what I should do next."

"Come talk to Darien. He'll know."

"I don't think the regent was very impressed by me when we met."

Zoe laughed. "Oh, believe me. He'll be impressed now."

Zoe wanted Rafe to return with them immediately so they could lay the burden of his identity on Darien's broad shoulders, but Rafe declined. "I need to think this through on my own," he said.

"All right, but I'm going to tell him," she said cheerfully. "And then he'll do whatever he decides to do, whether or not that's what you want. Darien can be somewhat high-handed."

"I'm not used to letting someone else make my choices for me," he said.

"No," Zoe agreed. "But you'll find that Darien works around your choices if he thinks it's important enough. He's hard to circumvent."

Rafe held up a hand. "Please. I'm dealing with enough challenges at the moment. I can't think about dealing with the regent, too."

Zoe laughed. "Well, I think things have just gotten very exciting! No wonder you've been showered with extraordinary blessings. You clearly are an extraordinary man."

Finally, *finally*, Zoe and Corene left, but Josetta still had no time to draw Rafe aside for a private conversation. It was practically the dinner hour, so all hands were needed in the kitchen. Even Josetta's. Even Rafe's.

"Do you think Callie will let me carry platters and wash dishes once she learns I'm a prince?" Rafe asked when Callie was out of earshot.

"Well, I'm a princess, and she makes me scrub the floors, so I don't see why not," Josetta responded. "But we can't tell her yet. The more people who know, the more dangerous your life becomes."

"It still seems impossible. That anyone could care if *I* lived or died."

They were chopping vegetables and throwing them into a big pot, a job that seemed endless. Josetta gave Rafe a stern look. "Your brother cares if you live or die. Your stepfather does. *I* care."

"It's not the same thing."

Josetta laid her knife aside, rested her hands on the cutting board, and leaned forward to underscore her words. "You're not a better person just because you have royal blood in your veins. The royalty of Soeche-Tas are *evil*, and I haven't formed the highest opinion of the court at Berringey, either. It's not what you inherit that makes you a worthy person. It's what you do."

She watched him think that over, still dicing onions and tomatoes as if it wasn't possible for his hands to stay idle. "That might be an absolute truth, but it's not a perceived one," he said. "We live in a society where heritage matters. Where what you *are*—down to your elemental blessings—defines how you are viewed." He glanced at her. "Even if I can't claim my birthright—and from the sounds of it, I don't want to! Even so, having it elevates me. Makes me into someone else."

"Do you *want* to be someone else?" she asked softly.

Now, briefly, she saw his hands pause in their ceaseless motion. His eyes lifted to hers again. "I want to be good enough to deserve you," he answered.

She felt her breath tangle in her throat. "I don't require a prince," she said. "Particularly one under a death sentence."

"What *are* you looking for, then?"

They studied each other a long moment in silence. Josetta had never seen Rafe's face so serious; she imagined her own looked much the same. "Someone with joy," she said at last. "Someone with kindness. Someone with purpose. Someone whose existence brings goodness into the world."

"I've never been that person," he said.

"You've never had purpose, I think," she answered. "But I've seen all the rest of those traits in you from the beginning."

He opened his mouth to answer, but Callie bustled into the kitchen. "Twenty people here for dinner already and it's not even firstday!" she exclaimed. "We're going to need a second kettle of soup. And more bread!"

The look on Rafe's face made Josetta laugh out loud. "Better get busy," she advised, grabbing an onion. "These vegetables won't chop themselves."

SEVENTEEN

It was scarcely noon the next day, and Josetta had just finished scrubbing the baths, when Darien arrived. Callie, who came running to fetch Josetta, seemed even more flustered by his appearance than by Zoe's.

"He doesn't look very happy," she said.

"Poor Darien. He often doesn't."

Darien was standing in the main room, his feet apart and his hands linked behind his back—the pose of a man braced to withstand a maelstrom, she had always thought. On his face was his usual expression of purposeful calm.

"I understand you're harboring fugitives," he greeted her.

She laughed and kissed him on the cheek. "I apologize for being dressed in rags, but I wasn't expecting visitors."

"I hope it doesn't sound rude when I say I didn't come here to speak to you. Where is Rafe Adova?"

"He doesn't *live* here, Darien. He has his own quarters southside, but I think he went back to the port this morning to continue training."

That caught Darien off guard. "Training?"

"Zoe didn't tell you? He's signed on with Kayle to learn to fly aeromotives."

She had the satisfaction of seeing Darien briefly speechless. "No. She didn't mention that part."

"So I assume he's at the harbor by now."

"Then that's where I'll go next."

"I'm coming with you. Give me ten minutes to change clothes."

I t was always a luxury to travel with Darien, because he owned the finest vehicles, whether horse-drawn or gas-powered. He had driven southside himself in one of his smaller, sportier smoker cars, which meant he hadn't bothered to bring any guards. But the car had a small back compartment that Foley could fold himself into, so they were soon on their way. Darien drove competently and extremely rapidly until they made it to the crowded streets of the port town, where he had to slow considerably, cursing under his breath.

Josetta remarked, "I've noticed that driving in traffic is one of the few things that makes you lose your temper."

He glanced at her, his face relaxing into a smile. "I hate inefficiency, and poorly regulated traffic is as inefficient as it gets."

"But it doesn't do any good to be angry. It doesn't make the other cars get out of your way. So *that's* a waste of energy, don't you think?"

"The fact that you're right doesn't make me any less irritated."

His irritation wasn't soothed much when they finally made it to the elaymotive factory, found Kayle, and asked to see Rafe Adova.

"He's not here," Kayle said. "He's at another facility."

"Take me to him."

Kayle's blue eyes blinked rapidly behind his lenses. He wasn't sensitive to nuance, but even he couldn't miss the autocratic tone. "Is something wrong?"

"I need to speak with him. You can listen if you like." He glanced fleetingly at Josetta. "I suppose all the primes will need to be informed, no matter how closely we try to contain the information."

"I am hardly a gossip, Darien," Kayle said with dignity.

"Good. Because a life is at stake."

They couldn't all fit in Darien's elaymotive, so Kayle called for another car, and soon enough they were on their way through the dirty, noisy, smelly city. Kayle was a terrible driver, though he did slow down when Josetta cried out as he almost ran over a pedestrian. When they arrived at a large building on the edge of town, Josetta thought she'd never been so relieved to step out of an elaymotive.

"We will need privacy," Darien said as they stepped into a cavernous space cluttered with ropes and pulleys and cylindrical containers. "Is there a place we can talk without being overheard?"

"I have a room in the back," Kayle said. A young man had hurried up to see how he might assist the prime, and Kayle told him, "Bring Rafe Adova to my office, then make sure no one disturbs us."

"I'll wait here," Foley said and stepped just outside the door.

Kayle showed them to a room that was just as cluttered as his office at the factory, though it was smaller, windowless, and had fewer chairs. Kayle, as always, seemed too restless to sit, and Darien too intent, but Josetta found a stool, dropped onto it, and simply waited.

When Rafe stepped inside five minutes later, his face instantly assumed what Josetta considered his gambler's expression—perfectly friendly and perfectly unreadable. He gave each of them a respectful bow, briefly met Josetta's eyes, then turned to face Darien.

"I suppose your wife has told you her discovery," he said. "Have you come to look for more proof?"

"Zoe's word is proof enough," Darien said. "Though I suppose Kayle could corroborate her theory."

"I could if I knew what it was," Kayle said.

Darien nodded at Rafe. "Your new pilot turns out to be related to Prince Ghyaneth of Berringey. From what we are able to piece together, a cousin, and directly in line for the throne."

Kayle looked regretful. "Well, that's bad news. He was a very promising pilot. I suppose now I'll need to find a replacement."

Josetta hid a smile as Darien said in an acid voice, "Indeed, replacements are in order. But that's not the urgent part of this story. The Berringese customarily kill off their close heirs, so there's no untidy scrambling for the throne. If Ghyaneth discovers Rafe's existence, Rafe's life will be forfeit."

Kayle brightened. "So then he might choose to stay on as a pilot after all."

Darien stopped trying to hide his exasperation. "Kayle. At the moment, I'm not concerned with your employment issues. First, I would like to know if you can validate Zoe's claim. And second, I thought we might discuss what we can do to keep Rafe Adova safe."

Kayle looked surprised. "I told him already. He's not from Welce, and neither were his parents. But there's not much else I can tell you."

"Still, that's useful to know," Darien replied.

Rafe spoke up for the first time. "I like the notion of staying safe, but I'm not sure there's much you can do for me as long as Welce has trading agreements with Berringey. Any Berringese merchant might see me on the streets and recognize me at any time."

Kayle looked at him doubtfully. "Really? Now that I study you, I notice something of a resemblance to Ghyaneth, but it's not so pronounced that strangers will gasp out in wonder."

Grinning, Rafe pushed back his hair to display his marked ear. "I believe this is what gave me away the last time someone tried to kill me."

Kayle stepped close enough to study the precise cuts. "Very artistic," he pronounced. "Though a little odd."

Josetta stirred on her stool. "But if no one at the Berringese court knows what Rafe looks like, can't we just disguise him? Perhaps a dollmaker can create a false ear."

"Perfect," Kayle said.

Darien shook his head. "Unfortunately, not perfect. I think once Ghyaneth knows you are alive and living in Welce, he will mount an intense campaign to have you found and brought to him, whether alive or dead. Simple disguises will not deter him for long. And if we as a nation do not aid him in the hunt, he will declare us his enemies and act accordingly."

"Declare war on us?" Kayle scoffed. "Surely you exaggerate."

Darien gave him a cool look. "We essentially are harboring a threat to his crown," he said. "Politically, we are in a tricky position. I do not want to anger the Berringese—but I cannot condone outright murder. We must think through our options and prepare for Berringey's hostility."

Josetta saw Rafe square his shoulders. "I suppose it would be easier for you if I left Welce."

Darien glanced at him. "Probably not. Unless we could prove you had gone somewhere else, Ghyaneth would suspect you were still here, merely in hiding."

"Then I'm not sure what you think I should do next."

Darien nodded. "I confess I haven't arrived at an ideal solution, though I do believe we need to surround you with soldiers, which means placing you in more defensible living quarters. But where? The palace is too obvious a choice, as is my house. We need a more out-of-the-way location."

"You could go to your stepfather's farm," Josetta said.

Rafe shook his head. "And bring trouble down on the heads of everyone who lives there? I don't think so."

"I was thinking a homestead of one of the primes," Darien said. "Zoe's house by the river, or Mirti's place in the woods. Not only are there plenty of guards on hand, but there is also some value in being under a prime's protection."

Josetta grinned. "Zoe could call up floodwaters to wash away anyone trying to kill Rafe."

"Exactly," Darien said. "And Mirti could topple trees onto an assassin's head."

"But—how long would you expect me to stay someplace like that?" Rafe asked. "Because I'll go mad if I'm buried away in the countryside."

"You might have to stay for some considerable length of time," Darien admitted.

"I have a better idea," Kayle said, his blue eyes sparkling. "Hide him here in an areomotive facility! No one would expect a royal heir to be training to fly. And *I* am a prime! He would be under my protection."

Rafe and Josetta laughed, though Darien did not appear amused. "I would value your advice, Kayle, if it didn't appear to be so drenched in self-interest."

"He might be right, though," Josetta said. "Ghyaneth seems the type who would think it was *much* more likely for royalty to seek shelter in the homes of the primes and the Five Families."

Darien frowned. "But surely we all agree that we cannot leave Rafe undefended. And if he is trailed by five or six guards wherever he goes, even if it's just to an aeromotive factory, someone will eventually notice."

"Then don't put me under guard," Rafe said. "I've survived up till now on my own."

Darien gave him a long, considering look. "Perhaps you have," he said. "But since you have now become my responsibility, it is unthinkable that I allow you to take such risks."

"I didn't ask to become your responsibility," Rafe replied quietly. "You can take me off your list."

Darien's voice was equally soft. "It is not for anyone but me to determine where my duties lie. You have become one of them, and I do not shirk my duty."

"Don't argue with him," Josetta advised Rafe. "You won't win."

Rafe threw his hands in the air. "Well, it seems like an impossible situation! I see no easy solution."

"If you would consider—" Darien began, but he stopped abruptly when the door flew open after the most perfunctory knock.

"This *is* where you're hiding," Nelson Ardelay said as he stepped inside and looked around disparagingly. "What an ugly room! I hope you don't spend much time here."

It was typical of Kayle to be immediately distracted from the issue at hand. "No, I'm rarely in my office at all," he replied. "Usually only when there's some kind of math I need to puzzle out."

"I'd be so full of despair I wouldn't be able to do sums."

"Arithmetic usually fills me with despair," Kayle agreed. He cocked his head. "Was I expecting you?"

"You were expecting me at the *factory*," Nelson said with exaggerated patience. "Where I was told you'd come *here* for the day. So, since I drove all the way from Chialto, I thought I'd track you down." The big, burly redhead put his hands on his hips, glanced around at the assembled company, and drew the obvious conclusion. "I suppose I'm interrupting something. My apologies."

Josetta stood up so she could kiss him on the cheek, a salute he returned with enthusiasm. There was always something bracing about Nelson's mere presence; it instantly made her feel more cheerful. "Hello, Uncle."

Darien, speaking more to the point, said, "You are, but your insights might be useful, so you may as well stay."

Nelson nodded in Rafe's direction. "I don't think I'm acquainted with this fellow."

"No, and despite his unassuming appearance, he's causing us all kinds of trouble," Darien said with a trace of humor. "Rafe, Nelson

Ardelay. The sweela prime. Nelson, this is Rafe Adova. Who is—" Darien's voice trailed off as he assessed the look on Nelson's face. The sweela prime was focused, frowning, and just a bit bewildered. "Ah. Perhaps you already know."

Nelson shook his head. "Usually I can get a sense of a person, if I'm standing close enough. I can pick up strong emotions and recognize thought patterns. But he's a blank to me."

"See? That's what I said," Kayle interjected. "Well, I said I couldn't hear him breathing, but it's practically the same thing."

Nelson sent an inquiring look in Darien's direction. "I didn't have much luck reading the Berringese delegation, either, though it was easy enough to tell what Ghyaneth was thinking most of the time." He nodded at Rafe again. "There's something about him that reeks of Berringey. Is that what you want me to notice?"

"Exactly," Darien said. "Zoe says he's close kin to Ghyaneth— most likely a cousin."

Nelson looked impressed. "Really! But didn't—" Now he frowned. "Didn't Ghyaneth say that he'd killed off all his cousins except one?" He pointed at Rafe. "So why is this one still alive? Did he run away?"

"As always, I appreciate your quick wits, Nelson," Darien said. "But it appears to be slightly more complicated. We believe his mother stole away with him when *she* realized his eventual fate. She died before telling Rafe his true story—which Rafe might never have learned if Zoe hadn't happened to meet him."

"Exciting," Nelson commented. "But something of a dilemma for you. Ghyaneth seems like the type to make a big fuss over Welce giving sanctuary to his enemies. Though I don't think you should hand him over to be executed."

By Darien's faint smile, Josetta guessed he was again pleased at how quickly Nelson had put the pieces together. "Right on all counts. We were just debating the best way to keep him safe without drawing attention to him."

Nelson ran a hand through his graying red hair. "You could send him to my place. It's remote enough."

"It's kind of you to offer," Rafe spoke up. "If the danger was immediate and short-term, I'd take you up on it. But for the rest of my life? I don't think I could bear it."

Nelson had cocked his head again, listening to the cadence of Rafe's words. "Now there. When you speak. I can hear Ghyaneth in your voice."

"They don't sound anything alike," Josetta protested. "Ghyaneth's voice is so much lighter, and he only spoke to us in Coziquela. Rafe talks Welchin like a native."

Nelson shook his head. "It's not the words. Not the timbre of their voices. It's the way their words reveal their thoughts. I can't explain it."

"We stray from the point," Darien said. "Which is: How do we keep Rafe Adova secure?"

"You don't want to assign a few guards to him? It seems the obvious solution," Nelson said.

Kayle waved a hand. "Darien thinks they'll only draw attention to him. Though no one ever notices guards, do they? *I* don't."

"Disguise the guards as pilots or workers in Kayle's factories," Josetta suggested.

Nelson glanced between them. "There's a reason Rafe Adova is spending his time in Kayle's factory?"

"He's training to be a pilot," Darien said dryly. When Nelson looked incredulous, he added, "Exactly."

"I don't want a bunch of royal guards pretending to be mechanics," Kayle said. "They'll only get in the way."

"I have a better solution," Nelson said. His eyes were sparkling as he pointed at Josetta, and she had a sudden foreboding. *I can pick up strong emotions,* he had just said. What had he picked up from her?

"Say there's been some threat against the princess," Nelson went on. "Assign a detail of guards to follow her everywhere. Then make sure Rafe Adova is always near Josetta. The guards will be watching *him*, though they seem to be watching *her*."

"I like that," Kayle approved. "It's elegant."

Nelson, Darien, and Rafe were all gazing at Josetta with varying degrees of speculation. "It might do for the short-term," Darien said. "But it would require Josetta and Rafe to become practically inseparable."

"Oh, I don't imagine either one of them would object to that," Nelson said affably. "I mean, if it saves his *life*."

Josetta was fiercely telling herself not to blush, but nonetheless she could feel the heat rising to her cheeks. "It might require us to change our schedules a little," she said, trying to speak coolly. "Rafe's been helping at the shelter now and then, usually on firstday, but he's in training most of the time."

"So he helps more and trains less," Nelson said. "Not a major obstacle."

Rafe seemed to be fighting amusement more than embarrassment. "And you did say you planned to watch my test flights," he reminded her. "You could tell everyone you've become obsessed by the aeromotives. You wouldn't necessarily be obsessed by *me*."

"Perhaps you could undergo some training of your own," Kayle suggested. "An elay girl! The perfect candidate!" He eyed her critically. "And you weigh so much less than most of my pilots. That would be another point in your favor."

Now she had to suppress the urge to succumb to hysterical laughter. "I don't want to fly, thank you very much," she said. "I'm afraid of your crazy machines."

"They're not crazy. When they're perfected, you'll be amazed at how exquisite they are. In fact, the new LNR—"

"Kayle." Darien cut him off. "That's a discussion for another time. I think Nelson's suggestion is a good one, if all parties agree."

"I'm not opposed, but where will we *put* all these guards you want to have trailing around after me?" Josetta said. "As it is, I scarcely have room for Caze and Sorbin—and Foley, don't forget him!"

"Zoe told me you were in the process of renting new quarters," Darien said, brushing this off. "The larger question is if you are willing to subordinate your schedule to Rafe's. It will require both of you to make some sacrifices."

Rafe offered a modest bow in Josetta's direction. "None of those sacrifices weigh with me," he said.

"Yes—of course—I want to do my part to keep him safe," she said. "It's just—but yes. I'm willing."

"It's just a temporary measure," Nelson said, grinning. He appeared to be enjoying himself hugely. "I'm sure we'll come up with a better solution eventually."

Darien glanced at Josetta. "Of course, this means you must bring him with you to court functions. He must attend you when the empress of Malinqua visits. You might want to construct an identity for him that renders his presence believable."

She gave him back a limpid stare. "I thought I had become obsessed with aeromotive pilots?" she said. "You don't think that's explanation enough?"

"Oh, and people *do*," Kayle exclaimed. "Arven *constantly* has women throwing themselves at him, showing up naked in his rooms, that sort of thing. You remember Arven, Rafe, he was the one who just crashed."

"Thereby making many ladies very sad, I'm sure," Darien said.

"He didn't die," Kayle assured them. "He'll be flying again in a few ninedays."

"I think 'aeromotive pilot' is identity enough," Nelson decided. "Some people will find him fascinating and others will find him repellent, but that doesn't matter."

"I think it would matter to me if people found me repellent," Kayle said.

Nelson pursed his lips and didn't answer. Darien hid a smile and said, "The final thing to determine. Who should know?"

"The primes, obviously," Nelson said. "Elidon, if you like. But I wouldn't think the other queens should be burdened with this knowledge." He glanced at Josetta. "Sorry, my dear, but your mother is a little too melodramatic to be trusted with a state secret."

"I agree with all my heart."

"Then I say, don't tell anyone unless there's some compelling reason to do so," Nelson said.

"That tallies with my inclination," Darien said. He glanced at the four others in the room, his gray eyes full of stern purpose. "Then I can trust all of you to speak of this to no one else? Not your siblings and heirs, not your friends?"

They all quickly agreed, though Josetta reflected that most of *her* family members already knew the truth. She would scarcely need to be keeping secrets at all.

"Then the next order of business is assigning guards and putting Rafe under their protection," Darien said. "Rafe and Josetta, will you return with me to Chialto, where I can organize a detail?"

Rafe hesitated, and Josetta saw him glance with longing toward the training facility on the other side of the door. "I will, of course, but—I had hoped to get in a few hours of work today."

"He needs the practice," Kayle said. "I'd like to try the LNR sometime during the next nineday, and he's not ready yet."

"Still, since our chief goal, we have all decided, is Rafe's safety—"

"Let him stay here today. I'll stay. Foley will stay," Josetta interrupted. "Send your guards straight to this facility. Even better, detour past the shelter and tell Caze and Sorbin to meet us here. He'll have a full detail in place by tomorrow morning."

Darien gazed at her a moment. "And you're prepared to spend the night here at the port, awaiting their arrival?"

She couldn't help laughing at him. "I believe I am."

He turned his hands palm upward, a rare gesture of concession from a man who never admitted defeat. "Then I suppose we have our plan."

It was a stranger day than Josetta had expected it to be when she woke up that morning, but—now that she thought about it—she could have said the same about many of the days that had included Rafe Adova.

Darien left almost immediately after they reached their decision. The two primes disappeared to talk business, leaving Josetta with little to do except watch Rafe's training exercises when they seemed interesting and talk quietly with Foley when they didn't.

"Darien's discovered something exciting about Rafe Adova, but I'm not allowed to share details," she told him as they sat together outside the training facility. It was late afternoon and the sun was low enough that the temperature was actually pleasant. "I need your help, though."

Foley nodded; of course he would help her. She went on, "It turns out the prince of Berringey might want to kill him. So Darien is assigning royal guards to protect him—but we don't want to draw attention to him. So the guards will follow me as if *I'm* in danger, and *I'll* follow Rafe like I'm a lovesick girl. They'll seem to be watching me, but they'll really be protecting him."

Foley glanced down at her. "I don't see any reason we can't protect both of you."

She smiled, then sighed. "In any case, we're going to be spending a lot of time at the port while I pretend I've fallen in love with an aeromotive pilot."

Foley's gaze dropped briefly to her fish bracelet before he lifted his eyes to hers again. "Will you really be pretending?"

She hadn't even realized he knew Rafe had given her the bracelet. They watched each other in silence for a long moment. "Maybe not," she said at last. "What would you think about that?"

"I'd think it was about time."

She was surprised into a laugh. "Really? Why?"

He seemed to consider how much to say. "I think you have led an extraordinary existence, which has made it difficult for you to have ordinary experiences. This seems to be one of the experiences you should have."

She nodded slowly. "I could say the same thing to you. What kind of life have *you* led, nothing more than a shadow of mine? Where is *your* lover, *your* house and family?"

"So far I haven't had a desire for those things," he answered. "Maybe one day that will change. But so far all I've ever needed in my life is purpose, and that's what I found when I came to Chialto to join the royal guard."

"It doesn't seem like it would be enough," she said.

"To me it's everything," he said.

She nodded again and leaned back against the sun-warmed factory wall, no longer meeting his eyes. "You know more about me than anyone else does, just because you're with me so much," she said. "And now—when I spend so much time with Rafe—you might learn other things. You might see me do things you don't approve of."

She heard the shadow of a laugh in his voice. "Then I'll look the other way. All that matters to me is that you're safe. The rest of it is none of my concern."

"From now on, keep both of us safe," she answered softly. "Guard him as you have guarded me."

"Majesty, I will."

. . .

Once the long day of training was over, they returned to the heart of the port city to find that the wayward Kayle had been unexpectedly efficient. He had commissioned Darby to find rooms for Josetta across the hall from Rafe's and to clear out nearby apartments for the guards. In fact, Caze and Sorbin were already installed, and once Josetta showed up, they hauled an assortment of boxes and bags from their room to hers.

"Callie packed almost everything you own," Caze told her.

"But I'll be back at the shelter for part of every nineday. We both will be."

"She figured you could sort out what you want to have where."

Josetta sighed and began hanging up rumpled tunics and arranging her toiletries. *Is this my fifth home? I'm losing count,* she thought. *Maybe I should buy a house of my own and stay there all the time. I won't visit anyone else. I might never even step outside the front door.*

But not yet. Her life was not designed to allow her to disappear.

Rafe knocked on the open door as she was smoothing the wrinkles from the last pair of trousers. "Looks just like my room," he remarked as he stepped inside. "Given how utilitarian Kayle's factories are, I was surprised at how comfortable the furnished quarters are. And I love the little touches of elegance." He pointed at one of the corners where the walls met the high ceiling. "You have butterflies painted on your walls. I have birds. Every time I look at them I smile."

"Sweela people are the hedonists who love rich luxuries, but elay folks require a certain kind of beauty in their living spaces," Josetta admitted. "Pleasing proportions. Restful colors. Sunlight. Their rooms might be austere, but they're always tranquil."

"I guess I haven't lived up to my blessings, then," he replied. "My living quarters were never what you'd call extraordinary."

"Maybe you should buy a lot of clocks," she suggested. "Though I honestly can't figure out how you'd represent triumph or synthesis."

"Melt a bunch of things together," he said promptly. "Metal and glass and oddments from the street. Turn them into little sculptures. Trophies. You know, the sort of thing you'd take home if you won a competition."

"Oh, yes. The perfect décor."

They were all hungry, so Rafe led Josetta and the guards to a commercial district that looked like a miniature version of the Plazas in Chialto—an open space where dozens of vendors had crammed booths selling everything from food to clothing.

"I could shop here in the morning," Josetta said. "I need more tunics. More everything."

"You could," Rafe said with a grin, "except I'm leaving pretty early to go back to the training facility."

She stifled a groan. "Then I guess I'll make do with what I have."

Back at Rafe's apartment, the five of them crowded around a small table and passed food around with a cheerful disregard for social standing. Caze, always the most talkative of the guards, didn't bother hiding his curiosity.

"The regent wants you watched by six men at all times," he noted. "Even *he* doesn't usually bother with that many guards when he goes out."

"Seems like I overheard something one night when I was gambling with the wrong people," Rafe said.

"Is that why those men were after you that night we found you? You knew something?"

"I suppose. But it took me a while to piece it together."

"It must be some pretty dangerous information," Sorbin observed.

Caze looked a little self-important. "It's up to us to make sure it's not *too* dangerous."

The soldiers ate fast and were on their feet as soon as the meal was over. "We'll keep a watch all night," Caze explained. "One in the hallway, the others close enough to rouse with a yell. Unless you want someone in the room with you."

Rafe looked horrified. "In the hallway is close enough."

Josetta made no move to stand up. "I'll stay awhile," she said casually. "Play a few hands of penta, maybe."

Foley gave her the smallest, briefest smile, then followed the other two out the door.

"Men in the *hallway* all night?" Rafe exclaimed in a low voice, locking the door and turning back to Josetta. "So much for my visions of sneaking into your room after everyone else was asleep."

She laughed. "We should have asked Kayle to give us adjoining chambers. Maybe with a connecting door."

Rafe looked at her a moment. "I was joking."

She smiled. "But I'm obsessed with you, remember?"

"A convenient fiction."

"Not so convenient," she said. *Not so fictional.*

He made a helpless gesture. "I know. You have to completely rearrange your life to accommodate me. I'm sorry for it."

"Well, it won't all be about your schedule, remember? Some of the time we both have to spend at the shelter. There's too much work there and I've neglected it so much lately."

"Callie must feel like you've abandoned her."

"Callie likes being in charge, I think. But there are decisions only I can make."

They cleared away the dishes, then seated themselves back at the small table. Rafe produced a deck of cards and suggested, "Penta?"

"Gladly. What kind of stakes?"

He intercut the cards over and over before answering. "I think the last time just the two of us played the stakes were pretty high."

"Dinner," she said, "or a kiss."

"Many dinners," he corrected, "one real kiss."

"Well, it seems pointless to bet for meals at this juncture," she said with a laugh, "since it looks like we'll be having most of them together."

"Then you need to place a different wager."

She gave him an inquiring look. "You don't plan to change your own?"

He shook his head, smiling. His hands never paused in their fluid motions.

"Maybe my stakes are the same as yours," she said.

That did cause him to grow still. Not just his hands—his whole body, his eyes, his breath. Completely stopped. He watched her, and the silence that ran between them crackled with heat.

She was the one to speak first. "You can hardly be surprised to hear that I like you, Rafe Adova," she said. "And stop asking me why."

"You're a princess."

"You're royalty yourself."

"Not royalty with a future."

She shrugged. "You intrigued me long before I knew you were heir to a throne," she said. "It's not your sudden elevation that has made me admire you."

"Maybe not," he said. "But it's made me feel more worthy of you. If only a little bit. Made me bolder."

She raised her eyebrows. "Bold? You don't seem to be anything of the sort."

He tilted his head back and stared at her for a long moment out of narrowed eyes. "For an elay girl," he said at last, "you certainly like to play with fire."

"My father was sweela," she retorted. She could feel herself smiling. "So I'm not afraid of flame."

"Maybe you would be," he said, "if you had any sense."

That made her laugh. Keeping her eyes on his, she flattened her hands and pushed herself to a standing position. Trailing her fingers along the edges of the table, as if she needed contact with something solid just to keep her balance, she circled around till she was standing right next to him, her knees touching his thigh. Then she bent and kissed him.

He didn't move, either to pull her closer or to push her away. His mouth returned the pressure of hers with a sort of guilty hunger, as if he had promised himself he would forgo all sustenance but he could not deny himself this one forbidden treat. She lifted a hand to touch his cheekbone, touch his jaw, run her fingers lightly down his throat to settle on his shoulder. His skin was hot as a sweela man's; she felt his blood running riot just under his skin.

When she straightened up, she left her hand on his shoulder just to hold steady. She felt dizzy enough to fall. "We didn't even play penta," she murmured, "and yet here we are, collecting on our bets."

He gazed up at her, somber as a man delivering news of death. "You might want to be careful," he said, "about how you play this particular game. You're gambling on my honor, but I've been known to cheat when the stakes were high enough. And I'll wager that this is another contest where I have more experience than you do."

"I'm sure you do," she said. "Maybe that's why I want you to teach me how to play."

"Maybe you need to think about it a little longer before you make that kind of bet."

She couldn't help it; she rolled her eyes and flung both hands in the air. "You're so exasperating!" she exclaimed. "Everything Alys said always made me think it would be easy to seduce a man."

His grin was a little shaky. "Maybe she picked a different kind of man."

"Well, one of them was Darien, and *he's* not easy to influence."

She was genuinely put out, which seemed to amuse him. At any rate, he seemed more sure of himself as he finally came to his feet. "Maybe he wasn't worried about the harm he might do to her by accepting her offer," he suggested.

"Darien worries about everything," she said in a grumpy voice, which made him laugh out loud. She felt a reluctant smile tug at her mouth. "But I suppose I should be grateful that you don't want to take advantage of—of the strange circumstances that have thrown us together."

"And will keep us together for the foreseeable future," he agreed. "You don't want to cross some line with me, and then regret it, and then be forced to smile and flirt and pretend you are enamored of me when you'd rather see me thrown in the Marisi and drowned."

She pretended to be much struck by this insight. "You're right! How could I have been so stupid! And it's not like I've spent any time with you in the past few ninedays—it's not like I have any sense of your personality *at all*. I could so easily be mistaken about you!"

"Happens more often than you might expect," he said, edging her toward the exit. "Now. Maybe you should seek your own room for the night and spend some time thinking about what you really want."

She allowed him to herd her toward the door, but before he could open it, she turned and placed one hand against his heart. "For what it's worth, this is all Nelson's doing," she said. "Remember what he said? How he can sense strong feelings? The sweela prime thinks we care about each other." She leaned in and kissed him again, quickly this time. "And he approves."

She opened the door and left him standing behind her, speechless.

EIGHTEEN

Though he had urged circumspection on her, Rafe was bitterly disappointed, the next four nights, to find that Josetta intended to exercise it. Oh, she left her apartment every morning when he left his, dutifully followed him to factory floor or training facility, shared dinner with him—and the guards—and lingered long enough to play a hand of penta or to talk over the events of the day. But she never again unsettled him with teasing kisses or half-articulated promises or even sideways, speculative smiles. He was left to wonder if he'd offended her or frightened her or mortified her so much she would never make the same overture to him again—and to curse himself for not taking her up on the offer when he'd had the chance.

It had seemed like the right thing to do. The honorable thing. But honor was vastly overrated late at night as he lay awake in his solitary bed, imagining what he could be doing instead.

During the daytime hours, training at least provided a distraction. His body had adjusted to the physical workouts, so most of the soreness was gone, and he could feel his arms gaining strength and flexibility. He had become adept at using the mock pilot's box, smoothly managing takeoffs and landings and the occasional rush of simulated bad weather. He wasn't sure what else he could do to prepare himself for actual flight—and when, near the end of that nineday, he said so to Kayle, the prime agreed.

"The LNR will be ready in a few days. I want you to take her up," Kayle said. "Secondday—thirdday at the latest. Are you ready?"

"I think I am."

So that was cause to celebrate with a bottle of really bad wine purchased from a street vendor. Josetta even presented him with a congratulatory gift—a pair of leather gloves and a jacket to help ward off the chill of altitude and the wind of passage.

"And I have a second present," she said, handing over a small packet. Ruins of dinner littered the table that sat between them; she hadn't even gotten close enough to touch his arm. "I thought you should have something elay with you since you are going to be defying the element of air."

Inside the packet he found three slim rings stamped with blessing glyphs. He still couldn't identify them by sight, but he could make a pretty good guess. "Yours?" he said. "Beauty and grace and joy?"

She nodded. "I thought you could wear them with all the others."

He instantly unfastened his silver chain and slipped the new rings on alongside Corene's blessings and his own extraordinary ones. It was fanciful, of course, but these three seemed to make the necklace lighter, not heavier, as if they really were made of air.

"Now I feel safe enough to fly," he said.

"Are you afraid?"

He thought it over. "I'd have to be a fool not to be nervous. It's a dangerous pastime, and so many things could go wrong. But I'm not actually afraid. Excited instead. I can't wait." He laughed. "So maybe I *am* a fool."

"Maybe you have merely found your calling."

B efore Rafe could take the LNR out for its first flight, they returned to the Chialto slums, where Josetta buried herself in work at the shelter. She seemed to be overwhelmed with all the details she needed to take care of, from finalizing the rental deal with the tailor to reconciling accounts for the existing building.

"There's no help for it," Rafe heard her tell Callie one day. He was sweeping the main room and the women were in the kitchen, but he could catch every word. "You're going to have to take over the book-keeping. I've been gone too much."

"It doesn't seem right for me to choose how to spend your money."

"Are you warning me that you might cheat me?" Josetta scoffed. "You, the woman whose blessings are loyalty, honor, and honesty?"

"Those might be my blessings, but I never lived up to them until I met you."

"Well, if you won't help me out, I won't have any blessings. I'll only have curses. Exhaustion and despair and lunacy. *Please* say you'll handle the money like you handle everything else."

Callie sounded like she was trying not to laugh. "Well, I will, but I'll tally everything down to the last quint-copper."

"Excellent. I know I can count on you."

Of course, there was even less privacy at the shelter than there was at the rental unit in the port. The new building wasn't ready to hold beds yet, so *everyone* was sleeping at the shelter—Josetta, Rafe, Foley, Callie, Bo, the six guards, and the couple dozen lost souls who had found their way to this safe haven and showed not the slightest inclination to leave. Rafe thought longingly of his room over Samson's tavern, but of course he couldn't spend the night there unless Josetta (and the guards) accompanied him, and he couldn't bear to put her through that inconvenience. So he unrolled a mat under one of the dining room tables and spent an uncomfortable few nights listening to strangers around him breathing in the dark.

Rafe felt a little bad about how happy he was when it came time to return to the port.

And then how close to ecstasy he felt when it came time to fly.

They practically required a caravan to travel from the port out to the giant facility where the aeromotives were housed. Kayle, Josetta, Rafe, Foley, Caze, Sorbin, a couple of Kayle's mechanics, and the four other guards required three smoker cars between them. The day was clear and sunny—cool enough at this early hour, but bound to heat up to oppressive temperatures once the sun edged past noon. Rafe was wearing a thin silk overshirt for the drive, but his leather jacket and gloves lay on the seat beside him, and he was already dressed in leather trousers and thick boots. Ready to fly face-first into a punishing wind.

Rafe and Josetta were mostly silent during the trip, but Kayle, who was behind the wheel and driving with his usual disregard for safety, talked incessantly. Rafe supposed that the elay prime was, in his own way, as nervous as Rafe, and this was how he showed it.

When they arrived, the mammoth doors had already been pushed back, but the slim silver bird was still inside the hangar. A crowd of about thirty people had already gathered outside, and they raised a quiet cheer when Rafe stepped out of the elaymotive. He waved and grinned in their direction, then pumped his fist in a gesture of victory. He wasn't displaying the kind of arrogance Arven had shown, not really; he just had to do something to relieve the tension gathering in his shoulders.

"Josetta, you wait out here with the others," Kayle instructed. "If they move back from the roadway, *you* move. There is always some danger that the craft will fall from the sky, but if you follow the others, you should be safe."

She gave him one expressive look. "Even if that's true, you shouldn't say so! Not right now!"

Kayle looked surprised. "But you *will* be safe."

"No! That the aeromotive might fall!"

"But it might."

She shook her head and turned to Rafe. "Is this my last chance to wish you luck, or will I see you again before you take off?"

"You'll see me, but not to say anything."

"Then good luck," she said. She put her hand behind his head and pulled him down to press her mouth to his. When she pulled back, she was smiling. "An elay kiss for an elay venture."

Kayle wore an arrested expression as he divided a look between them. "Well, that ought to keep you aloft," he said. "Come along."

Rafe gave Josetta one last sober glance before he followed Kayle across the paved entranceway into the cool dark of the hangar. There were maybe ten or twelve staffers in there, calling out numbers, checking fuel lines, checking rivets, checking struts. One—an elay woman with long silver-blond hair—merely stood at the front of the craft, rubbing her hands along its pointed nose and whispering to it as if reminding a fractious child that it had to behave nicely on a grand occasion. Rafe felt the skin prickle on the back of his neck, wondering if the machine might actually hear and understand her.

Finally, the chief mechanic approached Kayle. "Everything's in order. The LNR is ready for takeoff."

"Then let's move it out."

The workers positioned themselves behind the wheels and along the wings, cursing and grunting as they strained to budge the machine from its stationary position. Slowly, with the ungainly motion of a sea creature waddling across land, the slim silver craft creaked forward, gaining a little momentum as it crossed from the bottomless shadows of the hangar into the hard shellac of daylight.

The onlookers outside cheered again, more loudly. Rafe, strolling along beside the aeromotive—again, just like Arven—shot a quick look in their direction. Yes, there was Josetta, at the very forefront of the crowd, clapping and cheering like everyone else. He gave her a private smile and a quick wave and continued walking along at the LNR's maddeningly slow pace.

"Here! Turn!" the chief mechanic called out, and the workers shifted their grips enough to adjust the machine's trajectory. The goal, as Rafe could plainly see, was to line it up perfectly with the long, straight section of roadway. A few more shouts, a few more oaths, and the LNR was in position and at rest.

Kayle turned to Rafe and shook his hand. "Fly far and fast, and safely return."

"Thank you. I will."

He climbed into the pilot's box and settled into the padded seat. The space was so familiar from all the hours spent in training that Rafe felt some of his tension melt and his confidence ratchet up. He pulled out a silk scarf—another gift from Josetta—and wrapped it around his face, then nodded down at the mechanics. A moment later, he felt the great machine purr to life beneath him, trembling with a barely suppressed eagerness to be set free.

"And—she's—yours!" the mechanic bawled. There was a whirl of bodies at ground level as Kayle and the workers dashed for safety. Rafe waited long enough to be sure they were all clear, and then he slowly twisted the dial that would feed the machine more fuel.

Its purr grew louder and its trembling more pronounced. A harder pull, a quicker response, and in minutes he was *hurtling* down the roadway, faster than any elaymotive, jouncing along more roughly than he'd expected, but it didn't matter. Faster now and then even faster—top land speed. He gripped the altitude lever and pulled it toward his chest.

And all the rattling and bumping smoothed away as the LNR lifted cleanly into the air. Two feet—ten feet—twenty feet—a hundred, on a perfectly calculated angle. The land dropped farther below him, and the sun stooped closer to take a look. Higher. Straight into the untouched blue.

Simulated training was *nothing* like flying.

Oh, the hours in the practice box had taught him where to place his hands, how to compensate for the sudden quick shifts of wind; he didn't even have to think about it to correctly adjust the angle of his wings when a stiff breeze tilted him unexpectedly to the left. The rehearsal had even taught him how to adapt his body to the constant dizzying changes in height and speed, how to keep his sense of focus and direction, how to ride out the buffeting winds.

But it hadn't prepared him for the exhilarating way the air tore at his face as it raced by, hardly screened out at all by the scarf. It hadn't prepared him for the unbelievably fresh taste of the cold air, as chill and delicious as starlight. It hadn't prepared him for the assault on his senses, the almost battering effect of the rumbling motor and the shrieking wind.

It hadn't prepared him for the elation. He felt drunk with euphoria, light-headed with delight. *It might be altitude sickness,* he warned himself, keeping one hand on the lever that would bring him closer to the ground. He had leveled out at about a thousand feet up, though he was pretty sure the LNR could go higher. Indeed, it seemed to chafe under his restraint like a restive horse eager to break into a gallop. He had the thought that if he lifted his hands from the controls, it would point its nose upward and just keep going.

Those are crazy thoughts, he said sternly. *It's not alive. You're in control. You must think quickly and clearly or you'll crash and die.*

Those were never thoughts he'd had in the training facility, either.

He forced himself to focus, to concentrate, to shut down his sense of wonder and call up a sense of clinical detachment. He had traveled maybe a mile from the hangar in this short time; within another ten minutes, he thought, he would be able to see the ocean. Kayle hadn't thought he would get that far, but if he did, he was supposed to make a hard turn and follow the shoreline.

Bad enough to come down over land, Kayle had said with his usual bluntness. *But you certainly don't want to land in water. I can't imagine you'd survive.*

Shielding his face with one hand, Rafe peered over the side, trying to see any landmarks. But he was over open country, all green and brown in gentle hills and flat stretches of vegetation; not even a road or a pocket of civilization to give him any hints of his location. He knew by the placement of the sun that he was still heading south, though, and he had to think that any moment—

There it was! The great dark bruise of the ocean, spilling over the horizon ahead of him, eating up more and more of the skyline as he made his rapid approach. Rafe muttered under his breath as he fought to turn the craft west, using both hands to pull on the controls that would tilt his right wing downward and enable him to pivot. The machine fought him, bucking against the energetic wind blowing off the sea. Rafe tasted the salt air and wondered briefly if the heavy humidity this close to the ocean could clog his fuel lines this quickly. He was close enough to the shoreline that he could see the waves foaming against the sand; another minute and he would be over the water.

He came to his feet and pulled the lever with all his weight, and the LNR made a slow, graceful curve to the right, losing a little altitude as it did. Rafe kicked the throttle open and lifted its nose again, and it climbed back to a more comfortable height. But he found it harder to keep the craft steady as they hugged the coastline, cutting across all the vagrant breezes that rolled in off the ocean. Rafe glanced down to gauge how close he was to the water, and saw the shadow of the aeromotive sliding along the ruffled surface of the sea.

Impossible but true. He was flying.

He followed the coastline for another mile, but it was hard work. The wind was so strong that it constantly rocked the aeromotive, and the repeated pulling on recalcitrant levers was rubbing his hands raw, even through the leather gloves. He had lost altitude again and was having a harder time regaining it, and his fuel gauge was hovering at the halfway mark. Time to head for home.

The aircraft acquiesced more courteously this time when he asked it to turn. At first they had the sea wind at their backs, pushing them along even faster, but that died off within a half mile. In fact, the air was so calm, the sky was so clear, and the aeromotive was so responsive that Rafe had almost relaxed into the smug exuberance of a successful flight when the motor failed and the world grew silent and the LNR began to fall toward the earth.

Rafe had a single blank moment of absolute terror before he remembered that he had practiced this moment a hundred times. He worked the fuel pump and hauled on the controls, hoping to reignite the engine, while desperately seeking to catch any errant winds that might help him glide down instead of plummeting. With a sudden roar, the motor growled to life; Rafe's head was slammed against the back of the seat by the pressure of acceleration. Relief and euphoria flooded his veins, and he instantly tilted the craft skyward again, hoping to make up for lost altitude. A glance at his gauge showed that the maneuver had gulped down a good portion of his remaining fuel. He needed to get back to base, and without any more detours.

He was still on high alert, the adrenaline singing in his ears, so this time he caught the first warning sounds of impending disaster—a cough and stutter in the steady chugging of the engine. His hands were already on the throttle, throwing it wide open, his foot jammed on the fuel pump. Almost immediately, the engine caught again, and the craft surged forward with renewed energy.

But Rafe had a sense of cold certainty that he was on borrowed time. The LNR was struggling. He didn't know how much longer it could stay aloft or how many more times he could coax it into restarting in midair. He had thought to keep the craft as high as he could, to give himself more time to recover if the engine failed again, but now he realized he'd better start looking for a landing spot and bring the LNR down as soon as he had a clear, straight stretch of road. While he actually had the power to direct it.

Accordingly, he canted to the right, edging eastward, hoping to intersect the main road some distance from the hangar. Hoping there was no other traffic between the port and the assembly building. Hoping the LNR had another mile in it at least, maybe two . . .

Twice more the engine shuddered and fell still, and twice more Rafe was able to flood the fuel lines and spark it into life again. By now he was sweating with heat and effort and fear; his scarf had unraveled from around his face, and his skin was burning from a combination of wind and sun. The glare was bright enough that he was having trouble seeing, and he had lost all sense of time and distance. All he knew was sound—that choke and gurgle in the engine's full-throated roar—and altitude. Which was lower. And lower. And lower.

He was actually astonished when two landmarks appeared on the horizon simultaneously—the long dark ribbon of the paved roadway, and the hunched silhouette of the hangar. He'd traveled farther than he'd thought, or faster. He was within sight of haven. He felt his heart lift with hope, and the aircraft's nose lifted with him.

Then the craft fell ominously silent as the engine cut out again. Rafe stomped on the fuel pump and saw his gauge spin to zero. He was too low to hope the engine would catch in time to power the LNR upward again—too high to hope he would land in anything less spectacular than calamity. Probably didn't have to worry about fire, though, since there wasn't anything left to burst into flames. So Josetta wouldn't have to stand there and watch him burn to death—

Josetta—

Knowing it would do no good, he jumped on the fuel pump with the full weight of his body, hauled maniacally on the gears, trying to get the slightest bit of lift, just enough power to cruise those final yards. But the LNR, which had seemed so sentient before, was nothing now but a lifeless metal coffin careening toward land. Rafe felt like his head was about to detach from his body from the force of the rapid descent. He wrapped his hands around his chain of blessings and prepared for catastrophic impact.

Then a mighty force slammed against the LNR and hurled it sideways, lifting it a hundred feet in the air and spinning it like a leaf. Rafe loosed an inarticulate shout and grabbed the steering mechanism, trying grimly to avoid being pitched over the side. Now the craft was flung in the opposite direction, rocked on a furious wind. Rafe's head smashed against the wheel, against the back of the seat, against the metal sidewall. He was too dizzy and jostled to operate the controls, to try with levers and rudders to steer into the gale that had swept in to keep him aloft. He merely held on grimly as he was thrown from side to side, shaken like a child's toy, then dumped to the ground in a screeching, bumping, endlessly spinning tumble.

When everything finally stopped moving, Rafe sat motionless, trembling, panting, half blinded, and damn near deaf. He wasn't sure which direction was up and which was down, though he thought the LNR's right wing was tilted skyward, which must mean the left one had gouged itself deep into the soil. He knew he should try to extricate himself from the wreckage, clamber down the folded sides of the aircraft, show everyone in the watching audience that he had survived, but he didn't think he could do it. Couldn't free himself from the crumpled edges of the pilot's box, couldn't figure out how to lower himself to the ground, wasn't sure his legs would take his weight.

Wasn't sure, to be honest about it, that he actually *had* survived.

His first piece of affirmative proof was pain. His arm was on fire. His rib cage felt like someone had run a sword from his armpit to his hip, slicing precisely through each individual curved bone. His head was booming, every pulse of blood through his veins searing like a lightning strike. His right hand felt strange, both hot and sweaty; he had a feeling that if he managed to pull off his glove, he would find it filled with blood.

His second form of proof was sound. Muffled and dull—more nuanced than the grinding, wordless belligerence of the engine—and growing louder. Voices. Questions. *Rafe! Rafe! Are you all right? Rafe, can you hear us? Can anybody see him?*

He was alive. The elay prime—he knew it for a fact—had called up the winds to blow him to the roughest kind of safety. He had gambled his life and almost lost it, but he had had a hidden wildcard all along. The thought made him smile even as he closed his eyes and slipped into darkness.

NINETEEN

This is becoming altogether too common, Rafe thought as he swam fuzzily to consciousness. *Waking up in an unfamiliar place half dead from injuries.* The last time had been when he was attacked in the slums of Chialto. Recently enough for him to remember how wretched the experience could be.

It was no less painful this time—maybe slightly worse. He thought it was possible his head would crack right open, and the whole left side of his body felt as if it had been stripped raw. But the setting was different. Bigger, brighter, bustling with more purpose, and crowded with more people. The quality of the light made him think he'd been transported inside the aeromotive hangar and not much time had elapsed.

"His eyes are open," someone said. A woman leaned over him, her head blocking out almost everything else.

"Can you talk? Do you know your name? Do you remember what day it is?" she asked solemnly.

"Rafe Adova. It's the middle of the third nineday of Quinnahunti. My brains haven't been scrambled."

"That's good. Can you wiggle your fingers? Move your feet?"

He was tempted to not only flutter his fingers, but to lift his hands and wrap them around her throat. Maybe outsized irritation was a side effect of the concussion she clearly worried he might have. "Yes. See? Is anything broken?"

"Couple of toes. Maybe a couple of ribs, but I think you just flayed some skin off. I'm more worried about your head. And the possibility of internal bleeding. Let me know if this hurts."

She proceeded to apply pressure to various spots on his torso and seemed pleased when he didn't cry out. He wasn't paying as much attention as he should have been, maybe; he was trying, without lifting his head, to look around the room and figure out who else was in it and where exactly he might be. He spotted a man and a woman nearby, holding what looked like medical supplies, but neither of them, unfortunately, was Josetta. The space was too clean and brightly lit to be Kayle's office. Maybe they kept an infirmary right at the hangar. They probably had need of one often enough.

"What happened to the LNR?" he asked, grunting as the medic poked at his stomach.

"Worry about that later," she said. "Can you sit up?"

He struggled a bit, but with the man's help he made it upright. His senses reeled and for a moment he thought he might throw up, but then the nausea passed. That was the point at which he realized he was wearing nothing except a strategically placed sheet and an impressive array of bandages around his left leg, left arm, right hand, and chest.

"What happened to it?" he insisted. "Is it beyond repair?"

"Still being assessed," the man said briefly.

"You should be more worried about whether or not *you're* beyond repair," the woman said with grim humor.

"I feel all right," he said. He didn't, of course. He meant *All right for someone who crashed an aeromotive.* "Did anyone else get hurt?"

"Only you," the medic said.

"Where's Josetta?" he blurted out.

"The princess is waiting outside," the medic said. "Very worried about you."

"Can I see her?"

"When I've finished examining you. Do you feel like you might pass out again?"

"No."

"Do you feel dizzy? Like you might fall if you stand up?"

"A little."

"Want to try?"

"Sure."

He required help for this maneuver, too, but after a few moments he was able to stand without assistance. The stone floor felt cool beneath his bare feet. He tucked the sheet more securely around his waist and put his weight gingerly on his left leg. It didn't buckle; all the pain must be coming from scrapes and bruises, and not a broken bone. Well, that was cheerful news.

"How's your head?"

"Hurts. A lot."

She nodded. "I imagine it does. I have drugs I could give you for the pain—but they'd mask any dangerous symptoms you might develop, and I don't want to take the risk. Do you understand?"

"Of course I understand. I'm not an idiot," he snapped. Her face relaxed into a smile, and he caught the sound of muffled laughter from the other two.

"Well, that's a good sign," she said.

"So can I go home?"

"Not yet," she said. "I want to watch you for a day."

He glanced around the small space. Yes, it was clearly a sickroom. There were cabinets of medical supplies against one wall and the brisk scent of the powerful kind of soap people only used when they wanted to keep a place *really* clean.

"Here?" he said faintly.

She smiled again. "You wouldn't be the first to stay overnight."

He didn't have the strength to protest—or, for that matter, to keep standing upright. With a sigh he sank back to a sitting position onto the narrow bed. "Can I at least get dressed?"

She glanced at her assistants. "Can someone fetch him some coveralls?"

"What's wrong with my own clothes?" he asked as the other woman slipped out the door.

She looked at him again. "The bits of them that weren't ripped to shreds or covered in blood had to be cut off your body so we could tend to your wounds."

"Oh."

He didn't have a chance to ask another question because the door opened again and Josetta peered inside. "Is he—Rafe! You're awake! How do you feel?" She didn't wait for permission, just hurried inside and grabbed his hands with both of hers. "Look at you, you're so beat up, but you—well, for a few moments there, I was—that was terrifying to watch."

Her presence acted like the best kind of drug; for a moment, he forgot all his dreadful pains. He even found the strength to squeeze her fingers in return. "It was terrifying to live through."

"So are you all right? How soon can we leave?"

"He seems fine, but there's a chance of internal bleeding—most dangerous if it's inside his skull," the medic interposed. "I don't want to risk a brain hemorrhage on the drive home, so I want to keep him here overnight."

Just like Rafe, Josetta sent a doubtful glance around the room, but she didn't bother protesting. "All right. Maybe I can camp out in Kayle's office for the night."

"You can come back for him tomorrow," the medic answered. "You don't have to stay."

Josetta's fingers wrapped more tightly around Rafe's; she gave him a private smile. "Oh, yes I do," she murmured. "I'm not leaving him behind."

The rest of the afternoon passed in an unpleasant combination of pain and tedium. Rafe imagined it was less painful but more tedious for Josetta, who was mostly allowed to sit in the room with him but frequently chased out when the medic wanted to check his condition again. Even when the princess was sitting beside him, he wasn't capable of much conversation. His headache was back, his body hurt all over, and his mind was almost blank. She didn't seem to mind. She sat beside him when she could, her hand wrapped around his or resting on his arm. Sometimes she read. Sometimes she talked in a low voice to the medical staff. Sometimes she appeared to be lost in thought. He watched her when he was awake and dreamed about her when he slept.

It was morning before he realized night had crept up and slipped past while he wasn't paying attention. Early morning, to judge by the angle of sunlight, and he was entirely alone. Josetta and the medic must have found semi-comfortable accommodations elsewhere to bed down for the night. His headache was markedly better, though the left side of his body felt worse. For the moment, he considered that a good trade-off.

He cautiously pushed himself to a seated position and felt a certain elation when that didn't bring on vertigo or nausea. He was just debating whether or not to try to stand when the door swung open and Kayle Dochenza strode in. He was pale and disheveled enough to have spent the night sleeping on the hangar floor—though, of course, he always looked pale and disheveled, so it was hard to tell.

"That was bad," Kayle said without preamble. "I hope it didn't give you a distaste for flying."

Rafe wanted to laugh out loud because the comment was so perfectly in character for the elay prime. "Not at all. It's made me want to do a better job next time. If you'll trust me with another aeromotive."

Kayle nodded. "You're the best pilot we've got right now. You were aloft that whole time? No one else has kept a machine in the air that long."

"I made it to the ocean and then west about a mile. But once I turned to come back, the engine kept cutting out. Maybe six times."

Kayle looked thoughtful. "Maybe the fuel doesn't feed well once the tank is half empty."

"I need to thank you," Rafe said, "for saving my life."

Kayle just focused those blue eyes on him and said nothing.

Rafe went on. "I know you called the wind. It was violent and messy, but it kept me from crashing."

"You still crashed," Kayle pointed out.

"Not quite as spectacularly. I don't think I would have survived if I'd come down any harder."

"No, probably not. Wind isn't difficult to control, but it's not very precise."

"I keep thinking—there should be a way to eject from the pilot's box. A way to get free of the plane before it goes down."

"You'll still die if you jump out when you're a few hundred feet in the air," Kayle pointed out. "And you'd probably land on the wreckage anyway."

"Yes, but—" Rafe snapped his fingers. "The flying bag! If a pilot has one of those strapped on to him, he can shoot up out of the plane while it's going down. It might not carry him very far away, but even fifty feet would be enough."

Kayle looked intrigued. "That's very good," he approved. "We'll make flying bags a part of every pilot's equipment. So when will you be well enough to fly again?"

This time Rafe did laugh. "I don't know, but I think my injuries have to heal first."

Kayle glanced at him in an assessing manner. "Some bruises and sprains? That shouldn't take too long."

Rafe just grinned. "That's what I'm hoping."

The trip back to the port required only a single elaymotive, since Kayle had lent Josetta one of his big private cars that could hold up to twelve people. Still, the journey was agony incarnate, because whenever the vehicle hit a bump or rut, Rafe felt the impact on every inch of his battered body. Good to her word, the medic had finally handed over a small sack of drugs that she said would ease the pain, and he swallowed two of them before they were halfway to the port. The only thing that kept him from taking more was that she had limited him to four a day.

When they finally arrived back at their rented rooms and Foley had helped him up the stairs, Rafe mumbled an apology and headed straight for his bed. "I'll take care of things," Josetta promised as she kissed his cheek and smoothed the blanket over his shoulder. He figured that meant she would shop for food and maybe some replacement clothing, but he couldn't think about it too long. He just slept.

This time when he woke it was closer to dark, he felt a little less like the specter of death, and he wasn't alone. Josetta sat across the room at the small table, where she was busily engaged in writing notes or adding up sums or doing something else productive. The last horizontal rays of the setting sun lanced through the window and sizzled around her head, turning her pale blond hair to white fire. Serenity radiated from her like heat from a hearth; it was a perfume as heady as spring. He took a deep breath and felt tranquility settle into his bones.

"Josetta," he said, and she immediately jumped to her feet.

"How are you?" she asked, coming over to place a cool hand on his face. The fish charms from her bracelet tickled against his skin. "I'm supposed to check in case you develop a fever," she explained.

He covered her hand with his own. "Doesn't feel like fever."

She smiled. "What does it feel like?"

"Falling off a mountain onto a pile of rocks."

"Are you hungry? The medic said that if you hadn't started vomiting by now you'd better eat something. It's been almost two days since you've had a meal."

Maybe that angry feeling in his stomach wasn't pain, it was hunger. "Food sounds like a good idea," he said

"Can you make it to the table or do I need to spoon-feed you while you're lying there?"

"Well, I like the idea of you fussing over me while I'm in bed," he drawled, which made her laugh, "but I think I can manage to sit at the table. Anyway, I need to get up. I have a few other needs to attend to."

Caze was in the hallway when Rafe opened the door. "Look who's up! You must be feeling better. Need any help getting down the hall?"

"I think I can manage, thanks."

In the common bathing room, he cleaned up as thoroughly as he could around the bandages. There was a decent-sized mirror on one wall so he took stock of his injuries, which felt better but still looked spectacular. He appeared pitiable even once the dried blood was washed away. The whole left side of his body was one dark bruise; even his left eye was ringed with purple. And, of course, the abundance of bandages made him look pathetic as well. He slipped on a loose tunic and trousers and tried to return to the room without favoring his left leg. Caze gave him an encouraging nod as he stepped back through the door.

Josetta had laid out a simple meal, complete with the fruited water that he had always considered a sign of high elegance. "I'm supposed to tell you that you should have Kayle's physician check you out tomorrow," she said as they took their seats. "The medic gave me the name and address."

"I think I'll be fine."

"I think you'll go see him."

He sipped from his water and watched her for a moment in silence.

"I think I don't like the fact that for half the time you've known me, I've been beaten up and broken."

"You do seem to lead an eventful life," she agreed.

He gestured at the dressings mostly covered by his clothing. "Always needing medical attention. It makes me seem weak."

"Careless, maybe. Unlucky. Not weak."

"I'd rather seem dashing and adventurous."

"Oh, I'd say an aeromotive pilot is very dashing." She toyed with her food, then glanced at him. Her voice was carefully casual. "Did yesterday's disaster make you rethink the idea of flying?"

"It made me want to figure out how to make it safer, but no, it didn't scare me off. The opposite, really. I can't wait to get back into the pilot's box and do it right this time."

She nodded. "That's what I thought you'd say."

He waited a moment, then challenged her. "Were you hoping I'd give it up? Would you rather I did?"

"It's not up to me—"

"I'm going to make my own decision," he interrupted. "I just want to know what you think. Honestly. Whether or not you think it'll make me mad."

She nodded. "What I think is that my heart almost stopped when the aeromotive was coming down. What I think is that every time you fly another one of Kayle's machines, you'll be just as much at risk and I'll be just as terrified. Do I wish you wouldn't fly again? Yes. Do I think I should stop you? No. As soon as you climbed into that machine, I could tell it's what you're supposed to be doing. You were made for a chancy life. It just makes things harder on the people who care about you."

He could tell that his grin was lopsided. "There haven't been that many people who cared about me, up till now," he said. "I haven't been used to considering how they might feel."

"There's your brother."

He shrugged. "I'm a small part of his life. He wouldn't notice so much if I wasn't in it."

"Well, I'm used to having people care about me. And I'm used to nodding gravely when they express their concern about me—and then going off and doing what I want anyway. You can't be bound by other people's worry."

"Then what should you be bound by?" he asked softly. "If you want to be connected to someone else?"

She lifted her eyes and met his intense stare with an equally intense gaze of her own. "Affection. Honesty. The promises you make—the promises you keep."

"I haven't been used to making promises, either."

"Well, start with small ones. They're easier."

"Any that you might suggest?"

She gave him a faint smile for that. "How about, 'I'll see Kayle's physician tomorrow'? That shouldn't be too hard."

"All right. I swear I will. Now it's your turn."

"To make a promise to you?"

He nodded.

She leaned back against the chair and seemed to debate her options. "I'll take care of you while you're recovering from your latest injuries."

"Will you promise to come watch the next time I take up an aeromotive?"

She made a noise of protest, then sighed. "I'll go with you, but I can't guarantee that I'll actually watch."

"Good enough." He waited a moment, but she was silent. "Now it's your turn to ask me something."

She nodded, but she still didn't say anything.

"Josetta?" he prodded.

"It's just that I can't think of any lighthearted and meaningless things to ask for just to keep the game going."

His breath caught, but he shouldn't have been surprised. Josetta so rarely bothered with *lighthearted* and *meaningless*. "You could ask for something serious and important," he suggested.

Now she offered that faint smile again. "Oh, the only things I can think of are *too* serious and important."

His heart slammed against his ribs, its impact almost as sudden and forceful as an aeromotive crashing to the ground. "Well, that's got me curious," he managed to say.

Smiling now, she shook her head, and light flickered around her yellow hair. Gaslight, he realized; it was true night now, dark everywhere that some kind of man-made illumination wasn't making a valiant stand. "It's getting late," she said, coming to her feet. "And you're still an invalid. I'll go to my room so you can sleep, and I'll check on you in the morning."

He stood up so quickly his head did a little spin. "I'm not sleepy," he protested. "If you leave, I'll just be bored."

"Lie down," she suggested. "I bet you're more tired than you think."

She turned toward the door, but he was close enough to head her off. He didn't quite dare to grab her arm and hold her in place, but he did step in her path and crowd her back toward the middle of the room.

"I bet I'm not," he said. "Won't you stay a little while? Long enough to play a game of penta, maybe?"

She wasn't meeting his gaze, but she didn't move away from him, though their bodies were almost close enough to touch. "Last time we were going to play penta, we couldn't agree on the stakes. It's no fun unless you're gambling."

He reached out a finger and tilted up her chin. "We agreed on stakes," he reminded her. "We just didn't bother playing."

Now she did lift her eyes to his and he was astonished to see them bright with tears. "That's right," she whispered. "A kiss. How could I have forgotten?"

"Josetta—"

She stretched up and pressed her mouth to his, and he forgot anything else he might have wanted to say. The kiss kicked the blood through his veins at a galloping pace; it riled up every bruise he'd sustained, but it stirred other, far more pleasurable regions of his body as well. His skin ran with heat and his brain was steeped in desire. Heedless of bandages and bruised ribs, he wrapped his arms around her, drew her closer, and kissed her for all he was worth.

Only when he paused to draw a long breath did he remember that he was battered and realize that she was crying. "Josetta," he repeated, alarmed now. "What's the matter? I'm sorry, was I too rough—"

Shaking her head, she clung to him with a mute appeal that made him hold her tighter still. "It's just that—I was so *afraid*," she wailed. "I saw the aeromotive falling, and I thought you would die, I *knew* it, and I couldn't help you and I couldn't do anything, and I thought my heart would break! Right there! And then you didn't die, you're alive, and I'm so grateful, and I want you to know how I feel—but you're all beaten up and hurt and I don't know what to do—"

There was an easy answer for that sad, disjointed speech. He kissed her again, harder, ignoring the protest of his ribs as he crushed her to his chest. Her mouth was fervent on his, her hands insistent, pulling at his arms, seeking a way under his tunic. He thought she truly must be a creature of air alone, because he didn't seem to need to breathe; all he had to do was kiss her, and that was enough to sustain him.

They might have stood there all night, passionately embraced, except he shifted his weight to keep his balance and practically yelped with pain as he twisted his ankle. She broke free, apologizing madly, and he had to grab her wrists and pull her back to prove he was fine.

"Just a little twinge, nothing to worry about—"

"I'm so sorry! You don't even have the strength to stand, and here I am, throwing myself at you—"

He laughed at her. "This is the best I've felt since the LNR went down," he declared. "Let's tell all the medical folks! Euphoria is the best opiate there is."

She laughed weakly, resting her head against his chest. "I should go."

"I don't want you to go."

"You're hurt."

He drew back and she lifted her head enough to meet his gaze. "Not as hurt as I'll be if you walk out the door."

She was searching his face, looking for reassurance; she was offering him her own expression of unvarnished honesty. "I thought I had lost my chance to be with you," she said softly. "I thought you would die, and the only memories I'd have would be a kiss or two. I want more. I want all of you. But if you—"

He kissed her again before she could finish the sentence. He didn't know if she was going to ask about his injuries or question the state of his heart, but it didn't matter; his answer would be the same. *Nothing will stop me from making love to you tonight.*

It turned out he needed to breathe, after all, but it was only reluctantly that he lifted his head to gasp for air. Josetta kissed the stubbled curve of his chin and whispered, "You seem enthusiastic about the idea—"

"Oh, *very* enthusiastic," he panted.

"But last time I—I offered myself to you, you practically chased me out the door."

"And cursed myself every day since."

She brightened. "Really?"

"I wish I had the strength to sweep you into my arms and carry you to the bed, where I would prove how much I want you. But I'm afraid you're going to have to walk alongside me as I hobble over."

"Let me help you to the bed, my wounded hero," she said. "Maybe it's even more romantic this way."

"It's not," Rafe said, "but I'm not going to complain."

The bed was reasonably sized and reasonably clean, and Rafe suffered only a few easily overlooked spikes of pain as they tumbled into it together. "Clothes, clothes, clothes, clothes," he muttered, yanking off his tunic and slipping out of the loose pants. Josetta was down to a single thin undergarment but she got distracted by the stark evidence of his recent misadventure.

"You're covered with bruises!" she exclaimed, running her palm very lightly over the discolored patches of skin visible among the bandages. "It's even worse than I thought!"

"That's not the part of my anatomy I want you to notice," he said.

She choked back another giggle and widened the range of that questing hand. "Very nice muscles," she said, trailing her fingers along his arms and shoulders. "Broad shoulders. Slim hips. And—and—other interesting body parts."

"The most interesting," he agreed. He was tugging at her last silky piece of clothing, and she paused long enough to pull it over her head with one quick motion. This half of the room was in darkness, but there was plenty of light to see her slim shape, and he greedily drank in all the details—narrow shoulders, small breasts, pale skin as smooth as worn ivory. She looked like a treasure in some rich man's cache. He remembered suddenly that she was young, that she was royal, and that she was very likely a virgin.

"Josetta," he began, and he knew she could hear the remorse and worry in his voice. "Maybe this isn't—"

She stopped his mouth, practically stopped his heart, by laying her body next to his and pressing a kiss on his lips. She was capable of great reserve, but she had never been shy, and she was not shy now. "No more talking," she whispered against his mouth. Her hands were busy touching him again, and she needn't have bothered with the prohibition; he was incapable of saying a word. "Just show me how to love you."

Silently and willingly he began the demonstration, and silently and willingly surrendered her his soul. He wouldn't ask for promises, he wouldn't offer them, but they were already written on his heart.

TWENTY

When Josetta woke up the next morning, the first thing she did was squeeze her eyes shut tight again. No, no, no, she did not want it to be daylight, she did not want it to be time to get up, leave the bed, move away from Rafe's side. She wanted to lie there forever, curled next to him, feeling the amazing sensation of body to body, skin to skin. She wanted to think over the events of the night before, remembering each sensation, each new surprise.

She had long believed that she would enjoy making love to a man, and she'd been right, but her imagination had been woefully limited. She hadn't realized how consuming the experience could be, turning every other concern insignificant, at least for that precise moment. She hadn't expected it to leave this particular emotion behind—a sense of well-being, of satisfaction, that left her feeling almost smug.

It was enough to turn her sweela, she mused, to change her into a creature of pure physical hedonism. She thought if she were to draw a set of blessings now they would all be stamped with the glyphs for fire. Or maybe there would be a torz trait thrown in—the sign for contentment, perhaps. She lifted her arms over her head and stretched as high as she could. She felt magnificent.

Rafe lay on his side next to her, sound asleep, but one arm still curled protectively over her waist. He had been so sweet last night, funny and tender, careful and ardent, explaining, exploring, exhilarating. It had been easy to trust him, easy to make love to him. Easy to fall asleep beside him and wake up beside him, conscious of only a single regret—that it was morning already.

But it would be night again soon.

She kissed him on the cheek and whispered, "I'll be back in a minute," then extricated herself from his loose embrace. She slipped on her overtunic and stepped into the hallway, where one of Darien's soldiers was keeping guard. She nodded at him nonchalantly, then headed down to the common room to clean up. There, she locked the door and immersed herself in the water, washing her hair, washing away the last traces of lovemaking. She wrinkled her nose at the idea of putting on her dirty clothes again—well, she'd make a quick detour to her own chambers, get dressed, then be back in Rafe's room before he'd even woken up.

She stepped into the hallway and found Darien waiting for her.

"Good morning," he said affably enough. "I'm glad to find you awake so early."

For a moment she could only stare at him, her mind an utter blank. She hadn't seen him when she emerged from Rafe's apartment. Had he seen her? Had he figured out what they'd done last night? Did she care?

"Darien," she answered finally. "Why are you here?"

"I had business at the port," he said. "And I wanted to talk to you."

She pulled her wits together. "Give me a few minutes," she said, brushing past him toward her own door. "I need to get dressed. And then I need to check on Rafe. I assume you heard what happened yesterday—no, the day before?"

Darien nodded as he fell in step beside her. "Rafe crashed, but survived more or less intact."

"He's in a lot of pain, but I think he'll be fine. He knows he's lucky."

"I hope he's learned how ridiculous it is to want to fly an aeromotive."

"I don't think so. He says he can't wait to do it again."

Darien shook his head. "Some people are hopeless."

She was fishing in the pocket of her overtunic—where, by some great stroke of luck, she had left the key to her room—and she laughed as she unlocked the door. "Not everyone can be a wise, practical hunti man."

"No, but they don't have to be half-wits."

He took a seat at the table, facing the window while she hastily selected clothes, dressed, and tied back her wet hair. A glance in the mirror showed her face was a bit pale from too little sleep, but still shaped by that hint of smug delight. Zoe might notice—Corene certainly would—but she didn't think Darien had picked up on anything in her expression.

She rummaged through the area set aside as a kitchen, where she had a loaf of bread, half a round of cheese, and a stoppered pitcher of water. She was starving. "Are you hungry? Thirsty?"

"I'm fine."

She made a small breakfast plate for herself, then pulled up a chair across from him. "What did you want to talk to me about?" she asked.

"Do you want to come with me to visit Romelle?"

She had to swallow a mouthful of food before she could speak her surprise. "At Taro's? Why?"

He tapped a finger against the table. He was edgy and displeased—also a little worried—and it was rare for Darien to display those emotions, even if he felt them. "She went to Mirti's over the last nineday for some event. Mirti had explicitly told her to bring Odelia, and Romelle said she would, but when she arrived, it was Mally who came with her."

That *was* astonishing. "Did she think Mirti wouldn't know the difference? A *prime*?"

"She made some excuse. It was such a small gathering, she didn't think it would matter—Odelia had been coughing and feeling poorly—the usual reasons."

"Maybe Odelia really does have a lot of ailments," Josetta commented. "Vernon was pretty sick in those final years, you know."

"Yes, thank you so much for reminding me, I had practically forgotten," Darien snapped. It was Darien who had had the desperate task of trying to keep Vernon alive as long as possible while concealing from the entire court how weak he really was. "And it has not occurred to me *a single time* that Odelia may have inherited his poor constitution."

It wasn't funny, but she couldn't help laughing. "Well, it doesn't do any good not to acknowledge the truth."

"No, which is why I want to confront Romelle at her home, when she can't possibly fail to produce Odelia."

"Do you plan to arrive unannounced?"

He nodded. "It sounds cruel, I know, but I have the feeling I cannot allow her time to prepare. Perhaps she would whisk Odelia away somewhere before I could see her."

"But to what end? She can't be afraid *you* will harm the princess."

"I don't know. That's what I want to find out."

"And why do you want me to come with you?"

His face softened into the smile that always made Josetta forget how difficult Darien could be. "Because we miss you, in my household. Zoe, Corene, Celia, and I. We're not used to you being gone so many days in a row."

"And you're *all* going to see Romelle? That might be another reason she won't be pleased when you show up at her door."

Darien shrugged. "She lives with the torz prime. His household should be set up to entertain a hundred unexpected guests. I don't imagine *she'll* be the one making up extra beds and ordering enough supplies in the kitchen."

She sipped from her water glass, watching him. "Rafe Adova must come with me, of course."

"I haven't forgotten that."

"*And* Foley. *And* all the other guards."

"I always travel with an escort. Taro can accommodate whatever numbers we bring."

"How long would we stay there?"

Darien's expression sharpened and he stared at her, not even trying to be subtle about it. "Why? What pressing matters do you have to attend to here or in Chialto?"

She stared right back because you always had to meet Darien's strength with strength, or he could flatten you. "What I *have* is my own life. Which I have sorely neglected while playing this charade with the Berringey prince. I would like to know how long I'll be gone so I know how long it will be before I can go to the shelter again."

Darien rubbed his eyes, for a moment looking as tired as he probably was. "I don't know. Say it's a two-day trip in each direction. Say we stay three days or less. So—not even a nineday. Does a journey of *that* length fit in with your plans?"

She tried not to smile. "I believe I can manage it. And it's a good time for Rafe to be away, since he's too bruised to fly *or* train for a while."

"Then it's settled. You may as well ride back to my house with me. I'd like to set out tomorrow morning."

Josetta pushed herself to her feet. "Then let's see if Rafe's awake, and let him know what delights are in store for him."

Rafe was indeed awake and standing in the middle of the room, wrapped in a blanket, looking a little lost. His face showed both relief and apprehension when Josetta stepped through the door.

"There you are," he said. "When I woke up, I thought—"

"Darien's here," she interrupted before he could say anything too damning. "He came to check on you."

"Hardly that," Darien said, following her in. "But I *am* glad you didn't die in the aeromotive disaster. That would have been difficult to explain to Prince Ghyaneth."

"He probably would have offered you a reward," Josetta said.

Darien was giving Rafe a critical inspection. "You look fairly wretched. Are you well enough to travel?"

In three seconds, Rafe's expression had gone from worry to high alert to the calm amiability that Josetta thought of as his professional expression. "I don't see why not. Where am I going?"

Very smooth, Josetta thought. The man was so adaptable, so open to surprises, he should have been coru. "To visit the princess," she said.

He smiled at her. "*You're* a princess."

"The heir," she specified.

He glanced at Darien. "And there's a reason you think I need to meet her?"

Darien shrugged. "I want Josetta's company. You're just a collateral benefit."

It was easy enough to read Darien's tone. *I don't care if you meet Odelia or not, but this is the course we've chosen, so we're stuck with you*. Rafe's face showed perfect comprehension, and Josetta concealed a smile.

Rafe said, "Let me wash up and pack a bag, and I'll be ready to go."

It was frustrating beyond description to have no chance to talk privately to Rafe, and it took no great prescience to realize that they might not have another opportunity to spend the night together until this trip was over. Josetta had never been less happy to have Darien interfering in her life, but she had not been fooled by the casual nature of his invitation. He wanted her on this trip, so she would end up going, whether or not she wasted any energy in protesting. It was easier to acquiesce.

Though she could get her way in small things. "Rafe needs to see Kayle's physician before we go," Josetta insisted. "I don't want him to succumb to infection while we're on the road."

Darien agreed readily enough, so once they had loaded the elaymotives—again, a caravan of three to carry all the personnel—they set off to find the doctor. He operated out of a squat stone building of absolutely no exterior charm, situated on a narrow, noisy street.

"I'll wait here," Darien told them. "I assume this won't take very long."

Josetta accompanied Rafe inside, where the ambience was a little more welcoming, and soft chairs and softer lighting helped combat the clinical smell of strong detergent. A spare, efficient woman whisked them to a small room as soon as they mentioned Kayle's name—and they suddenly had a few moments alone.

"I'm so sorry about Darien," Josetta said instantly. "And this trip. But there's no help for it."

He didn't waste time with words, he just put his arms around her and kissed her thoroughly. She felt that sense of satisfied well-being flood back through her veins, sharply flavored with rising desire. "That's what a man does when a woman deigns to spend the night with him," he murmured against her mouth. "And then you were gone this morning! Are you all right? Are you—"

"I'm fine. I'm wonderful," she interrupted, putting her arms around his neck. "I liked that so *very* much. Let's do it again."

He laughed and kissed her once more. "Oh, if only we could! But since your brother-in-law seems to have designed this trip just to keep us apart—"

The door clicked open and Josetta tore herself out of Rafe's arms. The man who entered was small, slight, and gray, and his sharp eyes were so expressive that his personality made an immediate impact. Sweela, Josetta guessed. He had the look.

"Well, you can't be *too* sick, if that's how you're carrying on," he said dryly, "but let me examine you anyway."

After a rapid but thorough inspection, he pronounced Rafe free of fever and lucky to be alive. "I'd restrict my activities for a few days if I were you," he said, giving them both a pointed glance, "but pain is your best guide. If it hurts, don't do it. And if it hurts a lot, come see me again."

Fifteen minutes later they were back in the elaymotive, heading toward Chialto. Josetta watched sympathetically as Rafe squirmed a little on the padded seat; the doctor had rebandaged his ribs, which seemed to have reminded him how much they hurt.

Darien glanced over. "Better get comfortable," he advised. "It's going to be a long day."

In fact, it was a long three days by the time they finally arrived at Taro's property in the middle southern provinces of Welce. It hadn't been physically unpleasant—Josetta didn't think the trip could have been accomplished more luxuriously if the point had been to prove to Rafe how much extravagance the royal court could command. It was just wearisome.

For the two days of the journey, Darien had commandeered a pair of royal elaymotives, each consisting of a long, narrow, enclosed compartment pulled by a smaller powered vehicle. The compartments were like very small houses, with distinct and lavishly furnished living spaces such as bedrooms and kitchens. The guards and teams of drivers traveled behind them in less opulent transport vehicles, and by swapping out drivers at regular intervals, they were able to travel with very few stops.

At night, the men of the royal party slept in one car and the women in the other, but Rafe usually joined the women during the day while they were in transit. His presence proved to be very entertaining.

"Let's play penta," Corene demanded the first time the four of them were assembled in the women's car. "But you have to remind me of the rules."

"Gladly," Rafe said, pulling a deck of cards from his pocket. "What are the stakes?"

Zoe had Celia against her shoulder, trying to convince her to fall asleep, but Rafe's question made her look up in assumed indignation. "What, it's not enough for you to be taken on a fabulously exciting journey through the farmland of Welce—country so beautiful that your counsin Ghyaneth couldn't stop raving about it? You want to win our money, too?"

He grinned. "Maybe I won't win. Corene has a real knack for the game."

"I do," Corene said complacently. "But I don't have any coins with me. And I don't know if Darien will give me any if I tell him what I want them for."

Rafe's restless hands were shuffling the cards over and over. Josetta thought he was making a real effort not to look in her direction. "You can gamble on something else you want," he said. "Doesn't have to be money."

"I know what I'll bet," Zoe said. "If I win, all of you have to change the baby's diapers for the rest of the trip. Give the nursemaid—and me—a break."

Rafe laughed at her. "You think I don't know how to do that, but I do. I had a little brother."

"If I win, I want Darien to stop in a *real* city so we can have a *real* meal for dinner at least one night," Josetta said.

"Since Darien's not playing, you can't make him do that," Zoe pointed out.

Josetta gave her a sweet smile. "But *you* can persuade him."

"I like that dinner idea," Rafe said. "Maybe that will be my bet, too. Corene?"

Corene wore an expression Josetta had always thought of as wicked. "I'll get to ask everyone a question, on any topic I choose."

Zoe and Josetta exchanged looks of alarm. "I'm not sure we should agree to that," Zoe said. "Corene's liable to say anything."

"She always does," Josetta agreed. "Even when she's not gambling."

Corene shrugged. "All right, I'll just ask the questions anyway."

"No," Josetta said quickly as the other girl took a quick breath. "Let's just play. Maybe you won't win."

"Tournament style," Rafe suggested. "So no one is declared winner until we're at the end of the trip."

"I like that," Zoe decided. "Let's play."

Penta became their obsession over the next two days, to the point that they almost hated to break for meals. Darien seemed amused by their intense interest in the competition, but on the whole, relieved that it meant they weren't complaining to him about small inconveniences. Josetta found it remarkable that the luck of the individual players seemed to fall so evenly. By late afternoon of the second day, when they were only about an hour from their destination, the four of them had almost identical scores.

"I think you're doing something to the cards," Josetta accused Rafe when he won the hand that put him slightly in the lead.

"How could I do that? We've all taken turns dealing."

"I don't know, but I think you are."

He was shuffling the cards again, but Zoe took them away from him one-handed. With the other hand she was holding the baby on her lap. Celia's huge unblinking eyes had been following the game with apparent fascination, and Rafe had already predicted she'd be playing penta before she was three—winning, too.

"Then let's just make sure he doesn't deal again for the rest of the day," Zoe said. "He doesn't touch any cards but his own."

Rafe was grinning. "You malign me."

"On the contrary, I think I've formed a very accurate impression of your personality," she retorted. "Corene, you deal."

Three hands later, Corene took the last round with a wildcard that everyone but Rafe had forgotten she had, and he hadn't had the trump to stop her. "I win, I win!" she exulted. "Now you all have to pay up."

Celia chortled with delight and waved her little fists in the air, but the rest of them greeted the news with apprehension. "I'm filled with dread," Zoe said.

Corene turned to her first. "Do you like Romelle?"

Zoe's face turned thoughtful. "I used to," she said. "She seemed the most open and the least *scheming* of Vernon's wives. But there's something furtive about her these days that makes me not trust her. And I have a hard time liking people I don't trust."

Corene nodded, then looked in Rafe's direction. "Do you secretly wish you could go to Berringey and be prince? Be *king*? If you wouldn't die for it?"

Rafe narrowed his eyes, thinking that over. "I'd like to know what Berringey is like," he answered at last. "I'd like to see the place where I was born and meet people who might share my bloodline. I don't particularly want to leave Welce, but if I could visit there and not be afraid for my life? I'd go. I would."

"Would you want to be king?" she persisted. "If you could?"

"I don't think I'd be a very good king, to tell you the truth. You need someone with a certain kind of—focus. Resolve. Vision, maybe."

"But you'd have all that money! And power!" Corene exclaimed. "You could make people do whatever you wanted or have them put to death."

"Yes, and that whole business about putting people to death is exactly the reason I can't go there," he answered with a smile. "I think most people can't be trusted with that kind of power. I wouldn't want the temptation."

"I don't think Darien suffers from that kind of temptation," Zoe mused. "Oh, I'm sure he sometimes uses power to make small annoying problems go away—but he's so virtuous. So incorruptible. So *hunti*. He schemes, and he definitely keeps his secrets, but his motives are always pure."

"Yes, he's an inspiration to all of us—when we don't want to hit him," Josetta said, and the three women laughed.

"Now you," Corene said, looking Josetta's way.

The other questions hadn't been so bad, but Josetta steeled herself anyway. "Yes?"

"Are you in love with Rafe Adova?"

There was a moment of stunned silence, broken only by the sound of Celia babbling to herself. Then Zoe exclaimed, "Corene! That's unacceptable!"

"You agreed I could ask any question."

"But I expected you to have enough decorum not to embarrass your sister—or our guest! Ask her something else."

"But they *act* like they're in love," Corene insisted. "He touches her hand when he deals the cards to her. And every time she walks past his chair, she puts her hand on his shoulder. Haven't you noticed?"

Zoe sent Josetta one quick look, apologetic but brimming with laughter. "Well, yes, I have noticed. It's just not polite to point such things out."

Josetta could feel the blush heating her cheeks, but she willed her embarrassment to slink meekly away. Corene was like Darien; you had to face her down. "We said you could ask any question, but we didn't say we had to answer," she said brightly. "So I'm not going to."

Corene gazed speculatively at Rafe, and he laughed. "Hey, I already answered mine," he said.

She flounced back in her chair. "Well, the truth is obvious anyway," she said.

"Then you shouldn't have wasted your time asking," Josetta said.

Corene gathered up the cards. "Let's play another game," she suggested.

The collective "No!" was almost lost in the sudden jolt as the elaymotive lurched to a halt amid a series of squeals and clatters. Zoe was on her feet as soon as the vehicle stopped shuddering. "Looks like we've arrived," she said. "Time for this uncomfortable meeting to begin."

TWENTY-ONE

J osetta had always loved the entrance to Taro Frothen's estate. The main courtyard more closely resembled a garden, offering an exuberant display of flowers and bushes and trees that rioted with a heady mix of scents and colors. This area subtly fed into a wide stone patio shaded by a trellis hung with grapevines, honeysuckle, and wild ivy. It was easy to miss the point where you stepped from the patio into the *kierten*, which was filled with potted shrubs and climbing plants that wound their way up the walls and halfway across the ceiling.

It could hardly have been more obvious that this was the homestead of the torz prime.

Servants instantly appeared to usher them through the *kierten* and into an equally lovely room filled with afternoon sunlight and groupings of plush, comfortable furniture. Josetta recognized the steward, a solid-looking, eminently practical woman who had been there since Josetta was a child. "I'll tell the prime you've arrived," she said tranquilly. "I don't believe he told me you were coming."

"He didn't know," Darien replied.

Zoe waited till the steward was out of the room before she said, "He won't be entirely surprised, though. When I'm at my grandmother's house, I can sense the presence of other people as soon as they've drawn within a mile. I can feel their heartbeats. Taro will have some similar way of sensing our proximity."

Darien lifted his eyebrows. "Will he have had enough time to sequester Odelia?"

"Maybe," Zoe replied. "But I don't suppose that matters. Since you're not going to leave until you've seen her."

Darien turned toward the door, because they could all catch the sound of purposeful footsteps striding down the hall. "No," he said, "I'm not."

Seconds later, Taro barreled through the door, bringing such force of personality that Josetta, Corene, and Rafe all stepped backward. The torz prime was annoyed and not bothering to hide the fact. His normally sleepy, agreeable face was drawn into a frown, and he was consciously using his bulky body to express a certain latent menace. This was a man who would win any physical competition that required brute strength or endurance, and he was not above reminding his visitors of that fact.

"Darien," he said, his voice a low rumble of barely restrained displeasure. "How kind of you to drop by."

"You can hardly be surprised to see me," Darien answered quietly.

"And yet I am." Taro nodded at each of the women in turn. "Zoe. Princesses." If he saw Rafe, he gave no sign. Josetta thought that maybe, like Kayle, he found Rafe invisible, his foreign flesh impervious to Taro's particular brand of perceptive magic. "How long do you plan to stay?"

"Long enough to reassure ourselves that Princess Odelia is well and healthy."

Even as he said the words, Romelle hurried into the room. She was so plainly dressed she might have been working in the garden five minutes earlier, or sewing in the linen room. Her hair was pulled loosely back from her face in a girlish style. She looked so young, Josetta thought. Scarcely more than twenty-five, and could have passed for nineteen. Young and defiant and more than a little afraid.

"You *are* here!" she exclaimed. "Goodness, we're not prepared for guests, but—we're happy to have you, I suppose."

Taro turned to her, communicating something with his eyes. "They want to see Odelia," he said.

"Oh! Well, of course! She's playing outside, but I'll just have one of the maids fetch her—"

"Odelia," Taro repeated, a note of finality in his voice. "Zoe will know."

Romelle stared back at him for a long moment, while her shoulders drooped and all her defiance seemed to leak away. She opened her mouth as if to say something, but all she could manage was a gesture, lifting both hands and letting them fall.

Taro turned back to the unwelcome visitors. Some of his own anger seemed to have faded; Josetta thought now he just looked sad. "Follow me. It goes better if we bring *you* to *her*."

Josetta exchanged a look with Zoe, who wasn't troubling to hide her apprehension. Darien wore no expression at all as he fell in step behind Taro and Romelle. Corene touched Josetta's arm and whispered, "I don't like this. Something's wrong."

"I think something's been wrong for a while," Josetta whispered back. She glanced at Rafe, who looked baffled and uncertain. They had explained the situation to him, but she doubted it had the same resonance for him. He had not been brought up at court; he did not understand what it meant for an heir to be compromised.

Their small parade wound through Taro's warm and welcoming house. There were flowers everywhere, and small nooks holding statues of laughing children, and window seats covered with tumbles of books. Josetta could understand why Romelle frequently refused invitations to come to court; if she lived here, she might always want to stay, too. It felt nourishing, somehow—safe. A place where you could stay forever and not be afraid.

They traversed the entire bottom story and headed up a polished wood stairwell to the third floor. The wide landing looked much like the *kierten*; it was an open, sunny place brightened even more with buckets of fresh flowers. A couple of hallways led to what appeared to be smaller rooms, probably bedrooms, but most of this level was taken up by a large chamber directly in front of them, guarded by a half-open door.

"This is where Odelia spends most of her time," Taro said quietly. "Mally has rooms downstairs, where the rest of the family lives, but Odelia prefers solitude and silence."

Romelle had hurried ahead of them into the big room. Josetta saw her confer briefly with a woman inside—a nursemaid or tutor, perhaps—and then turn back to give Taro one brief, despairing look.

"She's inside?" Darien asked, and, when Taro nodded, he strode forward. The rest of them followed, dragging their feet, not sure what they would find on the other side of the door.

At first, Josetta thought it was nothing out of the ordinary. The room was large and bright, with sunlight pouring through banks of wide windows. There were furniture groupings and piles of toys lining the walls, but the majority of the room was given over to open space—just polished hardwood flooring and great squares of sunlight. It took a moment to realize that the windows were a little higher than you might expect them to be, that all the furniture was soft, upholstered, without a sharp edge on any table or armrest.

Odelia knelt in the middle of the open space, her eyes closed, maybe humming a song to herself. She looked very much as Mally had the last time Josetta had seen her—she had the same dark hair that twisted into natural curls, the same milky-rose complexion that looked so much like Romelle's. She probably had the same dark eyes, but it was impossible to tell, since her lids remained closed even once they all stepped into the room.

Darien started forward, as if he would crouch down and interrogate her, but Taro flung out a hand to hold him in place. "Wait," he said, and his quiet voice was so forceful that even Darien obeyed.

Romelle had approached Odelia cautiously and dropped to her knees. "Hey, baby," she said in a low tone. "There are some people here who'd like to meet you."

Odelia didn't answer or open her eyes. If anything, she seemed to rock a little faster.

Romelle tried again. "Do you think you could stand up and be introduced to them? It's your sisters Corene and Josetta. And Zoe. Do you remember Zoe?"

"What's wrong with her?" Darien asked Taro in an undervoice, but Taro just shook his head.

Romelle put her hands on her daughter's shoulders and spoke in a firmer voice. "Odelia. Do you hear me? I want you to come meet some people."

Odelia lifted her hands to cover her ears, and began humming loudly enough for them to hear. Except she wasn't producing a song—it was more like a thin, high wail that trembled over a couple of notes, and she only stopped long enough to take a breath and then resume.

Romelle came abruptly to her feet, pulling Odelia up with her. "Stop that. You know how to behave when there's company. Come meet our guests."

Without answering, Odelia jerked her head and pulled free. Still keeping her hands over her ears, still singing that atonal song, she began spinning around in a tight spiral, not looking at her mother, at the nursemaid, or at the strangers clustered in the doorway, who were staring at her in slowly growing consternation and dread.

Romelle pressed her lips together, and then gazed hopelessly at Taro. He turned to Darien. "When she gets like this, it's sometimes an hour before she stops," he said quietly. "Sometimes she gets so dizzy she falls to the floor, and then she curls in on herself and cries until she falls asleep. And when she wakes up, she stands up and starts spinning again. This can go on for days."

"But she—what causes this behavior? How often does it occur?" Darien asked. "Was she simply nervous because she realized strangers were in the house?"

Taro stared at him. "This *is* her behavior," he said. "Some days less extreme. Some days she will tolerate having others in the room, though she won't speak to us or meet our eyes. We've thought that perhaps she doesn't realize we're actually present. Other days, she's like this. Like one raw exposed nerve, and any noises, any rapid movements, certain kinds of light, make her frantic. She sings and spins, I think, to shut out those sounds and motions. Sometimes she can't endure the feel of clothing on her body. Sometimes she can't endure the taste of food. And she never speaks."

"Taro—how long has she been this way?" Zoe asked, her voice full of wretchedness and compassion.

"Maybe two years. She wasn't quite two when she started developing these behaviors. Before then, she seemed like every other child I have ever held, and I have known hundreds. Clever and engaged and happy enough. But she gradually began to withdraw from us, more and more every quintile, every nineday, and now I couldn't tell you the last time I saw the Odelia that I remember."

There was a long silence while Darien watched Odelia make her ceaseless clumsy pirouettes in the oblivious sunshine.

"You should have told me," Darien said at last.

"Should I?" Taro replied. "When I didn't understand why the change had started and I didn't know if it might reverse itself? To tell you would have been to raise doubts about her status as heir. I did not want to take away her birthright for what might be a condition that healed itself."

Darien gave him one long, stern look. "And do you acknowledge now that the passage of two or more years argues against the possibility that this is temporary?"

"I believe she still might improve," Taro began, but when Darien's face showed incredulity, he nodded, and bowed his big head. "I believe she might," he went on, "but not enough to assume the duties that would fall to the queen."

"Then we have some hard decisions to make," Darien said.

Josetta was amazed that he could move on so quickly from shock and sadness, where she was currently mired, and begin focusing on future considerations. But she supposed he had no choice. None of them did.

"We need to assemble the other primes and discuss what needs to be done next," Zoe said in a subdued voice.

"Which leads me to the next question," Darien said. "Besides the people in this room, who knows of her condition?"

"My wife and three women from my estate who share the primary burden of watching her. No one else."

"Mally? Natalie?" Zoe asked.

Taro shook his head. "We have kept them segregated from her for more than a year. We have been too afraid of what they might in all innocence say about Odelia when they are at public functions. Mally is too shy and obedient to ask many questions, but Natalie has been very vocal about wanting to know where her sister is. At least—she used to be." He sighed and rubbed a big hand across his face. "Now Natalie has gotten used to calling Mally 'Odelia' and she sometimes seems to forget there are two different girls. But twice in the past quintile we have found her coming up these stairs, so I believe she knows there is something strange in the house. She just doesn't know how strange."

As they spoke, they continued watching Odelia spin and sing, completely lost in her own private world. Josetta watched Romelle as the queen watched her daughter, her face a study in loss and devastation. When Odelia overbalanced and tipped to the floor, making no attempt to get up again, Romelle looked as if she couldn't bear it any longer. Instead of sitting down to comfort the girl, Romelle turned away, covering her face with her hands.

It was, strangely, Corene who stepped forward, ignoring Zoe's outstretched hand and Darien's "Corene, no." Her face solemn, her approach gradual and unalarming, she drew closer, then dropped to her hands and knees and crawled the last few yards to Odelia's side. She seemed to be speaking, but her voice was so low, Josetta couldn't catch a word. When she put her arms around Odelia, the little girl first started a wordless shrieking, flapping her hands as if to fly away. But Corene persisted, picking her up, pulling Odelia into her lap, wrapping her arms around the girl and bending her red head over the dark one. Enclosing her, almost, in a living cocoon of warmth and safety.

Josetta could hardly believe it, but within a few minutes, Odelia stopped wailing, grew almost calm in Corene's arms. She still wouldn't speak. She still wouldn't glance up at Corene, or even seem to acknowledge that the other girl was present. But she settled against her sister as if she had found a haven when it had seemed no such thing as a haven existed.

They moved the conversation back to the lower level of the mansion, to one of those big cheerful rooms with soft furniture and plenty of light. Taro's wife—an ample, smiling woman of great serenity—joined them only long enough to order refreshments and tell them she was having servants carry in their luggage.

Zoe exclaimed, "Oh—and Celia—I left her with the nursemaid in our elaymotive, but if she's fussy—"

Taro's wife patted her reassuringly on the shoulder and said, "I'm usually pretty handy with a baby."

"We have some decisions to make," Darien said again as soon as she was gone. "And we must make them quickly."

Taro gave him an inquiring look. "I don't understand the hurry. You did not expect Odelia to inherit the throne for almost twenty years. Surely we have time to consider our course."

"The empress of Malinqua will be here within the quintile and she is a stickler for protocol. She has expressed an interest in meeting all the princesses—and she has already familiarized herself with their names and likenesses."

"Mally may still stand in for Odelia until we come to a decision," Taro said.

Romelle had joined them, her eyes red with weeping, and some of her defiance rekindled. *"Mally!"* she exclaimed with bitterness. "The only good that will come of this whole disaster is knowing that I will no longer have to pretend *she* is my daughter!"

Josetta and Corene exchanged looks. Corene had been right when she declared that Romelle loathed Mally, though the reasons were far more complicated than they'd imagined.

"I suppose she will have to," Darien said, answering Taro. "Until we have decided what to do about Odelia."

"What to *do* about her!" Romelle responded with great affront. "You don't need to *do* anything about my daughter. She's beautiful. She's perfect. And I love her with all my heart, just as she is." Zoe reached over to hug her, but Romelle shook her off, glowering at Darien. "You can't come here and tell me that she doesn't deserve the best possible life."

"No," Darien said. "I would want her to be happy and cared for as long as she lives. But she isn't fit to be queen."

Romelle still seemed to be feeling belligerent. "Well, who wants to be queen anyway? All those gossips, all those terrible people trying to catch you out in a lie—it's a miserable existence."

"I agree in some respects, but that's not the point at issue here," Darien said. "Odelia was named heir by virtue of being Vernon's true daughter. If she cannot rule, we need to publicly say so. And then we need to determine who *will* be in line to take the throne."

Taro glanced around the room. "The other three heirs are all on the property," he said. "I suppose that's not an accident. Shall I bring Natalie into the room as well?"

Which was when Josetta realized exactly why Darien had wanted her to accompany him on this trip. *We miss you,* he had said. What he had meant was, *It is your duty as an heir to the crown.* Trust Darien to only give you partial information no matter how much you wanted to know the whole truth. She would have glared at him across the room except she knew he wouldn't care.

"We do not need Natalie's presence in the room, but, yes, I thought there might be some value in having all the princesses in one place," Darien answered. "When the primes certified Odelia as heir, they also determined the order of the succession. First Natalie, as Odelia's half sister by blood—then Josetta, as the eldest of Vernon's supposed daughters—then Corene. If that order still stands, do we need to begin more intensive preparation for Natalie? Do we need to find a decoy princess to occasionally substitute for her? Do we reconsider Josetta, who is so close to her majority? What is our course of action?"

Now Josetta looked straight at Rafe. He had been so silent since this whole strange interlude began, keeping himself so effortlessly out of the way, that even she had started to forget he was present. But she felt his sudden involuntary spasm when Darien put her forward as the likely queen. His face was flooded with dismay, and she could practically read the thought in his mind. *I might be a prince in hiding, but I'm not fit for a queen.* She gave him a small smile and nodded. *Oh yes, you are. Wouldn't that be the biggest gamble of your life?*

"Darien," Zoe said, and there was a note of urgency in her voice that made everyone in the room sit up straighter. "Yes—that was the original plan—but not everybody was satisfied by it."

Taro nodded. "I remember. The thinking was that if we had gone to so much trouble to make sure the heir was definitely Vernon's daughter—flesh of his flesh and bone of his bone—that Odelia's heir should also be from Vernon's line."

For a moment, Darien lost his usual look of calm certainty. "That's inconvenient," he snapped. "Whose idea was *this*?"

Taro and Zoe frowned at each other, as if trying to remember. "Nelson's, I think," Taro said. "It's a sweela sort of argument."

Darien put his hand to his temple as if his head hurt. "Then Nelson must have thought there was some advantage to his own family to promote such a plan," he said, sounding weary. "For instance, was Vernon in some way related to the Ardelays? That would explain Nelson's eagerness."

"Of course Vernon was related to the Ardelays—*all* the Five Families have intermarried over the generations," Zoe said. "I can tell you that the Lalindars and the Frothens and the Serlasts also carry some blood from that line, but it's very diluted. That can't be why Nelson would push for Vernon's heir."

Taro glanced at Josetta. "In fact, I would have expected Nelson to have favored Josetta's claim, since she is his brother's daughter."

"If it matters," Josetta said, "I don't want the throne."

"It doesn't," Darien told her. "Well, who *would* be Vernon's closest kin? He didn't have siblings or even first cousins—it was one of the reasons his advisors were so concerned when he failed to produce children of his own. But he must have relatives *somewhere*. This must all have been researched before Josetta was even born."

"It was," Zoe said faintly. She had a hand across her mouth and looked as if she had seen smiling death dancing around her wedding dress. "Oh no. Oh no no no no *no*."

"That could hardly be more ominous," Darien said. "Tell us."

"I touched his arm. At some function back in Quinnelay. And I noticed it then, but it was faint—Vernon's ancestry, yes, and a healthy percentage of Ardelay blood. I can't believe that Nelson—but the Ardelays were out of favor for so long that maybe he thought this was a way to right the balance—"

"Zoe," Darien said sharply.

Her expression was wretched as she glanced at him, at Corene, and back to Darien. "Dominic Wollimer. Alys's husband. He's Vernon's closest living relative—that I know about, anyway."

"I won't have that imbecile taking the throne of Welce no matter how many primes certify him!" Darien exploded.

Zoe shook her head. "Not him. His child. Alys's baby."

. . .

Darien stared at Zoe a moment. Josetta could almost see him putting the puzzle together, piece by piece. "She knew," he said flatly, and Zoe just nodded.

"She knew what? What are you talking about?" Taro demanded.

Darien was having a hard time controlling his anger as he returned his attention to the torz prime. "You told me that only a handful of people were aware of the situation with Odelia, but you lied," he said. "Obviously, Alys knew as well."

Taro clearly resented the tone. His voice was cool when he answered, "As far as I know, she didn't."

"Then why would she marry a man with nothing to recommend him but his distant connection to the late king? And why would she choose to have his child?"

"Alys is pregnant?" Romelle exclaimed. "She didn't tell me that!"

Darien swung his attention her way. "You and Alys are in the habit of confiding in each other, are you? I thought you disliked her."

Romelle looked a little guilty. "I used to. When we lived at the palace. She could be so *cruel*. But we've become much closer since Vernon died and we don't have to play all those political games."

"*You* might not be playing them, but *she* is," Darien replied. "Alys never stops intriguing."

Taro put a hand on Romelle's shoulder. "She knew about Odelia?" he asked, his voice gentler than Darien's.

Romelle nodded. "I didn't tell her—she found out. It was almost two years ago, and everything with Odelia was so new and raw. She stopped by one day—just like you, Darien!—on her way somewhere else. And she found us in the playroom, and she saw Odelia and she—she—I was so afraid! I begged her not to tell anyone, I said I was sure Odelia would get better, and she was so *kind* to me! She said only a mother could ever understand how terrifying it was to watch a child grow up and worry about all the dreadful things that could happen. She said she would never tell a soul. And she hasn't. Every time she sees me, though, she asks after Odelia, and it's such a relief to have *one* person I can confide in, *one* person I can be honest with."

"And one person scheming to take away the throne," Darien shot at her.

Romelle lifted her chin. "You said it yourself, Darien. Odelia will never be queen. So why do I care who inherits the crown?"

"She must have gone straight from this house to Chialto and started romancing Dominic Wollimer," Zoe said. "She probably didn't even stop to wash the travel grime off her face."

"But I don't understand," Darien said, frowning again. "How did Alys realize that the primes were considering supplanting Vernon's other daughters as heirs? It can't have been widely known."

Not known at all, Josetta thought, *if I didn't even realize it.*

Now Zoe looked a little angry. "My cousin Rhan would be my guess," she said. "He and Alys have always gotten along famously. So Nelson told his sons, Rhan told Alys—" She shrugged.

Taro still looked disbelieving. "So Alys figures all this out—more than two years ago!—and proceeds to marry Dominic Wollimer just in case the other princesses are put aside? That takes some cold-blooded calculation and long-range thinking."

"She is capable of both on a grand scale," Darien said grimly.

"If she wanted the prestige of being mother to the next queen, why didn't she put her effort into convincing us that Corene was the right one?" Taro asked.

"Because Corene is mine," Darien said, "and she knew she couldn't control me."

"No," Zoe said, sounding weary. "Because she doesn't care if it's one of her daughters on the throne. All she cares about is being in the middle of the excitement of court. Corene is old enough to make her own decisions—she doesn't need Alys at her side. But a baby? Everyone will have to come to *Alys* to beg for favors and sue for attention. She regains all the power. Which is all she has ever wanted."

"Well, she's regained nothing, because that child will never take the throne," Darien declared. "I won't allow it."

Taro fixed him with a sober stare. "Pardon my bluntness, Darien, but you don't have anything to say about it. The primes make that decision."

For a moment Darien looked so hostile that Josetta thought he might throw something at Taro. "Fine," he bit out. "But if you choose

Alys's unborn child, *you* can see it through the next twenty-four years of its life. I will not be regent, I will not be advisor—I will not even be living in Chialto. I'll repair to Zoe's estate in the mountains, and I won't leave again."

"Who needs you, anyway?" Romelle burst out. "All you do is cause trouble and make everyone else unhappy."

The look he turned on her should have scorched her flesh, but all he said was, "Indeed. Those are my highest aspirations."

"I think we've allowed our emotions to run a little high," Taro interposed, raising his hands in a gesture of peace. "Maybe it is time for you to withdraw to your rooms to recover and prepare for dinner. It has been a difficult day for all of us."

"All this drama could have been avoided if you had been truthful with us," Darien said.

"Maybe so," Taro said. "Discretion seemed like the best course at the time."

"I suppose it was never true?" Zoe said suddenly. "That story you told about the woman sneaking into Odelia's room and cutting off a lock of her hair?"

Romelle looked self-conscious, but Taro merely nodded. "A fiction to explain our choices."

"Nelson thought you were lying," Zoe said. "But I couldn't believe it."

He gave her a tired smile. Josetta thought that, despite all the anger in the room, the two primes still remained allies. Somehow that made her feel hopeful. "It was more difficult than I thought it would be," he said. "The words were ashes in my mouth."

Romelle started edging toward the door. "Do you need me?" she asked pointedly. "Or can I go?"

Darien looked like he wanted to protest, but Taro nodded, and she slipped away. "There is still so much to decide," Darien began, but Taro shook his head.

"Not now. Not tonight. In the morning. And perhaps over the following nineday, and the nineday after that. But for now, we are all tired, and sad, and ready to spend some time apart. I will have my wife take you to your rooms."

In fact, his wife must have been loitering in the hallway, waiting for some signal, for at that precise moment she stepped in. "I have put you all in rooms in the east wing," she said. "I think you'll find them very comfortable."

They made another trek through the house, but this time only to the second story, where, indeed, they found their bedrooms to be richly furnished and stocked with every amenity. "I hope you will join us for dinner in about an hour," Taro's wife said. "Let me know if there's anything you need."

Josetta made a point of noticing who was shown to each door so she could—if she chose—find anyone else at a moment's notice. Rafe caught her eye and grinned; he was clearly engaged in the same exercise. They were across the hall from each other. Josetta was sure she didn't have the nerve to attempt a tryst when most of her family was only a few yards away, but it was an illicit thrill just to contemplate the idea.

The others disappeard so quickly into their own rooms that Rafe and Josetta were suddenly alone in the hallway. That brief moment of solitude was all the encouragement Rafe needed to take two steps to her side and draw her into a close embrace.

"This has been a hard day," he murmured into her hair as she buried her face against his chest. "My body still aches, but everyone else is in a different kind of pain. I think I prefer the physical wounds."

"At least you know they'll heal," she agreed.

"It was very strange," he said. "To see this story unfold and be so removed from it—but at the same time, it was so raw that it hurt to watch."

"It's not like Darien to permit strangers to witness his battles," Josetta said. "I think he sometimes forgot you were in the room."

Rafe laughed softly. "I don't think Taro ever realized I was in the *house*. He never looked at me and no one introduced me. I'm surprised to learn I have a room of my own—though, to tell you the truth, I was almost hoping I didn't."

She lifted her head, and he took the chance to drop a quick kiss on her mouth. "No one introduced you? How rude! I'm so sorry!"

"I've gotten used to being ignored by primes," he said. "I'd be disappointed if one of them came right up to me and shook my hand."

"Mirti will," she promised. "She's like Darien—relentlessly focused on the components of power. She never overlooks anyone."

"Just like Darien? Then I can hardly wait to meet her," he said dryly.

She giggled. "She's his father's sister," she explained. "And even more hunti than he is." She kissed him briefly and reluctantly let him go. "I need to change clothes."

"Will I see you later tonight?"

"I doubt it." She glanced up and down the hallway. "Considering exactly where everyone else is placed—"

"Then I won't expect you," he said, "but that won't keep me from hoping." He touched her cheek. "See you at dinner."

She sighed. "And what a delightful dinner I imagine it will be."

Inside her room, Josetta hurriedly changed into a formal tunic and tried to comb her hair into some semblance of style. When it resisted her best attempts, she headed to Corene's room two doors down.

"Do you have a hair clip I could borrow?" she asked as Corene let her in.

"I was just going to ask if *you* had one you could lend to *me*," Corene answered. "I look ghastly."

Josetta laughed. "Hardly that. You look—" She paused, because now that she inspected her sister's face, Corene did look unwontedly pale and pinched. At the same time, her eyes glittered with an emotion that was hard to read. Anger. Or maybe grief. They also held a clear warning for Josetta not to ask what was wrong. "You look like you've been traveling," she ended awkwardly.

Corene turned away. "Fortunately, Taro doesn't really care what people look like. And I get the feeling Romelle doesn't care about *anything* these days."

"No. It's very sad and shocking, isn't it?" Josetta said, furiously reviewing the conversations of the afternoon to try to figure out what had upset Corene. "Though you were so good with Odelia! I was really impressed."

"Oh, well, I sort of know how she feels," Corene said airily. "No one's ever going to want her to be queen."

Of course. That was what had made Corene look so drawn and hurt and unhappy. The conversation about the next heir—and the revelation that Alys had been doing her best to supplant any of the existing candidates. Including her own daughter. Just one more piece of proof that Alys didn't love her.

Josetta's heart ached for Corene, but she knew better than to say so out loud. "Well," she said, her voice as light as she could make it, "I don't think we know *who* the primes are going to pick to sit on the throne next. I predict a lot of arguing and maneuvering and lying and plotting. Just the sort of thing I hate."

"My father hates it, too," Corene said.

"Fortunately, he's very good at it," Josetta replied.

Corene actually laughed. "Yes, he is," she said a little more cheerfully. "Let's go down to dinner and watch him do it."

TWENTY-TWO

Rafe could not wait to leave Taro Frothen's manor house behind, and he wasn't the only one. Despite its plush furnishings and the kindness of their hostess, the place reeked of sadness and worry. After the one oppressive dinner, which taxed all of their conversational abilities to the limit, it was clear none of the visitors wanted to stay any longer than it would take to load up their elaymotives in the morning.

He did have one interesting and unexpected exchange with Taro, though. It came after dinner, when all the women accepted an invitation from Taro's wife to visit the conservatory where she was able to grow flowers year-round. Only Darien, Rafe, and the torz prime remained behind.

That's when Taro fixed his gaze on Rafe and said, "You're an odd one. I can't quite get a read on you. Why'd they bring you along?"

Rafe glanced at Darien, who answered. "Oh, surely you can do better than that, Taro. Zoe and Nelson were able to figure it out. Even Kayle. I'll be disappointed if you can't."

That made Taro raise his eyebrows and resettle his bulk as he stared at Rafe appraisingly. "I don't think you're from Welce," he said at last. "If you'd take my hand, I could probably learn more."

"Certainly," Rafe said, and stretched across the table to meet Taro's grip. The heavy eyebrows shot up, then Taro released him and sat back.

"Kin to Ghyaneth of Berringey," he said. "Now there's a mystery in need of an explanation."

"You see I am dealing with other issues nearly as confounding as Odelia's secret," Darien said. "Harboring fugitive royalty might put the kingdom at almost as much risk as squabbling over who should inherit the throne of Welce."

"He might be an asset, not a liability," Taro said.

"How so?" Darien demanded.

Taro shrugged. "A living creature is always a thing of possibility. A dead one is not. You just have to remember that living things sometimes have minds of their own—something you, Darien, tend to find an inconvenience."

Instead of being annoyed, Darien looked amused. "I think the world would run more smoothly if they did not."

"It might run the way *you* want it to," Taro said. "Not always the same thing."

That exchange was the last bit of lightheartedness for the evening. Once Rafe retired to his room, he waited hopefully, but Josetta did not appear. In the morning, after the briefest of breakfasts and almost curt farewells to their host and hostess, Darien said to Rafe, "You're riding with me."

So there was really nothing to enjoy about any part of the return journey, and Rafe was beyond grateful when the three elaymotives pulled up in front of Darien's city house late on the following afternoon. "You could come in and eat something," Zoe said doubtfully as servants began unloading luggage.

"No," Josetta said without hesitation. "This trip has been far too long as it is."

Zoe gave her a quick hug, but didn't press them to stay. "Don't forget. Darien says that the empress of Malinqua will be here in a couple of ninedays. Which means *you* must be here—and you, Rafe."

"I don't think I'm enjoying all my time with royalty," he answered. "I always thought it would be more glamorous."

"It does seem that way from the outside, doesn't it?" Zoe agreed. "But really, close up, politicking is an ugly business."

Rafe had to give Darien credit for running an efficient household. It wasn't twenty minutes between the time they pulled up and the time he and Josetta were on their way again, in one of the big transports that could carry them as well as their guards. Rafe cared less what the soldiers thought than what Darien might think, so as soon as they were out of sight of the big house, he slid closer to Josetta and put his arm around her.

She sighed and leaned her head against his shoulder. "I didn't think it would be fun but I didn't expect it to be *horrible*," she said. "But it was. Every minute of it. Except the card games on the ride up," she added.

"Yes, I found the outbound journey more enjoyable than the homeward one, when it was just the regent and me not speaking in our elaymotive," he said.

She offered a tired laugh. "You don't like Darien."

"Oh, I'm gaining a great deal of respect for him. I think he's brilliant. He's like some impossibly skilled street performer. He never loses track of all the very different things he's juggling—and if one of them explodes on him in midair, well, he just picks up something else and moves on. He doesn't waste his tears."

She tilted her head up to look at him. "He's kinder than that makes him sound," she said seriously.

"Maybe," Rafe said. "But that's not a side of him that everyone gets to see."

They had turned on the Cinque and headed south, then east. Not until they missed the turnoff toward the port did Rafe realize their destination was the shelter. He kept his disappointment to himself. During the past six days, his body had accomplished a fair amount of healing, and he was itching to get back to the training facility—or back in an aeromotive. But even he realized they'd been away from the shelter too long.

Josetta answered his unvoiced sigh. "Just for a couple of days," she said. "I've been gone so much."

He kissed her forehead again. "I wasn't complaining. I'm looking forward to seeing how much work has been done on the tailor's shop."

"You're not," she said, "but it's good of you to pretend."

"Anyway, it might be nice to have a couple of days that aren't filled with drama and excitement. No spectacular crashes. No terrible revelations."

"No family members watching your every move."

"That's what I'm *really* looking forward to," he agreed.

So neither of them was prepared to step inside the shelter and find Steff waiting for them in the dining hall. Well, actually, sanding the edges of a newly constructed wooden table and explaining to Callie's son, Bo, how to fit together the joints of a broken chair, but clearly engaged in these activities merely to pass the time until the moment they arrived.

"Steff," Rafe said blankly. "What are you doing here? How did you find this place?"

Steff laid down his tools and came over, brushing his hands on the back of his work trousers. "I went to the tavern first, and that man told me to try this address." He glanced around. "And Callie told me it might be a few days before you got back, but I could make myself useful while I waited."

That certainly sounded like Callie. "Does Bors know where you are?"

Steff nodded. "He's not happy about it, but he knows."

"How long have you been here?"

"Three days." He jerked his head in a northerly direction. "Mostly I've been working over at the tailor's shop. Helping put up walls and fix the stairs. I like it better than working on farm equipment."

"Who wouldn't?" Josetta said, smiling at him. She held out her hand. "Since your brother looks like he's not going to introduce us—"

"Sorry, sorry. Josetta, as you've guessed, this is my brother, come up from the country to complicate my life."

"That's *not* why I'm here!"

"And, Steff, this is—" Rafe hesitated. How to explain Josetta?

"I knew you must be seeing someone," Steff said with satisfaction. He'd shaken Josetta's hand and let her go, but he was still watching her with admiration. She was tired, and her travel clothes were rumpled and plain, but there was still a fineness to her skin and an elegance to her bearing. And then, of course, there was that hair. "Last time you visited, you couldn't wait to rush back here."

"That's how I always feel. You of all people should understand. Anyway, this is Josetta."

"Josetta? Do you spell your name like the princess does?"

She was laughing. "Exactly like that!"

"And, yes, we've been seeing each other," Rafe said, because that was the story they'd devised—and because it was true. "But it's complicated."

Steff glanced at the soldiers who were just now tramping inside. Sorbin was arguing with one of the newer members of the guard unit, but without any heat; it sounded like they might be trying to set up a sleep schedule for the next few days. "Who are all these fellows?"

"That's why it's complicated," Rafe said.

"Why don't we all sit down and talk?" Josetta suggested. "Steff, are you hungry? I'm starving. And this might take a while."

No one was supposed to know the truth about Rafe, so they went with the fiction they'd told the soldiers: Rafe had overheard some incriminating information during a late-night session of penta, so the regent had assigned him an armed guard, with a royal heir thrown in to disguise the reason. Steff seemed less agitated about Rafe's danger than Josetta's identity

"But—you're—the princess?" he stammered. "I should have—I didn't bow! I should—"

"You should just be courteous, which you have been," she said with a smile. "I'm not a very picky princess." He still seemed overwhelmed so she tried to put him at ease. "What do you plan to do while you're here? Are you looking for a job? Do you need somewhere to stay?"

Steff looked uncertain. "I slept at Samson's tavern for the first night, but I like it better here."

Rafe shook his head. "This is why I haven't wanted you to come to the city. I don't have a place that's suitable for you."

"Take him to your apartment in the port," Josetta suggested. "Maybe Kayle would even give him a job."

"Any job," Steff assured them. "I'll work hard."

Rafe thought it over. "That might be feasible. How do you feel about doing maintenance on machines?"

Steff's eager look changed to consternation. "Farm machines? Here in the city?"

Rafe started laughing. "Oh no, much better. Smoker cars and aeromotives. Kayle runs a bunch of factories where he builds them."

Now Steff's face lit with delight. "Aeromotives," he breathed. "That's what I want to work on."

"I can tell you're brothers," Josetta said.

Rafe told Steff, "Wait till you hear what I've been doing lately."

Despite the fact that both Rafe and Steff were dying to get to the port, they spent three days southside while Josetta finished stacks of paperwork and checked on construction at the tailor's shop. Rafe had expected Steff's presence to make things more awkward with Josetta, but it didn't. For one thing, Rafe thought, Steff was still young enough to be fairly self-absorbed; he didn't care too much what was happening to other people unless it had a direct impact on him.

For another, Josetta handled the whole situation with the easy diplomacy he figured she must have learned at court. "Rafe stays in my room, of course, but you can pick where you'd rather sleep," she told Steff on that very first night. "Here in the shelter—where it tends to get very crowded lately—or over at the construction site, where Callie says most of the workmen have been staying."

Steff nodded. "That's where I was the past couple of nights. Suits me fine."

"Good. Then you can head over after dinner and we'll see you in the morning."

They had their meal, played a few hands of penta, and saw Steff off, accompanied by a couple of the other construction workers. And then it was time for Rafe to follow Josetta up the stairs to her room, shut the door, and take her in his arms. There had to be more than fifty people settling down at various places in the building, some of them, like Foley and Callie, barely a thin wall away. But it didn't matter. Rafe forgot they were nearby, forgot they even existed. He was alone with Josetta, and there was nobody else in the world.

Since he had to keep himself occupied while Josetta was busy, Rafe spent the next three days with Steff at the tailor's shop. He had never had much chance to work alongside his brother, and he was impressed at the boy's steady hands and quiet self-confidence. Some of the older men—clearly recruited from the ranks of potential tenants—even went to Steff for advice on how to handle certain tools or complete tricky joints. Steff showed his skills to advantage in those interactions: His instructions were clear, his patience unlimited. Rafe was pretty sure Kayle would find Steff a worthy hire.

But. "Maybe you should attend one of the training schools, really learn how to do this stuff," Rafe told him.

"Maybe later," Steff said. "I just—I want to get started *now*. I feel like I've wasted too much time already."

It was a sentiment Rafe could definitely understand.

Rafe was also impressed by how much had already been accomplished at the new location. An outdoor stairway had been constructed to lead residents to the upper levels, where the open spaces had been neatly divided into small bedrooms. On the bottom story, a long, narrow bathing room had been built along the back wall. Of course, there was no water yet, and the tailor asked them several times a day when the coru prime would return to fulfill Josetta's promise.

"When everything's ready for her," was the standard response of the bald, burly man who seemed to be overseeing the job. "Got to make sure all the pipes and sewers are in place."

But either that was a stall tactic to shut the man up, or the pipes and sewers were miraculously completed overnight, because Zoe showed up late in the afternoon of the third day. She was accompanied by Corene and a couple of guards.

"Well! Isn't this nice!" Zoe exclaimed as she insisted on touring the entire site before living up to her part of the bargain. "I wouldn't mind staying here myself some night."

"It won't be quite as nice once it's filled with Josetta's usual patrons," Rafe reminded her with a smile. "It will be crowded and noisy and full of questionable characters—"

She smiled at him. "I might like it even better then."

Corene had made the whole circuit at Steff's side, while Zoe and Rafe followed a few feet behind. Steff hadn't had much chance to be awed at the appearance of *another* princess in his life, since Corene had greeted him with: "Are you as interesting as your brother?"

"I don't know," Steff had replied, taken aback. He glanced at Rafe. "I never thought he was that interesting."

That made Corene laugh. "No, you never think your siblings *are*. They're usually just annoying."

"He wasn't around enough to be annoying. I just always thought he was lucky, because he got away."

She glanced around the construction site. "Well, it looks like you got away, too."

When they were done inspecting the upper floors, they trooped downstairs to find the tailor and his sons impatiently waiting. Zoe exchanged a few words with the big bald worker—confirming, Rafe supposed, that the all-important pipes really were in place.

Then she wandered into the bathing room and simply stood there a few moments, wearing a faraway expression, almost a look of bemusement. The rest of them crowded around the doorway, watching her, but she didn't recite incantations or seem to strain against heavy invisible burdens. She just looked as if she was trying to recall a not-very-interesting conversation she'd had a few ninedays ago so she could manage to say something polite to the woman she'd met on that occasion, if she happened to see her again.

Then she gave her head a small shake, turned to smile at the tailor, and said, "I think that takes care of it."

The tailor was suspicious. "You didn't *do* anything! Was it all a lie? Are you really the prime?"

"I should have the guards arrest you," huffed Corene, clearly offended, but Zoe just laughed.

"Try the spigots," she invited.

Still scowling, the tailor pushed through the doorway and wrenched at one of the faucets in the communal shower. He shouted and jerked back as water spurted out and doused him from above. Excited, his sons followed him into the room, running from faucet to faucet, opening each to its maximum flow. Water gushed from all of them, pattering onto the stone floor and slowly filling the room with steam.

"There's a hot spring that runs right under this part of the city," Zoe said with satisfaction. "Such a luxury in a place like this."

The tailor and his sons were laughing and hugging each other, but Corene splashed up to them, disregarding how soaked her trousers and

Royal Airs  S 289

her shoes became. "You should apologize right now to Zoe," she commanded. "Zoe *never* makes promises she doesn't keep."

Callie prepared a special dinner to celebrate the arrival of water in the second location, though Rafe thought the happy mood owed as much to the four bottles of wine he'd slipped off to buy. Well, he never actually "slipped off" anywhere these days; he was accompanied by Steff and trailed by three guards, and they drew no little attention as he stopped at a nearby tavern to make his purchase. Then again, the bartender didn't try to cheat him on the price, which was more or less routine here in the slums, so he supposed there were some advantages to always having an armed escort.

The meal was convivial, even Callie and Foley consenting to join them, though the cook jumped to her feet the minute the meal was over and Foley joined the other guards to divide the evening shift.

"When will people start moving into the second building?" Zoe asked.

"Sometime in the next nineday," Josetta said. "I won't be here, though, since Rafe and I plan to go down to the port tomorrow." She glanced at him. "He's been very good, but I can tell he's itching to climb into another aeromotive."

"I don't want Kayle to replace me," Rafe said. "Arven's probably all healed up by now and ready to take my place."

"I want to see you fly. Can I come, too?" Corene asked.

"If you want," he said. "If Zoe says you can."

"Well, I'd like to see such a thing myself!" Zoe exclaimed. "If we come with you tomorrow morning, will you be flying by afternoon? I don't want to be gone from Celia too long."

"I don't know when Kayle will schedule the next flight," Rafe admitted. "I know there was another model almost ready to go, but there are so many factors that determine a launch."

"Can I go even if you don't?" Corene asked Zoe.

"No. If I can't have fun, you can't have fun."

Josetta was laughing. "Send a note to Darien and tell him you've been called away for a few days and *he* will need to take care of the baby. Because it's obvious you want to come with us."

Zoe was wavering. "Well. Maybe if we arrive early in the morning. If Kayle says no flight for another nineday, we go home. But if there's a flight tomorrow, we stay."

"Excellent," Rafe said, refilling their glasses with the last of the wine. "Off on another adventure."

Steff and the princesses were clearing the table when Zoe drew Rafe aside for a private conversation.

"I like your brother," she said. "Did you tell him your story?"

He shook his head. "I was sure Darien wouldn't want me to. But I'll admit I'm worried. If it turns out that my mother was the royal, not my father, I'll have to. He'll be in just as much danger as I am. It didn't seem so risky when he was down on the farm, but if he's in the city where anyone might see him—"

Zoe nodded. "I was sure that was on your mind. So I made a point of taking his hand this afternoon."

"And?"

"None of Ghyaneth's bloodline in him at all. Steff is safe from Berringese justice."

Rafe felt a peculiarly powerful sense of relief; he hadn't realized how deep his fear had run. Steff didn't bear any telltale markings, of course. No one would have been able to identify him as a Berringese heir just by sight. Still, Ghyaneth sounded like the type to be frighteningly thorough, and if he had ever learned of another claimant to the throne . . . "Good. Thank you. I'm glad he's just an ordinary young man."

Zoe was smiling. "I'm sure, like you, he's extraordinary in his own way."

Of course, Zoe and Corene had to share Josetta's room, which meant Rafe followed Steff back to the tailor's shop to spend the night. So, the next morning, no one looked particularly rested by the time they assembled their caravan of one prime, two princesses, one prince, one brother, eight guards, and two drivers.

"When I think how simple it used to be to just walk out the door and *go* somewhere," Rafe marveled.

"I know," Corene said. "That was one of the reasons I loved traveling with Barlow and Jaker! It was just us and Foley. So easy."

"Who are Barlow and Jaker?" Steff asked her. As the youngest, they had been relegated to the cramped back bench of Zoe's elaymotive. Corene had seemed displeased at this arrangement until she realized Steff would be sitting beside her, and then she'd become almost complacent. Rafe figured she could tell how much Steff was dazzled by her, and she liked soaking up his adoration.

"Merchant traders that Josetta and I traveled with one winter," she said, and then launched into the whole story.

The rest of them carried on their own conversation, and the trip to the port passed in a much less tedious fashion than it usually did. They found Kayle at the factory, conferring with one of his designers, but he broke off his conversation to greet them.

"Are you finally recovered?" he demanded of Rafe. "When can you fly again?"

"This afternoon, if you've got a machine ready," Rafe answered with a laugh. "I've brought a few friends who'd like to witness a flight."

"Not today," Kayle said, shaking his head. "Not enough notice for the crew. Tomorrow, though. The K5 is ready to go."

Corene grabbed Zoe's forearms with both hands. "Can we stay? Please? It's just one more day. *Please?*"

"You and Corene can sleep at my house," Kayle told Zoe. "And then you and I can talk."

Zoe had looked undecided at first, but those last words convinced her. Rafe reflected that the primes had no end of conversation ahead of them. She said quietly, "You've heard from Darien?"

Kayle nodded. His face softened more than Rafe would have expected; the elay prime never seemed like the empathetic sort, but maybe he'd had tragedies of his own. "A sad business all the way around," he said. Then his mouth twisted. "And more *politicking* to follow. The very sort of conversation I hate the most."

"Yes, you and I are not good at all the plotting that comes so naturally to Nelson and Mirti," Zoe agreed. "Our strengths lie elsewhere. But we must work together for the good of the kingdom."

Kayle sighed and agreed.

. . .

Rafe returned to the training facility for the afternoon to discover that enduring a crash and passing a nineday without any strenuous exercise had left him weaker and slower than he liked. He was sore and sweaty by the time he joined Josetta, who had dutifully followed him to the facility, though she'd brought a stack of books to while away the time.

"Sorry, I know that was boring for you," he said, bending in to give her a brief kiss, careful not to drip perspiration on her tunic. "I hope the others had a livelier day."

Indeed, it turned out that Zoe, Corene, and Steff had passed a most delightful afternoon. When Zoe learned that Steff had never seen the ocean, she borrowed a boat from some Lalindar relative and took the young people sailing. Over dinner, Steff rhapsodized endlessly about the joys of being out on the open sea and wondered whether he should sign up to be a sailor instead of a factory worker.

"I thought I sensed a little coru in your blood," Zoe said, amused. "But I confess I didn't think you would take to the ocean so whole-heartedly."

"What *are* your blessings?" Corene asked.

"Mostly coru," he admitted, "including travel and surprise. My father would laugh and say those were the wrong blessings for a torz man. But I was never torz."

"What's the third blessing?" Corene wanted to know.

"Synthesis."

There was a short silence at the table. "Interesting," Josetta said. "That's one of Rafe's blessings, too."

"I didn't think you *had* blessings," Steff said to his brother.

"Josetta picked them for me."

"Josetta always picks the best blessings," Corene said.

There was a little more talk, but everyone was tired, and Rafe thought Zoe was eager to get to Kayle's place and discuss state matters with the elay prime. The first time Steff yawned, Josetta pushed herself to her feet. "Well, we're leaving here very early tomorrow, so you two should probably be getting to Kayle's," she said. "See you in the morning!"

Rafe had resigned himself to the notion that he would be sharing his room tonight with Steff, not Josetta, but the princess was not so easily defeated. As soon as her sisters were out of sight, she gave Steff her usual friendly smile and said, "You won't be nervous if you're here alone, will you? Rafe and I will be just across the hall."

Steff yawned again and shook his head. "I'm fine. A little privacy will be nice after the past few days."

"Then we'll see you in the morning, too."

TWENTY-THREE

Rafe wondered if it would ever become a casual thing to climb into the pilot's box of a live aeromotive and prepare for take-off. His brain was singing with adrenaline, his stomach was clamped with nerves, but all in all he would describe his state as elated rather than fearful. He forced himself to do a final check of all the gauges and dials, reminding himself of all the ways the K5 was different than the LNR. It was bigger, for one thing, no roomier in the pilot's box, but with a broader wingspan and heavier drag. Noisier, too. The throttle placement was farther to the left, and he'd already knocked his knee against it once.

But the biggest difference for this takeoff was that Rafe was outfitted with a piece of safety gear—one of the flying bags. The yoke with its flat container of chemicals had been clamped across the open pilot's box, and as soon as Rafe settled himself into the padded chair, he fastened its straps around his chest. If the K5 went spiraling for the ground, he could rip the yoke free, yank on the string that would combine the chemicals in the bag, and be lifted skyward by the sudden explosive burst of power. In theory, anyway.

Rafe was devoutly hoping he wouldn't have the opportunity to put the invention to the test.

He took one last look around—at the open road before him, the crowd of well-wishers behind him, the cloudless sky overhead—and nodded at the mechanics. He felt the engines rev up to takeoff speed and watched the mechanics dash for safety. Then he pulled on the throttle and felt the K5 leap forward.

Yes—faster and more powerful than the LNR—he reached takeoff speed in about half the time and lifted into the air with a guttural roar. For a few moments, Rafe felt like he was wrestling the big craft upward with his own body strength, forcing the nose to angle above the horizon. Then the machine seemed to steady, to find its own buoyancy—or, more truly, its own *joy*. It was as if the elaymotive was a wild animal that had been penned up too long and suddenly realized that its gate had been left open. It shot into the hard blue heavens with blistering euphoria.

Kayle had cautioned Rafe not to go as far this time. *We'd rather have you return safely than have you bring back stories about seeing the ocean,* he'd said. Together they had decided he would be wise to stick to the road until he got too close to the port and ran the risk of encountering land traffic. Following the paved surface also ensured he had a better chance of finding a landing site if the K5 developed any trouble.

Accordingly, he flew a southeasterly route, never letting the road get out of sight. Three times he passed over traveling elaymotives, once over a horse-drawn carriage. He was close enough to ground level that he could see the miniature people jump out of their vehicles and stare up at him, pointing and waving. Not sure if they could see him in return, he leaned over the side and waved back. He knew they weren't near enough to see him grinning like a fool.

Once he could make out the shapes and shadows of the port, he brought the K5 into a wide sweeping circle and guided it back toward the hangar. He glanced at his fuel gauge; still three-quarters full. The K5 ate through its reserves more quickly than the LNR did, but its hold was bigger. He should be able to fly just as far and maybe a little faster.

The engine chugged on with a reassuringly steady grumble as he retraced his route. But he wasn't nearly ready to come down again by the time he spotted the wide, flat roof of the hangar ahead of him. Accordingly, he kept the K5 at a cruising altitude and sent her straight over the compound. He could see the crowd gathered below pumping their fists in the air. He thought that, over the roar of his engines, he could catch the sound of their cheering.

He continued another mile northwest, but this was practically untracked wasteland—loose, sandy soil that didn't support much vegetation and would be hell on an uncontrolled landing. Anyway, his fuel gauge had slipped below the halfway mark. Time to subdue his rebellious spirit and head on home. He made another huge half-circle turn, tilting his left wing down and pivoting on its axis, and began the return trip.

He found himself unexpectedly nervous; this was when the LNR had begun to have trouble, and superstitiously he braced for similar problems with the K5. But the larger aeromotive held steady as he steered it back toward the hangar, back toward the road, dropping gradually lower. Once he cleared the rooftop, he descended more precipitously, not wanting to run out of the absolutely straight section of roadway before his wheels were on the ground.

He was probably going a little too fast when he touched down. The world suddenly became a windy blur of wild motion as the K5 careened along the pavement, metal shrieking, wheels bouncing, everything streaming by at an impossible speed. Rafe fought to keep the plane centered on the roadway, though his eyes watered with wind and his arms felt as if they were being torn from their sockets. The right wheel hit some kind of obstruction and the whole machine lurched into a violent spin; Rafe was almost flung out of the box. But when the dizzying motion ground to a stop, he was still inside the K5, he was still on the road—and he was still alive.

He'd actually done it. He'd taken off and landed safely, not a hundred yards from where he'd intended to put down. His machine was intact, and so was he. Even though no one was near enough to hear his victory shout, he threw his head back and whooped with exultation.

Kayle was all smiles as he roared over in a small open elaymotive. Behind him, like a splendidly variegated wake, the dozens of onlookers rippled toward Rafe in a spreading V of running motion. Rafe searched their faces until he could spot Josetta and Steff, Corene and Zoe right behind them. They were all waving madly, and he returned the gesture with equal energy.

"Perfect, wonderful, exactly what I hoped for!" Kayle called as he pulled up with a flourish that almost tipped his little vehicle to its side, then raced over to help Rafe climb out of the pilot's box. Rafe was surprised to find himself a little wobbly, as if he'd just tumbled down a mountain or run an exhausting race. Apparently flying an aeromotive successfully could leave a pilot almost as exhausted as crashing one. "Did you have any trouble? Tell me what happened while it's still fresh in your mind."

One of Kayle's assistants arrived on the scene, panting, and began taking notes as Rafe reeled off everything he could remember about wind resistance, hiccups in performance, hesitations, inefficiencies. "But, as I say, no real problems," he finished up. "This machine is born to fly."

Kayle beamed at him. "I think *you* are born to fly," he said. "That was spectacular."

Rafe laughed. "When can I do it again?"

Rafe probably could have stayed another few hours at the hangar, discussing the minutest details of the flight, but it was already close to noon and he could tell Zoe was anxious to start her trip back to Chialto. So they loaded up their caravan again and headed back to port.

"That was the most exciting thing I've ever seen," Corene said once they were on their way.

"Does it make you want to become a pilot?" Rafe teased her.

"No," she said flatly. "But it makes me want to come watch you the next time you fly."

"I want to do that. Do you think I could do that? I might want to be a pilot," Steff chattered. "Except—I'm a little afraid of the height. And the speed. But I definitely want to help build the next aeromotive!"

"Did you ask Kayle for a job?"

"Yes! And he said to come talk to him tomorrow."

"Did you tell him you were coru?" Josetta asked, twisting around from her seat so she could see Steff in the back. "I think he only hires elay mechanics." When his face fell, she started laughing. "I'm joking! I'm sure he hires all sorts of people!"

Rafe made an equivocal motion with his head. "We-ell. He has sweela workers, I know. And hunti, I think. But coru? I'm not so sure."

"Then I'll just get different blessings," Steff said. "Whatever it takes."

Zoe and Corene had left their belongings in Rafe's apartment, so they went inside quickly to gather their bags and wash up before setting off for home. While waiting for them to return to Rafe's room, Josetta wandered over to the big window that overlooked the ocean, and Rafe trailed behind her.

"A little less frightening for you this time?" he asked, resting a hand on her shoulder.

She tilted her head to smile up at him. "Not really. I was terrified the whole time you were out of sight, and even more terrified as you began to land. Of course, the fact that you didn't come plummeting down made it a little less scary, but I don't think I breathed until you arrived at a complete stop. Without bursting into flames."

"I loved it," he said. "Every single minute. I can't wait to do it again."

On those words, Zoe and Corene stepped back into the room. "Maybe that's what it means when a man has only extraordinary blessings," Zoe said. "It means he's a lunatic. Because only lunatics would want to fly."

Steff spoke up from where he lounged on the sofa. "Does Kayle Dochenza have extraordinary blessings? Because he's the one who built the machines."

"Well, elay folks," Zoe said in a dismissive manner. "Everyone knows *they're* crazy."

They all looked toward Josetta to get her reaction, but she was focused on something she could see out the window. Taking in her frown, Rafe followed her gaze out to the harbor. All he could see was the familiar sight of hundreds of ships crowded up to the docks, with more in the distance dotting the blue expanse of ocean. "What's wrong?" he asked.

She didn't answer. "Zoe? Do you recognize this flag?"

Zoe joined her at the window. "Which? Darien was just telling me that Welce trades with something like twenty other countries and I should really learn to . . ." Her voice trailed off.

Now Corene came over to see what they were staring at. Frowning,

Rafe returned his attention to the harbor. As Zoe had said, the ships gathered around the docks appeared to come from a couple dozen different nations, judging by their flags and the slight variances in their construction. Rafe recognized the most obvious ones, the merchant ships from Cozique and Berringey, and four or five others that he could name. And there, a whole cluster of ships with the distinctive heraldry of Malinqua, a red field divided into quarters by crossed swords; the militant message was somewhat softened by the small white flowers that marched symmetrically across the cloth. It looked like there were six or eight Malinquese ships docked in the harbor all at once. And there were another four or five hovering a half mile or so offshore—or, rather, another ten or twelve—a whole fleet, actually—

Rafe looked over at Zoe. "I thought the empress of Malinqua wasn't coming for at least another nineday."

"That's what Darien thinks, too," she said. Her eyes never left the harbor.

"She's certainly brought a large escort," he added.

Zoe nodded. "Much larger than Ghyaneth's, and he made a point of being followed around by twenty guards wherever he went."

"She's not—I mean, she's not *invading* us, is she?" Josetta asked, her voice uncertain.

"I don't think there would be enough soldiers in those ships to really mount an offensive," Rafe said.

"No," said Zoe slowly. "But there could be another hundred ships out in the deep ocean, just waiting to be summoned."

There was a beat of silence. "We have to tell Darien," Corene said.

Zoe nodded. "You know your father keeps spies here in the city. One of them is already racing to Chialto with the news. But *we* need to get back with all speed."

Josetta nodded and turned away from the window. "We can help you carry your bags downstairs. Do you want to take any food with you?"

"Oh no. You're coming with us," Zoe said.

"But—"

"Darien's going to want you back under his protection the minute he hears that the empress has sailed into the harbor with all colors flying." She jerked her head in Rafe's direction. "He's got to come, too, of course."

"Can't we join you in a few days?" Josetta asked.

"Kayle's expecting me in the morning," Rafe put in.

Zoe almost laughed in their faces. "Where do you think *Kayle* will be headed tomorrow? A foreign dignitary has arrived on Welce soil, bringing a formidable force at her back. *All* primes, *all* heirs will be convening in Chialto—with all haste."

Josetta sighed and gave Rafe a look of resignation. "We'd better start gathering our things."

Rafe nodded over at Steff, who was still sitting on the sofa, but looking a little anxious as the conversation progressed. "I need a day to get Steff settled. I can't just abandon him in a strange place."

"I'll be fine," Steff said, but he didn't sound convinced.

Zoe was smiling. "Bring him along. We have a big house. Plenty of room."

"I'm not sure Darien Serlast will—"

"Darien Serlast will be happy to have him. Come on. Everyone start packing."

Before long, they were all piling back into the elaymotives again. Rafe had thought it might be brotherly of him to sit beside Steff in the back of Zoe's big vehicle so he could point out the sights of Chialto. *Here's the Cinque. There's the Plaza of Women. If you follow that road halfway up the mountain, you'll arrive at the palace—can you see it? Splendid, isn't it, with the river making that spectacular fall right beside it.* But when he offered, Corene said, "I don't mind sitting back here with him. I'll tell him what everything is. You'd probably just get stuff wrong, anyway."

He'd glanced at Josetta with lifted eyebrows, and she'd smiled. "Well, you probably would," she said softly. But he could tell she was having the same thought that was uppermost in his mind: *Corene rather likes Steff.* The princess was indulging in a mild flirtation with the country boy. Who would have expected that?

Rafe tried to judge his brother with dispassionate eyes. Steff was good-looking enough, he supposed—taller and thinner than Rafe, but more muscled from a lifetime of hard physical labor. Rafe always thought of him as a little sulky and dissatisfied, but he'd been the complete opposite during these past few days. He'd been good-natured, hard-working, deeply interested in the events unfolding around him, and generally agreeable. Well. Maybe the princess was enjoying his company after all.

As before, they made good time in the royal elaymotives, but there was still a fair amount of ground to cover. It was almost the dinner hour by the time they pulled up in front of the tall, gracious Serlast manor and everyone began spilling out of the elaymotives. Foley organized the guards and hustled them off to some post in the back of the house, while silent, efficient servants unloaded the cars and made their luggage vanish.

Darien was awaiting them inside the *kierten*, his arms crossed and his expression sardonic. Zoe didn't wait for him to speak first.

"Darien, have you heard?" she demanded. "The empress of Malinqua is at the harbor, at least a nineday before we expected her!"

"Yes, I sent for her, hoping her presence would goad you into returning home. Since nothing else appeared likely to," Darien replied.

He didn't sound angry, and Zoe didn't look remotely contrite. "Well, you would have stayed, too, if you'd had a chance to see all the wonders *I* saw," she said. "But what are we going to do about the empress?"

"Welcome her, of course, but with perhaps a little more *presence* than I had planned," Darien responded. "I've called up some of our naval fleet to sail down to the harbor, and I'm bringing more troops into the city. Just to be safe. I can't think she's planning an assault, but she's obviously trying to make a point. So we must make one of our own."

"Will you call Romelle and—and Mally in?"

"I'm not sure," he admitted. "I had originally considered the presence of the heir to be essential, but with that situation in so much turmoil, Romelle's attendance might be more trouble than benefit. If the empress seems offended, I can use her own tactics against her and say her unexpected show of force made me reluctant to put our smallest princess at risk. I think it is an argument that will carry some weight with her."

They were all still standing in the *kierten*, but Zoe made brushing motions to urge them deeper into the house. "Let's get everyone settled into rooms, and then, I hope, find something to eat. We only had travel rations on the road, and I'm starving. How's Celia?"

"As she always is—alternately delightful and temperamental, and unfailingly vocal," Darien said. He nodded over toward Steff, who was standing in Rafe's shadow and trying not to gawk at the understated luxury of the house. "I don't think I know this young man."

"He's Rafe's brother," Corene explained. "He came to Chialto to visit Rafe, and he's been having adventures with us."

"'Adventures'?" Darien repeated, glancing at Zoe.

She grinned and tugged Steff forward. "Steff, this is my husband, and Corene's father, and the regent of Welce, Darien Serlast. He tries to be intimidating, but don't let him alarm you. He's not as hostile as he seems."

"Sometimes I am," Darien said in a pleasant voice as he eyed the boy critically. "But I didn't realize there was a brother! Are you very much like Rafe?"

He glanced at Zoe when he posed the question, and Rafe realized he was really asking her about Steff's bloodline. *Is this another Berringese prince we will have to protect? And does he know his heritage?*

"I guess we're a little alike," Steff said nervously.

But Zoe was smiling and shaking her head. "I've only spent a couple of days with Steff but I feel certain he's very different," she said.

Rafe thought the regent relaxed at the words. "Welcome to the house in any case," Darien said.

"Enough talking in hallways!" Zoe exclaimed. "All of you follow me upstairs while Darien makes sure dinner is served as soon as humanly possible. Then we can talk and talk and *talk* until we run out of things to say."

Rafe reflected later that this particular clan probably never *did* run out of things to say. The meal wasn't exactly boisterous, but Josetta and her family members all vied with each other to fill what moments of silence inexplicably occurred. They had no end of topics to discuss, from what to do about Romelle and Mally to what kind of tone to take with the newly arrived empress of Malinqua. Darien wanted to hear specifics on their "adventures," which led to talk of Josetta's shelter and Rafe's aeromotive exploits. Then they all wanted to catch up on any gossip Darien had heard while they had been gone. Even Celia, sitting in Zoe's lap for the meal, expressed herself frequently and vociferously, though not particularly intelligibly. Rafe figured it was only a matter of time.

Rafe found his opinion of Darien rising as he viewed the man in this setting, surrounded by the women who loved him. He was still autocratic, peremptory, and overconfident, but he was also warm, humorous, and affectionate. It began to make more sense to him that the wayward and generous Zoe might want to be married to him.

"Well, I expect the next few days to be chaotic in the extreme, and all of you look like you're ready to fall asleep in your chairs," Darien said as the meal drew to a close. "Except Celia—I imagine she'll be awake till midnight. But the rest of you might as well seek your beds."

"Gladly," Corene said through a yawn. "Oh, but—wait. Steff, I want to show you Zoe's favorite room in the house. You're coru, so you'll like it—it's got a river."

"A river? Inside? I have to see that," Steff answered, and the two of them jumped to their feet and disappeared out the door.

Darien turned to Zoe. "I have asked the other primes to join me in the morning. I expect only Taro to be missing, since he has some distance to travel. But the rest of us can debate some of our many, *many* concerns in what time we have before the empress arrives on our doorstep."

"Does she have a name?" Zoe asked. "It seems so odd to just call her 'the empress.'"

Darien nodded. "She does indeed have a name. Filomara Marita Subriella. Which sounds much gentler than I believe she is."

Rafe felt shock go through him with the force of a crash landing. Years of card-playing enabled him to keep his face impassive, show none of his astonishment or confusion. But he was more than familiar with some of those soft syllables. Subriella had been his mother's name.

TWENTY-FOUR

Josetta didn't like the empress of Malinqua any more than she had liked the prince of Berringey. She remembered how intensely she had hated the viceroy of Soeche-Tas and wondered if perhaps she just despised royalty. Or people who wielded power. During the past five years, her sympathies had become much more allied with the poor and powerless. It made it harder to sit at state dinners and play the part of princess.

The empress had arrived in Chialto in the morning, escorted by a hundred of her own men and fifty of Darien's, who had been on hand to greet her when she disembarked. The Welchin soldiers had brought her directly to the palace, where she was welcomed by a hastily assembled cast of queens, princesses, and primes.

"Sorry to arrive before I was scheduled," she said to Darien, speaking in Coziquela and not sounding particularly sorry. "The winds were so favorable we could hardly hold back the sails."

"We're delighted to have you, no matter when you appear," he replied, not sounding particularly delighted, either. He gestured at the men behind her, filling the courtyard with their red-and-white uniforms and their prominently displayed weaponry. "You must have been forced to leave some of your guard behind! Surely there were more men than these on the many ships you brought to harbor."

Her eyes gleamed with understanding and malice. She was a tall, solid woman with iron-gray hair and a square, unsmiling face. Unlike Ghyaneth, she hadn't bothered to array herself in resplendent dress for this final leg of her journey. She was wearing black trousers and—even in the heat of Quinnahunti—a long black jacket embroidered with red and white flowers. The clothes were well-made but hardly luxurious. She had dispensed with a crown or any other distinguishing headpiece, but across her chest and shoulders she wore a heavy chain of interlinked metal plates, each as big as a hand and studded with rubies. It was substantial enough to make Josetta think of armor, which she had to believe was the intent.

"I admit, I am a cautious woman, and I have been treated poorly by other heads of state," the empress said. "I have no reason to think you mean me ill, but I assume you are more likely to treat me well if you know my archers could burn down your city in a matter of hours."

"And yet other heads of state have shown you disrespect," Darien marveled.

She gave a sharp bark of laughter. "There are many who believe a woman on the throne must be weaker than a man," she said. "I would not want you to make that mistake."

"I never underestimate women," Darien replied. "I think it is my greatest source of strength."

One of those women sailed forward almost upon the words. "Let me welcome you into our capital," said Elidon. "We have prepared rooms for you and thirty attendants. We must discuss where you would like us to billet your remaining soldiers."

Filomara glanced around the courtyard. "This will do."

"It will not," Elidon said with great courtesy and utter inflexibility. "But there are several barracks outside the city, and you may take your pick."

"If I cannot have my troops around me, I cannot stay," said Filomara.

Elidon didn't even hesitate. "Then you may return to the port so that you can have them on your ships nearby. We will happily join you there while we conduct negotiations."

There was a long silence while Filomara appeared to be weighing Elidon's words, testing them for any hint of bluff. "Thirty of my soldiers with me in the palace, twenty in the courtyard, and the rest at a city barracks," she said finally.

Elidon turned her head to speak to an attendant hovering at her elbow. "We will be relocating to the port this afternoon. Can you begin gathering my wardrobe?" She glanced at the elay prime, standing a few feet away from her, his pensive expression making Josetta believe he was thinking about some problem with an aeromotive and not about the current confrontation. "Kayle, I assume you can house the members of the royal party for a few days?"

Kayle turned to her, his blue eyes rapidly blinking. "Well, I *can*, but I don't want to. All of you? You and the princesses, maybe. And Darien, of course. But I can find you rooms somewhere else."

It was so typical of Kayle that Josetta had to bite her lip to keep from laughing out loud. And she couldn't risk a look at Zoe. Elidon seemed neither amused nor offended. "Good enough," she said, and returned her attention to Filomara. "Would you like to stay for some refreshments before we leave?"

Again, Filomara's face showed both comprehension and malice. Josetta wondered if the empress had expected this little game to play out differently—if she was pleased or exasperated to find her hosts adept at maneuvering for power. *Ghyaneth thought we were provincial, so she probably does, too,* Josetta thought. *It makes me wonder what their cities are like.*

"We will stay," Filomara replied. "The barracks will suit after all."

Dinner that night was as full of pomp and excess as the first dinner with Ghyaneth but, as far as Josetta was concerned, with two major improvements. First, she hadn't been singled out by visiting royalty, so she didn't have to sit next to the empress on the main dais; and second, Rafe accompanied her to the meal.

"One more person among two hundred will hardly be noticeable, and we've brought him here to keep him safe, so let's keep him safe," Darien had said that morning as they made their preparations to move to the palace. "I don't suppose he has anything suitable to wear."

He didn't, of course, but Darien either lent him clothes from his own wardrobe or tasked one of his extremely efficient servants with outfitting Rafe for the night, because the next time Josetta saw Rafe he was very properly attired. The finely made tunic and trousers were both an unrelieved black, and the dark color added interesting contours to his face. One of the servants had also found a couple of rings to slip on his fingers and a silk ribbon he could use to tie back his hair. Josetta could not help staring when he joined her in the *kierten* of the palace, where they had all been assigned rooms for the next few days.

"I think I would *recognize* you, if I just happened upon you like this, but you look completely different," she told him, coming close enough to touch his shoulder through the black silk.

"In a good way or a bad way?"

"Definitely good."

Corene's assessment was even more blunt. "Oooooh, I didn't know you could look like this!" she exclaimed. "Just like a prince, but a *handsome* one."

"Glad to know I won't embarrass you at the dinner," he replied.

"For the first time," Corene said disparagingly, and then burst into laughter.

As Darien had predicted, there were two hundred people at the meal, and Josetta knew that Rafe was only acquainted with a handful. So she spent much of the evening identifying the major political players in Chialto for him, and following up names and titles with tidbits of gossip.

"That's Mirti Serlast. Darien's aunt and the hunti prime. I need to introduce you as soon as I can . . . The woman wearing the very blue headdress? Queen Seterre. My mother. When you meet her, say something nice about the feathers . . . And *that* is my cousin Rhan. Nelson's son. See him flirting with Alys? That's why Zoe thinks he told her about the succession."

"Where's her husband? That Dominic fellow?"

"Darien won't allow him at any function where Corene will be present."

"And she agreed to that?"

"Darien had guards take him away when he tried to accompany Alys to some event recently. So she didn't have a choice."

"Things are going to change if—" He didn't finish his sentence.

Josetta nodded. "Oh yes. One way or the other, things are going to change."

So the first meal wasn't bad and there was better news to come. It turned out Filomara had little patience for sumptuousness, as she made plain the very next morning.

"Spare me the expensive and pointless assemblies of your rich and powerful," the empress said to Darien as a much smaller group finished up a delicious breakfast. They were in Elidon's quarters in the queen's wing, a place where Josetta had spent uncountable hours watching the four queens spar and maneuver for precedence. She still hated this room. "I will take it as a given that you wish to do me honor, but I would be spared the tedium of experiencing it."

"You are not the only one who benefits from such events," Darien said in a mild voice. "Invitations to attend receptions at the palace are prized among the members of our Five Families."

"Let them find some other form of social currency," Filomara said.

Darien glanced around the room, making brief eye contact with Elidon, Zoe, Mirti, Kayle, and Nelson. He didn't bother glancing at Corene or Josetta, who had retired to a divan pushed against the east wall, or at the empress's attendants, who had taken a rather uncomfortable set of chairs on the other side of the room. He was looking for consensus from the power brokers of his circle. "Certainly we do not want you to be either bored or overwhelmed," Darien said. "We will drastically curtail the activities we had planned for you. As long as *you* are satisfied with the treatment you receive at our hands."

"If you speak sense and listen to mutually beneficial proposals, I assure you I will be satisfied," the empress replied.

"Then let us proceed."

Now Filomara glanced at the other Welchins at the table, and turned her head to take a long, deliberate look at the princesses. "And these are the people who make the decisions in Welce?" she asked, not bothering to hide the fact that she was unimpressed. "Now that the king is dead?"

"Some of us were deeply involved in making decisions even while the king was alive," Mirti said dryly. "Particularly in his last two years, when he was not well."

"So if there are issues you would like to raise, we are the ones you may speak with freely," Darien said with an edge to his voice.

When the empress spoke again, it was clear she had been counting noses. "But there are missing faces," she said. "I understand that you have five primes and four princesses. And assorted queens. They are not all here."

"Of Vernon's wives, only Elidon still keeps her hand in politics," Darien said. So he had decided to do without Romelle as well as Alys, Josetta thought. That was interesting. Seterre had long ago given up any hope of being included in Darien's calculations. "The fifth prime is on his way."

"And the missing princesses?"

"One is not quite five and one is almost seven. I doubt you would find their counsel useful."

The rest of them could not look at each other, thinking about how unlikely it was Odelia would ever have much conversation to offer in an assembly like this.

"But they are healthy, both of them, young as they are?" the empress pressed.

At that point, Josetta noticed, Nelson narrowed his eyes and fixed his gaze on Filomara's face. Everyone else was too busy being annoyed to wonder what she might mean by her interrogation, but the sweela prime had caught a hint of the thoughts uppermost in her mind. And didn't much like them. But he stayed silent and let Darien handle the conversation.

Which he did with his usual ability to lie with ease. "They are quite healthy. Those of us who have known them from birth are amazed to realize they have grown so quickly."

"Children do," Filmomara said, a dark note in her voice.

Mirti stirred impatiently in her chair. "So then," said the hunti prime, who could match anybody for bluntness, "are we enough for you, or do you want to wait until the table is full before you offer us your proposals?"

Filomara nodded once, sharply, and said, "This is enough to begin with. I am looking for allies. Berringey has been making extensive trade agreements with Cozique and a few of the island nations, and there is some thought they are making pacts of aggression as well. There is no love between Malinqua and Berringey. I am looking to find my own allies that I can call on if I am suddenly pushed into war."

That was an honesty so rough as to be almost brutal, and Josetta knew her own face showed shock. But Darien was nodding as if he had expected her to say exactly that. "We are a small country, and while we deploy enough military might to protect our own coasts, we have never looked for war outside our borders. Apart from skirmishes with Soeche-Tas many years ago, we have been an entirely peaceful nation."

"I envy you the geography that has made peace a viable option," Filomara answered. "But Malinqua has many nearer neighbors, some of them warlike, and we have a long history of conflict."

"I am sorry to hear it," Darien said, "but I am not eager to share it."

Filomara's mouth quirked. "You may not be eager to, but you may all the same."

"Please," Darien said, his voice edged in sarcasm, "speak plainly."

Filomara leaned back against her chair. "I know Ghyaneth Kolavar visited here this spring. You think he wanted to talk trade, but he was assessing Welce for its assets and its strength. Is the country rich in anything Berringey would like to have, and if so, how much trouble would it be to seize the nation through war?"

"That's an interesting theory," Darien said.

"And when he left here, he traveled to Soeche-Tas, did he not? A country that is not overfond of Welce, due to a diplomatic disaster five years ago."

Nelson spoke up. "Congratulations on your network of spies," he said. "You're singularly well-informed."

Filomara snorted in disdain. "You have spies in my cities as well. Or if you do not, you should."

Darien didn't answer that. "At any rate—" he began

Filomara interrupted. "At any rate, I think it would not take much to rouse Soeche-Tas against you, particularly if Berringey promises aid. At which time, you would be glad to have allies like Malinqua at your back."

"Well, I don't know," Kayle said, unexpectedly entering the conversation. "What would it cost us to have a treaty with you? What are *you* looking for?"

"I want a blood alliance," she said flatly. "I want one of your princesses."

There was a long silence in the room. Josetta felt Corene go rigid with shock, but she didn't think anyone else was surprised. Darien, in fact, looked perfectly relaxed, almost sprawled back in his chair.

"And what would you do with one of our girls?" he asked softly. "You have no sons of your own to marry them off to."

So Filomara had been right, Josetta thought; Darien *did* have spies in her cities. Somehow, she wasn't surprised.

"No, no sons, and no daughters living, either, though I bore two," Filomara said heavily. "But I have nephews, and brothers who are eager to see one of their sons take the throne. I would marry one of them to one of your girls."

"And promise her the crown?" Darien asked.

"I have some years left before I have to yield my place," Filomara responded. "I have not yet made final determination on my heir. But that would not make the bond between our countries any less strong."

"With our abundance of princesses, we have also had the luxury of wondering which one to name heir," Darien said, which earned him sidelong glances from all of his advisors. "What if we offered a counterproposal? One of *your* blood relations marries one of our princesses and they take the throne in Chialto?"

Zoe and the other primes were now openly staring at Darien, which made Josetta realize he had come up with this plan without discussing it with anyone. Corene poked her in the ribs and, when Josetta looked over, opened her hands in a gesture that meant, *What is he doing?* Josetta shook her head. *I have no idea.*

She glanced at her uncle Nelson again. Now he was frowning in concentration as he tried to figure something out. He looked from Darien to Filomara—and over at Josetta, where his gaze lingered. Without knowing why, she felt her stomach tighten.

What was going on here?

Filomara's face hardened and her shoulders straightened. "That is not an arrangement that appeals to me," she said. "Besides, I am looking for brides for my nephews to strengthen *my* royal line. I am not as interested in how you shore up your own."

"I think you are merely afraid of repeating an old mistake," Darien said. "And you want to make sure you control any future power alliances between you and another nation."

The empress scowled and her attendants buzzed, and it was all too much for Mirti. "Darien, for once stop playing games," the hunti prime burst out. "The empress has spoken openly. You could at least do the same."

"The empress has not been honest with us," Darien said. "I will accord her that courtesy when she extends it first."

There was a long silence in the room, broken only by the sound of Filomara drumming her fingers on the table. Nelson had sat back in his chair, a certain satisfaction showing on his face, but now Kayle leaned forward, almost as if he was sniffing at a bouquet. His blue eyes blinked rapidly behind his glasses as a look of excitement crossed his face.

"Darien," he began, "this woman—"

"I know," Darien interrupted. "Let her tell us in her own time."

Josetta felt Corene's grip on her arm. "What is it?" Corene whispered. "What have the primes figured out?"

"I don't know," Josetta whispered back, "but Mirti and Zoe don't know it yet. So it has to be something they could only analyze by touch, and neither of them has laid a hand on her."

Finally Filomara loosed another short bark of laughter. "So you're not quite as unsophisticated as you seem," she said.

"If by that, you mean I, too, keep international informants, then you're right," Darien answered.

"Please," Elidon said, managing to sound soothing instead of pleading. "Obviously Darien would like you to share some details before we can proceed. We are at an impasse unless you tell us more."

"Well, it's hardly a secret," Filomara said in a rough voice. "I bore two daughters, named the eldest my heir, and married the younger one to a likely prince. But my eldest daughter died of a fever and my youngest was murdered by her husband. Which is why I am not eager to see any of my other heirs take up residence in foreign nations."

That was when Zoe got it; Josetta could tell by her sudden start and her look of astonishment, quickly hidden. But she sent one quick, marveling look Darien's way.

Elidon was offering official condolences. "What terrible tragedies. My heart goes out to you for the losses you suffered."

"It was more than twenty years ago," Filomara said gruffly. "I am past the heartbreak, but I do not forget the betrayal."

"No, and how should you?" Darien agreed. "No wonder you despise the people of Berringey."

"*Berringey!*" Corene exclaimed, as every last person in the room now put the pieces together. "But—"

Darien stopped her with a single icy look before addressing Filomara again in a smooth voice. "I knew your daughter died, but I had not realized she was murdered," he said.

Filomara nodded bleakly. "In good faith, I married her to the queen's second son, and she bore him a child. But they have odd customs in Berringey. They kill off some of their heirs when they become too numerous, and my daughter and her son were among the ones deemed expendable."

"Sad indeed," Darien commented. "If only your spies would have known about such customs before you agreed to the wedding."

The resulting silence was even more toxic than the last one. Filomara glowered and everyone else, even Kayle, looked a little unnerved, but Darien still seemed wholly at ease.

Sitting there with Corene still tugging on her arm, Josetta worked out the rest of the puzzle. *Darien probably knew their customs, even before Ghyaneth arrived this spring, even though the rest of us had no idea. So Filomara must have known, too, before she married her daughter to Ghyaneth's uncle. She took the risk in the hope that her daughter might become queen. Did her daughter know before the wedding? Maybe she didn't. Maybe that's why she came to Welce instead of returning home—because she realized her mother had been willing to risk her life.*

Filomara finally spoke again. "I told you I can be as ruthless as any man. But I have paid the price for folly and ambition. Now I am looking to repair damages and build alliances. I have several fine nephews, aged eighteen to thirty-three." She gestured at Josetta and Corene, who sat motionless as marble when everyone looked their way. "You have two princesses old enough to marry, and two young enough to provide you some security. Send one of them to me, and bind our nations together for the following generations. It is an arrangement, I promise you, that will benefit us both."

"I would like to make a highly unusual counteroffer—one I doubt you would have even considered," Darien began.

That was when Corene startled everyone by jumping to her feet. "I'll go," she said. "Let one of them marry *me*."

Naturally, there was chaos for the next few minutes. Zoe was on her feet saying *"No!"* even before Darien had had a chance to react, and almost everyone in the room had also jumped up and started chattering. Josetta grabbed Corene's arm and hauled her back, exclaiming, "Are you *mad*?" Nelson was arguing, though it wasn't clear who was listening, while Mirti and Elidon had their heads together as they whispered strategy. Kayle looked around, seeming wholly bemused by the hubbub.

Darien and the empress of Malinqua merely sat at the table, staring each other down.

"So you have at least one adventurous soul in your provincial little capital," the empress said, needling him a little.

Darien was not to be provoked. "We have many. But princesses aren't generally allowed to decide whether or not they would like to be adventurers. Certainly this one cannot make that choice for herself."

"Shortsighted for a regent."

"Oh, but surely you knew," he said. "I am her father as well. And, alas, I cannot claim to be as ruthless as you when it comes to my daughters."

If he meant that as a slap, she took it without flinching. "You were willing to marry her off five years ago," she said. "When she was barely twelve. And you would cavil now, when she is old enough and smart enough to know what she wants?"

That hit home, Josetta could tell, though Darien managed to control his anger. Of course. "You received incomplete information about that debacle," he said, "if you believe I was ever in favor of that alliance."

Filomara shrugged. "It is in the past. It is the future we are concerned with now. What would it take for you to agree to a wedding between one of my nephews and your daughter?"

"Nothing you possess among your incentives," Darien replied in a deliberate voice.

At this point, Corene succeeded in wrenching free of Josetta's hold. She ran across the room, Josetta right behind her. Darien and Filomara came to their feet at her approach, and everyone else fell silent to hear what she would say.

"I meant it—I'll go," Corene said.

She looked jaunty and confident, but Josetta guessed at her unspoken thought. *Nobody here wants me anyway. My mother certainly doesn't.* She spared a moment to hate Alys with all her heart.

For a moment, despite the commotion in the room, Darien put his hands on Corene's shoulders and gave her his full attention. "You are not to speak another word to anyone from Malinqua until we have had a long talk," he said. He leaned in and kissed her forehead. "Now go with Zoe. I love you."

"But I—"

He signaled to Zoe, who came over to take Corene in a hold that was half embrace and half restraint. They could hear Corene protesting all the way out the door.

Filomara seemed grimly amused. "Your daughter has more courage than you do, regent."

"Yes, it is one of her blessings," Darien agreed. "And it has characterized her for her entire life."

"Darien, we need to talk," Mirti said, coming up on his right elbow. She glanced at the empress. "Amongst ourselves."

"I had imagined you would want an opportunity to discuss my proposals before responding to them," Filomara said. "I will withdraw."

"I will be happy to assign someone to take you to some of the sites of Chialto," Darien said. "It cannot compare to Malinqua's capital city, of course, but it has many charms."

Josetta expected some kind of sneering rejoinder, but Filomara nodded. "I would enjoy an excursion, I think. Perhaps Princess Josetta could be my guide?"

"She'd like that," Darien replied. "Josetta, why don't you gather a suitable escort and take the empress to see the Plazas? Perhaps your friend Rafe would like to accompany you. And, of course, as many guards as the empress needs to feel secure."

She had never in her life wanted so much to hit somebody. Only years of rigorous training allowed her to answer with easy courtesy. "Of course. Majesty, would you give me thirty minutes to organize myself? We can meet in the castle courtyard. It's quite warm outside—you might want to dress in something lightweight."

The empress looked amused. "I will endeavor to find suitable attire." Without another word, she turned for the door, her attendants hurriedly trailing after her.

"Darien, we have to talk," Mirti said again, more urgently, as soon as the visitor was out of earshot.

"I don't know if anyone else realized it," Kayle put in before Darien could answer, "but that woman! She's closely related to my new pilot. Rafe—Rafe—I forget his last name."

"Adova," Darien said. "She's his grandmother. I believe everyone eventually figured it out."

"Everyone except the empress," Nelson said. He appeared to be delighted with the complex knot of intrigue. "Did I understand that right? She thinks he's dead?"

"She does."

"Then we would appear to have an advantage over her, though I'm not entirely certain how to use it."

"That's one of the things we need to talk about," Mirti said.

Josetta took Darien's arm, ignored everyone else in the room, and held his gaze with a glare that would have melted his bones if he hadn't been hunti. "Send them away," she said in a low, fierce voice. "Because I need to talk to you alone."

He nodded, not even bothering to look surprised. "Elidon, would you kindly give us the room? This will only take a few minutes."

"Certainly," the queen said. "Should we go down the hall to Mirti's chambers? Darien, join us as soon as you can."

Josetta waited until the room was emptied and she heard the definite click of the door latch engaging. Then she gave him a hard push designed to send him crashing against the wall. It only sent him a couple of inches backward.

Hunti. Unyielding. Immovable. Infuriating.

"You *knew!*" she exclaimed. "You knew he was Ghyaneth's cousin and Filomara's grandson! How did you know? How long did you know? And don't lie to me, Darien."

"I saw the markings on his ear the first night I met him," Darien said. "I knew that meant he was related to the Berringey crown. So I investigated the history of the Berringey royal house. The wedding between nations was documented fact, not hard to uncover. From there, it was easy to unravel the story."

"Why didn't you tell me? Why didn't you tell *him*? You knew he was in danger. And yet you practically let him be killed on the streets—"

"I took steps to keep him safe," Darien answered. "Why do you think I had Caze and Sorbin sent to the slums? Why do you think they happened to arrive in time to save his life?"

She stared. "You sent them to—to—guard *me*. To guard the shelter. That's what you *said*."

"And of course I was happy to think you were also under their protection," Darien replied.

She came close enough to shove him again, with even less effect. He barely swayed. "Then did it occur to you to tell him just because he would want to *know*? Why keep the information a secret?"

"Because I habitually keep information a secret when I can," he said impatiently. "Because, as Nelson said, I hadn't yet determined how to use the knowledge to my advantage."

"That's so selfish! It's cruel!"

"How is it cruel? He lived to be twenty-seven without knowing certain facts about his existence—as long as he was safe, why couldn't he survive another quintile or two without that knowledge?"

"Oh—and you planned to tell him sooner or later, I suppose. When there was an *advantage* to you."

He smiled. "I knew he had become enmeshed in your life. I knew that meant it was only a matter of time before Zoe would insist on meeting him. And I knew what would happen then. And you see I was right."

"You didn't want him to be 'enmeshed' in my life!" she exclaimed. "You thought I was—you thought that he wasn't—" Her voice trailed off. "But if you knew he was an heir to Berringey, you wouldn't have minded so much. Darien, tell me right now you didn't plan for me to fall in love with Rafe Adova."

"I don't think it's ever possible to *plan* for someone to fall in love," he said. "I admit I wasn't unhappy to see that you seemed to like him."

She put her hands to her forehead and turned away from him, so angry and confused that she could hardly think. "I can't believe this," she said. "I always knew you manipulated everyone, but I didn't think you'd play those games with *me*."

He caught her arm and pulled her back to face him. She shook off his hold but didn't move away. "I haven't manipulated you," he said gently. "It is true I have watched events unfold around you without providing you with all the information I possessed, but I can't think you would have made any of your decisions differently. If you would have, I am sorry. But this is the place where we have arrived now."

She lifted her eyes to his, hostility in hers. "This is the place where the primes begin another long argument about who should be named heir, isn't it?" she demanded. "Odelia is obviously no longer in the running. Natalie was always the next one in line, but only because of her connection to Odelia, and that's looking like a liability at the moment. You're obviously going to fight as hard as you can to keep Alys's child out of the succession. And you *love* the idea of marrying a Welchin princess to the newly discovered prince of Malinqua. I think the arrow is pointing straight at me."

"You have spent most of your life as the most likely heir to the throne," Darien said. "You can hardly be surprised."

"I don't want the job. I never wanted it, even when I was growing up, even when I was supposed to be coveting the crown, proving myself to Vernon and the queens. I hate the palace, I hate the royal life, I hate the lying and the pretending and the scheming—all the things that come so naturally to *you*."

That was meant as an insult, and he responded with heat. "They don't come naturally—I learned those skills when I had to. When I believed the kingdom teetered on a precipice and that only a strong hand could keep it from tumbling down. When I realized that my country needed me and that I had no choice but to serve. A man doesn't walk away from a responsibility like that—neither does a woman."

"I could," she said.

"No, you couldn't," he said. "You are as steady as they come."

They stared at each other a long moment. She had no idea what he saw on her face; on his, she read the usual unflinching determination, the bone-deep commitment to whatever task he had taken on as his. Darien had never shied from a hard chore, never shirked a responsibility, no matter how much it cost him. She could not remember a time when he had not, at least in some peripheral fashion, been part of her life, but for the past five years, as Zoe's husband, he had been far more central; and in all that time, he had been an unfailing source of strength and counsel. She might be furious with him, but she could trust him— to always lead her the right way, and to always tell her the truth, if he bothered to tell her anything at all.

She felt the world re-form around her, weight shifting under her feet and inside her heart; she felt long-held but unused knowledge shake free from a dusty corner, preparing to come to her hand if she ever had need of it again.

Oh, but she didn't want to take it up again, didn't want to feel its burden across her shoulders, heavy as Welce itself.

Nothing was settled yet, she reminded herself.

"You cannot pick who will take the throne just because she suits you," she said at last. "The primes are deeply invested in that decision, and they might make another choice."

"They might," he agreed. "But I plan to use my considerable persuasive powers to convince them that Alys's child should not be the next one to wear the crown."

"That doesn't mean they will choose me."

"I think you must accustom yourself to the notion that they very probably will."

She sighed and put her hand to her forehead again. "I can't take it all in. There is too much to think about. And I must go meet the empress of Malinqua and give her a tour of Chialto."

"Be sure and bring Rafe with you," Darien said.

"Though, of course, I can't tell her why I want him along! So when *do* you plan to tell her that she has a living grandson?"

"I haven't decided yet. When the moment seems favorable. That is generally when I share information."

"She might not believe us. There must have been pretenders to her throne in the past."

Darien shrugged. "That's not my concern. Though I imagine the primes could put on a fairly convincing demonstration, sorting out who is related to whom among her swarm of attendants. That might impress her enough to make her believe us."

"Though we could still be lying about Rafe," Josetta pointed out. "If she knew you well enough, that's exactly what she'd suspect."

He laughed out loud. "I see it will take me some effort to return to your good graces! Go collect that troublesome young man and take the empress on a shopping expedition. Maybe she'll buy something fashionable. And, Josetta," he added, as she turned away to do his bidding. "If you can bear it, perhaps you could refrain from telling Rafe the secret of his parentage."

The words were so sweet they tasted like candy in her mouth. "He already knows."

TWENTY-FIVE

In fact, Josetta was only guessing that Rafe knew about his connection to Filomara, because he hadn't been any more honest with her than Darien had. All he had told her last night was that his mother must have hailed from Malinqua, because she shared one of the empress's names.

"Subriella," he added. "I always thought it was so pretty. I imagine it's fairly common in that country."

"Like Josetta is here," she agreed. "And Corene and Natalie and Odelia. You can find dozens of them in any classroom in Chialto."

"But none of them are as delightful as you," he said, kissing the top of her head. They were lying together in his room, where she had arrived after a long and stealthy trek through the palace. The queens' wing, where all the single women were billeted, extended off of one end of the great hall; the king's wing was built off the other. She had encountered a few servants and a few soldiers on her journey through the shadowy corridors, but no one had stopped her.

"Your mother must have been well-born, though, to marry a foreign prince," Josetta replied. "Perhaps Filomara could tell you who she was."

"Oh, yes, I can just see having a nice casual chat with her some afternoon," he said. He had trailed a line of kisses across her temple and down her cheek, and she had thought he was just eager to return to lovemaking, but now she realized he had wanted to distract her. He had figured out the truth, but he didn't know what to do with it, and he didn't want to share it until he did.

If I'm ever queen, all that's going to change, she fumed as she hurried to her room to slip into comfortable shoes. *I will pass a law that everyone has to be honest all the time. Anyone who lies will be thrown into the Marisi to drown.* She figured Darien would be the first to go into the water, though Zoe would probably save him. Too bad.

One of the palace servants was hovering near her door, and she asked the woman to find Rafe and have him meet her as soon as possible in the courtyard. "Oh, and tell him to bring his brother. We're going to escort the empress of Malinqua around Chialto."

Ten minutes later, a small group set out in one of the royal elaymotives, followed by *two* transports carrying ten guards from Welce and ten from Malinqua. The empress had brought personal attendants of her own, briefly introduced as her cousin and his wife. Then she eyed Rafe and demanded, "And who's this?"

Josetta placed her hand on Rafe's arm and managed to produce a girlish giggle. "Oh—this is Rafe Adova. He's my—well, there's nothing official yet, but we—my family likes him very much. And this is his brother, Steff."

Filomara's shrewd eyes took in Rafe's expensively tailored clothing and handsome face, and she drew her own conclusions. "You're not going to want to come to Malinqua and marry any of my nephews, I suppose," she said.

Josetta could feel Rafe's start of surprise, but his expression, as always, remained pleasantly neutral. "I didn't know such alliances were even being discussed," he said.

"They were the topic of today's conversation," Josetta replied.

Filomara nodded sharply in Josetta's direction. "Your sister, though. Did she mean it when she said she'd come?"

Now both Rafe and Steff looked at her in surprise. "Corene?" Steff asked, sounding a little anxious.

"She might think she meant it," Josetta said. "But Darien will have something to say about it. And what he'll say is no."

Filomara grunted. "I liked her. She has a certain fire to her. And bravery in her soul."

Josetta laughed. "Indeed, she's entirely a sweela creature, and one of her blessings is courage."

Now Filomara frowned. "All this talk of blessings! It's very annoying. What does that even *mean*?"

So Josetta launched into a quick explanation and ended up by offering to take the empress to a temple to draw her own. "Or, rather, we will draw them for you," she finished. "Because the blessings have more power when they are bestowed upon you by a stranger."

Filomara seemed reluctantly intrigued. "That seems like an exercise that might be entertaining," she conceded. "I would be willing to do that."

Josetta smiled. "But first let's stroll through the Plaza of Women and shop."

Filomara didn't seem like the frivolous type who would enjoy spending hours sorting through fabrics and considering jewels. So they just made one quick pass through the open bazaar of the Plaza and a more leisurely stroll through the shop district where the very expensive boutiques had their permanent locations. Josetta couldn't resist taking the empress to the cobbler's shop run by Zoe's old friends Melvin and Ilene, because she knew how much Ilene would relish a chance to wait on visiting royalty. And, in fact, Filomara was so pleased with the selections on hand that she bought three pairs of shoes in fifteen minutes. Josetta thought it might have been the first time she had seen the empress smile with real pleasure.

From the cobbler's shop they headed straight to the little temple Josetta had last visited when she pulled new blessings for Corene. She pointed out to Filomara the subtle touches that reflected the five elements—the fountain, the flowering plants, the hovering butterflies—but Filomara just nodded briskly and stepped inside. This clearly was not a woman who bothered much with nuance.

"You can take some time to move from bench to bench and meditate yourself into a state of balance," Josetta said, speaking quietly so she didn't disturb the three people inside who appeared to be doing just that. "Or we can simply draw blessings for you and go."

She wasn't surprised when Filomara said, "Oh, let's just get this done with. Draw the blessings."

So the six of them clustered around the barrel, though the cousin and his wife expressed no desire to participate in the ritual. Josetta nodded at Steff, who looked nervous at being the first one to pick a blessing for the empress. He took his time rummaging through the barrel before pulling a coin and handing it to Filomara. She studied it by the smoky temple light, then showed it to Josetta.

"What does it mean?" she asked.

"Endurance," Josetta replied. "It's a torz trait—a symbol associated with flesh and earth."

Filomara made a sound that seemed to indicate approval. "I like that. I feel like I have endured a great deal in my life."

"Now Rafe," Josetta directed. He took a little longer than Steff had to toss through the blessings; Josetta suspected he was trying to avoid pulling a ghost coin, so he might be fingering each disk in turn. When he finally made his selection, he presented it to the empress, who again held it up for Josetta's inspection.

"Power," Josetta said, smiling a little. "A hunti trait—wood and bone. Again, it would seem to be accurate."

"I like the notion of power," the empress agreed.

Josetta dipped her hand into the barrel. "And I will pick your final blessing," she said. She had thought the coins might be recalcitrant, as they had been for so long with Rafe, unwilling to grant blessings to a foreigner. But her arm was barely wrist-deep in the pile before she felt a disk scalding against her palm. She retrieved it and held it up for everyone to see.

"The glyph for surprise," she announced, and it was all she could do to keep from laughing. Even Rafe, who was always so adept at schooling his expression, had to bite his lip and look away. "A coru sign. Water and blood."

The empress looked somewhat displeased, though she accepted the coin from Josetta's hand. "I don't care for surprises," she said.

"No, I have had my share of unpleasant ones," Josetta admitted. "But now and then—there have been a few big, spectacular ones that I rather liked. Maybe the same will be true for you."

Filomara stood for a few moments gazing down at the coins in her hand. "So what do I do with them now?" she asked. "Keep them? Return them?"

"It's up to you. People who are just looking for guidance on one particular day usually toss their coins back into the barrel, unless they've drawn one that they especially like. People who are receiving their random blessings for the first time often keep them as souvenirs. Though they frequently have the blessings reproduced in more permanent and specialized forms."

Josetta touched her necklace, drawing Filomara's eyes to the charms hanging there, and added, "Zoe wears a bracelet holding her blessing glyphs. Corene wears rings. Some people have them made into artwork. If you like, we can return to the Plaza and shop at jewelry stores that will carry the charms in many sizes and several kinds of metal."

She fully expected Filomara to toss the coins away and say, "No, I'm done with this nonsense," but the empress lived up to her final blessing. "I would like that," she said. "A necklace, perhaps, to remind me of my sojourn in Chialto."

"Excellent," Josetta said, leading the way out of the temple. Foley, who had stationed himself at the door to await their reappearance, barked a command, and all the other guards instantly deployed around them. "We could go to one of the stalls in the Plaza or one of the fancier boutiques in the shop district."

"Something simple will do," Filomara said.

"Then the Plaza it is. It's easier to walk there, unless you'd rather take the elay—"

Before Josetta could finish the word, their cavalcade was plunged into violence. There were horses—riders—the sounds of men shouting and metal clanging and weapons firing. Josetta hadn't even completely registered what was happening before rough hands grabbed her and thrust her toward the haven of the temple. She barely recognized Foley as he deposited her there and charged back into the fray.

"Rafe!" she cried, because she couldn't see him in all the commotion. "Steff!" She knew Foley wanted her to cower inside the temple, but she couldn't, not until she knew what was happening to the others— *why* it was happening. She strained to see through the swirling mass of bodies and animals, flinching every time another firearm detonated.

There seemed to be five soldiers on horseback, dressed in unfamiliar black livery, trampling through the Welce guards and the Malinquese escort. *Is someone trying to assassinate Filomara?* Josetta wondered, looking around frantically for the empress. But Filomara had been shoved out of the way by her own guards, four of whom formed a tight circle around her while the others engaged in fierce combat.

It wasn't Filomara the soldiers had targeted. It was Rafe.

She realized this just as one of the men on horseback raised a weapon to his eye, clearly sighting down a long barrel aimed straight in Rafe's direction. *"Rafe!"* she shrieked, abandoning the protection of the temple to scramble toward him. But one of the Welchin guards caught her before she could take three steps and hauled her firmly back. She heard the loud report of the weapon firing and she screamed again.

"Let me go to him!" she cried, fighting against her captor, whom she finally recognized as Sorbin.

In reply, he dragged her closer to the temple door and struggled to open it against her mad flailing. In the end, he contented himself with shoving her hard against the doorframe and flattening himself over her. No harm could reach her without going through his body first. She could just see over his left shoulder and, helpless, she watched the rest of the battle play out.

Five against twenty made terrible odds for the attackers, but they had two enormous advantages: They were on horseback, and they had more sophisticated weaponry. City guards tended to carry swords, not firearms, a custom that could cost them dearly in this encounter. The street was littered with bodies in the uniforms of Welce and Malinqua, but only one of the riders had been brought down. As Josetta watched, another one of the weapons made its distinctive explosive sound, and another Welchin soldier fell.

Where was Rafe? *Where was he?* Josetta breathlessly scanned the mass of heaving bodies, trying to find his face. He couldn't be dead—*surely* he couldn't be dead—or the invaders would have ridden off by now.

There—dodging through the milling bodies to evade two riders charging at him from different directions. Josetta screamed his name again, and Sorbin fearfully gazed over his shoulder to watch the action behind him. The riders were fast, but the cluttered terrain impeded them. Rafe slipped off the roadway and into the waist-high ornamental shrubbery that lined it along both sides.

He had figured it out, then. That these men were after him. Some of Ghyaneth's soldiers, probably, having tracked him down at last. Head ducked low, he dove through the thick, prickly bushes, the foreigners in close pursuit. But the thorns on the stubby branches grabbed at the horses' legs and caused them to rear and snort. Just as one pursuer quieted his mount and lifted his weapon to fire, Rafe plunged straight back at them, making the horse shy and almost unseat his rider.

Josetta thought Rafe would run back into the covering chaos of the general fight, but he surprised her—he surprised the attackers—by grabbing the stirrup of one rider and swinging himself up. The horse made a furious sound of distress and stumbled badly, crashing deeper into the shrubbery. The wild, unbalanced weight on its back seemed to madden the creature, and it bucked and reared as it tried to dislodge both riders. The two men were punching and clawing at each other, and it was impossible to tell who had the advantage, though Josetta could see that the foreigner had tossed away his weapon so he could use his hands at close quarters. The nearby soldier divided his attention between trying to calm his mount and readying his weapon in case Rafe proved victorious—or offered a clear target.

A ragged cheer dragged Josetta's attention back to the bigger conflict, where she saw only one rider remaining on horseback. He was surrounded by a furious mob of defenders from both nations, and it was clear they were willing to sacrifice every last man if it meant pulling him to the ground. He wrenched his horse away from a Malinquese soldier and got off another shot at a man in Welchin livery, but he was done for; even Josetta knew it.

There were terrible sounds of an animal screaming, men shouting, and large bodies falling, and Josetta's gaze swung back to Rafe's desperate battle. She was horrified to see him lying on the ground a few feet past the line of shrubbery, his body limp and still. One horse and its rider lay spasming a few yards away, where they must have fallen when their gyrations caused the animal to crash. The remaining soldier steadied his mount with his knees and used both hands to lift his weapon.

Josetta hadn't even drawn breath to shriek when a body hurtled from the general melee and dragged the attacker off the horse, then pivoted to fling him straight into the tangled border of thorns. There was a struggle, the hard sounds of grunts and curses, and then a strangled cry of a man being choked to death. The unearthly sound was almost the only noise in a place grown suddenly, eerily quiet.

Josetta risked a quick look around. All the horses were riderless. All the Welchin and Malinquese soldiers were brushing themselves off, investigating their own wounds, or dropping to the ground to check on their fallen comrades. Filomara's phalanx of guards were straightening up and moving away from the empress to join their fellow soliders in assessing the carnage left behind.

"Let me go now," Josetta panted, shoving at Sorbin, and he swiveled aside to free her.

She was so frantic to get to Rafe that she slipped and almost fell as she dashed away from the temple. There were so many bodies on the roadway; she knew she should stop to see how many brave souls had perished defending her. But all she could think of was Rafe, still lying facedown and motionless on the ground. The man who had saved him now pushed himself to his hands and knees and crawled to Rafe's side, his hands going to Rafe's exposed neck to search for a pulse. As Josetta tore through the shrubbery to reach them, he looked up at her.

Foley. Foley who had dedicated his life to protecting Josetta, and was now determined to protect anyone else she held dear.

"He's alive," Foley said as she dropped down beside him in the dirt. "Bad shoulder wound, but that might be the worst of it."

She wanted to burst into tears, but she didn't have time. "I'll attend to his cuts. Send someone for help. Then make sure the empress and her attendants are safe inside the temple. And Steff! Where is he?"

"I'm here," said a voice behind her. She turned to see Steff standing there, his face pale with shock, his left hand pressed to a long, ugly graze on his right arm. "Is he—is—"

"Alive," she said quickly. "But I need to bind him up."

He came to his knees beside her and for a second she thought he might pass out; maybe his own wound was deeper than it looked. But he pressed his lips together and drew on some inner source of strength and said, "I want to help."

"Good. Then help me turn him. *Very* gently."

In the background, Josetta heard the sounds of battle cleanup—soldiers conferring, officers shouting, horses being captured and calmed, bodies being dragged to the side of the road—but she focused all of her attention on the task before her. Rafe's shoulder was a mess, pierced by a projectile, which appeared to have gone straight through his body. The blood flow was already starting to slow, but there was black residue on his skin, and dirt and debris ground into the wound.

"I need water," she said as steadily as she could. *I need disinfectanct. I need Callie! I need a true doctor!* "And the cleanest cloth anyone can find, to serve as a bandage."

Water and cloth miraculously appeared. She suspected one of the Welchin guards had run to the nearest home or shop and stormed in, conscripting supplies on behalf of the crown. And surely another one had been sent off to the nearest medical facility, and true help was even now on its way. Rafe was not the only one injured, although he was the only one she could think of at the moment. Surely there would be a whole convoy of transport elaymotives arriving very shortly to take all of the injured to an infirmary.

She cleaned the wound as gently and thoroughly as she could, directing Steff to hold Rafe down when he flinched away from her touch. He groaned, which she took as a good sign, but he didn't open his eyes. Which she took as a bad one.

Once she had bound his shoulder, she began investigating his other wounds. A long cut on his left arm, both legs badly scratched through the thin silk of his trousers. But none of those other injuries seemed severe. There was a streak of blood on his cheek, and when she wiped it away, she found a long, shallow slice that ran from his cheekbone and down his neck. Someone had been aiming to cut his throat, she thought, but Rafe had managed to turn away.

She dampened the cloth again and cleaned the rest of the dirt and blood from his face. His long hair had spilled behind him on the ground, making the bones of his face more prominent, exposing his right ear with its distinctive serrations.

You were almost killed because someone recognized this pattern, she thought, finding a clean patch of the cloth and catching a drop of blood that was trickling toward the thin gold hoops. *How can we ever keep you safe?*

Behind her, she heard someone step off the paved roadway and break through the bushes while soft voices spoke imploring words in a language Josetta didn't understand. When she reluctantly looked away from Rafe's face, she wasn't surprised to find Filomara closing in on her, clearly as unwilling as Josetta to sit tamely in the temple until rein-forcements arrived. Steff scrambled to his feet in a gesture of deference, but Josetta remained kneeling at Rafe's side.

"Attacks on the street in broad daylight in public venues!" the empress spat out in Coziquela. "Good thing I *did* have my own soldiers with me, because we *all* would have been dead if we'd had only your men to protect us."

Josetta felt her own spurt of anger in response, but she kept her voice cool. "Indeed, I was grateful to know your men were protecting you, but Welchin soldiers fought valiantly."

"And died bravely," said Foley's voice from behind them. Josetta thought he might have seen Filomara bearing down on her and hurried over to offer his protection from a very different kind of foe. "Five of our men are dead, and two of the Malinquese soldiers."

"I'm astonished you have any soldiers left at all if such attacks are everyday occurrences," said the empress. "I will not feel safe the rest of the time I'm in your wretched city."

This time Josetta's tone was sharp. "Such things hardly ever hap-pen. I have lived in Chialto my whole life and never been assaulted." She gestured back toward the roadway, where even now bodies were being lined up for inspection. "Has anyone identified the attackers yet? I am guessing we will find clues that they're from Berringey."

"Berringey!" the empress exclaimed. "So, Ghyaneth opens up war on Welce, after all, though he is still talking alliances."

It was extremely undiplomatic, but Josetta couldn't contain her hot reply. "Or he has merely opened his war on *you*. Perhaps *you* were the target of this display."

The empress's eyes narrowed as she stared down at Josetta. "Per-haps, but they largely left me alone, and I was visible enough," she replied slowly. With one booted foot, she pointed at Rafe's hip. "*He's* the one they seemed most interested in. Why? Merely because a crown princess fancies herself in love with him?"

"I hardly know," Josetta began, but something in that still body had caught the empress's attention. Filomara dropped to a squat and stared intently at Rafe's face.

"I kept thinking he looked—in a certain light he looked—and lying this way, with his face just so—but it can't be," the empress muttered.

Alarm sparked through Josetta, and she looked around for allies. But no one here knew everything she knew. Not even Steff, who had drawn closer as if to overhear Filomara's thoughts. He was watching the empress as closely as she was watching Rafe.

"Tell me his name again," the empress demanded.

"Rafe Adova."

She shook her head. "That's not right. He's—"

Then her voice stopped. Perched on the balls of her feet, she swayed forward, had to put a hand to the churned ground to catch her balance. Josetta knew without trying to follow her gaze what the empress had seen.

"Lerafi Filoman Kolavar," the empress whispered. "My grandson."

TWENTY-SIX

Once the doctor convinced Josetta that Rafe would be fine—sore, maybe feverish, and damned uncomfortable, but out of danger—she was able to enjoy the fight between Darien and the empress of Malinqua.

First, of course, it was always a pleasure to see Darien's carefully orchestrated plans upended. Whatever he had decided about when to inform Filomara of Rafe's parentage, he certainly hadn't envisioned such a dramatic denouement.

Second, Filomara was every bit Darien's equal in terms of fierceness, intransigence, and cunning. Darien could wear down most other people or he could outmaneuver them or he could convince them he had only their best interests at heart. But Filomara he could not exhaust, outwit, or charm.

"He's met his match," Josetta whispered to Zoe as they paused outside the room that used to be King Vernon's study, listening to the rise and fall of voices through the door. It was close to dinnertime, and the two had been arguing for at least an hour. Ever since the battered cavalcade of bloody soldiers and shaken royals had arrived at the palace courtyard with their recital of calamitous news.

"Good," Zoe said.

Josetta searched her sister's face in the soft gaslight of the hallway. "You don't seem worried or nervous about what's going to happen next."

Zoe shrugged. "I think it's out of my hands. Out of Darien's and Filomara's, too. The only person whose opinion is going to matter is Rafe's."

"I don't know—I'm not sure—he was shocked enough to discover his connection to Ghyaneth. Now to find that he's the heir to two kingdoms—well, I don't know how clearly he'll be able to think it through. Especially because people are trying to kill him all the time!"

"And maybe that's a consideration that will weigh with him heavily," Zoe said. "Where will he be safest? In Welce, flying Kayle's aeromotives? Or in Malinqua, sitting on the throne?"

Josetta caught her breath because she hadn't considered that aspect of it. "In Malinqua, of course," she whispered. She felt a hand squeeze hard on her protesting heart. *While I am imprisoned inside the palace in Welce . . .*

"Maybe," Zoe said. "But maybe Rafe doesn't care about his safety."

"Maybe other people have to care for him, then," Josetta said dully.

Zoe smiled. "Now, that's something I learned a long time ago," she said. "Despite what Darien thinks, you can't always get people to do what you tell them. Even when it's indisputably the best thing for them. The most solid, the most dependable, the most hunti man has a little coru in his veins. And no matter how wayward a course of action might be, in the end, he'll do what he wants."

From behind the study door came the sounds of glass breaking and Filomara's angry voice rising. Zoe's smile grew even wider. "I don't think they're going to be done any time soon," she said cheerfully. "I'm going to check on the baby." She patted Josetta on the arm. "You go find Rafe."

Rafe was right where she'd left him, in his room in the men's wing of the palace. He was awake, sitting up in bed, and being tended to by Steff and Corene. Although Josetta thought Steff and Corene were arguing with each other more than they were seeing to Rafe's comfort.

At any rate, he looked vastly relieved to see her. "Finally, someone with a little sense," he said. "Tell me what's going on here. These two are telling the wildest stories."

"They're not *stories*," Corene said. "They're true."

"You weren't even there this afternoon!" Steff responded. "You don't know *anything*!"

"I know a lot more about palace intrigue in Welce than you do!"

Josetta ignored them and perched on the edge of the bed to put her hand on Rafe's forehead. "How do you feel? No fever yet. That's good."

"I. Feel. Horrible," he said. "Like I've been stabbed and trampled and burned, and then drowned for good measure." He closed his eyes briefly to wait out a clutch of pain, and then opened them again to gaze at Josetta. "Why is it that every time you see me, I've been beaten up or knocked senseless?"

"You're always senseless," Corene contributed from the foot of the bed. "I don't know about the beaten up part."

Josetta leaned forward to give him a brief kiss. "You're not always battered and broken," she said. "And maybe this will be the last time."

"I hope so."

"But what *happened*?" Steff demanded. "Were those men really trying to kill Rafe? And what did the empress mean when she said— when she said—"

Josetta spent another moment with her hand on Rafe's cheek, her eyes on his face, convincing herself that he was going to survive this latest misadventure. Then she nodded and moved to a chair. Corene and Steff pulled their own chairs closer to listen. Josetta had tried so hard to keep this story from Steff; now he had to learn Rafe's complex heritage along with his own.

"As best I understand it, Filomara's daughter Subriella was married off to one of the princes of Berringey about thirty years ago," she began.

"Wait," said Steff. "Subriella. Our mother? She was the empress's daughter?"

"Yes."

Steff stared at his brother accusingly. "And you *knew* this? And you didn't *tell* me? We're—we've got royal blood? *Both* of us?"

Rafe was grinning. "Yeah," he said, "but I'm even more royal than you are. Let her tell the story."

Josetta resumed. "It's not clear how much Subriella or her mother knew about the customs that govern Berringey's royal house, but it turns out that after they've identified one clear heir to the throne, most of the other ones are killed off. Once Rafe was born—excuse me, once *Lerafi* was born—someone at the palace had his ear marked with the royal pattern. A couple of years later, Rafe's cousin Ghyaneth came along and was named the crown prince. That's when Subriella realized that Rafe didn't have long to live. She somehow escaped with her baby and made her way to Welce. Filomara was told that both of them were dead."

"And you *knew* this? All this time?" Steff demanded. "She told you about it when you were growing up?"

Rafe shook his head. "I just found out about the Berringey connection a couple of ninedays ago. I just found out about Malinqua—yesterday."

"You should have told me."

"I found out because someone from Berringey spotted me on the streets and tried to kill me," Rafe said soberly. "Darien Serlast decided that the fewer people who knew the truth, the safer I'd be. But that's why he's had me followed by guards all this time."

Josetta nodded. "Darien thinks mercenaries recognized Rafe because of the markings on his ear. When they weren't able to kill him, they did the next best thing—they told Ghyaneth he was still alive. He's been hunting Rafe ever since."

"It looks like he's going to continue to hunt me," Rafe said.

Josetta kept her voice even. "Maybe. But Filomara came to Welce because she's focused on the succession in Malinqua. She was hoping to find a royal bride to take back to one of her nephews, since all of her direct descendants are dead. Or so she thought. Now that she knows you're alive—she's going to want to take *you* back instead."

"I'm not going to Malinqua," Rafe said instantly.

"Why not?" Corene asked. "Maybe you'd like it."

"Because I don't know anything about Malinqua! Because the people are strange to me and the customs are strange to me and everyone would be watching me, wondering if I was really who I pretended to be—"

"There's your ear," Corene pointed out.

"Sure. I bet I could cut your ear to look just this way."

"I do wonder if Filomara will think you're an imposter," Josetta agreed. "But if she accepts you as her grandson, she might be able to do something we haven't managed here in Welce. She might be able to keep you safe from Ghyaneth's revenge."

Rafe narrowed his gaze and watched her a moment. "Not enough of an inducement," he said at last. "I don't want to leave Welce."

"You mean you don't want to leave Josetta," Corene said, as always speaking straight out loud the things other people could hardly admit to thinking. "But that's stupid. Once you're *king*, you'll find all sorts of women you can marry, and I'm sure you'll like them just as much as you like Josetta."

"As you can see, my sister has a romantic heart," Josetta said.

Steff spoke up. "Why not take Josetta with you? If the empress is looking for an alliance with Welce, you can marry her, and then everybody's happy."

Because Darien thinks I'm destined to be the next queen of Welce, Josetta thought. Instead of saying that, she turned her gaze on Corene. "Because there's another princess who's already volunteered to go to Malinqua."

Corene looked defensive, stubborn, and anxious, all at once. "Well, I don't see why I shouldn't," she said. "I think it would be exciting. I'm tired of boring old Welce."

Josetta didn't have Corene's ability to speak a devastating truth with ease. So she kept her voice gentle. "You think there isn't a place for you in Chialto because your mother is having another child," she said. "But there are so many people here who wouldn't want you to go. Darien. Zoe. Me."

Corene hunched her shoulders. "Everybody was perfectly fine with the idea of me going to Soeche-Tas five years ago, and Malinqua sounds like a much better place."

"Everyone was *not* fine with that idea!" Josetta exclaimed. "In fact, I think Zoe reacted pretty drastically to the announcement."

Corene produced a faint grin. "So maybe she'll flood the city again if I say I'm leaving with Filomara."

Steff spoke up in a reasonable voice. "Well, if Corene wants to go and Rafe ought to go and the empress is looking for a bride for her heir, wouldn't the solution be for Corene to marry Rafe?"

"No!" everyone else in the room answered at once. They all looked at each other and laughed.

Then Rafe spoke up more forcefully. "No. I'm not going to Malinqua. I've finally found the life here that I want to live, and I'm not giving it up."

"I'd go," Steff said enviously. "I've always wanted to see the rest of the world. After all those years on my father's farm—" His words trailed off as they stared at him. "What?"

"You *can* go, of course, don't you realize that?" Josetta said. "You're Filomara's grandson, too. You're her other direct heir."

Naturally, Darien had not forgotten for a second that Steff was related to the empress of Malinqua; he must have realized it the moment he met the boy. Josetta wondered just how he had slipped that information into his grand quarrel with Filomara and what her reaction had been. But it was clear that she had somehow learned of the connection, because before dinner had been announced, she sent a note to Rafe's room, asking him and Steff to meet her within the hour.

Since Rafe's injuries would make it difficult for him to navigate the long corridors of the palace, Filomara had received Darien's permission to use his study in the men's wing. Steff and Josetta practically carried Rafe there, ignoring his muttered curses and grunts of pain. They had just enough time to situate him in a comfortable chair before Filomara strode in.

She was dressed in her usual drab colors, but her stern face held a look of unwonted excitement. She came halfway into the room and then stood stock-still, her gaze flicking between the two brothers. Josetta saw her hands tighten as if to curb traitorous yearning; she didn't offer either one an embrace.

"In many ways, Malinqua is much more advanced than Welce," were her opening words. "We have techniques to test a man's blood and determine if he is, in fact, who he claims to be. So if you are not my daughter's sons, you will be found out quickly enough. I advise you to stop pretending now."

Steff looked indignant, but Rafe nodded. "My mother's name was Subriella, though my stepfather always called her Subi," he said. "I know she was Steff's mother because I was there when he was born, and I truly believe I am her son as well. Was she *your* daughter? I don't know. It seems to be true, though the story is almost too fantastical to credit."

Filomara seemed to relax at this calm rejoinder. "Then you are willing to come to Malinqua to be tested?" she said gruffly.

"*I* am," Steff replied.

"I would happily submit to testing," Rafe said, "but I am not interested in leaving Welce."

She gave him a sharp look, then cut her eyes toward Josetta, who had prudently taken a poorly lit seat in the back of the room. She had offered to leave, but Rafe had begged her to stay and, well, she was dying of curiosity to see how this interview would go.

"I think you should take a look at the alternate version of your future before you decide you have already found the life you want," the empress said.

"I've already abandoned one possible future because I didn't like what lay before me," Rafe said. "I'm content with the one that's finally moved into view."

"Come anyway," Filomara said. "Come see Malinqua. There is a plain outside the royal city where the grass grows as purple as plums. There is a mountain so tall that no one has ever seen the top of the peak, because it is always hidden in clouds. The royal palace is twice the size of the one you have in Chialto. All of it could belong to you."

"I think you have other heirs who have been brought up to believe it could all be theirs," Rafe answered. "My time in Malinqua might be very short."

Filomara's eyes glinted. "I am not as ruthless as your Berringese cousin, but I can still control the members of my court. You will not be in danger."

"I am still reluctant," he said.

Filomara turned all the considerable weight of her attention to Steff. "And you?" she said. "Are you also reluctant to cross the ocean and explore your heritage?"

"No," he said eagerly. "I want to come. If you'll have me."

She nodded. "Of course I'll have you—Steff? There must be more to your name than that."

"Steffanolo Kordan Bors Adova. But no one ever calls me that."

"That's your father's name? Adova?" When he nodded, she prompted, "What's he like? Not a royal man, I take it?"

"No. He's very plain," Steff answered. "He says what he thinks. He works hard and believes everyone else should work hard and he doesn't have much imagination, but you can trust him. He's all torz, but you'd think he was hunti, he's so strong. He'd never fail you."

Josetta heard the catch in his voice and thought this might be the first time Steff had tried to describe his father to someone who didn't know him—the first time he truly realized what a good man his father was. And the first time he realized that journeying to Malinqua would mean leaving his father behind, maybe forever.

She judged by Filomara's slight smile that the empress was thinking something similar. "He sounds like someone I would like and respect," said the empress. "I am very plain myself."

"You could meet him," Steff said doubtfully.

Filomara actually laughed. "I intend to meet him," she said. "You and I shall visit him before we set sail for Malinqua. With, I hope, your brother alongside us."

Everyone in the room looked at Rafe. He shook his head. "I told you. I am happy where I am."

Filomara turned her gaze on Josetta. "Perhaps if you offered to accompany him, he would change his mind," she said. "And who knows? You might find Malinqua more to your taste than you expect."

"The regent needs me to stay, and I have promised him I would," Josetta replied. "But I agree with you. I think Rafe should visit Malinqua before he makes any decisions."

Rafe's head whipped in her direction. "You never said that! And it doesn't make sense."

Josetta kept her eyes on Filomara's face. "I'll do my best to persuade him. You and Steff visit his father. By the time you've returned, Rafe will be ready to go."

The complicated work of convincing Rafe to leave her behind had to be put on hold, however, because the very next morning, Josetta was swept back up in her *own* life. Taro had arrived in Chialto, and all the primes had been called to the palace to discuss their own succession issues, which appeared to be even more tangled than those in Malinqua or Berringey.

"I am *tired* of sitting in rooms and listening to people argue about who belongs on what throne where," Corene complained to Josetta as they made their way to Elidon's quarters shortly after breakfast. Taro had been accompanied by a dozen companions, although Romelle, Natalie, and Mally were not among them. Nonetheless, Darien had insisted that the other two princesses be on hand for the discussion.

"So am I," Josetta answered with a sigh. "As soon as we can, let's slip off and go somewhere no one can find us."

"The river flats," Corene said instantly.

"Zoe could find us there in five minutes!"

"Not if we don't put our feet in the water."

"And we have to bring Foley."

"Well, of course we'll bring Foley," Corene said. "But nobody else."

"All right, then. As soon as we can."

Elidon's lovely yellow-and-white room didn't seem sturdy enough to accommodate all the strong personalities gathered inside for the meeting. Taro alone seemed powerful enough to shove the walls outward with his bare hands, bringing down the whole ceiling, and he looked irritable enough to try it.

"I hope you had a pleasant trip," Nelson greeted him as they settled around the table that was the centerpiece of the main room. Josetta had spent countless hours at that very table while the queens bickered and sparred. She couldn't imagine this meeting would be much more cordial.

"No, I didn't have a pleasant trip," Taro snapped, his rumbling voice threaded with annoyance. "How many times am I going to be summoned to the city before the quintile is up? Can't we just settle on someone once and for all and be done with these games?"

"You have been summoned to Chialto to do honor to the empress of Malinqua, but we may as well discuss our own issues while we are all present," Darien said, casually taking his seat. Elidon always sat at the head of the table, and Darien had positioned himself at the foot. Staking out his position of power. "And I would like to point out that securing the succession of the kingdom is hardly a game."

Josetta would have preferred one of the chairs by the window overlooking the butterfly garden, but she took a place at the middle of the table, Corene beside her. Zoe dropped down in the seat on her other side, and Josetta instantly felt more optimistic. Nothing *too* bad could happen to her as long as Zoe was nearby.

"No, but it's very tedious," Kayle replied earnestly. "I agree with Taro. Let's just settle it so we can get back to more important things."

"And I agree with Darien!" Nelson cut in. "What could be *more important* than the fate of the kingdom?"

"Let us first review the facts that have come to light," Elidon said. "Odelia, the only princess who is Vernon's daughter by blood, has a condition that makes her unsuitable to rule. We must look about us for alternatives."

"Josetta is the eldest. Name her and let's be done with this," Kayle said.

Mirti frowned him down. "And is that how the Dochenzas choose the next elay prime—in five minutes—because that son or daughter happens to be the *eldest*?" she demanded.

Even Kayle looked a little chastised. "No," he admitted. "It is a very delicate process."

"Then naming the next ruler of the country should be approached with equal care," she said.

"If there are three princesses, there are three choices," Darien began, but Nelson cut him off.

"We can cast a wider net than that," said the sweela prime. "And if our goal is to choose an heir who is related to Vernon by blood, we must."

Darien gave him a long and level look. "And is that our goal?" he said in a mild voice.

Nelson showed surprise, an emotion Josetta had to assume was false. "Isn't it? Isn't that why we were all so pleased, once Odelia was born, to find that she had been sired by Vernon when all the other princesses had not?"

"Of course it was," Mirti snapped. "What's your point?"

Nelson glanced around the room, making sure his gaze touched everyone else at the table. "Vernon had no close relations but his bloodline is far from extinguished. We should look for his next of kin—"

"Spare us all the pretense," Darien said. "You know his nearest living relation is Dominic Wollimer. Who is no more fit for the throne than Odelia is."

"I agree, but he has an heir of his own, who will be born by Quinnelay," Nelson responded, not at all flustered by Darien's manner. "That child deserves serious consideration."

Mirti spoke up in a heavy voice. "The primes did agree that we would recur to Vernon's bloodline if we ever needed another heir. But that's before we looked ahead at who might be parenting that child."

Elidon had just now worked out the genealogy. "What—*Alys's* child? To sit on the throne? Certainly, if you want to see the kingdom in ruins."

"*Corene* is Alys's child and I assume you think she is still in the running," Nelson said. The glint in his eyes convinced Josetta he was just trying to stir up trouble.

Elidon glanced at Darien. "Her father's strengths outweigh her mother's defects."

"If we are going to choose a queen based on which of her parents we like best, we will never come to an agreement," Taro said. "We must choose based on the abilities of the candidates."

"We must choose based on bloodlines, because that is what the people value!" Nelson exclaimed.

Mirti leaned across the table to respond in an equally loud voice. "You've never cared what the people value! What you're looking for is an advantage to the house of Ardelay! And both Dominic and his scheming bitch of a wife are sweela creatures with Ardelay connections."

"That's offensive!" Nelson bellowed, slamming a fist to the table, then gesturing at Josetta. "If I was trying to control the throne, wouldn't I choose my own brother's daughter?"

Zoe spoke up for the first time. "Not if you've spent much time with her," she said coolly. "Josetta isn't often amenable to persuasion."

Kayle was watching Nelson, his expression bemused. "Is that really true?" he asked. "Are you favoring Alys's child because of some Ardelay connection? I might have backed you up on Vernon's bloodline, but not if you're just being sneaky."

"Nelson is always being sneaky," Taro said.

Nelson threw his hands in the air. "I argue for purity of blood and you accuse me of crass self-interest!" he exclaimed. "Choose your own heir, then, and be damned to you all!"

"Well, there are clearly four choices," Taro said, enumerating them on his fingers. "Josetta. Corene. Natalie. And Alys's child."

Mirti shook her head. "Aside from all other considerations, do we really want to wait another twenty-four years to see Alys's baby grow to adulthood? And what if that child falls ill or proves unsuitable in some fashion? Think of all the time we will have wasted!"

"That is an issue that must be considered," Darien said, his voice silky smooth. "How stable *is* Vernon's bloodline? Vernon himself was very unreliable in his final years—physically sick and mentally uncertain. He sired only one child, which raises questions about the virility of his line. And that child has certain deficiencies of her own. Is that really the heritage we want for the next king or queen?"

Oh, he's been waiting for just the right time to raise that particular question, Josetta thought, feeling reluctant admiration as she glanced around the room. Kayle was wide-eyed as he pondered this new thought, Mirti and Elidon were nodding in agreement, and even Nelson looked somewhat uneasy. Taro appeared to be already convinced—and there had never been any doubt about Zoe's opinion.

"I move that we strike the unborn child from the list," said Taro.

Nelson spoke up quickly. "If you cannot stomach Alys as mother to the next ruler, Vernon had other connections, a little more distant than Dominic Wollimer—"

Taro fixed him with a fierce stare. "I move we strike *all* of Vernon's relatives from the list."

"I agree," said Mirti. "We have plenty of choices as it is."

"Let's examine them one by one," Zoe suggested. "Natalie."

Nelson shook his head. "Too young," he snapped, "if you're already weary of *waiting* for the next heir to grow up."

"What concerns *me*," said Elidon, "is how she has been raised." When Taro rumbled in annoyance, she continued, "Oh, spare me your protests! You know as well as I do that Romelle has had almost no attention to spare for the girl in the past three years! Natalie has hardly ever been at court, she is shy and difficult around strangers, and she is almost as wild as a girl who has been raised by animals! She could be trained and molded, perhaps, but not by Romelle. If we choose her, she must come to Chialto—and *I* must be the one to prepare her for her role."

There was a short silence while everyone imagined what that would be like. Corene looked over at Josetta with one expressive glance. *Nobody deserves such a dreadful fate.* Josetta was certain they weren't the only two thinking it.

"Then we are down to two," Darien said at last.

Everyone was staring at Corene and Josetta.

"Either one would be acceptable," Taro said. "Either one has *always* been acceptable."

"Corene has the fire, but Josetta has the vision," Mirti said.

"Corene is too reckless and Josetta is too cautious, but those are both faults that could be balanced by thoughtful advisors," Elidon added.

As if we aren't actually sitting here! Josetta thought indignantly.

"Josetta is the eldest," Nelson said. "Just as Kayle said."

Taro gazed at him with contempt. "So *now* you'll back your dead brother's daughter. Still looking for that Ardelay advantage."

"If you don't want my input at all, just say so," Nelson shot back. "If you're going to question my motives every time I offer an opinion—"

"I question everyone's motives every time *anyone* offers an opinion," Elidon interrupted. "Everyone has some self-interest at play. The trick is to set that aside as much as possible to consider the welfare of the kingdom."

"Well, I don't know why Welce even needs a king or queen," Kayle said, his voice petulant. "I mean, we haven't had one for five years—longer, if you add in Vernon's final years on the throne—and we've managed just fine, haven't we?"

Mirti cast him a look of irritation. "We've been governed by a regent and an advisory council as we waited for the heir to grow to a suitable age."

"And the regent and the council have managed just fine, haven't they?" Kayle repeated. "There's been no civil discord. There's been no financial crisis. We've treated and traded with foreign nations. Why do we need someone to sit on the throne?"

"Well, because—" Elidon began, and then stopped. Mirti was frowning, and Nelson looked thunderstruck. Taro and even Darien looked as if they were having trouble processing what he'd said.

Zoe, of course, was laughing. "Kayle raises an interesting point," she said. "*Do* we need a royal ruler for Welce? Can the primes and selected advisors adequately manage the kingdom?"

"You are talking about overthrowing an entire government and starting from scratch," Darien said. Josetta thought he actually sounded breathless. "You would need—systems for choosing advisors and guidelines for when to get rid of them. And you would need—you would need—a constitution of some sort, a document, rules that everyone agreed to. And you would need to determine who would vote on this government. And you would need—*everything.* You would need to redo it *all.*"

"He's right. It's too much work," Kayle said.

But the others were shaking their heads, looking at each other with a certain degree of speculation. "It's certainly worth considering," Taro said. "It would save all this nonsense about choosing an heir."

"There would be just as much scheming and maneuvering," Nelson warned. "I am not the only one constantly jockeying for advantage! A throne changes hands once every two or three generations, if you're lucky. But an elected government—well—that can turn over every few years."

"Yes, but the primes stay in place for decades, usually," Elidon pointed out. "They would provide a great deal of stability on any council."

"So who would be eligible to take a seat in this governing body?" Mirti asked. "How long would they stay? What would they be empowered to do?"

"All of that would have to be decided," Darien said. "It is a monumental task."

"Well, we are intelligent people," Elidon said. "I think we're up to the challenge."

The debate was not nearly done by the time servants began bringing in luncheon trays. Josetta imagined it might go on for days, as the primes and their advisors hammered out the details of what a new government might look like. She formally asked to be excused and Corene hastily jumped up beside her, equally eager to escape. Darien caught Josetta's wrist as she brushed past him on her way to the door.

"Don't think you're out of this—either of you," he said. "You're both too important to Welce, even if you're just very visible figureheads. Don't think you'll be running off to live in obscurity somewhere."

"You read my mind," Josetta said, and Corene merely smirked.

Two steps out of the room, Josetta inhaled deeply and said, "I can hardly *breathe* in there. Let's get out of here before Darien finds a reason to call us back. Where should we go?"

"Like I said. The river flats."

"Let's do it."

They made a quick detour through the kitchen, where the cooks packed them a light lunch, and picked up Foley as they were crossing the courtyard. He commandeered a small elaymotive and drove them down the winding mountain road that served the palace, and from there they followed the Cinque to the river flats. Josetta was practically starving by the time they parked as close as they could to the wide, depressed stone apron that fanned off from the Marisi here on the lowest corner of Chialto.

It was, as always, a colorful, chaotic scene. Especially in the warm weather seasons of Quinnahunti and Quinnatorz, the flats were crowded with itinerants and beggars, people with no better place to stay and people who simply preferred to live on the river. There were hundreds of small tents, narrow mats, and impromptu campsites laid out in random fashion along the river's edge. Josetta supposed there might be a couple thousand people living there, and all of them appeared to be in motion: walking, cooking, fetching water, talking in small groups. The sparkling Marisi ambled past, slow enough to bathe in at this point in its journey. The early afternoon sun was hot enough to be uncomfortable, but the breeze off the water turned the air delightful.

"Let's find a spot and eat," Corene said, crouching down and vaulting easily from the overhang to the stone apron. Josetta and Foley were right behind her.

The river residents might have recognized them, or they might simply have decided not to tangle with Foley. At any rate, no one approached them as they picked their way through campsites until they found a relatively clear and level spot. Foley, it turned out, had remembered to bring blankets, so they sat in comfort as they consumed delicacies from the palace kitchen. There was plenty left over; Josetta started skimming the faces of the nearby campers, trying to pick one or two who might need extra food.

"So did the primes settle everything, then?" Foley asked, gathering up plates and linens and stuffing them back in the food basket. "Have they decided who will be the next heir?"

"No!" Corene exclaimed. "Kayle—of all people!—asked why they needed a king or queen at all, and now they're talking about setting up a whole new government!"

Foley looked impressed but not particularly anxious. Josetta imagined that most of the people of Welce might feel the same way. As long as the country continued to function smoothly, did they care who ran it? Maybe not.

"Big changes," he said. "But does that mean you two are no longer princesses?"

"I don't know what it means," Josetta said. "I just hope it means I don't have to be queen. I'm so relieved I feel dizzy. I feel so light and happy I could float away."

Corene gave her a quick sideways glance. Whereas Josetta had taken off her overtunic and stretched out on the blanket, reveling in the feel of the sun on her bare arms, Corene was still in a sitting position, her knees drawn up and her hands linked around her ankles. She did not look nearly as relaxed as Josetta felt.

"Really?" Corene said, her voice soft. "I'm disappointed."

Joestta was astonished. "You wanted to be queen? You never said so."

Corene shrugged and fixed her eyes on the river. "It was never going to be me. It was always going to be you. And then Odelia was born and it was going to be her, but at any rate, it was never *me*. I was always the troublesome one. You heard Elidon. I'm reckless—and I have *Alys* as a mother. No one would ever trust me on the throne." She set her chin on the top of one knee. "But I always wanted it. From the time I was a little girl."

"Well, I suppose if you'd gone to Soeche-Tas like they planned, you could have been queen there—or whatever they call the viceroy's wife," Josetta said.

Corene made a scoffing sound. "Ugh. He was horrible. And I was so afraid of him! No, I didn't want to go to Soeche-Tas. I wanted to be queen in Chialto and have a suite as big as Elidon's and decorate it in sweela colors. But I didn't mind just being a princess because there was always the *possibility* I could be queen, even when I was really old. And now—" She turned her head, resting her cheek on her knee; her voice was muffled when she spoke again. "And now I'm just another ordinary girl."

Josetta's heart twisted; she didn't know what to say, though she knew better than to offer outright sympathy. As she cast about for some kind of light reply, Foley unexpectedly spoke up.

"It doesn't matter whether or not you have titles, I'll never think of either one of you as ordinary," he said. "Both of you will always be princesses to me."

Corene laughed and Josetta smiled and the difficult moment passed. "Princesses who are late for their next engagement," Josetta said, standing up and pulling Corene to her feet. "We'd better be getting back."

They made it to the palace a scant hour before dinner and separated instantly so they could wash up and change clothes. Josetta hurried through her preparations so she could slip over to the men's wing and look for Rafe. Who, it turned out, was sitting in the great hall of the palace, perched glumly on the bowl of the fountain, trying to figure out how to find *her*.

She didn't quite have the nerve to kiss him in public, but she did squeeze his hand. "How's your shoulder?" she asked, sitting down gingerly once she made sure the edge of the fountain wasn't sprinkled with water.

"Pretty awful," he said. "But if I don't move too quickly, I can bear the pain."

"I suppose that's good," she said doubtfully. "So tell me about your day."

"I spent it with my brother and my grandmother, hearing about the marvels of Malinqua," he said.

"Did that make you want to visit it?"

He was silent a moment. "Yes and no," he said at last. "A part of me does want to go. Wants to get a glimpse of that—that alternate life, just to see what could have been mine. But part of me wants to dig my heels in and *plant* myself in Chialto. Get so entrenched that there's no way to dig me up and move me anywhere else."

"Which part of you is winning?"

Again he was silent, but she read misery on his face.

She stretched up to kiss him on the cheek. Well-dressed, wealthy people were beginning to gather in the hall, waiting to be summoned to dinner, but no one was paying them much attention. "I'm sure your grandmother is very persuasive," she said gently. "You should go. You need to *see* it, at least, before you decide to throw it away. Especially if the only reason you *don't* want to go is me."

"Not the only one," he said. "But the biggest one. The thought of leaving you behind makes me feel sort of panicky. Makes me have a hard time breathing."

"I'll still be here if you decide to come back," she said calmly, though the words scraped her throat on their way out.

"*When* I come back," he corrected.

She didn't bother to argue. Instead she asked, "How soon do you think you might set sail?"

"Filomara wants to meet Bors, and that's a trip that will take a couple of days in each direction, not to mention however much time they spend on the farm. But I don't imagine she'll want to linger long once they're back. I think she'd like to be gone before another full nine-day is up."

"Maybe you should go with them to see Bors," she said, still speaking in that tranquil voice. It was an almost unbearable effort. She felt like she was drowning, suffocating, utterly adrift. This man had been part of her life for barely a quintile, and yet he had become indispensable to her. How could she encourage him to leave her, how could she smile and wave goodbye as he boarded one of those tall-masted ships bound for Malinqua? Once he set foot in that ancestral homeland, she was sure, it would lay an ancient enchantment on him; it would waken some dormant longing deep in his soul. Once he left, he would never come back. How could she kiss him and let him go?

His fingers tightened on her hand. "Maybe I should," he said. "But I want to spend every minute I can with you."

"Good," she whispered. "Because I want to spend all those minutes with you, too."

TWENTY-SEVEN

Despite his determination to slow down time—to stop it, even—and to register each separate moment with such detailed clarity that it imprinted itself on his memory for all eternity, Rafe felt the next nineday slip away in a frenzied haze. He had managed to refuse Filomara's strongly worded request that he accompany her and Steff to Bors's farm, but he had acceded to her desire that he immediately begin studying the Malinquese language. So he spent part of every day with Filomara's cousin, learning grammar and verbs and hearing about the incomparable beauties of Malinqua.

It did, indeed, sound like a gorgeous spot—and it was both alluring and sobering to think that one day he might be master of the entire realm. But anytime he felt a flare of excitement, it was overmatched by a spurt of dread. How could he leave Josetta behind? He had wanted to turn himself into someone who was worthy of a princess. Now, by any genealogical measure, he could be considered her equal—but the elevation could put her even more surely out of his reach.

Only if he stayed in Malinqua, of course. Which he wasn't going to do. He could tell that Josetta believed that once he sailed away, he would never return, but he knew that wasn't true. There was no treasure in any other kingdom in the world that could compare to what he had gathered right here.

Steff and Filomara returned from their journey to the countryside, both of them seeming oddly satisfied. Filomara had liked Bors, Rafe realized. Maybe she had appreciated his gruff honesty; maybe she was deeply grateful that he had rescued her daughter in Subriella's darkest hour. Maybe it soothed her lacerated soul to hear him talk of Subriella's last ten years, which had been lived in modest surroundings but had seemed mostly happy. Filomara didn't seem to care much about happiness in general, but Rafe would have bet it eased some of her buried grief to know that Subriella had been granted a share of it.

As for Steff—well, that was easier to understand. He had received his father's blessing as he embarked on his new life. And he had gotten to know his grandmother better, formed a clearer picture of the life that awaited him in Malinqua. Steff didn't have any of Rafe's reasons for staying behind. He was all eagerness, all enthusiasm.

"Can we set sail *tomorrow*?" he demanded the very night they returned.

But Darien and the primes had decided that the Malinquese delegation should have an escort back to the port city, and it took some time to organize who would go and where they would stay. Taro had said flatly he was returning home and he might not come back to Chialto till *next* Quinnatorz, but the rest of the primes and Darien accompanied the Malinquese contingent back to the port city. Kayle had reluctantly agreed to house everyone, "if you don't stay very long." But Josetta and Rafe made it clear they were staying in their own apartments, along with whatever guards were assigned to them, and Filomara declared she and Steff would take up residence on her ship.

"One night only," she warned them, "and then I cast off for deep ocean. I am done with all this fretting and feting."

Rafe thought, *One more night with Josetta.*

They arrived in the harbor town early in the afternoon of the hottest day of the season. Everyone, from Zoe to the driver of the royal elaymotive, appeared to be in a bad mood inspired by the heat. Rafe watched with envy as Steff, Filomara, and her soldiers escaped toward the ocean; the temperature had to be ten degrees lower on the water.

"Perfect weather to gather in a dining room filled with warm bodies," Zoe observed as their caravan paused outside Rafe's rented lodgings. "I can hardly wait for the meal tonight."

"It will be much more pleasant than you expect," Kayle assured her. "I have been perfecting an air circulation system that cools down the whole house. It's the only thing that makes Quinnatorz bearable."

"A cooling system?" she repeated. "Why haven't you made *that* commercially available? *Everyone* would buy one."

Kayle looked surprised. "It's very expensive. Hardly anyone could afford it."

"*I* could," she said. "If it beggared me."

"Well, all right, we can talk about it over dinner," he said.

Their voices faded as they climbed back into the elaymotive. Rafe picked up his own baggage and Josetta's, and they headed for the door.

"No special air circulation system in *here*," he observed as they made their way through the stifling hallways and stairwells to his quarters. The curtains had been drawn before he left, so the darkened room was not quite as unbearable as the street outside. But the place was still stuffy to the point of oppressiveness.

"I know we can't do it," Josetta said, "but wouldn't you love to head down to the docks and go swimming?"

"I would," he agreed. "But I'm surprised to learn you know how."

Smiling, she turned back to face him. "My sister is the coru prime," she said. "She taught me."

"Of course."

"Though actually it's a longer story than that." He watched her debate whether or not to tell it, then she gave her head a slight shake. "Well, I don't think swimming is really an option, but it's too miserable to stay here. Is there anyplace you'd like to go on your last afternoon in Welce?"

His last afternoon in Welce. The very words made his breath catch. How could he possibly leave here tomorrow? How could he do it? "We could go to the training facility," he said, keeping his voice casual to cover his turmoil.

She looked amused. "*Really?* That's what you want to do?"

He nodded. "There are a couple of people there I'd like to say good-bye to. But that's not the real reason."

"Oh, do tell me."

He grinned. "Kayle's cooling system. He's got one at the facility, too. It'll be the best place in the city to wait out the day."

It was almost a shock to step from the malicious heat of the city into the palpable chill of the facility. Josetta actually gasped, and Rafe felt goosebumps roughen his skin.

"I should have brought my overtunic," Josetta said. "I might actually get cold."

"I'm sure someone could scrounge up an old jacket for you."

"Not yet," she said. "For the moment I like it."

A couple of his old trainers came over as soon as they recognized him. "So, the prince of Malinqua has come back for one last session," said the one named Clay. He was a stick-thin bald man of indeterminate age, so focused and so odd that he had to be pure elay, but he was Rafe's favorite of the entire crew. "We heard the news."

"Yeah, I don't think they have any aeromotives in Malinqua, and I'm going to miss flying," Rafe said.

Clay gestured at the contraption currently suspended above the floor by pulleys and chains. "We've made some modifications on the LNR," he said. "Even you wouldn't crash it next time."

"Very funny," Rafe said. "Who's going to take it up?"

"Arven, probably. Sometime within the nineday, we think. Would have been sooner but Kayle's been busy with the foreign empress. But I understand she's leaving tomorrow."

Rafe fought down a surge of regret. *So am I.* "So maybe life will get back to normal. Tell me about the modifications."

"Well, there's a new fuel system—two tanks that feed at different rates so you've got a backup in case one of the lines gets fouled. And the whole pilot's box is wider and clearer in case you have to eject and—oh, maybe you don't know! We redesigned the flying bags to make them easier to use. Come on, I'll show you. We've got one in the back room."

Rafe glanced at Josetta. "Oh, I don't know—"

She smiled and waved him away. "You go look. I'll find some nice dark spot and sit quietly. This is the happiest I've been all day."

He followed Clay back to a small, overfull office. The trainer pawed through what looked like a pile of discarded clothing and came up with a square, flat pack ornamented with straps and loops of fabric. "The new flying bag," he said proudly.

Rafe took it gingerly, holding it by one dangling strap. "How does it work?"

"You put it over your shoulders and buckle it in place. That way you're already wearing it if your machine goes down—you don't have to grab it. Here, put it on."

Clay settled the pack over Rafe's shoulders and belted it around his waist. His most recent wounds had almost completely healed, or else the bag was too light to cause him any discomfort at all. Clay said, "If you need to bail out, you pull this cord—here—and the chemicals combine. The bag inflates and you're *wrenched* out of the pilot's box."

Rafe craned his neck, trying to see over his shoulder. "But how do you guide it? The old one had the yoke that you could turn from side to side—"

"Right, but it didn't fit into the pilot's box. So, see these two straps? One on each side? Pull one to go left, one to steer right."

"All right. Good. How long do you stay in the air? What's your range?"

"We're not sure."

Rafe grinned at him. "So it's just a prototype?"

"It's experimental," Clay said a little defensively. "It hasn't been tested in the field. But it *should* work the way I've described."

A horrific metallic clangor suddenly issued from the main room, followed by a chorus of voices raised in dismay. "What's wrong out there?" Rafe demanded.

Clay didn't seem perturbed. "Probably someone was up in the training module and dropped a box of tools. Or maybe one of the chains snapped and a part fell off. It happens all the time."

"All the *time*?" Rafe repeated. "How do you—"

There was another clattering sound of metal smashing against metal, and more voices rising in something like panic. "That doesn't sound like something that just *dropped*," Rafe said.

He had just reached for the door when he heard Josetta's voice lifted urgently. "Rafe! Run! *Run!*"

"Josetta?" he cried, and charged out the door into the cavernous space of the facility.

Which was now a battleground. Between the pillars holding up the roof, the supports sustaining the practice capsule, and the boxes and barrels of equipment lining the floor, it was hard to get a clear view of the action, but Rafe could see soldiers and scientists engaged in deadly combat. The soldiers were winning, of course, beating back the mechanics with bludgeons and knives and the occasional shot from a noisy firearm, but the scientists were putting up an unexpectedly vigorous defense. They were swinging long poles and heavy chains against their opponents; they were flinging sharp-edged metal objects in deadly trajectories across the open floor. Rafe saw one of them snatch up a blowtorch and use its blue flame to set a few of his attackers on fire.

His attackers. Wearing the gold-and-white of Berringey. Here to find and kill Lerafi Filoman Kolavar.

Clay grabbed him by the arm. "Out the back," he said grimly. "Come with me."

Rafe shook him off. "Where's Josetta? I have to find her."

Heedless of Clay's cry of alarm, he plunged through the melee to the last place he had seen the princess.

At first no one noticed him. The scene was so noisy and chaotic that it was hard to keep track of anyone, and he darted around clashing fighters without drawing any particular attention. He spotted Welchin soldiers in among the Berringese, grimly and valiantly fighting, but they were wholly overmatched—ten, perhaps, to what looked like twenty or thirty.

He looked for Foley, knowing that he would be guarding Josetta. Yes, there he was—and Sorbin, too, charging and feinting and falling back to keep a small circle of safety around Josetta while Berringey soldiers milled around nearby. Oh, but Josetta wasn't cowering back in helpless terror. She'd ripped a canister of some noxious gas off the wall and was spraying its contents straight into the faces of the Berringese soldiers.

"*Josetta!*" Rafe screamed, snatching up his own improvised weapon, a long-handled pole that ended in something resembling a hatchet. He fought to Josetta's side, wielding his weapon wildly, knocking Berringese soldiers to the floor as he charged past

The fear on her face intensified as she saw him. *"Get out, get out!"* she cried, swinging around to squirt another stream of poisonous chemicals at a soldier creeping up on her left side. "Leave us! Go!"

For an answer, he smashed the sharp edge of his pole onto the shoulder of a soldier who was menacing Foley. The man dropped to the floor, blood spurting from a deep gash on the side of his neck. Rafe felt a moment of utter horror—would the soldier die? Rafe had never killed a man in his life. He waded forward through the blood.

"Rafe!" Josetta shrieked, and he spun around just in time to stave off a blow from behind. But there were three soldiers converging on him—four—all armed with swords and knives and those deadly firearms. Rafe swung his weapon in a wide and violent circle, fending them off, but he knew it was just a matter of time before they closed in on him. Killed him, right in front of Josetta. Maybe killed her, too.

If only he had left for Malinqua already! He wouldn't mind dying so much if Josetta could survive. The thought made him redouble his efforts, land the pole with bone-jarring force on another man's head, and another. But someone had him from behind, grabbing his throat with a grip so powerful that he instantly lost the ability to breathe. He dropped his weapon and clawed at the gloved hands around his neck, writhing and contorting with all his strength. Through the roaring in his ears, he heard Josetta's continued despairing cries. Through the gathering haze in his brain, he waited for the fatal blow to fall.

W hen Rafe regained consciousness, it was to utter darkness punctuated with pain and an odd, nauseating dizziness. *Concussion*, he thought. *My head's swimming.* It was a moment before he realized the random rocking motion came from outside his body, not inside. Another moment before he recognized the sounds and smells around him.

I'm on a ship. We're on the ocean. It couldn't be too far from land—he didn't believe he'd been out that long, and he could still hear the sounds of gulls and and other seabirds.

I've been kidnapped, not killed, was his next realization. Knocked out, trussed up, and carried to one of the hundreds of boats snugged up to the harbor. Probably one that had hid its colors for the past few nine-days as Ghyaneth's men looked for any chance to grab Rafe and run.

If he wasn't dead, maybe Josetta wasn't dead, either.

If he wasn't dead, maybe Ghyaneth wanted something from him. Maybe they could come to an arrangement.

Unless the only thing Ghyaneth wanted was a chance to witness Rafe's death.

Cautiously, because his skull was pounding, Rafe rolled to his knees. That made both his stomach and his head rebel, and for a moment he stayed as motionless as possible, panting as he tried to calm his senses. Even so, he could already get a better feel for his situation now that he was upright.

It wasn't dark; there was a heavy cloth bag over his head, blocking out light and air. His hands were tied in front of him, but his legs were unbound. His captors must have figured that, once they put out to sea, he would have nowhere to run even if he slipped his bonds. He shrugged cautiously, to see what other aches were woken by movement. He'd taken a knife in the ribs, judging by the sharp pain in his side, but he didn't think the gash was too deep. He was probably bruised on every square inch of his shoulders and torso, but he didn't seem to have sustained any real damage. Once his head cleared, maybe he could work his hands loose, maybe he could dive overboard, swim for shore—if they were only a mile out, maybe less, he could make it that far—

He heard the sound of approaching footsteps, a cluster of them, five or six people at least. Just as he braced himself for whatever was coming next, someone whipped the bag off his head, and he was blinking into the sullen glare of late afternoon sun.

And into the equally sullen glare of a pair of curious eyes. A man about his own age was bending down, staring at him, his whole demeanour one of hatred and disdain.

"So you're my cousin Lerafi," he said in Coziquela.

Rafe gazed up at him in turn. His first thought was that Corene had been right; he was wearing one of the turbans she'd described, and it looked pretty stupid. This one was made of soft gold cloth, wrapped in complex folds around his head and carefully arranged to cover the prince's ears. *Which are probably sliced just like mine,* Rafe thought. *My cousin Ghyaneth.*

His second thought was that they didn't look much alike. Ghyaneth had olive skin and dark slanted eyes, characteristics that Rafe's father had probably shared, though Rafe hadn't inherited them. The shape of the mouth was similar, but that was a subtle thing. No one would see them together and exclaim that they must be related.

"That's what I hear," Rafe replied. His voice came out as little more than a croak, and the effort of speaking made his throat hurt. That was when he remembered that one of Ghyaneth's men had tried to strangle him.

"I have gone to quite a lot of trouble to find you," Ghyaneth told him.

"You've tried to *kill* me," Rafe corrected. "I'm surprised I'm alive right now."

Ghyaneth's face showed dissatisfaction. "It would be better if you were dead," he agreed. "But my spies tell me you've become enmeshed with one of the princesses. I think Darien Serlast is less likely to fire on my ship if he believes you are on it. And alive."

"I'm a hostage to your safe passage."

"Exactly."

Rafe's eyes had had time to adjust and now he took a quick look around. Ghyaneth, a few of his soliders, and Rafe were clustered on the deck in the stern of a large, oceangoing ship. He could spot two even more massive vessels on either side, about a ship's-length behind them; their flags were down, but Rafe assumed they were escorts for the prince. On all three of them, the big white sails drooped, not even half full, as the wind was uncooperative on this sunny day. They were moving, but slowly, and the shore was indeed less than a mile behind them.

Which cheered Rafe up a good deal, but even more encouraging was the sight of twelve or fifteen smaller, faster ships in close pursuit, all of them flying the rosette symbol of Welce.

"Looks like you might have trouble outracing the Welchin navy," he observed, not even trying to keep the note of satisfaction from his voice.

"I doubt they will follow us all the way to Berringey. You cannot be worth that much to them."

Rafe agreed, though he wasn't about to say so, but Ghyaneth didn't wait for an answer. "Though I should not be running from them! I should be berating them," he declared, his voice aggrieved. "I thought we were treating in good faith, and yet I find they have been harboring my greatest enemy! They are without honor, and I will tell my father so. We will not make alliances with them."

"They didn't know I was your enemy," Rafe said, though he didn't think Darien Serlast needed Rafe's help explaining his motives. "*I* didn't know. I just found out who I am a few ninedays ago. There's no reason to kill me, because I never had any thought about taking the throne of Berringey."

"It doesn't matter what you thought or what Darien Serlast thought or what anyone in this backwater land thought," Ghyaneth said grandly. "You are a threat to the throne of Berringey, and therefore you must die."

Rafe shifted on the hard planks, trying to get more comfortable. It was something of a strain to tilt his head back to argue with Ghyaneth, but he didn't particularly want to stand up to confront his cousin. He didn't want to do anything to make Ghyaneth strike him dead.

Resettling himself on the deck made every separate bone and muscle shriek with protest. It also made him aware of a light, compact weight hanging from his shoulders.

The flying bag. Still strapped to his back.

How might *that* be turned to his advantage?

"So you're going to kill me yourself," Rafe said slowly. "I admit I'm surprised. I wouldn't have thought you'd spend all this time skulking around Welce, looking for me."

"I wasn't *skulking around*," Ghyaneth defended himself. "I've been in Soeche-Tas for a much more fruitful visit than the one I spent in Chialto. My men brought me word of your activities, and I decided to wait at the harbor for a few days to see if you could be found. And you were."

"I suppose my father is dead," Rafe said abruptly.

Ghyaneth added. "Of course. He took his own life, as an heir should, the night your mother fled with you." Ghyaneth's voice turned bitter. "He believed that both of you died at his side. He prepared potions for all of you—the gentlest elixirs, toxins that offer no pain at all, just a quick escape into a deep sleep from which there is no waking. The servants said your mother pretended to drink hers, pretended to feed your own portion to you—pretended to be sleeping at your father's side until the house was quiet. Then she slipped out and vanished into the night." He fell silent, still brooding on this monstrous injustice.

"She was courageous and clever," Rafe said.

"She was deceitful and wicked," Ghyaneth said sharply. "And if she minded death so much, why didn't she care that the entire household was executed after her disappearance?"

Rafe flinched, though he had been acquainted with none of the people who were sacrificed on his behalf and all of them had been dead more than twenty-five years. "From what I know of my mother," he said quietly, "she would have considered their blood to be on *your* hands, not hers. She had a pretty fierce sense of justice."

"Well, all of her machinations are pointless now," Ghyaneth said with a certain zest. "You will be dead soon enough."

Before Rafe could answer, a loud *boom* rang from one of the pursuing ships. A cannonball ricocheted off the starboard side of their craft and splashed noisily into the water. There were shouts all around them from soldiers and sailors leaping to assess the damage and take up combat stations.

"Looks like Darien Serlast doesn't care that I'm on board," Rafe said. "He'll sink you anyway."

Ghyaneth grabbed Rafe by the back of his tunic and jerked him to his feet, hauling him to the railing. Rafe was unsteady enough that the sight of the dark water churning below made him dizzy. Without Ghyaneth's grip, he thought he might have pitched overboard.

"We still have him and he is still alive!" Ghyaneth called to the pursuing ships. They were close now, maybe only fifty yards distant; no doubt Ghyaneth's voice easily carried that far. "If you sink me—if you set me on fire—he dies alongside me!" He shook Rafe hard enough to make his head wobble.

"Return him to us!" came the shouted reply. It was distorted by wind and water, but Rafe was pretty sure the speaker was Darien. "We do not wish you harm! But we will not let you take him."

"Do not interfere in matters that do not concern you!" Ghyaneth shouted back. "He belongs to Berringey, and you cannot prevent me from taking him!"

On the words, the ocean grew motionless as glass.

The sails, which had begun to strain and billow with sea air, lost their tautness and fell limply against the masts. The escort vessels were similarly becalmed. The three Berringese ships might as well have been on solid land baked hard by an unforgiving sun. They did not move at all.

Rafe heard the closest sailors begin to mutter and curse. He didn't understand what they were saying, but a few of them made gestures that looked like religious signs designed to ward off malicious spirits. He imagined the sailors on the other Berringese ships were engaged in much the same activities.

Ghyaneth shoved Rafe away from him and turned toward a nearby soldier, a tall, forbidding man wearing what Rafe guessed was a captain's insignia. The prince was angry and just a little apprehensive. "What is happening?" he demanded. "Why have our ships stopped?"

"The wind—" the captain began.

"We have rowers," Ghyaneth snapped. "Set them to work!"

The captain barked an order to an underling, who dashed away. Rafe permitted a smile to come to his face as he leaned against the railing, looking down at the satin-smooth surface of the water.

"You won't make any headway," he said. "It is not by accident you've stopped moving."

"What do you mean?" Ghyaneth demanded.

Rafe nodded toward the Welchin ships, which were rapidly drawing closer. "I'm guessing that among your pursuers are Kayle Dochenza and Zoe Lalindar. The primes of air and water. They control the wind and the sea, and if they don't want your ship to travel, it will stay here until the end of the world."

"That's ridiculous," Ghyaneth snapped. "No one controls the elements."

"Well, *they* do," Rafe said. "It doesn't matter if you believe me or not. You still won't move."

Below him, at the ship's waterline, he heard the sound of many oars splashing into the ocean more or less at once. Ghyaneth gave him a thin smile. "We'll see about that," he said.

Some sailor belowdecks bawled out a command followed by a rhythmic exhortation. *Row! Row! Row!* At each word, the oars swept through the water again.

The ship didn't travel so much as an inch. The water was so still that the craft didn't even rock on its hull.

"Ghyaneth!" came Darien's bellow from across the water. The lead Welchin boat was close enough now that Rafe could identify the figures standing in the prow. The regent, of course; Kayle and Zoe, as he'd suspected; and Josetta, Foley, and a dozen others. Maybe twenty soldiers massed behind them on the deck, and each of the other Welchin ships carried at least as many troops. "Release Lerafi Kolavar, and you will be free to sail away! But we cannot permit you to take and murder him."

"This is Berringese business, and none of your affair!" Ghyaneth called back.

"I have made it my affair," was Darien's reply. "As you see."

Indeed, the Welchin navy had surrounded Ghyaneth's escort, four ships to each of the Berringese vessels. The Welchin soldiers were clearly poised to board, waiting only on Darien's order. The Berringese soldiers were also preparing themselves for battle; Rafe could see thin streamers of smoke rising from braziers set up alongside the Berringese cannons. He spared a moment to wonder if Nelson Ardelay could damp those fires if he chose to—and another moment to wonder if the sweela prime was among the Welchin contingent.

"We will bring our ship alongside yours," Darien continued. "Return Lerafi safely to us, then be on your way."

There was a brief silence while Ghyaneth seemed to think this over. Rafe had a moment's hope that his bloodthirsty cousin would choose his own safety over an arcane tradition. But suddenly Ghyaneth whirled around and clouted Rafe across the face, driving Rafe to his knees with his head ringing and his bound hands braced on the planking. Ghyaneth had struck him with a weapon of some sort, he realized, probably the hilt of a heavy dagger. At any rate, it left Rafe as dizzy as he'd been when he first regained consciousness.

He heard feminine voices raised in alarm, their bright syllables skittering to him across the water. But he didn't have time to sort out if it was Zoe or Josetta pleading for his life, because Ghyaneth had crouched beside him, that same dagger now point-first in his hand. The expression on the prince's face was unadulterated, fanatical rage.

"You *shall* not take the throne of Berringey if I have to die to keep you off of it," Ghyaneth snarled, and he laid the tip of his weapon against Rafe's throat.

Rafe threw himself sideways to avoid the thrust, swinging his bound hands up to try to knock the weapon out of Ghyaneth's grip. He landed hard on his elbow and scrambled awkwardly to his knees, then to an ungainly crouch. As he struggled to keep his balance, he pawed madly at the straps across his chest, trying to find the one that would inflate the chemicals in the flying bag. Ghyaneth whirled around, grabbing a patch of Rafe's hair with his left hand and jerking Rafe's head backward to expose his throat. The dagger was still firmly clutched in his right hand.

"This blood should have been spilled long before now," Ghyaneth panted, and sliced at Rafe's neck.

With all his strength, Rafe yanked on a cord, and the world exploded.

TWENTY-EIGHT

Rafe shot up in the air so fast and so far that he couldn't help a shout of alarm, and he was moving so swiftly, so randomly, that he could hardly get his bearings. Sky—ocean—land—ocean—clouds—ocean—he was spinning and tumbling through the air as the flying bag whipped him through a wild and constantly shifting course. He thought that the chemicals were still combining, delivering little bursts of speed that jerked him in one direction or another. Higher. Closer to land. Farther out to sea.

There seemed to be a dozen straps dangling over his chest and he fumbled through them, trying to find the ones that Clay had said would offer directional control. But it was hopeless. He couldn't tell which one was supposed to do what, and all the cords kept flopping about anyway, as he dipped and dove and shot higher over the water. So he just yielded to the vagaries of the device and concentrated on trying to figure out where he was.

A fresh burst of chemical combustion spun him around again. Now he was facing land and it wasn't impossibly far away. He seemed to have migrated to a point equidistant from the ships and the shore. That was good, right? Once he came down, he'd be able to swim to the harbor.

Or he might have been able to, if his hands weren't tied.

And if he hadn't been attached to this great puffy ball of heavy canvas. Squinting against the sun, Rafe peered up at the flying bag, which, inflated, was about the size of a massive desk, though rather more spherical. What happened when *that* hit the water? How quickly would it drag him under?

Almost as he had the thought, the bag emitted a sour, soughing sound and seemed to collapse in on itself. Rafe felt himself plummeting toward the ocean with an ominous directness. Just as he gathered the breath to yell, he was jerked upward again as some late-firing chemicals gave off their own precious gases, momentarily slowing his descent.

Another terrifying plunge, another head-snapping reversal of course—another drop—another brief ascent. Rafe was so disoriented, nauseated, and terrified that he could hardly monitor his progress, but he could see the great sparkling immensity of the ocean growing implacably closer.

Ghyaneth kills me after all, he thought.

The flying bag made a sputtering, hissing sound and utterly deflated, settling lumpily over Rafe's skull and shoulders. Seconds later he went feetfirst into the water and continued downward a good distance under the surface. At first the shock of cold and the inability to breathe left him paralyzed; the water pressed in on him from all sides, eager to crush him.

Then his own natural buoyancy pushed him upward, and he regained both sense and will. He kicked hard for the surface, feeling the strain in his legs, his back, his lungs. His open eyes were slitted against the salt water as he strove for the pale strip of blue above him where sunlight played on the sea. His head burst clear and he gasped for breath, flailing with his hands and feet to try to keep his face above the water. The canvas flying bag spread out behind him like a spill of sewage, half-submerged, half floating, as a few bubbles of stubborn gas still kept it yearning toward the sky. But it was easy to see that soon it would take on enough water to sink toward the bottom of the ocean.

If I only had a knife! Rafe thought, trying not to panic. *I'd cut myself free!* It was another five seconds before he remembered he didn't need one. *Buckles. Buckles. The bag is held on with buckles.* He clawed at the straps across his chest, greatly impeded by the waterlogged ropes tying his hands together. His fingers were clumsy with cold and his head kept slipping underwater, making it hard to see, hard to function, hard not to succumb to mounting fear. The last little pocket of air seemed to sigh out through the seams of the canvas, and the whole bunched mass of material drifted below the surface of the water. Down— down—down, slowly but inexorably, pulling Rafe with it.

The top of his head was just fully submerged as he worked the last buckle free, tore the final strap from his shoulders, and kicked his way up to the light again. He took a few deep, shuddering breaths—swallowing more than a little salt water as he did so—and tried to figure out where he was and what he should do next. He was so low in the water it was hard to tell which way was land and which way was open sea. He was so cold and his muscles were so exhausted that he wasn't sure he'd have the strength to fight his way to shore even if he knew in which direction to go.

You can't give up now, he admonished himself, squinting at the sky, trying to determine where he was by the angle of the sun. *You can't escape Ghyaneth just to drown!*

That way. If the sun was setting toward the west, land had to be northward, straight in front of him. Rafe aimed his bound hands in the direction he hoped was home, laid himself out in the water, and kicked himself forward.

He began sliding backward through the ocean.

He let out another shout of dismay, momentarily convinced he'd become entangled in the heavy canvas, maybe even a thick weave of seaweed, that he was being pulled down as well as backward. But nothing dragged on his hips or ankles; he didn't slip below the surface. In fact, he seemed lighter all of a sudden, higher in the water—which had heated to a bearable, almost delicious, temperature. He continued to be carried away from land with an irresistible pressure.

Away from land. Back toward the boats. By a warm, vagrant current designed especially for him.

Zoe, he realized, suddenly suffused with a relief so dazzling it mimicked joy. The coru prime had dipped her hand in the water and commanded it to carry him straight to her side. He was safe. He would not drown after all.

. . .

Rafe had never in his life been so glad to see anything, *anything*, as the lead ship from the Welchin navy taking shape against the horizon line. Someone spotted him and began shouting and waving, and then the whole railing was crowded with people shouting and waving, and somewhere there was the small splash of a dinghy hitting the water. Moments later, two soldiers pulled up next to him and hauled him into the little boat, and then it was hardly any time at all before he was being raised to the deck by a set of straps and pulleys, because he was too exhausted to climb.

The minute his feet touched the hard planking, women fell on him from all sides. Josetta, Corene, and Zoe hugged him and chanted his name and hugged him again, heedless of his soggy state and the very real possibility that they would suffocate him. He could tell that the princesses were crying and he thought Zoe might be crying, too. He was laughing, when he could catch his breath, but he thought it wouldn't take much for him to start weeping as well.

"Enough—give him some room—he needs a change of clothes and a quick update on our situation," came Darien's voice, slicing cleanly through the feminine commotion. The women reluctantly moved aside to let Darien through, although Josetta kept her hold on Rafe's arm and seemed unlikely to ever release him. Which suited Rafe just fine.

Darien surveyed him a moment. "I commend you on both your luck and your quick wits," the regent said at last. "Kayle explained to us what unlikely invention made your escape possible—further explaining that it was wholly untested. You were brave and smart. And fortunate. We saw that scene playing out and were convinced you were going to die."

"Stop *saying* that," Josetta moaned, turning her face into Rafe's wet shoulder.

He patted her awkwardly with his lashed hands, and Darien made an almost imperceptible gesture. Instantly, one of his soldiers appeared with a knife and quickly sawed through Rafe's bonds.

"I thank you most gratefully for sailing to my rescue, but I don't know how many times you're going to want to save me," Rafe said gravely, shaking his hands to send blood back to his frozen fingertips.

"In the few moments I had to discuss my fate with my cousin, he made it clear that he will *never* forgo the desire to see me dead. Maybe I would be safer in Malinqua, I don't know. But I am afraid I will always be a hunted man."

"As to that, Zoe has some ideas," Darien said. "Once we have found some dry clothes for you, will you be up to discussing a deal with the prince?"

"Discussing—will he treat with you? Will he listen?"

"At the moment, he has no choice," Darien said. "He is in our possession."

"He is—" Rafe supposed it was the effect of the stress or the water but he was having trouble comprehending what the regent was saying. "What?"

Darien nodded to something over Rafe's shoulder, so Rafe twisted around to take in the whole tableau of Berringese and Welchin ships. All three of the big warships were surrounded by the smaller navy boats; it was clear soldiers from both nations were prepared for combat, but all of them were awaiting some kind of signal.

"One of the side benefits of your unconventional escape from Ghyaneth's hands was that you knocked him into the ocean as you shot into the air," Darien said. "Naturally his own men went diving after him, but—well. If a man is in the water, he is Zoe's to command. We brought him aboard our ship and we have him now."

"It's his fault I overlooked you for a few minutes," Zoe interposed. "I was concentrating so hard on bringing him *to* us and keeping his men *from* him that I didn't pay much attention to you once you went down. You had a bad few moments, I'm afraid, but I promise you were never going to drown."

"So Ghyaneth is actually aboard this ship?" Rafe said. "What are you going to do with him?"

"Oh, we're going to send him home again," Zoe said, "after we convince him that he's better off leaving you alone."

There was no such thing as a large room on a small boat. Once he had changed into a moderately clean tunic and trousers supplied by the captain, Rafe joined eight other people crowded into a space meant for about half that number. Among them were the regent, the princesses, and four of the primes, for it turned out that both Mirti and Nelson had joined the rescue party.

The other two people in the room were Rafe and his cousin.

Ghyaneth was bound exactly the way Rafe had been: hands tied in front of him and his feet free. Like Rafe, he had gone into the ocean, but no one had bothered to give *him* a fresh change of clothes. He managed to act as if it didn't bother him to sit upright in a hard-backed chair, his wet garments plastered against his body, his glare falling impartially on everyone in the room.

His turban had been lost in the struggle, and Rafe was sure he wasn't the only one taking surreptitious glances at the prince's ear. It had the familiar triangular pattern cut into the cartilage, though Ghyaneth hadn't bothered to decorate the pointed edges with hoops. The marks were enough for him. *By this you will know that I am royal.*

"I think, Prince Ghyaneth, it is time we had a very honest discussion," Darien said with his usual imperturbability.

Ghyaneth turned his bitter stare at the regent. "Just kill me and be done with it," he said. "Though I warn you. When my cousin Siacett takes the throne of Berringey, she will be just as determined as I am to see this pretender put to death. He is a threat to her and her children as surely as he is a threat to me."

Darien shook his head. "I am not going to kill you. I want to find a peaceful solution to our differences."

Ghyaneth nodded in Rafe's direction. "Then hand that man over to me and let me go."

"Since I have gone to considerable trouble to keep Lerafi alive, you must realize that is not going to happen," Darien replied. "We must discuss other options."

"He is an enemy of my people!" Ghyaneth burst out. "You know his heritage, but do you know *why* his bloodline is dangerous? Malinqua and Berringey have been rivals for generations. We have never declared outright war, but there have been incidents—ships mysteriously lost at sea, outposts raided, ambassadors murdered. Subriella's marriage to my uncle was supposed to bring peace between nations. But it only made things worse."

Ghyaneth raised his clasped hands to gesture in Rafe's direction.

"And now this man who *should* be dead is returning to Malinqua, possibly to sit on the throne? A traitor with Berringese blood in his veins ruling over the nation that is our greatest enemy? Perhaps *your* country may be safe from war, but war will come all the same, and thousands will die, if that man becomes king of Malinqua."

Probably Darien had something he wanted to say to that, but Rafe couldn't contain himself. "I won't go to Malinqua, then," he offered. "I'll stay in Welce. I won't look for a throne in either country. I never wanted to be king anyway."

Josetta looked at him sharply and then looked away; the stakes were too high, just now, to think about what such a promise might mean to the two of them. Anyway, Ghyaneth was regarding him with a sneer.

"You can swear any vows you like while we are talking treaties," he said disdainfully, "and you can break them the minute I sail away. I have learned all I need to know about the honor of the Malinquese."

Before Rafe could answer that, Darien took control of the conversation again. "If you could be convinced that Lerafi Kolovar would stay in Welce, never traveling to either Malinqua or Berringey, would that be enough to make you drop this blood feud? Would you agree to return to Berringey without him and make no more attempts on his life?"

Ghyaneth spoke aloud the exact words that were in Rafe's head. "It seems unlikely you could make such a guarantee."

"But if I could?"

Ghyaneth gave an elaborate shrug. "Then yes. I would allow him to live out his days here in your backward little repellent nation. But you won't be able to convince me."

Darien nodded at Zoe and she pushed her way to the front of the group. Her smile was friendly but, Rafe thought, rather wicked. "Rafe, show us your hand," she said. Mystified, he extended his right hand and turned it from side to side for everyone to see. It was raw from the straps and the seawater and the general abuse of the day, but he supposed that wasn't the point.

"Prince Ghyaneth, watch closely," she said, holding out her own hand. She didn't touch Rafe, but it was clear she was concentrating on him. He had the strangest sensation, as if he'd drunk an entire bottle of wine, or replaced his familiar blood with the burning salt water of the ocean. A dark stain quickly spread along his fingers and knuckles, and he felt a deep, dull pain.

Zoe had bruised him without laying a finger on him.

"I am the prime of blood and water," she told Ghyaneth in a chatty voice. "If I want to, I can pull the blood out of any man's body and leave him a dry corpse. I don't even have to touch him."

Behind him Rafe heard a sharp crack of laughter and Nelson's crow of delight. "I think I see where this is going," the sweela prime said to himself.

Zoe ignored him, taking one step closer to Rafe. "Bend your head," she instructed, and a little fearfully, he did. Her fingertip pushed gently through his hair and came to rest on the back of his skull. His head pulsed with a sudden sharp ache; he bit his lip to keep a gasp from escaping. The agony lasted only a moment, then she lifted her hand.

Rafe tilted his head back to stare at her. Her expression was still sunny. "I've made odd little tangles in a couple of Lerafi's arteries. If he tries to leave Welce, those tangles will burst apart," she explained. "There will be a little—" She seemed to search for the right word. "Explosion of blood in his head. It will kill him instantly. Lerafi will never trouble you in Berringey or Malinqua."

The expression on Ghyaneth's face was a cross between triumph and suspicion. "Most excellent," he murmured, "but only if I can believe you speak the truth."

"I don't think *Rafe* is the one who will be troublesome," Kayle said in a dissatisfied voice. "*Ghyaneth* is the one who's running around trying to kill people. He might try to harm Rafe even if he has this—this condition—and how will you stop him?"

"I concur," Mirti said. "Ghyaneth's sense of honor is different from ours."

"Oh, I agree with both of you," Zoe said. She placed one hand flat on the table and leaned across it, placing the tip of her finger against Ghyaneth's temple.

The prince jerked his head away. "What are you doing?" he demanded.

"Hold him still," Zoe said in a businesslike voice, and Nelson and Darien wrestled Ghyaneth into a tight hold. The prince thrashed noisily, but the two men held his head motionless while Zoe again laid her finger against his face. Ghyaneth kicked out against his captors and almost succeeded in upending the table, but Nelson and Darien were immovable. A few moments later, Zoe lifted her hand and they released him.

"What did you do?" the prince panted, staring up at her with fear and horror.

"Exactly what I did to your cousin. I put a few kinks in the arteries that feed your brain. If Rafe is murdered or dies under mysterious circumstances—" Zoe held out her hand, the fingers splayed, and then suddenly contracted them into a tight fist. Rafe felt all the blood in his own body snap in her direction, and by the murmurs of discomfort that went around the room, he guessed everyone else did, too. "If Rafe dies, I will cause those kinks to burst. And *you* will die."

"You can't do that," Ghyaneth said uncertainly. "Not from hundreds of miles away. No one can do that."

"Really?" she said quietly. She pointed a finger in the prince's direction, and he cried out in pain as a bruise blossomed on his exposed forearm. She pointed again, and he leaned over and clutched his ankle. Again, and he rolled to one side, now cradling his bound hands against his shoulder. "I think I can make your blood respond any way I choose, and it doesn't matter how far away I am. If Rafe dies, I promise you will learn that I am telling the truth."

"But anything could happen to him!" Ghyaneth cried. "He might be run over by one of your elaymotives! He might be robbed and killed by thieves! That would have nothing to do with me!"

"I think I can tell the difference between a tragedy and a murder."

"And my cousin!" Ghyaneth went on, even more desperately. "If she hears of this, *she* may well have him killed just so I am slain in retaliation and she takes the throne in my place!"

"That's not my problem," Zoe said. "*You* are my problem, and I have taken care of you."

Nelson had started laughing. "Oh, that's elegant, that is," he said, slapping his hands together. "I swear, Zoe, you have your father's sweela mind and your grandmother's coru heart."

Darien looked around the room. "Are we all done here? Is everyone satisfied with the parameters of our agreement?"

Rafe took a deep breath. It was probably his imagination that he could still feel Zoe's fingertip pressed against his skull. "I am," he said. "I will stay in Welce or know my life is forfeit."

Ghyaneth glared at Rafe, at Darien, at Zoe, at everyone in the room. "I am not satisfied, no, it is impossible to be *satisfied* when dealing with savages," he spat. "But I will happily depart this place, and I will leave my cousin in peace. If that's what you're waiting to hear from me. And because I am an honorable man, you have no cause to doubt my word."

"I believe him," Nelson declared. "He's speaking the truth."

"Good," Darien said. "Prince Ghyaneth, we will see you back to your ship and guarantee you fair winds and favorable seas until you are well on your way."

Darien helped Ghyaneth to his feet and the room quickly emptied out, only Josetta, Corene, and Rafe remaining behind. Rafe because he was too exhausted to move, and the princesses to keep him company.

"And *that*," said Josetta, "is the reason some people are afraid of Zoe."

"I see that now," Rafe said. "I had no idea she would go to such extremes. Or do you think it was Darien's idea?"

"Oh, no," said Josetta. "That was all Zoe."

"Well, I'm not sorry you're staying in Welce, but are you sad you're not going to Malinqua?" Corene asked him.

He managed a faint laugh. "I'm too tired and too unnerved and too beaten up—*again*—to figure out how I feel about anything," he said. "I'll miss my brother. I'll miss the chance to get to know my grandmother better."

"You'll miss the chance to be a *king*," Corene said. She glanced between him and Josetta. "Although—they might name Josetta queen of Welce. And you could marry her. And then you could be king. Unless she marries a lot of husbands, and then you could be *one* of the kings."

"I don't think I want a lot of husbands," Josetta said.

"Well, do you want to marry Rafe?"

The question hung in the air a moment while Rafe and Josetta studied each other. He could feel himself grinning, and she couldn't quite keep a smile off her lips.

"I don't know," she said at last. "Maybe. But I am very, very, *very* glad he won't be leaving for Malinqua."

TWENTY-NINE

Josetta had a hard time releasing her hold on Rafe's arm once they made it back to shore and the various heroes of the day began dispersing. Naturally, the regent and the primes needed to gather so they could discuss the ramifications of the afternoon's events, but Rafe declined to join them.

"I would like to spend a little time saying my goodbyes to Steff. And I must tell my grandmother what occurred and why I can't accompany her back to Malinqua," he told Josetta gently. They were standing face-to-face at the edge of the pier, holding hands, trying to ignore the surrounding turmoil of the general deboarding. "She will be disappointed—and angry, I think, with both Zoe and Ghyaneth. I will have to convince her that I am not so sorry events have transpired this way."

"I hope you're not," Josetta replied in a low voice. "In some ways you've become a prisoner of Welce, and I would understand if you didn't like that! But I just don't see—"

"I don't see many other options that would keep me safe," he interrupted. "And since this option keeps me near you—well—I am going to consider myself lucky."

"Josetta!" Darien's peremptory voice carried easily over the clangor of ships and men. "I would like you to join our conference!"

She kissed Rafe quickly on the mouth. "Come with your grandmother to the dinner tonight," she said. "If you're up to it. If not—I'll come back to your lodgings as soon as I can. But it might be late."

He touched his forehead briefly to hers and then released her. "I'll be waiting."

Corene had opted out of this particular meeting—Josetta wondered glumly how she'd managed that—but otherwise the usual group convened in one of Kayle's beautifully decorated salons. Subtle scents sweetened the air; invisible chimes occasionally drifted across the room. The temperature was delightfully cool in contrast to the muggy heat outside, and the repast Kayle had grudgingly offered was bountiful and delicious.

The primes, the princess, and the regent gathered around a highly polished table of wood and inlaid gold and reviewed the events of the day. The general consensus was that they had escaped with less damage than they could have and that the future looked promising, if not entirely free of difficulties.

"Berringey might stop all trade with Welce," Mirti warned. "And that will have an economic impact across the provinces."

"I understand," Darien said. "We have discussed opening new trade routes farther west. Now might be the time."

"We can step up our exports to Malinqua, too," Kayle said. "That horrible empress has already ordered three elaymotives and she's very interested in my flying machines. I'm sure she'll be willing to make other deals with us."

"Will she?" Nelson asked. "She was disappointed that we didn't fall in with her bridal plans."

"She was, but she brings a grandson home with her, which should make her happy enough," Darien answered. "We had some private talk last night and I came away believing she is generally pleased with the results of her visit here."

Josetta happened to be glancing in Nelson's direction, so she caught the sharp look he sent Mirti's way. The hunti prime nodded, and Nelson sat up straighter in his chair.

"If we're done rehashing Malinqua and Berringey, I suggest we return to the most pressing issue of Welce," Nelson said. "The succession."

Kayle threw his hands in the air. "Will we never be done with that topic? First we're to have a queen. Then, no, we're to throw out the whole government and start over again. I don't care. Let's just *settle* it."

"We have been a monarchy too long to throw it aside because one generation is problematic," Mirti said gravely.

"Kayle's right. We discussed all this," Zoe said impatiently. "We've managed just fine for the past seven years, when we didn't have a king at all."

"That's just it. We did," Nelson said. "We just didn't realize it."

"But we *didn't* have a king," Kayle protested. "It was Darien acting on Vernon's behalf and—*oh*. Darien! Oh, of course, I see that now. You want to name him king." He nodded.

It was the first time Josetta had ever seen Darien taken wholly by surprise. "You *what*? Nelson, what nonsense is this?"

"It's hardly nonsense," the sweela prime said. He was grinning widely. "You were the de facto ruler during the last two years of Vernon's life and the first five years of Odelia's. I'll tell you, watching you negotiate with Filomara and Ghyaneth gave me a whole new appreciation for your intelligence. Are you sure you aren't part sweela?"

"Hunti through and through," Darien snapped. "And this is preposterous."

"I agree with Nelson," Mirti said. "You possess every skill a king needs and you've had years of experience on the job. You've treated with foreign nations, kept civil order, helped the economy flourish— and produced an heir."

At this point in the conversation, Zoe started laughing uncontrollably. Josetta felt a smile curve her own lips; oh, this would be so much better than being named queen herself!

Darien still appeared to be shocked. "You cannot just—pick a man at random and stick him on the throne," he said. "What about all the posturing of the past nineday? Vernon's heritage and all that! How will you get around the requirements of blood?"

"Well, all you really have to do is persuade the primes to ratify you, and that should be easy enough," Mirti retorted. "You come from one of the Five Families and your wife comes from two of them, so your daughter has the blood of *three* primes running in her veins. If we can convince Kayle and Taro—"

"I'm convinced!" Kayle exclaimed. "If that means we're done with conversations about the crown, I'm happy to name *anybody* king."

"That's hardly civic minded," Darien retorted.

"Taro might be harder to win over, though," Nelson said thoughtfully.

Zoe had dropped her head to her hands, but now she looked up, showing them a face suffused with merriment. "Oh, surely we can find a way to prove Frothen blood runs in Darien's veins!" she cried. "I'm convinced I've noticed it in the past. I just wasn't paying attention."

Darien smiled at her reluctantly. "Maybe if we go back far enough on the genealogy charts—"

"*All* the Five Families are related," Nelson said firmly. "Somewhere there will be a convenient bloodline."

"Or marry Celia off to someone who's related to both the Dochenzas and the Frothens," Josetta suggested. "And *her* son or daughter will be related to all the primes."

"Excellent plan!" Nelson exclaimed, beaming at her. "Kayle, you and Taro get some heirs together and start making babies."

"I was joking," Josetta said. "Celia might want to find her own husband."

"It doesn't matter who Celia wants to marry because she's not going to be heir to the throne," Darien said firmly.

"Oh, I think she will," Nelson said. "There might be a few details to clear up—"

"A *few*!" Zoe wailed, still laughing. "Here's one you haven't thought of! Whoever marries the king or queen gives up all their own property rights. But I'm prime and I can't give up *my* property. And if my daughter is queen, she can't be prime after me—"

"Well, you can have another child, can't you?" Kayle said. "Or three or five or eight."

"Yes, of course, but the land—"

"We will have to figure out how to account for the property," Mirti admitted. "The laws were written to prevent the crown from gathering too much power—to keep a king from marrying all the primes, for instance, and controlling the elements as well as the throne. But we can come up with some kind of amendment. Perhaps we simply don't allow Zoe to be named queen. These are *our* laws, after all. They are here to serve our purposes."

"But—" Zoe started.

"As Nelson said, there will be many details to take care of," Mirti interrupted. "But the solution itself feels right. It feels solid. I vote in favor of Darien Serlast as king."

"As do I," Nelson said immediately. "Kayle?"

"I already said I was in favor of it! Yes, yes, I say yes! But what about Zoe?"

Everyone in the room looked at Zoe, who was still trying to compose herself. Josetta saw her pat her cheeks and bite her lips before she reached over to take Darien's hand.

"The day I met you, you invited me to come with you to Chialto to marry the king," she said, keeping her voice reasonably steady. She was still smiling, but the expression had grown tender instead of hysterical. "I knew fairly quickly that I didn't want to marry Vernon—but I *did* want to marry you. As coru prime, I agree with the others that you would make a splendid king. I vote in favor of Darien Serlast, too."

After the day's exhausting events, no one was particularly interested in one last lavish state dinner, but no one wanted to send Filomara off without a formal farewell. So they compromised with a modest buffet in one of Kayle's smaller dining rooms, and anyone who wanted a chance to say goodbye to the Malinqua contingent had a chance to do so.

Rafe sent his regrets, but Steff was there. He stuck close to his grandmother all night and seemed to be listening carefully whenever Darien or one of the primes stopped to talk to her. Josetta thought he might be practicing to be a prince, but he seemed to be enjoying the apprenticeship. It took her a moment to identify what seemed different about him, but eventually she realized that he was dressed in Malinqua clothing, more fitted and formal than the flowing tunics and trousers the Welchins wore. It made him seem taller and older somehow.

"I'll miss Steff, won't you?" Josetta said to Corene as the two of them sat together at the end of the table and finished their meals.

Corene lifted her eyes and studied the young man across the room. "I'm not sure I know him well enough to miss him."

"Really? I'm surprised. I thought you liked him."

Corene shrugged. "I'd miss *Rafe*. I know him better."

"I wonder how Steff feels knowing that he might never see his brother or his father again."

"Well, of *course* he can see them," Corene said irritably. "He just has to come back here for visits. And Bors can sail out to Malinqua anytime he wants. It's Steff's own fault if he gets so caught up in his new life that he forgets his old one."

Corene seemed determined to be more than ordinarily contrary, which made Josetta think her first guess was right. Corene liked Steff more than she wanted to admit. Josetta changed the subject. "Have you talked to your father since the meeting with the primes? Has he gotten over the shock of being nominated king?"

Corene's expression grew even more remote, and Josetta wondered what was wrong now. "Not yet, but I'm sure he'll get used to the idea quickly enough. It only makes sense, since, of course, he'll make an excellent king."

"And he's already been doing the job for seven years."

"And he's already produced *one heir*," Corene said with heavy emphasis.

Which was when Josetta figured it out. "Wait. Of course. The primes didn't even think of that! Darien has *two* daughters! That makes him an even better prospect!"

Corene's dark eyes were unreadable; she seemed to be struggling to speak in a light voice. "It doesn't matter if my *pretend* father or my *real* father is sitting on the throne, no one seems to think I should be the next one in line," she said.

"I think Nelson and Mirti were just so focused on the fact that Celia is related to three primes," Josetta said awkwardly. "They weren't thinking about *Celia* so much as the bloodlines."

"And my blood is always wrong."

"Corene—"

Corene stood up abruptly. "It's all right. I'm getting used to being the one nobody ever remembers."

Josetta jumped to her feet and caught Corene's arm. "*I remember you. You're my sister. You're my closest friend in the world.*"

Corene wrenched away and opened her mouth as if to spit out a recrimination, but then she hesitated, and the bitter line of her mouth softened. "And you're the best sister I could have ever had," she said. "I'd miss *you* if you sailed hundreds of miles away." She leaned forward to kiss Josetta on the cheek, then practically ran from the table, through the room, and out the door.

Josetta stared after her, then wended her way to Zoe's side. "I think you should check on Corene when you get a chance. She seems to be having a rough day."

"It's been a strange one for all of us," Zoe agreed. "I, for one, am ready for it to be over."

"Well, I'm going to make my goodbyes to Filomara and leave," Josetta said. "I'll see you in the morning."

"Darien wants to leave for Chialto no later than noon. We'll send the elaymotive to pick you up."

"Oh no," Josetta said, smiling. "I'm not going back to Darien's house. I'm heading to the shelter. And to my own life. And not even Darien will be able to change my mind."

When Josetta presented herself to Filomara, the empress was passably gracious and claimed she had enjoyed getting to know her. "Come visit Malinqua sometime," Filomara invited, keeping Josetta's hand in hers for a moment. "You'd like it, I think."

"Perhaps I will," Josetta said.

"I'll introduce you to all my nephews," the empress said with a speculative glance. "Maybe you'd like one of them more than you expect."

"I like your grandson Lerafi," Josetta said. "Is that good enough for you?"

Filomara laughed and dropped her hand. "Maybe," she said.

Josetta turned to Steff, standing in Filomara's shadow. "I hate to see you go, but I wish you all the best in your new life," she said, giving him a hug. "Come visit us often."

"I'll try," he said. "Take care of Rafe."

"I'll try."

Josetta knew she should make a quick round of the room, bid farewell to Darien and the primes, but she simply couldn't stand any more polite conversation. She slipped out of the room and through the cool high-ceilinged corridors of Kayle's house, stepping out the front door into night air that was still dense and sticky with heat. Instantly, Foley was at her side.

"Heading back to the lodgings?" he asked. "Do you want to walk or shall I find an elaymotive?"

"It's not that far. Let's walk."

They had traveled about five blocks in companionable silence when she realized Foley was her only guard. "Did Darien send Caze and Sorbin and the others ahead with Rafe, then? Or—"

"He's decided the prince is safe," Foley confirmed. "The Berringese boats sailed out of the harbor as soon as the tide was favorable, and the regent truly believes Ghyaneth will abide by his promise."

Josetta took a deep breath. "Wonderful! I can hardly imagine what that will be like—not to be trailed by a dozen soldiers every time I take a step."

Foley sent her a sideways glance. In the gaslights intermittently lining the streets, it was easy to see his amused expression. "Now you no longer have to keep him safe by pretending to be in love with him."

That made her laugh. "What a relief that will be!"

There was a moment when the only sound between them was the light patter of their footsteps. "I think you are in love with him, though," Foley said.

She couldn't entirely read the tone of his voice, but he didn't sound sad or bitter or lost or angry. He was merely making an observation. So she said, "I think I am, too."

"And that means the task of looking after you falls to someone else now. Not me," he said.

She came to a halt right there, one foot on an uneven section of brick, one on a carefully graded stretch of pavement. "You're leaving the royal service? Or just leaving the task of guarding me?"

"It's more complicated than that," he said. "There's someone else I need to watch over."

She felt a complex surge of delight, curiosity, and the tiniest, smallest, least attractive tendril of jealousy. Foley had cared for her so long it was hard to imagine him giving all of his attention to someone else. "You've fallen in love? Oh, tell me about this person!"

He shook his head. "It's not love. It's—responsibility. I believe someone else needs me more than you do."

She lifted a hand and pressed it against his heart. "Then whoever that person is, he or she will always be safe, because no one could be a better guard than you. I will miss you—but I am glad to see you moving on with your life."

"We both are," he said. "Everybody has to."

Josetta was close to tears by the time she let herself into Rafe's room. It was almost completely dark, with only a little light glancing up through the open windows from the gaslight below. She could tell by the even sound of his breathing that Rafe was already asleep, so she moved as quietly as she could while she readied herself for bed.

But when she lay down next to him, he stirred and came half awake. "All done with pomp and statesmanship?" he asked through a yawn.

"Yes, finally," she said, snuggling against him. The room was warm but not unbearably so, and she wanted to feel his particular heat against her skin. She wanted to be reassured that he was alive, that he had survived yet another dire adventure. "How are you feeling?"

"Sore and headachy and a little dizzy," he admitted. "But I'm not complaining! I could so easily be drowned. Or lying on the deck of a Berringese ship with my throat cut."

"Don't say such terrible things," she begged, clinging even closer. "I'm going to have nightmares as it is. Every scene from this terrible day is printed on my mind like paintings on a wall. I'll never forget a single one of them."

He kissed her forehead and wrapped his arms loosely around her shoulders. "I'm sure you'll find plenty of other things to think about as the days go by," he said comfortably. "So tell me if anything interesting happened since I left your side."

She started shaking with laughter. Anything interesting! "The primes have decided to name Darien king."

"*Really?* That seems like big news! Although as soon as you say it, it just sounds right. Of course he should be king."

"Of course he should," she echoed. "And Darien has called off all your guards because he believes Ghyaneth will leave you alone."

"I know. I figured that out when I came back here and no one followed me. I can't tell you what a relief it was."

"I thought you might be nervous."

"If I was going to be nervous, I'd worry about this blood knot your sister put in my head," he replied. "I'd worry about climbing back into one of Kayle's aeromotives. I can't say I've actually gotten over my fear of death in the past quintile, but I've certainly faced it down a few times. I don't think I can spend the rest of my life afraid of all the things that *could* go wrong. So I'm just going to go forward trying not to be afraid of anything."

"That's brave," she said.

"It doesn't feel brave. It just feels like—my new life."

She sighed faintly. "There's a lot of that going around these days. New lives."

"I suppose so," he agreed. "Steff's. Darien's."

"Foley's," she said. "He told me tonight that he's found someone else to guard with his full attention."

"Really? That's big news, too. Did he say who?"

"He didn't. Foley was always devoted to the crown more than the person, so I think it might be Celia. Since the primes want to certify her as the heir after Darien." *Not me. Not Corene.* She pressed her lips to Rafe's throat. "And he seemed to feel that he could safely leave me behind now that I have *you* to watch over me."

Rafe had become more and more awake as the conversation progressed, and now he returned her kiss with enthusiasm. "And I am *far* more devoted to the person than the crown," he said. "May I show you how?"

She laughed at him, running her fingers through his hair and pulling him down for another kiss. "Oh, I wish you would."

It was late the next morning when Josetta woke up, and then only because someone was knocking loudly. Rafe was already on his feet, cursing and stuffing himself into a pair of trousers. In the daylight, she could see that his torso was covered in scrapes and bruises; the straps from the flying bag seemed to have left permanent impressions in his skin.

"Josetta!" came Zoe's voice from the other side of the door. "Are you up?"

"Just a moment!" she called back as Rafe crossed the room to hand her the tunic she'd worn last night. He looked around the room in a comically desperate way, as if seeking a place to hide.

"What are they going to *think*?" he whispered as she climbed out of bed and shrugged into her clothes.

"I don't care what they think," she said. "I don't even know why she's here. I told her I was returning to the shelter today, not going back to Darien's."

"She seems to believe there's been a change of plans," Rafe said, heading over to open the door.

It was something of a relief to find only Zoe on the other side, looking worried but hardly shocked. "Are you two really just waking up?" she demanded.

"It was kind of a long day yesterday," Josetta replied. "Maybe you hadn't noticed."

"Never mind. Have you seen Corene?"

Josetta exchanged startled glances with Rafe. "Not since the dinner last night. She was upset, though, I told you."

Zoe nodded. "I talked to her before I went to bed, and she said she was just tired."

"She was acting like she wouldn't miss Steff, but I think she was just pretending. Maybe she went to say goodbye to him."

"Well, I doubt it, since the whole Malinquese fleet sailed out at dawn."

"Give us five minutes to clean up, and then we'll help you look for her," Rafe said.

Zoe nodded. "I'll be downstairs. Darien said he'd meet us here after he talked to the rest of Kayle's servants. Surely someone saw her go."

Josetta and Rafe hurried down the hall to wash up with great efficiency, though they took the time to put on fresh clothes before running down the stairs to find Zoe. The late morning sunlight was so determinedly bright, so jubilantly hot, that it took Josetta a moment to adjust to its weight and brilliance. She lifted a hand to shade her face as she gazed out toward the harbor. Zoe was right. All the Malinquese ships were gone. There were plenty of vessels flying foreign colors, but none of them boasted that bright red flag with the crossed swords and white blossoms.

"I have to admit I'm worried," Zoe said.

Josetta didn't answer because a small, private elaymotive was headed their way, bouncing too quickly over the uneven surface of the roads. The bad driving made her expect to find Kayle behind the wheel, but once the car squealed to a stop, it was Darien who stepped out. His face was set so hard Josetta couldn't tell what emotion he was trying to keep in check. Fear, maybe. Anger. Bafflement.

"Did you find her?" Zoe asked anxiously.

His voice was cool and controlled. "In a manner of speaking," he said, and handed her a folded piece of paper. Josetta crowded close to read over her shoulder. She recognized the large, well-formed letters of Corene's handwriting, but she had trouble taking in the words.

I've gone to Malinqua with Steff and Filomara. Foley's coming with me. Don't worry. Corene.